NOTHING TO LOSE

A Grey Justice Novel

Christy Reece

Nothing To Lose
A Grey Justice Novel
Published by Christy Reece
Cover Art by Patricia Schmitt/Pickyme
Copyright 2014 by Christy Reece
ISBN: 978-0-9916584-1-1

PROLOGUE

Houston, Texas

The man's plane landed at William P. Hobby Airport. Like any other businessman, he disembarked and headed with the seemingly endless throng of people toward ground transportation. Having no luggage other than his carry-on, he was standing in line for a taxi within minutes.

Innocuous looking, he blended into the mass of people as if he didn't exist. If a thousand people were later asked if they had seen a slender man of medium height with short, brown hair and pleasant features, most would say no. A few might say yes and yet be unable to describe him. Blending in was part of his trade, and he was very good at his chosen profession.

When an overaggressive traveler grabbed the taxi meant for him, he did nothing but step back and wait for the next one. Attracting attention would be unwise. The rude man would never know that he came in close contact with Death today.

Finally procuring a cab, the man gave the name of a hotel in the city. Nothing particularly expensive—just one of the many hotels on the outer edges of the big metropolitan area where one wouldn't be noticed.

After checking in, he followed a large family onto the elevator. All eyes were on the overexcited, squealing children. No one noticed the silent stranger in the corner.

Reaching his room on the third floor, he slid his key card into the slot and pushed open the door. A sniff of air brought a scowl to his bland features. He'd asked for a non-smoking room, and this one had definitely housed a smoker. A complaint or a room-change request would only bring unwanted attention and make him memorable. Shrugging philosophically, he set his bag on the luggage rack, withdrew his new, unused phone from his pocket, and punched in a number.

On the first ring, a male voice answered, "Yes?"

"I'm here," the man said. Not waiting for a reply, he ended the call.

Most people would unpack their clothing or check the television guide. Others might take a quick look over the room service menu. He did none of those. His total focus was on the job. Once that was finished, he would leave and go about his business. He wouldn't stay in the same hotel. Instead, he would head into the city and pay an exorbitant price for a one-night-only stay. Then he would return to his home and be someone else until another employment opportunity presented itself again.

Three minutes after making the call, a soft chime indicated he had a text message. Clicking on the message icon, he quickly took in the brief but significant information. Two targets. Both events were to look like random acts of violence—a specialty for him.

All relevant information gathered and memorized, he deleted the message, then efficiently and thoroughly demolished the phone. He would drop the decimated parts into a dumpster on the way to his first job.

After a quick check in the mirror to ensure his pleasant, nondescript appearance was still in place, he walked out the door with nothing more on his mind than to complete a successful business transaction—just like any other businessman.

CHAPTER ONE

Kennedy O'Connell stepped back to admire her work and released a contented sigh. *Yes.* Even though she'd painted only a quarter of a wall with one coat, she was almost sure this color was the right one.

"Oh holy hell, you changed your mind again."

Grinning, she glanced over her shoulder at her husband. "Eighth time's the charm."

His arms wrapped around her and pulled her against his hard body. As he nuzzled her neck, she could feel his smile against her skin. Kennedy knew if she looked at his face, his eyes would be dancing with good humor. Thomas O'Connell was a patient, even-keeled man, but her indecisiveness about the color for the nursery had put him to the test.

Snuggling back into his arms, she asked, "So do you like this color better than the last one?"

Without raising his head, Thomas growled, "It's perfect."

She snorted softly. "That's what you said about the first seven."

"That's because they were perfect, too. Anything you pick is going to look great."

She appreciated his faith in her. Having grown up in various foster homes, her priorities had been getting enough food to fill her belly and staying out of trouble. Surviving her childhood hadn't involved learning about colors, textures, and fabrics.

When she and Thomas had married, almost everything she owned was secondhand and ragged. Since then, she'd been learning little by little, mostly by experimenting, what she liked. She had delighted in setting up their home, creating a beautiful environment she and Thomas could enjoy together. Now that their first child was on the way, she wanted everything to be just right, so she had taken experimentation to a whole new level.

She was on winter break from her first year of law school. In her spare time, she freelanced as a researcher for several law firms. She had considered taking on some jobs to earn a little extra money while on break, but Thomas had encouraged her to take her time off seriously by doing nothing at all. Never one to be idle, she couldn't stop herself from working on the nursery. This wasn't dry contracts, torts, or mind-numbing procedure. This was relaxing and fun.

Thomas's big hands covered her protruding belly and caressed. At just over twenty-two weeks, she was all baby. The weight she had gained—thirteen pounds so far—had gone straight to her stomach.

"How's Sweet Pea doing today?"

Smiling at the nickname Thomas had taken to calling their baby, Kennedy covered his hands with her own. "Sweet Pea is doing wonderful." She tilted her head to look up at him. "But you know, if it's a boy, you cannot call him Sweet Pea, right?"

"It's a girl," he assured her. "As sweet and beautiful as her mother."

"I hope you're right, if only because everything I've bought so far is pink."

"I'm right." He kissed the nape of her neck. "So. No queasiness?"

"Nope. I think she's decided to take the day off."

Warm breath caressed her ear as Thomas gently bit her lobe. "I'd say that calls for a celebration."

Heat licked up her spine. Morning sickness that lasted long past morning had put a damper on their lovemaking lately. When she wasn't in the bathroom throwing up, she was concentrating on staying still to keep from getting sick. But today, for whatever reason, the baby had decided to give her a break.

Turning in his arms, she whispered against his mouth. "I've missed you."

His mouth covered hers, and Kennedy gave herself up to the delicious and familiar taste of the man she adored. Two years of marriage had only increased her love for him.

He raised his head and dropped a quick kiss on her nose. "Think that'll hold you till tonight?"

Her smile teasing, she winked at him. "Yes, but don't blame me if I get started early."

His gruff laughter was cut off abruptly as he kissed her once more. Before she could pull him in for a deeper connection, he backed away. "Save some for me."

Already tingling in anticipation of the coming night, Kennedy watched him walk away, loving how his swagger denoted confidence without a hint of conceit.

Thomas stopped at the door and looked over his shoulder. "I'll call you before I head home to see what you need."

Blowing him a kiss in thanks, Kennedy turned back to her project, blissfully unaware that it would be the last time she would see her husband alive.

Detective Nick Gallagher slid into the front seat of his car, started the engine and flipped on his headlights. Damn, it was already dark. He pulled out of the parking lot and headed in the opposite direction of his apartment, pushing the vision of going home for a quick shower out of his mind. In fact, he'd be lucky to make his date on time. This was the first time today he'd had a few minutes to himself. This morning he'd been tied up in court, waiting to testify in a murder trial. The minute he'd walked out of the courtroom after his testimony, he'd been called in on a double homicide.

He took all of that in stride. He had played this dice when he'd chosen his career path. Sometimes, though, a little downtime to handle personal issues would have been nice.

With that thought in mind, he grabbed his cellphone and punched the speed dial for Thomas. His best friend was a detective in the Narcotics Division. Lately, the only way they'd communicated was through text messages and emails. Yesterday, Nick had gotten an oddly obscure text from him that had put his cop instincts on high alert.

Thomas answered on the first ring. "You forget something?"

"How's that?" Nick asked.

Thomas chuckled. "Hey, Nick. Sorry. I was just talking to Kennedy. She's been having some wild cravings lately, and I figured she'd thought of something else she wanted."

"So you're headed home for the night?"

"After I make a stop at Bailey's grocery."

"Where's that?"

"Corner of Kendrick and Mulberry."

"That's on the other side of town. Why so far?"

"I'm on a mango run. I was in the area last week and picked up some fruit at the store. Kennedy went crazy over the mangoes and asked me to pick up some more. I think she's got some sort of special dessert in mind for tonight."

Nick didn't question his friend's need to please his wife. He'd seen Thomas's devotion to Kennedy firsthand…there was almost nothing he wouldn't do for her. And Kennedy was the same way about her husband. If anyone had the perfect marriage, it was the O'Connells.

"Sounds like you guys have plans for the evening."

"Yeah, something like that. Why? What's up?"

"I thought we might meet later and talk about that text you sent me yesterday. You know…about the Slaters."

The slight pause before Thomas answered told Nick that plans or not, his friend didn't want to discuss the subject. "It's nothing, really. I made a couple of calls, thinking I'd found something interesting, but nothing panned out. Forget about it."

Thomas O'Connell was the finest man Nick knew, but he couldn't lie for shit. Something was definitely going on. "What do you mean you made a couple of calls? To who?"

"No one…really. Just forget I mentioned anything, okay?"

"Look, I'll be the first to admit there's no way the Slaters are as squeaky clean as they pretend. But if you are right, they'll screw up big-time one day and get what's coming to them."

"Yeah, I know that. Like I said, it was just an idea that didn't pan out. I'm over it now. So who's the hottie of the night?"

The less-than-smooth effort to change the subject made Nick even more suspicious. Letting him off the hook for the time being, he said, "Louisa something or other."

"Where'd you meet this one?"

"Belden's party last week."

"Where're you taking her before you take her to bed?"

Nick snorted his disgust. His reputation of being a lady's man was mostly fictional. Yeah, he dated a lot of different women, because he enjoyed their company. Somehow, even Thomas was under the impression that it also meant he had a lot of sex.

"I don't sleep with all of them."

Thomas gave his own snort, this one of disbelief. "Yeah. Right."

Knowing whatever protests he made would only be construed as modest, Nick decided to go back to their original discussion. "Seriously, let's talk about the Slaters tomorrow. If you've got something on your mind, I want to hear about it. Want to meet for lunch at Barney's?"

"Um…yeah…sure, lunch sounds good. But I promise there's nothing to talk about. Gotta go. Catch you later."

Nick cursed softly at the abrupt end to the call. Thomas was definitely keeping something from him. Tomorrow he'd get in his face and make him talk. Screwing around with the Slaters wasn't a good career move. With their kind of influence, they could end a career with a phone call. On the other hand, if Thomas did have something significant on the family, then Nick wanted to know about it.

Mathias Slater and his clan were Texas royalty. Few people in America, much less Texas, hadn't heard of the Slaters. They were one of the oldest and wealthiest families in the country with descendants dating back to the first American settlers. Nothing seemed to tarnish their good image. Even the arrest and conviction of the youngest Slater, Jonah, on a major drug-smuggling charge had done nothing more than elicit sympathy. Shit bounced off of them like they had some kind of protective shield.

Nick knew almost nothing personally about the family—just what he'd seen on the news or read in the paper. One thing he did know was they had major connections. Hell, last week he'd seen a photo of Mathias Slater shaking hands with the president. The family had the kind of influence that most people could only dream of having.

A few months back, Thomas had handled the investigation of Jonah Slater and had given Nick the lowdown. Slater had been caught red-handed with a boatload of illegal drugs. In fact, he'd looked so stinking guilty that Thomas had said he would have suspected the guy had been framed if he hadn't been a Slater. According to Thomas, it'd taken almost no investigation or effort to put Jonah away. He was now serving a hefty sentence in Brownsville.

Mathias Slater had made the most of the publicity. He'd held a press conference, stating that he still loved his son and offered his full support. He'd even donated millions to a drug-rehab facility. Nick had caught the press conference on television and had seen more than a few people wipe away tears.

Thomas had described an incident the day Jonah Slater was sentenced. Said it had given him several sleepless nights. Jonah had been about to walk from the courtroom, his hands and ankles shackled, but he'd stopped in front of Thomas and said, "Hell of an investigation, O'Connell. Hope you didn't break a nail."

Nick agreed it was strange but had encouraged Thomas to let it go. Cryptic remarks from convicted criminals weren't exactly unusual. And prisons were filled with criminals who swore they were innocent. Few freely admitted their guilt.

As Nick pulled in front of Louisa's apartment complex, he glanced at the dashboard clock. Yeah, seven minutes late. Jerking the car door open, Nick strode up the sidewalk. Before he got to Louisa's front door, she had it open for him. Long-legged, honey blond hair, full pouty lips, and exotic eyes. She looked exactly like her magazine photo that had been splashed all over the country last month. Many men would have given their eyeteeth to talk with a cover model much less date one. So why did he want to turn around and walk the other way? Since he already knew the answer to that, he kept moving forward.

Giving her one of his stock smiles in greeting, Nick listened to her chatter with half an ear as he led her to the car. Had she been this talkative last week?

Thankfully, the restaurant wasn't far away. Within minutes of leaving her apartment, they were seated and had ordered their meal.

They were almost through with their appetizer when Nick had to stifle a giant yawn. For the past ten minutes, Louisa had droned on about her weekend in St. Moritz with some Hollywood celebrity. Taking a large bite of his ravioli so he wouldn't have to respond verbally, he chewed, nodded, and did his best to put on an interested expression, wishing like hell he'd never made this date.

"And then Maurice said the funniest thing. He—"

The abrupt ringing of his cellphone was a welcome distraction. Holding his hand up to stop her chatter, Nick answered, "Gallagher."

"Nick, it's Lewis Grimes."

Before he could wonder why the captain of the Narcotics Division was calling, the man continued, "There's been a shooting."

The fine hairs on the back of his neck rose. The instant he heard the victim's name, he went to his feet. "I'll be right there."

He threw a wad of cash on the table. "I gotta go. That should pay for dinner and a cab home."

Before she could open her mouth to answer, Nick was already running toward the door, his date forgotten. His mind screamed a denial, but Grimes's stark words reverberated in his head, refusing to allow him to deny the truth. "Thomas O'Connell has been shot."

CHAPTER TWO

Kennedy stretched her back and winced at its tightness. This kind of work was nothing to a full day of research at her laptop. Still, she was exhausted. The first coat of paint looked wonderful. The second one she would apply tomorrow would look even better. She couldn't wait to see Thomas's grin when he saw that she had indeed changed her mind once more. Apparently, the ninth time was the charm, because the jewel-toned lilac was perfect. The people at Lloyd's Paint and Wallpaper would probably be just as happy as Thomas that she'd at last made her final choice.

She might be tired, but tonight was going to be perfect. She had taken a break late in the afternoon and prepared lasagna—one of Thomas's favorite dishes. The delicious fragrance now wafted through the air, and her stomach grumbled—a reminder that her early afternoon peanut butter and banana sandwich was long gone. What a blessing to have hunger pains in place of queasiness.

Thomas should be home soon. She would have to rush through her shower, but she wanted to be dressed and ready when he walked through the front door. Or undressed, in this case. On her way back from the paint store, she'd slipped into Victoria's Secret and found a negligee on sale that would probably make Thomas forget all about dinner.

She dashed from the nursery and ran to the master bedroom. Toeing off her sneakers, she was about to unzip her jeans when the sound of the doorbell chimes stopped her. Could she ignore it? If she'd been in the shower, she wouldn't have even heard it. She shrugged resignedly and headed downstairs. Curiosity was the bane of her existence…she had to know. Besides, if she was still in the shower when Thomas got home, he could join her and they could get started even earlier than planned.

The delightful thought cheering her, Kennedy opened the door with a big smile on her face. Thomas's best friend stood before her.

"Nick! Hey! Come on in." Even as she said the words, she inwardly sighed, seeing the romantic evening with her husband fizzling fast.

He didn't speak. The odd look in his eyes puzzled her until she realized what a mess she must look. Her chestnut hair, pulled up into a halfhearted ponytail, had more than a few streaks of lilac in it. She had a feeling that she had a few spots on her face, too.

"I know I must look a fright, but I just finished painting the nursery." She stepped back. "Come in and see it. Thomas isn't home yet. I asked him to pick up a couple of things at the store, but he should be here soon."

When he still said nothing and just kept looking at her, she frowned. "Nick? What's wrong?"

The woman before him was disheveled, messy and absolutely lovely. She was his best friend's wife…one of the sweetest people Nick had ever known. And he was about to destroy her world.

He opened his mouth to speak, but before he could say the words, she started shaking her head and said a very soft but emphatic, "No."

"Kennedy, I—"

She backed away, head still shaking. "You are not here to tell me anything bad, Nick. You got that? Thomas is on his way home. He's not on duty. He is fine."

Reaching out his hand for her, he wasn't surprised when she tried to close the door. Unfortunately, closing him out wasn't going to stop the truth.

He grabbed the edge of the door to keep it from slamming in his face, the words grinding from his mouth, "There was a robbery at the grocery store. Thomas tried to stop it. He was shot."

Her head continued to shake. "No. You made a mistake. Thomas will be home any minute." She looked wildly around the room, as if trying to hold back reality. But her face had paled to a sickly color, and her mouth trembled with emotion.

He took a step inside the house, and she backed away again. Tears swimming in her eyes, she whispered, "This is all wrong. This can't happen. It. Can't. Happen. Do you hear me? It can't."

He reached for her. Wanting to hold her, comfort her. When she jerked away, his hand dropped, and he whispered hoarsely, "I'm so sorry, Kennedy. So damn sorry."

Kennedy turned away from the sorrow on Nick's face. This couldn't be happening. It just couldn't. As a cop's wife, she knew this kind of news could come at any time. She lived with that knowledge daily. Having lost both her parents as a child, she knew more than most people about unexpected tragedies. But this? This wasn't something she could ever have expected. Thomas had been in a grocery store, off duty. Just like any other citizen.

Nick's gruff voice penetrated her blurred thoughts. "I've called Julie…she's on her way."

Julie was her best friend, also a cop's wife. She had been in Julie's place before. Last year, Sara White's husband, Rick, had been killed in the line of duty. Kennedy had been there when they'd told Sara. Had held Rick's widow in her arms and whispered to her that everything was going to be okay. Kennedy now realized she had lied. Everything wasn't going to be okay. Never would be again. How Sara must have wanted to wail and scream those very words.

No! She refused to accept it. Kennedy whirled, shouted, "He's not dead, dammit! I won't allow it. I will damn well not allow it. You hear me? It's a mistake."

His eyes glittering with tears, Nick pulled her into his arms and whispered, "It's going to be okay, Kennedy. I promise."

Hysterical laughter bubbled in her chest, and Kennedy jerked out of his arms. "No, it's not. That's the funny thing about those words. They're only said when it's not going to be okay." Tears blurred Nick's face as Kennedy felt them come. She froze, held her breath…willing them away. She couldn't cry. If she did, it would be admitting the truth.

She gazed blindly around at her house, her happy home. The home she and Thomas shared together. The one their baby would soon share with them. This couldn't be happening!

A female voice, filled with sympathy and sadness, said, "Kennedy?"

Julie stood at the door, tears streaming down her face. Agony shot through Kennedy, almost bending her double. It was true. Oh God, it was true.

Thomas was gone.

Nick watched as Julie led Kennedy into the living room. As they got to the entrance, Julie twisted around and mouthed, "Hot, sweet tea."

With a nod, Nick headed to the kitchen, grateful to have a task. He'd never felt more helpless in his life. Nothing he could say or do would change the situation. Hot tea was about as good as anything.

He entered the kitchen and then stopped for a moment. How many times had he been in this house? Dozens. And they had all been happy times. Cookouts, dinners, the occasional brunch. Laughter had filled the rooms, and Kennedy had been the biggest cause of that. She had a dry, witty sense of humor and could deliver punch lines like a pro. She also had a smile that could light up the darkest of hearts, and not once had he heard her say an unkind word about anyone.

Every room in the house bore Kennedy's vibrant personality, but he'd always felt the kitchen showed the soul of the woman—sunny and inviting but with a calm serenity. He shoved his fingers through his hair. Hell, grief was turning him into some kind of lame-assed poet.

Nick opened a cabinet. Tea bags and sugar were to the left of the stove. Kennedy had once mentioned that her need for organization was rooted in the chaos of her childhood. Nick identified with her need to control her environment. Control gave power. And when your life goes to shit, control means everything.

He filled the teakettle, set it on the burner and sat down to wait for the whistle. As he waited, the memory of sitting beside his best friend as he bled out ran like a horror movie through his mind.

Nick's car had slid almost sideways into the parking lot, while the words "it's a mistake, it's a mistake" drummed like a mantra in his mind. The identification was wrong. It was someone who looked like Thomas.

He'd jumped out of the car and shoved open the store door, barely slowing to flash his badge. Uniformed and plainclothes cops had hovered around, their faces wearing the same bleak look of hopelessness.

"Back here, Gallagher," a voice called out.

Nick ran to the sound and then skidded to a stop. Thomas lay on his back, the front of his shirt covered in blood. His eyes were closed, and two EMTs were working on him.

"Dammit…no," Nick whispered.

Amazingly, Thomas must have heard him. His eyes flickered open, and he muttered a faint, "Nick…need to talk…Nick."

"We need to get him to a hospital," one of the EMTs stated.

The other EMT scooted out of the way. "Sit here. I'll get the transfer ready."

Nick knelt beside his best friend and could literally feel his own heart breaking. They'd known each other since college—cheerful, charming Thomas and angry, sarcastic Nick. Their friendship shouldn't have worked, but somehow it had. He gave Thomas all the credit. The man had tenaciously pursued him as a friend. For which Nick would be forever grateful.

Thomas's eyes glittered with a strange, intense light. Pain? Fear? Somehow, Nick got the idea there was another reason

"Need you…do me a favor," Thomas whispered.

"Anything. Name it."

"Take care of Kennedy for me. She's going to take it hard." He swallowed and added, "And our little girl. Please…take care of her."

His eyes stinging, Nick said, "I promise, Thomas. I'll take care of both of them."

"You're a good man." A small smile lifted his mouth. "Despite what your ex-girlfriends say."

Nick forced a laugh. "Always joking."

His eyes opened wider, and Thomas said softly, "Tell Kennedy…" He drew in a rattling breath. "Tell her…best…thing…ever happened to me. Love her…" His eyes closed, and then he opened them even wider. Grabbing Nick's arm in a surprisingly strong grip, he rasped, "Don't let them hurt—"

The hand on Nick's arm went slack, and Thomas gave a final gasp.

"Thomas!" Nick shouted.

"Back away."

Nick jumped out of the way and watched as the two EMTs worked frantically. When one of them said, "It's no use," Nick yelled, "What do you mean it's no use? Do something. He's a healthy man. He's got a wife…a kid on the way. Do something!"

"I'm sorry…he's gone."

Nick looked blankly over at Lewis Grimes. "What happened?"

Grief filled his eyes as he muttered, "Robbery. Thomas tried to stop it." He gestured to a black body bag. "At least he got the little bastard."

The whistle of the kettle drew Nick back to the present. Feeling like he'd aged a hundred years in the last hour, Nick prepared the tea and headed to the living room. Kennedy sat on the sofa, staring into space. Julie was talking softly to her, but he doubted any of the words penetrated.

He'd seen this reaction dozens of times. Had been there himself. First, there was the denial. The push back against a truth so horrific, your mind refused to acknowledge its existence. Then came the inevitable numbing shock. That was actually a welcoming place. Everything went on shutdown. You didn't think about the agony ripping at your heart. There was no knowledge of reality. You didn't think, period. You breathed in and out. You swallowed, occasionally nodded at the soft murmurings around you, even though you didn't comprehend the words. You just existed.

Nick had been eighteen years old when he had experienced that pain firsthand. His mother had been driving home from work, and some drugged-out bastard had decided to do a little target practice. Eight people had been shot. His mother had been one of three who'd died.

He had been home, cooking dinner, when the doorbell rang. Unaware that his life was about to be completely changed, he'd casually opened the door and faced two policemen. He still remembered their words, their solemn expressions... the sympathy in their eyes. He remembered the bellowing cries of their next-door neighbor, his mother's best friend. He even remembered the dog across the street that barked incessantly at all the cars and people who'd showed up a few minutes later. Those kinds of details—innocuous and unimportant—were ingrained in his memory.

Years later, even when the pain had dimmed, Nick knew Kennedy would remember these odd, unimportant moments, too. They lingered like small dark clouds. Not necessarily painful but just little reminders of life in all its messed-up glory.

He held the hot tea in front of Kennedy, wrapping both of her hands around the mug until she had a good grip. Assured she did, he dropped into a chair across from her and watched her carefully. Soon, the shock would wear off, and the truth would hit her once more. Only this time the pain would be harder to bear, because denial was no longer something to fall back on.

An ache developed in his chest as he watched her struggle to hold it together. He'd been a homicide detective for two years now, delivered news of a loved one's death to countless families. Though he'd always felt a measure of sympathy for them, he had always been able to hold himself apart. But there was no way in hell to separate himself from this tragedy. His best friend was gone.

Thomas had asked him to take care of Kennedy, and though it was something he would have done in the first place, the vow he'd made held extra weight. Nick would do whatever it took...give her whatever she needed, no matter what. From now on, Kennedy and her baby were his responsibilities. Whatever anyone said about him, no one could dispute that he took care of his own. And that's what Kennedy was now. *His.*

Chapter Three

"Okay, let's go over it one more time."

"I don't know what more I can tell you, Detective Gallagher. I mean…it happened so fast." The grocery store owner, Mike Bailey, looked as ravaged as if he'd been shot himself. Since the poor guy had seen two people die in front of him only hours ago, that was understandable.

"Just take your time, Mr. Bailey."

"One minute, that nice Mr. O'Connell…I mean, Detective O'Connell, was shopping for mangoes and the next thing I knew, I had a gun stuck in my face."

"And what did the gunman say to you?"

"He said, 'Give me all the money from the cash drawer.'" Bailey shook his head. "I've been held up before, so I thought about going for my gun. But then I remembered that Mr. O'Connell was a policeman. I figured he'd know what to do."

Nick had seen the video of the robbery. The grocer's words went along with what the footage showed. Miguel Ruiz, the punk-kid gunman, had shoved a .22-caliber pistol into the storeowner's face. The video hadn't picked up the audio, so Nick had to rely on Mr. Bailey's memory.

"What happened after he demanded the money?"

"I opened the drawer and was pulling the money out when Detective O'Connell came around from the back and told the kid to drop his gun."

"And then what?"

"He turned around and shot Mr. O'Connell." Tears flooded the old man's eyes. "He was such a nice man."

Nick shoved aside the emotion. He knew he shouldn't be investigating Thomas's murder. Other detectives were on the case. Personal involvement always blurred judgment. Didn't matter. He had to do something.

Thomas's funeral was tomorrow. Nick had been granted a couple of days' leave but hadn't been able to do anything but think about Thomas. He'd talked to the detectives on the case. They had the case virtually wrapped up already. A robbery gone bad. A man shot down in his prime. The loss of a good cop. End of story.

Nick turned and stared at the spot where Thomas had breathed his last breath. And on his last breath, he'd said something that haunted Nick. *Don't let them hurt—*

Hurt who? Who had he been talking about? Commonsense told him Thomas's pain-dulled mind had been focusing on Kennedy and their baby. That his words had meant something about not letting them hurt because of his death. That made sense. So why the hell did his gut tell him something else?

His focus returned to the store owner. "And you're sure it was the kid who shot first?"

"Oh yes, it was definitely the kid. Mr. O'Connell told him to put the gun down. That he didn't have to do this...that we all have choices."

"Choices? That seems like an odd thing for Thomas to say."

Mr. Bailey nodded his head. "That's because the kid said he didn't have any."

Adrenaline rushed through Nick. Wanting to question the man without alarming him or putting him on the defensive, Nick said casually, "That's interesting. Him saying he didn't have a choice. Wonder why he said that."

"I don't know. It was the strangest thing. He told Mr. O'Connell that he was sorry, but he didn't have a choice."

"So he apologized to him?"

"Yes. I told the other detectives that. They said it must've been because the kid was poor and felt he didn't have a choice but to rob the store for money."

Again, commonsense told Nick that was a possibility. Desperation made people do stupid things.

"What happened after the kid said he didn't have a choice?"

"That's when Mr. O'Connell told him that we all have choices. Told him again to put the gun down."

"And then?"

"The kid said, 'I'm sorry,' and pulled the trigger. It must've been only a half second later that Mr. O'Connell pulled his trigger, 'cause he and the kid went down almost at the same time."

That had shown on the video…the kid and Thomas fell at the same time. "But you're absolutely sure the kid fired first?"

"Absolutely. I had my eyes focused on the gun in his hand. I saw him squeeze the trigger."

Nick thanked the grocery store owner, took one last look around, and then walked out the door. He thought about going to Kennedy just to make sure she was okay but forced himself to turn in the other direction. Julie was with her, as were her other friends. He would just be in the way. This was the only productive thing he knew he could do.

He drove aimlessly, the kid's words of apology spinning around in his head. The detectives on the case had a point. The kid might've felt desperate for money, and saying he didn't have a choice could mean exactly that. So why were Nick's instincts saying something else? Was he nitpicking just to occupy himself? No matter what he did, Thomas would still be dead.

Seeing a break in traffic, Nick made a U-turn. No, there was something there. He had trusted his instincts way too long to ignore them now. Miguel Ruiz's parents had to know what was going on in their son's mind. He had to talk to them. He couldn't let go until he knew for sure.

Kennedy lay on the bed, still in her black dress. She'd managed to slip out of her heels, but that was it.

Night was falling, and as dusk settled around the empty bedroom, her thoughts were filled with Thomas. How they met, the first time he smiled at her, their first kiss. His brilliant smile when she agreed to marry him, the happy tears he shed when she told him she was pregnant.

Today she had said goodbye to him for the last time. In a way, the moment had been surreal. She had stood over his coffin and gazed down at the man she loved more than life. He had looked like her Thomas but not. The expression on his face had been much too bland and peaceful. She was used to Thomas's light blue eyes twinkling with laughter, his quick smile and animated features. It had been close to four in the afternoon and his beard should already have been showing. Usually, by the time he made it home at night, he needed a shave. His beard had stopped growing. She had touched his face…his skin had felt cold and smooth. Not like her Thomas at all.

Thomas's mother and sisters had been standing beside her. When Kennedy had asked for a few minutes alone with him, his mother had thrown her the same look she'd been giving her for the last two days—one of accusation.

Kennedy couldn't deny the blame was well deserved. When she had asked for the mangoes, she hadn't known that Thomas would have to go across town to get them. Stupid not to have thought about that before she had asked. And Thomas, being Thomas, hadn't complained. He had put her needs first—just as he had from the moment she met him.

If he hadn't been in that store, for her, Thomas would still have been alive. God, if only she could go back and relive that one moment. She would have given anything if that had been possible.

Thomas's family had left right after the funeral. His mother lived in Nebraska, and his four sisters were scattered across the country. They had barely taken the time to say goodbye before they'd marched out the door with their silent condemnation. Thomas had been the baby of their family and the only male. Kennedy had never felt close to any of her in-laws, and now that Thomas was gone, she didn't see things improving.

Despite her enormous guilt, Kennedy had been glad to see them go. Their resentment might have been warranted, but it had been more than she could handle.

The funeral had been well attended by non-family, too. The church she and Thomas attended each Sunday had always seemed quite large...today, the sanctuary had overflowed with mourners. No surprise. Thomas had been a favorite of many. Not only had his brothers and sisters in blue been in attendance, but also the many friends Thomas had made outside of work. Some she hadn't even known about. How many times had people come up to her today and told her what Thomas had done for them? She had known her husband was a phenomenal man. She just hadn't realized how many other people had experienced his wonderfulness.

Nick had been by her side the whole time. She knew he was feeling Thomas's loss almost as much as she was. She wished she could comfort him, but so far all she felt was a cold numbness that wouldn't go away.

She and Thomas had made so many plans, had so many dreams. They had a baby on the way and hadn't even started talking about names. She didn't even know if it was a girl or a boy. Thomas had said from the start that they were having a girl, and she supposed she had gone along with that because she knew it was what Thomas wanted. And now that baby girl would never know her father. Never know what a wonderful man he had been.

Kennedy twisted on the bed, trying to find a comfortable position. Thankfully, the sickness she'd had the past few months had passed, but the last two days had been stressful on her body. She ached in places she wasn't used to hurting.

Conversations, soft and muted, reached her ears. There were still people here. Probably the closest of Thomas's friends. She knew that Julie and probably Kathy Jenkins and Helen Carver were gathered in the kitchen, washing plates and tidying up. The men—Julie's husband, Hank, Jeremy Jenkins, and David Carver—were most likely in the living room and den, putting furniture back in place. And Nick... yes, Nick would still be here, too. Hurting and grieving.

A soft knock sounded at the door.

"Yes?" Kennedy said, surprised at how weak her voice sounded.

"Hey, it's Julie. Can I come in?"

Kennedy told herself to get up and answer the door or, at the very least, sit up. She couldn't make herself do it. She felt listless...so very tired. She called out, "The door's open."

Julie entered and then closed the door behind her. "How are you feeling?"

There were so many answers to that question...Kennedy gave the easiest one. "A little tired."

"I'm sure you're exhausted. Think you could eat something?"

"Maybe later."

"Okay, just remember that even if you're not hungry, you're eating for someone besides yourself."

That was true. Kennedy placed her hand over her protruding belly. She still had a part of Thomas with her. A beautiful, precious being that she and Thomas had made with their love for each other. As long as she had that precious gift, she would survive.

"You're right." She struggled to rise and only managed to prop herself up against the pillows a little higher. "I must be more tired than I thought."

"I'll bring you a tray. Okay?"

"Thanks. I'd appreciate that."

Julie turned at the door. "By the way, Nick was wanting to come up for a visit. That okay?"

"Absolutely. Tell him to come on up."

Hopefully, a nourishing meal and a good night's sleep would help her feel stronger. Sleeping without Thomas had been difficult. In two years of marriage, she had never slept apart from him. The last couple of nights, she had woken and reached for him, thinking she'd had a nightmare about losing him. Then, when she had found nothing but empty space, she had cried uncontrollably and been unable to go back to sleep.

She was scheduled to see her obstetrician tomorrow. Julie had called the doctor the day after Thomas's death, and he had advised that rest and nourishment were of utmost importance. She had forced herself to comply with both, but she was going in tomorrow just to make sure everything was still okay. The last thing she wanted to do was jeopardize her baby's health.

Another knock at the door, and she knew that Nick had arrived. His knock had a distinctive sound for some reason.

"Come in."

The door opened, and Nick's handsome, unsmiling face appeared, the pain in his eyes mirroring her own.

She waved him in. "Hey. How are you holding up?"

His mouth moved up in a halfhearted attempt at humor. "That's what I came in to ask you."

She scooted over slightly and patted the bed. "Come talk to me."

He sat beside her, took her hand. "How are you feeling?"

"Tired. Empty. Numb."

"I'm going to stay in the guest room tonight. That all right with you?"

Gratitude filled her. What a wonderful friend he was, but she shook her head. "Thank you, but I'd really like to be alone tonight."

His brows drew together in a dark frown. "I don't think that's a good idea. I—"

She held up her hand. Julie had stayed with her the last two nights, but tonight she felt the need to be by herself.

"I'll be fine." She glanced at her cellphone on the bedside table. "I promise, you'll be the first person I call if I need anyone. It's just…I really need to be alone tonight." She shrugged, unable to explain why this night in particular she needed to be by herself.

She could tell he wanted to argue, but thankfully he let it go with, "You need anything…anything at all, you call me. You hear?"

A surge of affection washed over her. "You're such a good man. Why have you never married?"

"Guess I've never found that perfect woman."

"There is no perfect woman."

She finally got a grin from him. "Well…see? There you go."

"Seriously. Thomas used to say you would never settle down, but I've always believed there's someone for everyone."

"Maybe." His awkward shrug showed her he wasn't quite comfortable with the conversation. Typical guy reaction.

Deciding to let him off the hook, she said, "Thomas was a good man, too, wasn't he?"

"The very best."

"Thank you for always being there for him." A thought occurred to her, puzzling and surprising. "It's weird. I've heard hundreds of stories about the stuff you guys got into while you were in college and when you went through the police academy together, but I don't think I ever heard how you two met."

A small smile tilted his mouth. "That's definitely a story you need to hear. Very dramatic."

Excited to be hearing a story about Thomas she hadn't heard yet, she snuggled into her pillow. "Really? What happened?"

"Thomas saved me from a severe ass-whupping."

Now that *was* a surprise. Even though Thomas had been a cop, tough when he needed to be, and in good shape, he hadn't been particularly muscular. Certainly not like Nick, who looked as though he lifted weights on a regular basis. As much as she loved her husband, if it came to a fistfight between the two, she would have put her money on Nick.

"How on earth did he do that?"

Nick shrugged. "It was my first semester at A&M. Back then I was mad at the world and always looking to get into a fight. I was one incident away from losing my scholarship and getting thrown out of school. I didn't care…didn't care a whole lot about anything. I mouthed off to the wrong guy and found myself surrounded by three giant jack-offs…uh, I mean, jerks, who were more than eager to pound me into the dirt."

Fighting a smile at his obvious attempt to clean up his language, she asked, "Thomas helped you fight them?"

"No, nothing like that. He used that wit and charm that was so natural for him. By the time he was through, the guys were laughing, and I was feeling more than a little foolish."

"And you were friends from then on?"

"Not exactly, but you know the man's persistence. By the end of that first semester, he'd torn through my tough-guy façade. He was Mr. Optimism, and I was Mr. Grouch, but somehow we became best friends."

Though his hazel eyes remained solemn, she saw a glint of amusement in them as he added, "He saved my butt in the classroom more than once, too."

"I always felt a little like that with him."

"How so?"

"That he saved me." She shrugged. "For the first time since I was ten years old, I had a family."

"You still have a family. Thomas's mother and sisters are—"

She shook her head. "They're not my family. His mother and sisters blame me for what happened. And they're right."

"It damn well wasn't your fault. It was the fault of some punk kid who couldn't handle being out of prison."

Yes, she knew the story behind the man who'd shot Thomas. Miguel Ruiz had gotten out of prison just a few days ago, having served eighteen months for attempted robbery. And, like too many criminals, had reverted back to his old ways. And Thomas had paid the price.

"If I hadn't asked for the mangoes, Thomas would still be alive."

"You cannot blame yourself for another person's evil. What happened was that kid's fault and no one else's. Got that?"

Still unconvinced, she nodded, knowing it would do no good to argue her point. Intellectually, she could agree with Nick. Emotionally was another matter.

"You've been such a good friend to both me and Thomas. I'm glad you were with him at the end."

Nick battled with himself to keep from reaching for her. She was trying so hard to be strong and brave. And all he wanted to do was hold her and tell her she didn't have to be. That he would do it for her...whatever she needed.

"He was still...awake when I got there."

"He was?"

"Yes, I talked to him."

She released a shaky breath. "What did he... Did he..." She swallowed hard and tried again. "Did he say anything?"

"Yes, he told me to tell you that he loved you. That you were the best thing that ever happened to him. He asked me to watch over you and the baby."

Her eyes closed, tears seeped behind her lids and slid down her face. He was beginning to think he should have waited to tell her when she was stronger. Then a beautiful smile curved her mouth, and when she opened her eyes, he saw gratitude and peace.

"Thank you for telling me. Even though we didn't get to say goodbye, now I feel as though we did."

His chest tight, he continued, "He also said...about the baby. How he wanted her to know how much he loved her."

"He would have been a great dad."

"Yes, he would have."

Nick purposely didn't mention Thomas's last words. What good would that do? Neither could he mention his questions and doubts about Thomas's murder. After talking with the Ruiz family, those doubts had increased a thousandfold. Constance Ruiz, the kid's mother, had still been in shock about what happened and had insisted her son hadn't had it in him to kill anyone. She claimed that his short stint in prison had changed him. He'd recently started a new job and had been turning his life around.

So why would a kid who'd finally been headed in the right direction give all of that up and go down such a drastic path? It didn't make sense.

Unfortunately, his captain didn't agree with him. Today, just hours before Thomas's funeral, Nick had presented his doubts. He had to give the man credit…at least he had listened. But after listening, he'd asked the question Nick had known was coming. The captain had wanted to know what proof Nick had, other than gut instinct telling him something was off. He had nothing. The crime, while senseless and tragic, wasn't uncommon. As far as everyone else was concerned, it was a done deal. Case closed.

"You have a tell, you know."

Jerked out of his grim thoughts, he turned his attention back to Kennedy. "How's that?"

"You get this little tick in your right jaw, like you're grinding your teeth. That's when I know something's not right."

Stunned that she'd interpreted him correctly, he said, "A tell, you say. And when have you seen it before?"

"Remember the time you brought that pishposh society girl over for dinner and she made a remark about the meal?"

Yeah, he remembered that night all too well. Hilary had seemed nice enough. They'd been out on a couple of dates. When he had invited her to a barbecue with the O'Connells, he'd thought she'd blend in okay. He had been wrong. She'd gone out of her way to ridicule the meal and had even made an offhand insult about Kennedy's décor.

He grimaced as he remembered his behavior. "That wasn't my finest hour."

"I thought what you did was very heroic. Not many men would call a taxi for his date and then demand she wait outside for it or he would pick her up and throw her out."

Nick chuckled as he remembered. "I'm not sure what surprised Hilary the most—me telling her to leave or you asking her if she wanted you to wrap up some of your lowbrow meal to take with her."

She grinned. "It was tempting to let her wear it home. You'll never know how close I came to dumping the potato salad on her beautiful head."

"Can't help but believe that would have improved her looks."

They were still laughing when Julie entered. "Now that's a sound I love to hear." She glanced at Kennedy. "Ready to eat?"

Sitting up, she straightened her clothes. "Thank you...yes. I'm suddenly famished."

Julie placed a tray over Kennedy's lap. "We're going to take off now. Nick's staying the night."

Kennedy gave Nick a telling glance. She didn't want Julie to know that he wasn't staying. He hadn't given up on changing her mind, but he went along with her unspoken request.

"Thank you so much for everything, Julie," Kennedy said. "You've been a godsend."

Julie kissed the top of her head. "Get some rest. I'll see you tomorrow."

Nick stood and gave Julie a hug, and then with one last encouraging, "Eat up," Julie walked out the door.

"Want me to leave you alone to eat?"

"No, stay with me if you don't mind." Her eyes dropped to her plate. "In fact, you can help me eat some of this. Julie took 'you're eating for two' quite literally."

"Eat what you can."

Nick was pleased to see that she was indeed diving into the meal with gusto. Color was coming back to her pale face, and that lost, shattered look had disappeared from her eyes, at least for a while.

Kennedy had been amazingly strong and brave throughout the funeral. He feared that tomorrow, though, when all the busyness of the last two days had passed, the pain would really take its toll. Trying to get back to normal when life was no longer normal could be hellish.

"That was good, but I don't think I can eat any more."

Nick took the tray from her, pleased that she had eaten more than half the meal. "Why don't you get dressed for bed? Sounds like everyone's gone. I'll go lock up for the night."

"Thanks for everything."

"I have my clothes in the car. One word from you, and I'll bunk down in the guest room. It'd make me feel better."

Again, she shook her head, and her eyes glistened with tears. "This may sound weird, but I just really think I want to be alone to say goodbye to Thomas. Just me and the baby. Okay?"

His chest tight, Nick nodded. "It doesn't sound weird at all." And it didn't. He'd done the same thing the night after his mother's funeral. He glanced down at her cellphone on the nightstand. "Call me if you need anything. I don't care what time it is or what you need. I can be here within minutes."

The sweet smile she gave him kicked him deep in the gut. Nick turned away and grabbed the tray before he did something stupid, like grabbing Kennedy, holding her close and promising nothing would ever hurt her again. He'd long ago given up on making promises he couldn't keep.

CHAPTER FOUR

A whisper of sound woke Kennedy, and she smiled sleepily. *Thomas.* He was talking in his sleep again. He hadn't done that in a while. She reached over to touch him as she had so many times in the past. The place where he slept was cold and empty. Frowning, she blinked open sleep-heavy eyes and looked around. The room was dark and still…empty. Where was he? Had he gotten up, and she hadn't heard him? She twisted her head slightly, and then it hit her, as it had the past three nights. Thomas was gone. She would never be able to touch or hold him again.

She turned to curl up in a tight ball, needing to release the grief. A low, dull pain in her back stopped her. She'd been feeling a little ache there all day but had thought it was because she had been on her feet too much in heels. Now she wasn't so sure. She reached behind her to rub the spot, and the pain increased. Another one followed, this time in her belly. Frantically, Kennedy placed her hand on her stomach. The baby had quieted down for the past few days, but that was all. She'd just been quiet…nothing more.

The pain hit her again, this time harder. Whatever the problem was, she needed to get to the hospital right away. Nothing could happen to her little girl. She swung her legs off the bed and grabbed her cellphone. Just one key to punch, and she would be in touch with Nick. He would be here within minutes and take her to the hospital. Agony struck. She grabbed her belly, the cellphone dropped from her hand. A streak of fire slashed through her, like the blade of a white-hot knife had been plunged deep within her womb. A warm gush of wetness flooded down her legs. No, no, no. This couldn't be happening. It couldn't.

Fiercely determined to save her child, Kennedy reached for the cellphone lying on the floor. She had to call someone…anyone. *God, please don't let this be happening.* Her fingers grazed the phone…excruciating agony ripped through her. She screamed.

In the midst of rifling through Thomas O'Connell's desk drawer, the man jerked up at the sound. *What the hell?*

Another unearthly bellow echoed through the empty house.

He glanced around the room. Fifteen minutes of looking through every file and folder in O'Connell's small study, and he had found nothing. Whatever information the man had, it wasn't here. Now he had a decision to make. Pretend he hadn't heard the screams and leave or go help?

Hell, he might be a heartless, unfeeling bastard, but even he wasn't that cold. Exiting the study, he ran upstairs toward the sound of the cries and shoved open the door. The flashlight in his hand speared the darkness. His eyes took in the woman on her knees beside the bed, almost bent double in her agony.

"What's wrong?"

She gasped out "Who are—" Pain distorted her face, and she cried, "My baby…something's wrong."

He reached for her, and she tried to back away. "No, who are—" She broke off and gasped out a soft, anguished sob.

He lifted her gently, laid her on the bed, and said firmly, "You have nothing to fear from me. I promise." Pulling pillows from the top of the bed, he placed them under her feet. Taking the cellphone she must've dropped on the floor, he punched in 911. With the other hand, he took Kennedy O'Connell's pulse. Rapid…way too rapid. When the operator answered, he told her the situation. She gave him instructions and assured him an ambulance would be there within ten minutes.

Ten minutes? Screw that. He could get her to the hospital in five.

"Okay, hold on. We're going to the hospital."

Scooping her into his arms, blankets and all, he rushed down the stairs and out the door. He placed her as gently as he could in the back seat of his SUV and then jumped in. It was past midnight…traffic was light. Ignoring every traffic light and stop sign, he pulled into the emergency entrance four minutes later and jumped out. Pulling open the back door, he cursed under his breath when he saw the blood. Damn…there was so much of it.

With soft utterances of reassurance that he knew in his gut were lies, he pulled the semiconscious woman into his arms and raced inside the hospital.

"I need help!" he shouted.

Nurses ran forward. A gurney appeared, and he relinquished his hold on the woman in his arms. Her face whiter than the sheets she lay on, her eyes closed into what looked like death. When the gurney disappeared behind closed doors, knowing he could do nothing more, he turned to leave.

A young woman in a nurse's uniform appeared before him. "Sir, would you step over to the desk, please? I have some paperwork that needs to be filled out."

He shook his head. "I don't know her. I was walking to my car and found her out front."

Her eyes widened—she'd bought his story. "Oh. Well, thank you for carrying her inside."

"She did manage to tell me her name is Kennedy O'Connell. That's all I know."

Taking advantage of the woman's inattention as she scribbled on the clipboard in her hand, he turned and strode quickly out the door. He was halfway to his car when he happened to catch a glimpse of his hands. Blood. Everywhere.

Shit. Memories he'd fought a lifetime to smother flashed before his eyes. With a loud, vicious curse, he dove into his car and sped out of the parking lot.

Nick sat in the waiting room, waiting for word on Kennedy. If not for fellow police officer Pete Stark, whose wife, Holly, was an ER nurse, he might not have even known Kennedy was here, fighting for the life of her child and possibly her own.

One minute after Pete called him, he'd been on his way to the hospital. Julie had already been here, pacing—the slippers on her feet a testament to her need to get to her friend as soon as possible.

Nick had barely even noticed that his own feet were bare until Julie had pointed them out. Thankfully, Julie's husband had been kind enough to bring him socks, shoes and a shirt before heading into work. Nick and Julie now sat in the waiting room, and in between jerking their heads up every time they heard a noise, they talked in soft, low tones about the damn cruelties of life.

A nurse had come by a half hour ago and given them the somber news that they were doing everything they could to save the baby but it wasn't looking good. When he'd asked about Kennedy, the woman had just shrugged and repeated the same words: "We're doing everything we can."

Nick gazed down at the paper cup of cold coffee in his hand. Hell, he didn't even remember how it got there. His total focus was on Kennedy. What was she going to do if she lost the baby? What if she didn't make it?

He shoved a hand through his hair, guilt eating at him like a ravenous beast. "Dammit, I should have insisted on staying with her last night."

Julie shook her head. "I've experienced Kennedy's stubbornness. Once she makes up her mind about something, talking her out of it is almost impossible."

"But why didn't she call me…or you? Why the hell would she drive herself to the hospital?"

"I don't know. Maybe she wasn't thinking straight."

Nick rubbed his tired, bloodshot eyes. No matter what Julie said, he blamed himself. If he had stayed, both she and the baby might have been fine. They might die because of his carelessness.

"Does she know you're in love with her?"

Flinching at the question, Nick twisted his head around to stare at Julie. "What the hell are you talking about?"

"Kennedy. Does she know?"

Hell, was he that obvious? Nick shook his head. "You got it wrong. She's Thomas's wife and my friend. Yeah, I care about her. I don't love her…at least not the way you're implying."

She gave a small knowing smile, shrugged. "My mistake. But just so you know, it's not a crime to love a woman."

"Might not be a crime, but it'd be damn wrong. Thomas was my best friend."

"You don't choose who you love."

"No, but you can make sure the love you have doesn't hurt someone else." Nick pushed up from the chair. "I don't even know why we're having this conversation. Kennedy is my friend. Nothing more."

"She's going to need you more than ever now."

"And she has me for as long as she needs me. I'll be there for her. Don't worry about that."

"And what happens to what Nick needs?"

He shrugged. His needs were way down on his list of priorities right now. "She's my only concern."

The sound of a throat being cleared had them both turning. A middle-age man wearing blue scrubs stood a few feet away. The deep furrows in his brow and grim set to his mouth made Nick tense up even more.

Almost afraid to ask, he said gruffly, "How is she?"

"You're her family?"

Before Julie could respond, Nick said, "Yes, we are."

"Mrs. O'Connell is stable. She lost a lot of blood, but she's going to be fine."

"And the baby?"

"I'm sorry, he couldn't be saved."

Nick closed his eyes. He was beyond grateful that Kennedy would be okay, but how in the hell was she going to survive losing both Thomas and their baby?

"She's been under a tremendous amount of stress," Julie said. "Her husband was killed three days ago."

The doctor nodded. "I saw that on her chart."

"Does she know about the baby?" Nick asked.

"Not yet. She's still under." The doctor lifted his shoulder in a tired, resigned shrug. "These things happen. She's a healthy young woman and should be able to have successful pregnancies in the future."

"Can we see her?" Julie said.

"Yes. Someone will let you know as soon as she's moved to a regular room. She'll be unconscious for at least another hour, though."

After the doctor moved away, they both dropped back into their chairs. "I can't believe all of this has happened to her," Julie said. "It's so damned unfair."

Even though Nick had long ago realized that life was rarely fair, this went way beyond even his realm of understanding. What the hell had she done to deserve this? Absolutely nothing.

Julie glanced down at her watch. "I really need to get home to the kids for a couple of hours. Can you stay here till I get back?"

"Yeah, no problem."

She patted his hand and walked wearily away.

Nick slumped down into the chair and covered his face with his hands. Even though he felt a huge relief that Kennedy would be okay, he couldn't help but wonder just how well she would recover. Losing Thomas had been gut-wrenching enough, but now their baby? How the hell was she going to be able to survive this? Just how much more shit could life throw at her?

Kennedy blinked her eyes open, wondering why she felt so groggy and weak. She moved slightly and then moaned at the soreness in her entire body. What had happened?

"Hey," a gruff male voice said.

Turning her head, she saw Nick sitting beside her. Machines surrounded her. An IV was attached to her hand. She was in the hospital. Her eyes swung to her stomach. It was flatter. Flatter than it had been for months. No, sweet God in heaven, no!

"I'm so sorry, Kennedy," Nick said huskily. "They did everything to try to save the baby. For a while, we thought we were going to lose you, too."

That would have been best. She had lost Thomas, and now she had lost their daughter. All that she'd had left of Thomas. Her sweet baby was gone.

"What was it?" Her voice sounded raspy and hoarse.

"What?"

"Was it…a girl?"

"No, a boy."

The tears came then. Thomas had been wrong. Would he have been disappointed? No, of course not. Thomas would have loved him and been the perfect dad, just as he'd been the perfect husband.

She drew in a trembling breath. She couldn't give in to the pain. Not yet, not yet. She managed a sad hiccupping laugh. "A little boy would have hated the lilac bedroom."

A small smile stretched Nick's mouth. "Yeah, I would think so."

"I've lost everything."

His large, warm hand covered hers. "No, you haven't. You have people who love you. Law school…a good job. You've got so much going for you. Yeah, life has kicked the shit out of you, but you're stronger than what it can do to you."

She didn't speak for a long time. Had no words that could express the grief. A part of her knew she was still in shock. Knew that when everything hit her, she'd lose all control. For right now, the numbness felt good. It was a relief to not feel anything.

"I wish you'd called me instead of driving to the hospital yourself."

Her brow wrinkled as she tried to remember. She had driven herself?

"I…what…" She shook her head to clear the haziness. "Are you sure I drove?"

"Your car was parked at the entrance to the ER."

She had been in such agony…her only focus had been on saving the child inside her. Maybe she had only imagined a tall, dark man bringing her to the hospital. But if that were true, how could she know he'd had a crisp, British accent and cobalt-blue eyes?

"Julie will be here in a little while to stay with you. Then I'll be back tonight. Is there anything I can get you from your house?"

Nick's words brought her back to the present. "No…please." She took a breath. "Don't be offended, but please don't come back tonight. And call Julie and let her know not to come. I really need to be alone."

His brow furrowed in disapproval. "Kennedy, I—"

"Please, Nick. Do this for me. I'm surrounded by doctors and nurses…I'll be fine."

He squeezed her hand again and shook his head. "No, I'm not leaving you alone. Not again."

"Please…I--." The lump in her throat impossibly large, she swallowed hard. "I'm begging you, Nick. I have to be alone. Do this for me."

"Kennedy, I…" His expression one of helplessness, he pressed a kiss to her hand and then stood. "Okay." He stood, leaned over and dropped another kiss to her forehead. "I'm here if you need me. I'll always be here for you. Just remember that." He pointed at the table beside her bed, much as he had last night. "Your cellphone is there with my phone number in it. Call me, no matter what time. Okay?"

How things had changed in a matter of hours. Last night she'd still had hope…a purpose. Now she had nothing. Unable to face him, to see his compassion and pain for her, she kept her gaze on the far wall as she managed another nod.

He stood for several seconds, as if unsure whether he should leave. Then, finally, he sighed heavily, and she heard the door close behind him.

Kennedy continued to stare straight ahead. She was alone. For the first time in four months, she was completely alone. No tiny little being living inside her, cocooned and safe within her womb. Her baby was gone, as was her husband. She was completely, utterly alone. Much the way she had been when she'd first met Thomas. He had given her everything she'd always dreamed of and now it had all been taken away.

A jagged, ugly sound echoed through the room, as if to emphasize its emptiness. Another sound, even uglier, followed. And at last, Kennedy rolled to her side, buried her face in her pillow, and allowed grief to consume her.

CHAPTER FIVE

Nick threw back another slug of coffee as he looked out the dirty broken window of the abandoned apartment building. Sad, lonely place to die. He turned back to the massacre on the floor. Three dead bodies. An execution? Gang shooting? Single bullet hole in the middle of each of their foreheads, close range. No discernible defensive wounds. Like they'd lined up willingly and then been gunned down, one by one.

"You look like day-old dog shit."

He looked over at his partner. Margo Gentry was as gruff and outspoken as any seasoned homicide detective, but beneath her rough edges lay a kind heart. He and Margo had been partners since he'd been bumped to detective. There was little they didn't know about each other and almost nothing they wouldn't say to one another.

He drained the last of his coffee, crushed the paper cup in his hand. "Been awhile since I slept."

"Why didn't you take more time off? Captain would've understood."

"Staying busy helps."

"Yeah, I know what you mean."

And she did. Margo had lost her sixteen-year-old son a few years back to leukemia.

She turned back to the bodies on the floor. "So, we've ID'd two of the perps as gangbangers from Delano. The other one, blond guy, is unknown."

"I know him…Stevie Miller. Busted him when I was a street cop. He was just a kid then."

Margo glanced down at Stevie's body. "Doesn't look older than seventeen now."

"He's probably in his late-twenties. Spent some time in juvie for possession. Can't remember how much. Apparently not enough to make a difference, though." Nick drew closer to the body lying beside Stevie's. Holy shit, he knew this one, too.

"What's wrong?" Margo asked.

"Just realized I know the one on the end, too. Frankie Chavez. Thomas questioned him when he was working the Slater case. I remember him from a photo Thomas showed me. He worked part time for the Slater family…was most closely associated with Jonah."

Nick stooped down for a closer look. Hell, this kid had been put through some serious pain. Fairly recently, too. Burn marks scattered around his neck, looked as though they went down his torso. Nick noticed a few knife scars—probably a couple of years old. But the burns were recent. Maybe only a day or so old.

"Looks like he was tortured before he was shot." He scanned the bodies of the other two victims. No burns. Nothing other than the neat little bullet hole in each of their foreheads. "Question is, who and why?"

"M.E. says time of death was between nine and eleven last night."

"What kind of information did this guy have for them to torture and then kill him?"

"Maybe when we know more about them…what they've been up to…it'll be clearer why they were killed."

"Yeah." Damn, this was too much of a coincidence, wasn't it? First, Thomas was killed by a kid, who from all accounts shouldn't have had any reason to rob a store, much less kill a cop. Now, a couple of days later, a kid Thomas had questioned who was associated with the Slaters is found tortured and shot to death. The brief conversation he'd had with Thomas an hour before he was killed rolled around in his brain. Could this have anything to do with the Slaters?

No, none of this made sense. Why would one of the most prominent families in America have anything to do with a gangbanger? Nick rubbed his gritty, tired eyes. Lack of sleep was making him see connections that didn't exist. Guys like these got killed every day. What could one have to do with the other?

Margo scribbled something in her notepad, thankfully not seeing anything odd in his behavior. She looked up to say, "Before I forget… Norm's birthday is today. We're having a little impromptu get-together. Why don't you come? It'll help get your mind off things."

"I thought you said he didn't want any kind of celebration."

"He did, but I woke up this morning pissed as hell about that. I won't make a big fuss, but it seems crazy to just pretend like it's a regular day. I figure throwing a few steaks on the grill wouldn't seem too fancy. He'll just have to get over the birthday cake I ordered from the grocery store."

"Wish I could come, but Kennedy's being released from the hospital today. I thought I'd go over and keep her company."

Compassion darkened Margo's eyes. "How's that dear, sweet girl doing?"

That was a good question, but one he wasn't sure he could answer with any degree of inside knowledge. Kennedy had amazed him with her strength. Just about anyone who'd gone through what she had experienced might have suffered severe depression or even worse. And though he had seen monumental grief, she had pulled herself together and seemed to be pushing through it.

"Better than anyone could have anticipated."

"It's amazing what the human spirit can endure. Sounds like she's a strong woman."

"She is, but…"

"But what?"

He couldn't answer that question. Kennedy brought out every protective instinct he possessed. He wanted to shield her from every hurt. He wanted to hold her, comfort her…be everything to her. No…hell, no. What was wrong with him? He couldn't think like that.

"Nick? You okay? You're looking a bit green about the gills."

"Yeah...yeah. I'm fine." He turned back to the three bodies on the floor. "Let's find out if there are any surveillance cameras in this area. Maybe if we're lucky, we can ID the killers and have this wrapped up by dinnertime."

Giving him a strange, knowing look, Margo went on to talk about what they'd found at the crime scene.

Nick pushed his insanely inappropriate thoughts away. Kennedy needed him as a friend...nothing more. It was time to prove his love for her by being just that.

Odd how everything could look the same but yet be so completely different. Kennedy stepped up on the porch. A silent Julie stood behind her. Knowing her friend, she was most likely struggling to say something encouraging and uplifting. If so, it was understandable she was so quiet. No amount of encouraging, uplifting words could fix this.

Turning back to the woman who'd been her friend the moment they'd met three years ago, Kennedy forced a smile. "Thanks for bringing me home, but I think I'd prefer to go in alone."

Unshed tears gleamed in Julie's eyes. "Absolutely not. I'm going to get you settled with a cup of hot tea, and then make you a good, nutritious lunch."

She started for the door, but Kennedy held out her hand to stop her. "Please, Julie. I appreciate you more than you'll ever know, but I need to do this alone."

"That's the thing you keep saying and you shouldn't. You don't have to do anything alone. I'm here for you. Loads of people are here for you."

"I know..." Kennedy swallowed the lump in her throat that had been with her for over a week now. "Believe me, I wouldn't have made it this past week without you. But this..." She looked over her shoulder. "This is what I need...for right now." Turning back to her friend, she said, "Please understand."

Even though her eyes flashed in disapproval, she thankfully backed away, saying, "Call me if you need me."

"Thank you."

Kennedy waited until Julie's car had backed out of the drive and disappeared before she turned to the front door again. At last, she could breathe. For days she had been surrounded by well-meaning people who wanted to do things for her. And while she appreciated her friends, she needed this time alone with her thoughts and her memories.

Four days ago she had buried her husband and lost their child. Yesterday, in a small private ceremony at the hospital chapel, she had said goodbye to the baby boy she'd named Thomas, Jr. and had him placed beside his father's grave. Daddy and son were together now.

She needed to be alone for one reason—to say goodbye to Thomas, their baby, and her dreams. That might have seemed odd to some people, but to Kennedy it made perfect sense. Her life with Thomas had been sheer fantasy...something she'd dreamed about growing up, sure that such a beautiful life could never come true. People without a family, like her, raised in foster homes, didn't get their heart's desires. Survival was the best they could hope for. Secretly she had known that...but still she had dreamed. And for a while, that dream had been reality. Was losing her loved ones more painful than never having had them in the first place? It hurt that she didn't know the answer to that question.

She stood just inside the entryway and allowed the memories to wash over her. The day they'd moved into the house, Thomas had carried her over the threshold. They hadn't had furniture yet and had eaten burgers and fries in front of the fireplace. Then they'd made love on the hardwood floor. It had been uncomfortable and absolutely wonderful.

Each step she took, another memory came. The sheer delight on Thomas's face when she'd told him she was pregnant. That night, and every night after, he'd gently kissed her belly and told their baby goodnight, too. She had never seen a man happier or more proud of impending fatherhood.

She stood in the middle of the hallway, and like a warm, gentle waterfall, more memories washed over her. Many were mundane and ordinary, but now extraordinarily sweet—like the time she'd had a bad cold and Thomas had snuggled on the sofa with her and watched three romantic comedies in a row without one complaint. Or the time they'd locked themselves out of the house and blamed each other. They'd both been in a bad mood, sniping at each other like kids, but by the time Thomas had hoisted her up into the kitchen window, they'd been laughing so hard that neither of them cared whose fault it had been.

Kennedy dropped her keys and purse on the hall table and took a deep breath. Even though she was so alone she literally ached to her soul, she felt instant peace at just being home.

Deciding that the hot tea Julie had mentioned sounded heavenly, she headed to the kitchen. The busyness of boiling the water and preparing the tea kept her mind occupied. When she sat to drink it, more memories threatened to assail her. And while she loved having them, she could deal with them only in increments. To distract herself, her mind returned to the alarming mystery of the man who had rescued her and taken her to the hospital. She remembered his reassuring words. His face was a blur, but if she ever heard his voice again or saw those strangely beautiful eyes, she would know him.

She had been in so much pain, so devastated by what was happening, she hadn't had the presence of mind to question him. She'd just been grateful for his help. By the time he'd gotten her to the hospital, she'd been unconscious. Now, in the clear light of day, with all of her faculties, she had to admit it was downright creepy.

Had the man been outside and heard her scream? If so, he would have had to have been on the porch…or at the very least in the yard. And the alarm hadn't gone off. Her mind might have been consumed with agony, but she would have remembered the blare of the security system. All she remembered were strong arms that had held her and a calm, masculine voice telling her to hold on, that she was going to be all right.

The hospital staff hadn't been able to identify him. The nurse who'd met them with a gurney had said she'd paid little attention to him as her focus had been on Kennedy. She remembered a man with a tough, authoritative demeanor. That was it.

Even the security cameras at the hospital had been no help. All they'd shown was a tall, muscular, rather imposing man. He'd worn a baseball cap, and a black leather jacket had covered his big frame. The man had stayed long enough to see Kennedy deposited onto a stretcher. He'd been about to leave when another nurse stopped him. He had talked to her briefly and then had walked out the door. The cameras hadn't been able to pick up any features. It was almost as if he had known where the cameras were and had avoided looking at them. He had wanted to hide his face.

The admitting nurse knew nothing other than he'd said he found Kennedy in the parking lot and had brought her inside. Her car had been found, parked haphazardly in front of the hospital. Blood had been on the driver's seat. How had her car gotten to the hospital?

She shook her head at the mystery, suddenly too tired to think about it any longer. She hadn't mentioned the incident to Nick and made a mental note to do so the next time she saw him.

She put away her mug and headed upstairs. First, she wanted to shower and then she would take a long nap. She told herself if she concentrated on the here and now, things would be less painful. She was almost convinced until she passed by the nursery. She hadn't been inside it since she'd painted it—the night Thomas died. And now there was no reason to go into the room ever again.

Telling herself she shouldn't, she twisted the doorknob and pushed open the door. She took a few steps inside. The lilac color really was pretty but she probably would have had to change it. Maybe to a light summer blue—the color of Thomas's eyes.

A giant pink rabbit sat in the white rocking chair in the corner, its blank, lifeless eyes a reflection of her life. Agony hit her like a bowling ball had been thrown into her at warp speed. Her baby was gone. Thomas was gone.

With a howl of grief, she dropped to her knees in the middle of the room, wrapped her arms around herself, let anguish wash over her. Harsh, jagged shards of sounds erupted from her throat. She screamed, cried, shouted and cursed, wailing at the top of her lungs. She had lost her husband, her baby. God…Oh God, why? What had she done to deserve this kind of punishment? Why, dear Lord…why?

Curling up in a fetal position, Kennedy closed her eyes and allowed herself the grieving she'd been bottling up for days.

The clang of the hallway clock woke her. Stretching gingerly, she looked around and realized she'd fallen asleep on the floor. The tears had been cathartic. She felt drained and empty but oddly peaceful.

Pulling herself up to her knees, then her feet, she walked like an old woman into the master bedroom. Everything ached. First, a hot, steamy shower and then…? She didn't know. For right now, she could think only about five minutes ahead. At some point, she'd think about the future. But not today.

CHAPTER SIX

Kennedy stood in front of the dresser and dried her hair. The hot, bracing shower had helped. The physical aches had eased…the emotional ones remained but were thankfully numb. The bed called to her, inviting her into its warmth. She couldn't. If she lay down, she had the strangest feeling she'd never get up.

Determined to not become mired in grief again, she pulled on a pair of jeans and a fleece sweatshirt. And because it was something mundane and normal, she applied makeup to her exhausted face. She still looked tired and way too pale, but at least she could almost convince herself she looked like the Kennedy she was used to seeing in the mirror and not like a woman whose perfect life had been ripped away from her.

Turning away from her reflection, she gazed about the room. What to do now? A laundry basket with freshly folded clothes caught her eye. She had done laundry a few days ago but never got the chance to put the clothes away.

Though the task would take only a few minutes, at least it was something. She opened drawers and placed the folded clothes in the correct drawers, ignoring the fact that half the clothes were Thomas's. *Don't think…just do.*

She dropped an armload of socks into Thomas's drawer, was about to close it when the top of her hand touched something. Puzzled, her fingers felt around. A small object was taped to the bottom of the drawer above. Carefully ripping the tape away, she removed the object and was shocked to see a small key in her palm. A safe-deposit box key.

Somewhat disturbed, she closed the drawer, stepped back, and stared at the object for several seconds. Not usually one to look for signs or believe in premonitions, the more she stared at the key, the more she felt the need to know the reason Thomas had hidden it. Why would he even have a safe-deposit box anyway? They had shared a bank account, and as far as she knew, he'd had no valuables that would require him to lock them away. To her mind, that meant one thing—he had valued something he didn't want anyone else to know about.

Without giving herself time to think…to wonder if she truly wanted to know what Thomas had hidden from her, Kennedy grabbed her purse and ran out the door. Even though there was no bank name on the key, it made sense that Thomas would rent a box at their bank. The main branch was downtown, which was where the safe-deposit boxes would be. The traffic would be heavy at this time of day, but she couldn't wait another minute to see what was inside the box.

Cyrus Denton tried to ignore the trembling of his hands as he made the call. His people had never messed up so badly before. His men wouldn't get the blame, though. This was on his head alone.

When the phone rang on the other end, he swallowed and forced strength into his voice he didn't feel. "She's headed to the bank. She found a key to a safe-deposit box. That must be where he hid the papers."

"I thought you searched the house. How did you miss a key?"

"We did a thorough search. Looks like he taped it to the bottom of a drawer."

"I don't want excuses. I want the problem handled. If there's anything in that box that incriminates the family…"

The threat remained unspoken but was clearly understood. Wouldn't do any good to mention that none of this would've been screwed up if Cyrus had been given the green light to act weeks ago. What was done was done. They'd all learned a lesson.

This Slater wasn't the one who concerned him. The one he was most scared of would make Satan himself wary.

"I'll take care of it. Don't worry."

"You damn well better. I don't have to tell you what's at stake."

"It's as good as done. I'll call you when it's over."

"I'll look forward to the call."

He dropped the phone on the seat beside him and blew out a breath. He'd been taking care of the Slaters' problems for more than a quarter of a century, had done things for them that would make a normal man puke. He rarely thought about it anymore…the job was what it was. In a way, the Slaters were his family—not by blood but by loyalty. Still, this particular case was beyond distasteful. Nevertheless, it was his job to get done.

Ignoring the knowledge that he was adding another stamp to his one-way ticket to hell, Cyrus followed Kennedy O'Connell's silver Ford Taurus as it headed downtown. He didn't worry about being spotted. His older model Chevy van was an innocuous navy blue, blending in seamlessly with the heavy work traffic.

They had known for some time that incriminating evidence had been leaked. The "who" had been discovered several days ago, but the "what" was still in question. He had a feeling the "where" was about to be answered.

During O'Connell's funeral, his people had combed every inch of that damn house and found nothing. Even though he had been positive the place had been clean, he'd been around the block too often to take chances and had ordered cameras to be placed in some strategic areas. Once again, his experience had paid off.

He hadn't yet figured out how this would go down. Fortunately, he was good at improvising. By the end of the night, two things would happen: He'd have whatever incriminating information Thomas O'Connell had been hiding, and the man's lovely widow would join her husband in the afterlife.

Thinking about that gave him chills. He felt a softness for the woman he didn't usually feel for people. While his men had been searching O'Connell's house, he'd gone to the graveside service. The young widow had held up like a stoic soldier.

When she'd leaned over the coffin and caressed it lovingly, he'd seen her lips move. She had been saying one last goodbye to her husband. Despite his own cold, dead heart, a lump had developed in his throat.

Thomas O'Connell's death had been unfortunate but necessary. Using the discretionary funds for jobs such as this, Cyrus had paid for the hit with only a small amount of regret. O'Connell had messed with the wrong people. It was as simple as that. The man had known enough about the Slaters to realize that you tangled with them at your own risk.

Killing O'Connell's widow was a different matter. It wasn't because she was a woman. Lord knew he'd arranged for more than a few females to disappear over the years. No, what Cyrus was having trouble with was her very innocence. Never had he taken anyone out who hadn't been either dirty or a threat to his employer.

Unfortunately, by association, the O'Connell woman was now a threat. Hell, after what she'd been through, maybe she'd be happy to join her husband. When he thought of it like that, killing her would actually be a gift.

Working like hell to focus on the report in front of him, it took two tries before he heard someone yelling, "Hey! Yo, Gallagher!"

Nick lifted his head. "Yeah?"

"Some guy's on the phone, asking for you. Says it's urgent. I'm sending it over."

Nick barely grunted an acknowledgment. Phone to his ear, he growled, "Gallagher."

"Uh...this Nick Gallagher?

"Yes. Who's this?"

He heard what sounded like a nervous swallow, then, "Thomas O'Connell's friend?"

Nick stiffened, his attention now fully on the caller. "That's right."

"Um, I got some information."

"Information about what?"

"I can't say over the phone."

"You'd damn well better say something. You called me."

"Can we meet?"

"Not until I know what this is about."

A long pause followed. Was this some kind of crank call?

"I think Detective O'Connell's murder was a hit."

Nick was on his feet before he realized it. "What the hell are you talking about?"

"That's all I'm going to say over the phone."

"Where and when?"

"In half an hour. Doug's Diner at the corner of Fifty-Fourth and Archer. Come alone."

Though a dial tone followed, telling him the guy had hung up the phone, Nick continued to hold the receiver. He looked around at the desks and people surrounding him. They were all going about their business while his entire universe had shifted yet again. His gut instinct had been sound. Thomas's murder had been a hit. By whom? And why?

Kennedy stood at the entrance to the safe-deposit room. She had ignored the frowns of the bank employees who wanted to lock the doors. They were justifiable since she had arrived five minutes before the bank was due to close. That couldn't be helped. Assuring the young bank employee that she wouldn't take long, she showed her identification and within seconds was led to the room. Inserting her key, she waited for the young woman to insert the bank's key. She heard the click as it opened and was surprised at the rapid beat of her heart. What on earth could Thomas have wanted to hide?

Telling herself she would be prepared for and could handle anything, she pulled the box out, opened the top and stared at the contents. Two envelopes. One letter-size, with her name scrawled on the front in Thomas's scratchy handwriting, the other brown, legal-size and very thick.

Whatever these envelopes held had been important to Thomas and so private, he'd felt the need to hide them. With the knowledge that her perception of her life with Thomas might well change, and refusing to allow that to happen in a bank, Kennedy dropped the letter-size envelope into her purse. The larger one wouldn't fit, so she clutched it to her chest and hurried out of the bank. She would go home and open the envelopes in private.

The instant she stepped outside, a clap of thunder blasted overhead. Already jittery nerves ramped up to warp speed. Heart pounding, she raced to her car, barely making it inside before the sky opened up and torrential rain exploded as if a dam had burst in heaven.

Despite the frantic need to get home, Kennedy took a moment to calm down. This was all so silly. The envelopes were probably nothing more than some stocks Thomas had forgotten to mention to her. Or maybe he'd planned to surprise her on their anniversary with an island he'd bought in the Caribbean.

Her heart lightening slightly at the whimsical thought, she cranked the engine and pulled from the parking lot onto the street streaming with traffic. She was overreacting because her emotions were on edge…it was nothing more than that.

Traffic was now in full rush-hour frenzy. With the heavy rain, it would take twice as long to get home. Stop-and-start traffic continued for what seemed like hours. Fifteen minutes in this mess, and she had traveled about five miles. The tension in her shoulders and back had returned. By the time she made it home, she'd be one giant knot of nerves.

The windshield wipers beat with a furious, frenetic pace as they tried to keep up with the heavy deluge pouring down on them. Hoping to get out of the traffic gridlock, Kennedy made a right turn onto Elk Road. Any other time she would have taken the interstate, but at this time of day and with this weather, it would be one giant parking lot. This two-lane road was bumpy, curvy and not a straight shot home, but at least she was moving forward.

Darkness had swallowed all light, and her headlights barely penetrated the thick curtain of rain. With total focus on the road ahead of her, she had no clue of danger until something slammed into her rear bumper. Suddenly, instead of heading straight on Elk, she was skidding sideways. Horns blared a warning. Oncoming traffic was within mere seconds of crashing into her.

On instinct, Kennedy punched the gas and shot forward, passing within inches of the semitruck barreling straight for her. She let out a little scream, realizing the only thing in front of her was a giant gaping hole of nothingness. The bridge! She was going off the bridge into the bayou below!

With all the strength she could muster, Kennedy wrenched the steering wheel to the right. Even as she prayed to avoid going into the bayou, she also prayed that she didn't hit some unsuspecting driver going the other way. Either one could mean certain death. At the last minute, she closed her eyes, braced herself for the end result.

The car came to a crashing, shuddering stop. Opening her eyes, she gazed around, amazed. She had somehow avoided both scenarios and found herself on a grassy area several yards away from where she'd spun out of control. Other than the terror-laced adrenaline still rushing through her veins, she was safe, unharmed.

Her eyes took in the area around her. What had seemed like an eternity had probably happened in a matter of seconds. And despite coming within a hair of dying a horrific death, she watched the traffic continue to flow as if nothing had happened.

Willing her heart to slow, she took in another breath. As she did, the event prior to her losing control of the car halted the breath. Someone had hit her from behind.

Movement in her peripheral vision caught her eye. A man was running toward her car. Darkness and heavy rain obscured his face, but she could tell he was focused on her. Was he the one who'd hit her?

In seconds he had reached her car. Expecting him to come around to the driver's side and ask if she was okay, she was startled when he pulled on the handle at the passenger door. Without thinking anything of it, she flipped the lock.

The door was jerked open, and a face appeared before her. Kennedy gasped and jerked back. Not a face. A man wearing a ski mask.

"You should be dead."

"What?"

He glanced behind him and cursed. Turning back to her, he spoke in a soft, menacing tone, "This was a freebie, little lady. You won't get a second chance." He grabbed the large envelope from the seat beside her and shoved it beneath his jacket. "You tell anyone about this, you and whoever you tell is dead. If you're smart, you'll forget this ever happened." With that, he turned and ran away.

"Hey! Wait! You can't just—"

A fist pounded on the driver's window. Swallowing a scream, Kennedy twisted around. A man shouted, "Are you all right?"

She hit the button, allowing the window to open only a crack and said shakily, "Yes...I'm fine." Turning her head again, she searched for the man who'd just stolen the envelope. "That man...did you see him? He stole my—"

The man looked up toward the road and muttered a vicious curse. His attention returned to her. "You're sure you're all right?"

"Yes, I'm just—" Before she could finish her sentence, the man turned away and disappeared. Stunned, she could barely comprehend what had just happened. Someone had tried to kill her. Had threatened her. And had stolen one of the envelopes.

And the second man—the one who'd asked if she was all right. It had been too dark to see his face, but she would recognize that accent anywhere. He was the man who'd taken her to the hospital.

What the hell was going on?

Unwilling to have someone else come to the car, Kennedy eased her foot on the gas pedal and was relieved to feel the tires gain traction. She drove up to the road, and the instant a break appeared in the traffic, she zoomed back onto the roadway and headed home.

Ten minutes later, she parked in her garage. Rushing inside, she locked the door leading to the garage and turned on the security system, then made a mad dash to the kitchen, where she pulled open the drawer beside the refrigerator and removed the handgun Thomas had given her not long after they met. With quick efficiency, she made sure it was loaded. Still not feeling comfortable, she ran from room to room and ensured that all outside doors and windows were locked, all blinds closed.

Back in the kitchen, she stood in the middle of the room and finally allowed herself a long, ragged, relieved breath, feeling a slight sense of safety. Whatever was going on, she vowed never to be so unprepared again.

Her eyes shifted to her purse she'd dropped on the table. She still had the small envelope from Thomas. More than ever, she knew the contents wouldn't be just anything. Whatever had been in the lock box was something someone had been willing to kill for.

Determined to be in the dark no longer, Kennedy plopped down at the table and pulled the envelope from her purse. Her hands shaking, she withdrew a letter from Thomas, noting it was dated the day before he died. She took a breath and read:

My darling Kennedy,

If you're reading this letter, then it means that I have screwed up massively. It was never my intent to put you in harm's way. I am so very sorry for pursuing something that has obviously cost me my life. However, it will not cost you or our child your lives.

With the information attached to this letter, you will find everything you need to ensure your safety.

Before I begin my explanation, I am begging your forgiveness for causing you heartache and putting our family's lives in danger. You deserve only happiness and I have taken that away from you.

A little over a year ago, I worked a case involving Jonah Slater. He was convicted of drug trafficking and is now in prison. I always thought the case was fishy—too easy. After his conviction, I began my own secret investigation of the Slater family. The more I dug, the more I realized that the family is up to their eyeballs in more crimes than I ever imagined, yet I had no substantial proof. Yesterday all of that changed and many of my suspicions were confirmed.

Within the large envelope is enough dirt on the Slaters to ensure a thorough investigation and hopefully several convictions.

Tell no one but Nick about this. He's the only man I trust to do what needs to be done. He knows nothing about it yet. I texted him that I had something but then I got to thinking that my phone and computer might be compromised. I suspect the Slaters have eyes and ears everywhere. Please tell him how sorry I am for not being able to tell him sooner. He'll be mad as hell, with good reason.

Once you give the information to Nick, I want you to leave Houston. You and our child are my life. I love you both more than anything and therefore must protect you at all cost. The actions I want you to take will break several laws. I don't care. They are for your protection. I have listed everything you must do, the order you must do it, and the people you can trust to carry it out. I know this will be difficult for you, but it's the only way to ensure the safety of you and our child.

I know what you're saying to yourself right now. That it's not possible. That you don't want a new life. That you can stay safe. I am telling you that you cannot. Someone will come for you, Kennedy. I know they will. If I am dead, it was because of the Slaters. I can't bear for anything to happen to you. Tell no one what you're going to do…not even Nick. If he knows, then you'll be putting your life and possibly his in jeopardy. Take each step in the order I've given you and don't look back. Your safety must be the only priority.

In closing, my darling, I beg your forgiveness again. You gave me such joy in our life and if I had known that my investigation would endanger what I treasured most, I would have dropped it. I will love you long past eternity.

Yours forever, Thomas

Kennedy's heart pounded so hard, she feared it might explode. But Thomas's death had been a random robbery. Hadn't it? He had tried to stop a man with a gun at the grocery store.

Could that have been faked or set up? She knew little to nothing about hired killers, but didn't they usually take the shot and run? They didn't try to rob grocery stores, and they most certainly didn't stick around and get killed, too.

But…what if someone had wanted it to look like a random act of violence? If so, why would the man who killed Thomas sacrifice his own life? Or had he not been meant to die?

Her thoughts scattering in a thousand different directions, Kennedy pushed her fingers through her hair. How had she not known about Thomas's investigation? She had slept beside him every night. They had talked endlessly on a variety of different matters regarding his job. No subject was off-limits for them. They had shared every secret. Thomas had always been honest and up front with her. How could he have kept this from her?

If he had been so worried for her safety, why had he hidden the key from her? She'd only found it by chance. Had he meant to give it to her and hid it away until an opportune moment? Even with the dire warnings in the letter, perhaps even Thomas hadn't realized just how much danger he was in.

And now what was she to do? Thomas wanted her to begin a new life? Get a new identity?

A wave of fury swept through her. This time it was directed at one person only. *Thomas.* He had done this to them. If he had just let things go, he would still be alive. Their baby might still be alive. Instead of being totally alone, she'd still have her beloved family, her happy home. How could she not be furious with him?

She brushed aside the anger. That would have to wait. Feeling as though a new destiny awaited her, Kennedy began to look through the pages attached to the letter. Her eyes scanned the lengthy and detailed list Thomas had provided. A new identity, with a new name, birth certificate, Social Security number, etc. Everything she would need to become someone else and the names of people who could apparently make that happen.

Additionally, he had listed diversionary tactics for her to use to ensure she wouldn't be followed, along with names of people who would assist her with that, too.

He had thought of everything, and even though it was obvious what Thomas wanted her to do, this had to be her decision. Her choice, no matter which one she chose, would be monumental. Stay and fight, putting her life and those she cared about in danger? Run and hide, change her identity and start all over again?

Or was there a third possibility?

Despite her disappointment and anger at Thomas, the blame wasn't his. It belonged to the Slater family. These people obviously believed they could do anything they wanted and get away with it. She refused to allow them to have control over her life. They were finished playing God.

She had to call Nick and give him what information she knew. It wasn't much. Apparently, what had been in the large envelope was what had gotten Thomas killed. But, still, Nick needed to know what had happened. Then she would do what she had to do to survive.

The man who'd run her off the road had been trying to kill her—his words had indicated as much. It was beyond a miracle that she wasn't dead. He had obviously known what was inside the envelope he stole. But how had he known that she would go to the bank today? Or that she had found a lock-box key?

She froze as the answer came to her with the force of a wrecking ball: She was being watched. There was no other explanation. Somehow they knew she had found the key and was going after the information Thomas had hidden. If that was the case, it could mean only one thing. There were cameras inside her house. *Sweet Lord!*

Suddenly, she felt their eyes on her. Who were they? The Slaters? Someone who worked for them? Thomas had feared they had eyes and ears everywhere. Had they been able to read the letter? Did the man know he hadn't taken the only information Thomas had left? Were they coming for her?

Should she just run out of the house now? Take nothing and leave forever?

She took a breath to steady herself. Yes, she did need to leave but not in a panic. Even though she felt that any second armed gunmen would burst through her door, Kennedy calmly stood and walked upstairs. She packed quickly and efficiently, taking only what she felt she couldn't live without.

Gun in one hand, a large suitcase in the other, she went into the garage. Hoping to time it just right, she cranked the car and pressed the garage door opener. The instant the doors were clear, she backed out and then zoomed out of the driveway. Thankfully the rain had stopped, but clouds covered the sky, making for an ink-dark night. Were they following her? Every headlight behind her had her tensing up. Would the man who'd slammed his car into hers try to finish the job?

Finally miles away from her house, with no visible car following her, Kennedy allowed herself to think about her next move. A plan began to form—one that would most certainly have horrified Thomas. She had no experience in things like this. She was a law student, not a cop. But she was something else, too—a born researcher. How many times had the law firms she freelanced for told her she was worth her weight in all the information she supplied them? She knew how to dig deep for obscure information. She could do this.

But could she really? Did she have the stamina? The courage to see it through? A small voice inside her screamed a resounding, *Yes!* She had already lost the love of her life and her precious child. Everything she had always dreamed of having had been taken from her. She had nothing left to lose. It was time to turn the tables and take her power back. So, could she really do this? The answer came in a firm, definitive: Oh hell yes, she could. And she would.

CHAPTER SEVEN

Milton Ward gnawed at the hangnail on his pinkie finger as he waited for Detective Gallagher. Every noise had him turning right or left. The Slaters were a powerful family and had spies everywhere. They were looking for him…he had no doubts about that.

Doug's was quiet this time of day. Too early for dinner, too late for lunch. Only a few people sat at the counter, seeming uninterested in him as he cowered in the back corner booth, nursing his coffee and jumping at every sound. He kept his eyes on them, taking no one for granted. The Slaters were as crafty as they were crooked.

He'd hightailed it out of the city the day before Thomas O'Connell's death. After hearing through the grapevine that two hits had been ordered, it didn't take a genius to know that he'd been one of the two. He didn't bother to question how the Slaters had discovered that he had snitched on them. His only thought had been to get away. It had bothered him that he hadn't let O'Connell know. Then when he'd heard about the man's widow losing her baby… That was some bad karma shit. It was too late to save O'Connell, but that didn't mean the Slaters should be able to get away with murder.

He was taking a big chance on coming back to Houston, but his conscience had made him return. O'Connell hadn't deserved to die. If Milton hadn't contacted the man and told him about the papers he'd stolen, none of this would be happening.

But when he'd heard from a friend that O'Connell was doing some poking around on the Slaters, he hadn't been able to resist. And now, look what had happened.

But what was done was done. Main thing was to give the information to someone he could trust and hide till the Slaters got what was coming to them.

The squeaking door alerted him that someone had entered the restaurant. A tall, broad-shouldered man with a hard, uncompromising expression on his face headed toward him. His thick brown hair glistened with rain, water dripped from the black leather jacket covering his large frame. Fear clutched at Milton's chest, turned his bowels to liquid. Had the Slaters' hit man found him?

Apparently reading his terrified expression, the big man said, "Relax. I'm Gallagher."

Breath whooshed from Milton's body as he slumped back into his chair. "I hope nobody followed you."

Gallagher sat across from him and seared him with a fierce look. "Like who?"

"If I tell you, you'll have to offer me the same deal as O'Connell. And protection, too."

"Tell me what this is about, and we'll talk about whether I can give you anything."

Figuring that was the best he could hope for right now, Milton said, "I was a clerk in the offices of McClusky and Hendrix."

"And they are?"

"The accounting firm that handles the Slater family."

A dangerous light flared in Gallagher's eyes. Milton swallowed hard and continued, "One night after everybody was gone and I was working late, I went into Hendrix's office to see if he had a file I was looking for. I sat down at his desk, and my knee bumped something underneath. I looked down and saw this little cubbyhole with this file sticking out of it. My curiosity got the better of me, so I pulled it out. It was a file detailing some of the Slaters' dealings."

"If the accounting firm is used for tax purposes, all those holdings would be legitimate."

Milton shook his head. "Oh, there's legit stuff, too. I've handled a couple accounts for them. I had no idea any of this other stuff was happening till I came upon that file. From what I could tell, Hendrix is in deep with the Slaters. In cahoots, I guess you could say. The file was full of documented shipments to and from various ports, along with the contents of each shipment."

"Such as?"

"You name it, they shipped it."

"In other words, everything illegal."

"Exactly."

"You told this to Detective O'Connell?"

Milton nodded. "We met a few days ago. I gave him copies of all the documents. I was even willing to testify, only—" Milton broke off, embarrassed to admit that he'd run like a scalded cat when he'd heard they were on to him.

"But you heard that the Slaters found out you had snitched on them and you ran."

"Yeah. I don't know how they found out, but a friend of a friend heard about it and gave me the heads-up. I was gonna call O'Connell and let him know as soon as I got someplace safe. Then I saw on the news about him getting killed. I know it was supposed to be a robbery of some kind, but it seemed too much of a coincidence to me."

Gallagher's face had gotten grimmer with each additional detail. Cold eyes roamed over Milton's face, and he swallowed hard again. *Damn.* O'Connell had been no pushover, but this guy looked as ruthless as any stone-cold killer the Slaters might hire.

"So what's in it for you?" Gallagher asked.

"What do you mean?"

"I mean, are you just trying to be a good citizen or is there an ulterior motive?"

"O'Connell promised me a reward…monetary."

"Nice try." Gallagher stood, threw down a dollar for the cup of coffee he hadn't touched and turned to walk away.

"Wait!" Milton called out, panicked. Okay, so the guy was no dummy. Even if he got nothing for his troubles, he still needed protection. Gallagher was the only man O'Connell had said he trusted. "Can you at least keep me safe?"

The big man turned back to him. "I can do that."

Milton blew out a long, jagged sigh. So maybe he couldn't make any money off this deal, at least he'd be alive and his conscience would be clean.

"You still have copies of the information you gave Detective O'Connell?"

"Yeah. It's in a safe place. I didn't bring it with me in case you weren't on the up-and-up."

Gallagher nodded toward the door. "Then let's go."

"You want to follow me?"

"No, we go together. Stay behind me till we get to my car."

Milton walked out the door behind the detective, sticking to him like he was glued to his back.

"My car's over there." Gallagher pointed to a dark sedan only a few feet away.

His head down to avoid the pounding rain and feeling safe for the first time in days, Milton stepped around Gallagher and ran toward the car.

Gallagher shouted, "Wait!"

A pop-pop-pop sounded. Milton whirled. Gallagher was lying faceup on the wet sidewalk. Blood mixed with rainwater swirled around his head.

Survival instinct kicked in… Milton took a running step. Too late. A blinding, piercing agony exploded in his head. And then nothing.

Kennedy gripped the phone. Nick wasn't answering his cellphone. She had considered calling him at work, but Thomas had said trust no one. What if someone heard him talking on the phone call? She couldn't take the chance.

The only thing she could do was leave a vague voice mail. "Nick, it's Kennedy. I need to talk to you."

The man behind her muttered something. She bit her lip and continued with her message, "I'll call you back."

She turned to the little old man staring up at her with worried eyes. Everett Meacham was the first man on Thomas's contact list. He was apparently going to get her started on a new identity.

"I'm sorry, Mr. Meacham. I didn't hear what you said."

"I'm just wondering if you're sure you're doing the right thing. I mean…um… are you sure you're thinking…um…rationally?"

Rationally? No, she couldn't say with any degree of confidence that her thinking was remotely rational. In the span of just over a week, she'd lost her husband, her baby, and the happy life she treasured. She had just learned that her husband's death had been a hit, and now she was on the run from people she didn't even know. So, hell no, she wasn't thinking rationally. She was acting on instinct and a whole lot of fear. Both were telling her to hide. But something else transcended her need to run and hide—full-blown fury.

"All I know is what Thomas told me to do. He said you could help me. Was he wrong?"

"Oh, no, ma'am. Thomas O'Connell was a good man. He helped get my boy on the straight and narrow. I'd do anything for him."

"This is what Thomas wanted."

Nodding, he said, "That's good enough for me." An amazing change came over the man's craggy face. He might not have felt comfortable consoling a grieving widow, but he was in his element when it came to his expertise—helping people disappear.

His eyes targeted the object in her hand. "You need to get rid of that right quick."

She gripped her phone…the last link to what was dear and familiar. It contained texts, emails and voice mails from Thomas. And it had all of her contacts.

"Give it here."

"But I still need to call a couple of people."

With one hand, he snatched the phone from her grasp, and with the other hand, he plunked a small plastic bag holding three phones onto his desk. "Use these. They're burner phones. Can't trace 'em…usually. To be on the safe side, make the calls short. No more than thirty seconds. And as soon as you finish with a call, do this."

Pulling a wooden mallet from his desk, he whacked her cellphone, obliterating it. He then gave her a narrow-eyed glare, as if waiting for her objections.

She blew out a fragile, shaky breath. There was no point in protesting what was already done.

"What do I need to do?"

"You got a place to stay?"

She shook her head. "Not yet."

"You got cash?"

"Yes." After driving around the city for an hour, making sure she wasn't being followed, she'd stopped at an ATM and withdrew the maximum allowable amount for a single transaction. Her shaking hands pulled the wad of bills from her coat pocket and shoved them toward the man.

"I don't want your money, darlin'. Thomas O'Connell done paid with what he did for me and mine years ago. I just wanted to make sure you got cash. No more credit cards."

Yes, she knew that much, but there was one slight problem. Thomas's life insurance company had been amazingly quick in paying, and she'd deposited the money into her savings account. "How can I get into my savings? I'm going to need it to live."

"You got your account number?"

She nodded and withdrew the card from her wallet. It never occurred to her not to give it to him. Thomas had trusted him—she had no choice but to do the same.

"I got a man who can get it for you. Don't ask how. He'll want payment, though. And he ain't cheap."

Negotiating a price for doing something that was most likely illegal was beyond her knowledge and expertise. "I'll pay him."

"You go on now and get you a good night's sleep. Come back tomorrow night. I should have what you need."

"Thank you, Mr. Meacham." Feeling as though she'd lived a thousand lives in the last few hours, Kennedy returned to her car and took a moment to think. First, she had to try Nick again, to explain what was going on. He had most likely dropped by the house to check on her. There was no telling what he was thinking.

She took one of the phones from the plastic bag and tapped in Nick's cell number. After three rings, his voice mail came on again. Why wasn't he answering? She left another message, once again telling him that she would call back in a few hours.

She had one more call to make. One she dreaded. She'd been told to keep it short, but how do you tell your best friend that you're disappearing and might never see her again? She could explain nothing.

Julie answered on the first ring. The thick huskiness of her voice made Kennedy wonder if her friend was coming down with a cold.

"Julie, it's me. I—"

"Kennedy, where the hell are you? I've been calling you for hours."

"I'm sorry. I had to turn my phone off because I—"

"Then you don't know?"

"Know what?"

"Nick's been shot. It's been all over the news."

If she hadn't been sitting down, she would have fallen. "What happened?" she asked faintly.

"There are almost no details. He was getting into his car. There was another man shot, too. That man was killed."

"And Nick?"

"He's hanging on…but it's not looking good. He's in coma. You need to come to the hospital. We're all here in the ICU waiting room on the third floor."

A sob built up in her chest, waiting to explode. *Nick.* Did this have anything to do with the Slaters? Had he been targeted, too? He was the one person Thomas had trusted. Had Thomas told him something and had Nick been shot because of it? Or had they just assumed he knew something?

"Kennedy, you there? What's going on?"

"I can't come to the hospital right now, Julie. I—I'm not even in town. I left a few hours ago."

"What? Where? Why?"

"I just needed to get away. I've got to go. I'm sorry."

"What? No, wait… I—"

She ended the call before she lost it completely. Dear, wonderful Nick. The one man she could count on and trust was fighting for his life.

Kennedy's forehead pressed into the steering wheel. Her fingers gripping the leather with a punishing force, she whispered softly, "Oh, Thomas, what have you done to us?"

Hours later, a slender, shadowy figure crept up the stairway to the third floor. Dressed in navy sweats and a dark hoodie that covered her hair and most of her face, she was unidentifiable. A lone nurse sat at the main desk, staring at a computer screen. Silent as a whisper, Kennedy slipped into the supply room and five minutes later, emerged wearing scrubs and a surgical cap. Clipboard in hand, she walked with an air of confidence toward the intensive care unit. Stopping at another supply closet not far from the locked ICU door, she stepped inside and waited. Five, ten…fifteen minutes. She didn't care how long it took. She had to see him. At last, two nurses emerged from the unit. Deep in conversation with each other, they never glanced her way as she caught the door they'd exited before it could close.

She peeked into several rooms before she found the right one. The sight that met her eyes caused a small cry to slip out. Prone and lifeless on the bed, Nick looked paler than death. Half of his face was covered in bandages. Had he been shot in the head, his face? Machines beeped, oxygen pumped air into his lungs, and tubes filled with life-sustaining fluids were attached to both of his arms.

Swallowing a sob, she drew closer. The last time she had stood beside a hospital bed and seen someone so seriously injured, she had been ten years old and her daddy had been barely clinging to life. He had never woken up. Would that be Nick's fate, too?

Nick had always treated her with affection and respect. He had been a part of her life almost as long as Thomas. The last few days she hadn't been sure she would have survived without him. Her heart breaking, she uttered a small, fervent prayer for his recovery.

Knowing she could be caught at any moment, Kennedy leaned over and whispered a promise in his ear, "I'm going to get whoever killed Thomas. And if they hurt you, too, I'll make them pay double. I swear I will, Nick." She pressed a kiss to his unbandaged cheek and then a soft kiss to his firm, masculine lips.

She then turned with a new determination. She had made a promise, and she would keep it. The Slaters had messed with the wrong people. And they would pay.

Chapter Eight

Twenty months later

Nick steered his car toward home, his thoughts as grim and bleak as the flat, barren landscape. He'd seen a lot of shit in his life. A person didn't grow up in one of the most dangerous areas of Houston and not see his share. But he'd had the kind of mother who could turn the sorriest piece of news into something good. And though he couldn't say he had inherited her optimism, for the most part he had always felt some kind of hope for a better day. All of that had gone to hell. He had felt nothing positive in months and didn't see a change in attitude coming his way anytime soon.

His recovery had been a long and arduous journey. After waking from a five-day, drug-induced coma, he'd barely known his own name, much less what had happened. It'd taken more than a week to remember. When the memories had rolled in, a tidal wave of panic had followed.

Kennedy was in danger. He was sure of it. When he had demanded to see her, he'd learned just how much was being kept from him. She had disappeared. No one knew where the hell she was—not even Julie, her best friend.

The panic had morphed into something else. With a howl of fury, he'd ripped tubes and wires from his body and flung himself out of bed. Three steps from the doorway, all hell had broken loose inside his body. He'd keeled over, unconscious. He'd learned later that he had been rushed to the operating room for another seven hours of surgery.

When he'd finally been coherent again, he'd asked for news. There had been nothing.

The first few weeks after his release from the hospital, in between rehab, Nick had spent hours trying to track Kennedy down and again, found nothing.

When he'd been able to return to work, he had been deskbound for months. That hadn't stopped him from demanding a thorough investigation into Thomas's death. Most everyone, including his captain, had looked at him as if he was crazy. There'd been talk of brain damage, PTSD, hallucinations. He hadn't given a shit what people thought. He had insisted and finally got grudging approval to move forward. Of course, implicating the Slaters hadn't made him popular or appear any less crazed. The top brass especially hadn't been thrilled with the target of his investigation, but they had allowed him leeway. Wasn't long before Nick figured out why. He couldn't find one damn thing.

Whatever evidence Milton Ward had possessed was long gone. Nick had tracked down the man's last known address, an apartment on the south side of the city. The three-room apartment had been tossed, not even a scrap of paper could be found.

The accounting firm, McClusky and Hendrix, did confirm that Ward was a former employee but they claimed he was let go because of poor job performance. When Nick had asked questions about the Slater account, he'd been met with a stony silence. With nothing and no one to back him up, he'd had no choice but to walk away.

The lack of information and cooperation was infuriating but did help him understand Thomas's secrecy. Hell, there had been nothing to tell. The evidence that Milton Ward had provided had probably felt like answered prayers. Unfortunately, it had gotten both Ward and Thomas killed.

Nick had the gut-wrenching feeling that unless another snitch stepped up to rat out the Slaters, Thomas's murder would remain unsolved. True, the bastard who'd fired the gun was dead, but the people who'd hired the hit were still running free. And, apparently, that's the way it would stay. Thomas's murder was officially closed as a robbery gone bad. Nick's own shooting and Milton Ward's death had gone to cold case. Speculation that Nick had been targeted for a bust he'd made years ago had become the standard party line.

The shooting of the three gang members, including the kid associated with Jonah Slater, went down as a rival gang shooting. Everything got tied up with a neat little bow.

And once again, the Slaters had gotten away with murder.

For Nick, this would never be over. He would search until death to find the people behind Thomas's murder.

On his own time and dime, Nick had dug deep into the Slaters. Investigating the family was a lot like eating cotton candy. You could stuff a lot in your mouth, but it disintegrated into a whole lot of nothing. If he hadn't been shot and Milton's head hadn't exploded seconds after implicating the Slaters, he wouldn't have believed they were involved either.

He would've handled everything a hell of a lot better if he could have been sure that Kennedy was safe. The three voice mail messages she'd left on his phone had been terrifying and frustrating. The first two had been "I'll call you back" messages; the third one had been a vague, "I'll be fine. Don't worry about me, just take care of yourself."

He'd heard the fear and despair in her voice. He had listened to those messages at least a hundred times. He could only imagine how alone and cornered she must have felt. And he hadn't been able to do a damn thing to help her. After all the promises he'd made to her and to Thomas, he had failed them both.

Arrogantly, he had assumed that because she was an amateur, she would be easy to find. He knew she was intelligent but had underestimated her ingenuity. Air and train tickets purchased and not used. Car rental reservations made without the car being picked up. Her car had been found in a grocery store parking lot in Hobbs, New Mexico. And at some point, in the middle of the night, someone had come and cleaned out her house. According to her neighbors, one day the house had been filled with furniture, and the next it stood empty, as if no one had ever lived there.

Where was the evidence Ward claimed to have given Thomas? Had Thomas hidden it somewhere? Or had one of Slater's people gotten to it?

Nick had searched every square inch of the O'Connells' empty house. If that's where Thomas stored the documents, they were long gone. Did Kennedy have them? Was that why she had disappeared?

How the hell could a young woman with no covert experience vanish so thoroughly? There was only one answer—she'd had help. Someone had guided her actions and helped her disappear. She had created a mass of leads that had him running around like a rat in a maze. And though the dead ends had been as frustrating as hell, they had reassured him. If, with his experience and resources, he couldn't find her, then no one else could either.

Yeah, it was tepid, shallow optimism…these days, he took what he could get.

Nick opened his apartment door and headed straight to his bedroom to change into a pair of shorts and an old sweatshirt. About the only way he had to battle the hopelessness inside him was to beat the hell out of his boxing bag and work himself into exhaustion. He was halfway to the kitchen for a bottle of water when he realized he wasn't alone. The dark figure of a man sitting in a chair in the corner caught his eye.

Cursing his inattentiveness, he grabbed the closest weapon—a bust of Sherlock Holmes—and turned toward the intruder.

"Before you allow Mr. Holmes to bash my head in, wouldn't you like to know why I'm here?"

The crisp British voice sounded familiar, but he couldn't place it. Nick replied coolly, "I'm more of an attack-first-and-ask-questions-later kind of guy."

"Pity. You don't seem the type to go off half-cocked."

"Depends on the situation. Having some asshole break into my house is the type of thing that pisses me off."

"Understandable, but you can often learn more things if you wait awhile."

"Or you can get yourself killed. Now, tell me who the hell you are and why you're here."

"Let's talk first. Then we'll decide if we want to exchange personal information."

If the man was going to shoot him, he would've done so by now. Nick lowered the statue to his side but held on to it just in case. He reached for the light switch on the wall.

"No lights."

"So I'm not allowed to know your name or what you look like?"

"Not yet. Have a seat."

Despite the aggravation of having a stranger break into his house and the man's numerous rules, Nick was intrigued. He pulled his hand back from the light switch. "I'll stand. Now tell me what the hell you want."

"I want what you want—to bring Mathias Slater and his goons to justice."

If he hadn't captured Nick's attention before, he sure as hell had it now. "What do you know about Slater?"

"That he's into more shit than anyone could ever imagine."

"And why do you care?"

"Let's just say that seeing bad guys get what's coming to them is a hobby of mine."

"And how can you assist me in seeing that Slater gets what's coming to him?"

"By giving you access to information you can't get through your channels."

"You mean illegal channels."

"Semantics. What you see as illegal, I see as creative license."

Still wary but more interested than ever, Nick returned the statue to the end table and dropped down onto the sofa. "Okay, you have my undivided attention."

"Excellent. However, we need to come to an agreement before we go further."

"Such as?"

"If you decline my proposal, this discussion never happened."

"Agreed."

"Excellent."

"You're just going to take my word for it?"

"I wouldn't be here if I didn't already know you can be trusted, Mr. Gallagher."

Where and how he'd gotten information on Nick could wait till another time. "Okay, I'm listening."

"Mathias Slater and his antics hit my radar several years ago. I've tried penetrating his tight-knit circle. Unfortunately, I've gotten only so far before someone ratted out my informant."

"And how can I help? If you know that much about me, then you already know that I've run into a road block in every avenue I've taken against Slater."

"That's true. However, you have an avenue you don't even know you can take."

"And what's that?"

"There's a folder on the table in front of you. Take a look inside."

Nick didn't move…considered what could be inside.

"I'm glad to see that my informants were correct. You have a short fuse, but it's tempered with a deliberative cautiousness."

"I'm assuming that I'll be allowed to turn on the lights to look at the folder."

"That's correct. Another reason why your deliberation is important. You turn on those lights, you will have information that could destroy not only me, but negatively impact the lives of thousands."

Nick reached up and flipped on the lamp beside him. Light illuminated the man sitting in the corner and he knew why the voice had sounded so familiar. This was a man known to millions. And he was right—if anyone discovered the truth, thousands of lives would be affected.

Deciding to mull over the man's identity later, Nick grabbed the folder and opened it. The instant he saw the first photograph, everything within him froze. He looked up at the man who sat so calmly across from him and whispered hoarsely, "What do I need to do?"

CHAPTER NINE

Grey Justice wasn't a man easily impressed. Nick Gallagher had managed to do that on more than one occasion. The detective had been researched thoroughly. Before he brought people into his confidence, he had to know what they were made of and if they could be trusted. Gallagher had the forthrightness to tell it like he saw it, but he also had integrity. Having a few notable contacts in the Houston Police Department, he had learned many things about the detective over the last few months.

Raised by a single mother, Gallagher had never had it easy. The majority of people in the world didn't, but challenges didn't reveal character. How a man chose to deal with those challenges showed his true self. Some allowed their circumstances to conquer them; others battled for all they were worth to rise above them. Nick Gallagher was a man who had fought to overcome the odds.

Recovering from the bullet wound hadn't been a painless path, either. Few people survived the kind of injury Gallagher sustained…much less regained their health. A combination of luck, stamina, and determination were required to overcome that kind of trauma.

He noted that Gallagher took his time, looking through all the photographs in the folder as if memorizing each one. There shouldn't have been that many, but the woman was extraordinarily photogenic. His photographer had obviously enjoyed his assignment.

It was telling that Gallagher knew the woman's identity immediately, especially since she looked almost nothing like she had before. Hair that had once been brownish red, reaching well past her shoulders, was now a mass of short platinum-blond curls. The style suited her, highlighting exquisite cheekbones and enhancing wide brown eyes. The woman wore glasses, most likely thinking they gave her an aura of seriousness. She also wore more makeup than she had in her previous life. Either way, she was a lovely woman and would attract many men.

Grey had briefly considered approaching her instead of Gallagher, but had changed his mind. She had little reason to trust him. Nick Gallagher was probably the only person she completely trusted.

If not for the trained eyes by some of his employees, he might never have found her until it was too late. She'd come a long way from the frightened, emotionally battered woman she had been when he'd first met her, and he couldn't help but be impressed by her ingenuity and determination. However, she couldn't know what she had taken on. She was in a nest of vipers. One slipup, and she'd be eliminated without a second thought.

He'd mucked things up before…underestimating her. He didn't intend to do that again. Gallagher was his way in.

Coming to the end of the photographs, Gallagher raised his head. "How long has she worked there?"

"Over a year. She started at an entry-level position, but with her intelligence and drive, she's already received several promotions."

"What the hell is she trying to do?"

"I don't know. My guess is she's either going to find a way to destroy Slater financially or she's going to get information she needs to prove his guilt."

"So she's not working for you?"

"No, she did this on her own. Impressive that she was able to infiltrate even this level. The Slaters have stringent hiring procedures. Her cover is impressive and airtight."

"I can't believe she's working right under their noses."

Grey shrugged. "It's the talent and backbone of the person that makes or breaks a cover. She's very talented…and determined."

For the first time since they'd begun talking, he saw a small crack in Gallagher's stony veneer. Though fleeting and covered up almost immediately, the agony in the man's eyes was almost painful to witness. Another piece of the puzzle was solved. Gallagher had deep feelings for the woman. That might complicate things a bit but could also be used to his advantage.

Ruthlessly using people had become a way of life for Grey. Some saw him as a heartless bastard with no conscience. Others saw him as a generous, kind man who assisted those in need. In his opinion, he was neither. He was just a man on a set course who did what he had to do to accomplish his goals. He cared little about other people's opinions. Though, on occasion, he caught a glimpse of the man he'd once been—with a conscience, morals and ethics—he would never let that prevent him from taking advantage of others' weaknesses to get the job done.

"If she's not working for you, then why are…?" Comprehension came quick, fury followed. "You son of a bitch. You want to use me to get to her."

Grey shrugged. He would make no apology for his methods. "She doesn't trust easy…especially after what happened to her husband. She trusts you."

"Forget it. I'm not going to put her in danger just to further whatever agenda you have."

"Not even to bring down the people responsible for Thomas O'Connell's death?" Grey asked softly.

It took every ounce of Nick's self-control not to fly across the room and slam his fist into the man's face. The fact that Grey Justice was one of the wealthiest men in the world made no difference to him. The bastard wanted to use Kennedy.

"Before you fulfill that need to beat me to a pulp, you need to realize that Mrs. O'Connell is already in danger. She chose to pursue Slater. Whatever Thomas O'Connell intended for his wife, I doubt it included working for the enemy."

That much was true. Thomas would have been furious at what Kennedy had done. And Nick couldn't help but be furious with his friend for putting her in this position in the first place.

"What exactly does Kennedy hope to accomplish?" Nick asked. "You said yourself you've not been able to infiltrate Slater's tight-knit organization. If she's working in a low-level position at one of the family's many companies, how does she expect to succeed? Hell, she'll never even get close enough to do any damage. He's probably got thousands of people working for him that he's never met."

"Exactly. That's one of the things you're going to have to address with her. I don't know her plans."

"But you already know what your plans are for her. Right?"

"Yes, we have an entry for her, but she'll need to trust us. That's where you come in."

Nick cocked a brow. "Sorry, asshole, but if you think I'm going to trust you because of your money or reputation, you're barking up the wrong tree."

Humor lit Justice's eyes. "I've been known to do my share of barking, but I don't believe it will be necessary in this case."

"I'll hear you out. That's all I'll promise."

"Good enough for me. But there's something else I'd like you to consider as well."

"And that is?"

"Working for me."

Nick shook his head. "I'm a cop."

"And a good one." Justice shrugged. "I'll let you ponder your career choice. I'm hopeful you'll change your mind."

Not one to make decisions without knowing all the facts, Nick wasn't going to say one hundred percent that he wouldn't change his mind, but it would take a hell of a lot of persuading to get him to make a change of that magnitude.

For right now, his main concern was Kennedy. While seeing Thomas's killer get what was coming to him was high on Nick's list of priorities, Kennedy's safety and welfare trumped those things to hell and back. What on earth was she doing working for the Slaters?

"Let's talk about the Slaters. I already know they're the scumbags responsible for Thomas's death, Milton Ward's murder, and my shooting."

"They are much more than that."

"Such as?"

"Did you ever wonder why you could find nothing—not a shred of evidence—that sullied the Slater name?"

Hell yeah, he'd wondered. It'd been driving him crazy for months. "What about his son Jonah? He sure sullied it."

"You never thought that was strange? An anomaly?"

Thomas had thought it was suspicious, but proving someone's innocence hadn't exactly been on Nick's must-do list. He'd been looking for a way to nail all the Slaters, not investigate one who'd already been proven guilty.

"The guy was caught with a shitload of cocaine and heroin. Not much mystery there."

"True. But when you piss Papa Slater off, you pay the price."

"You're saying Slater set up his own kid? Why? And how do you know this?"

"Because Jonah Slater works for me."

Nick wasn't buying it. "You're saying the son of Mathias Slater is a good guy who was set up by his father to take a fall as punishment? Somebody sold you a crock of shit."

"I assure you, Mr. Gallagher, I don't deal in crocks, shit or otherwise. Jonah went against the family. He was punished for his sins. It was either send him to prison or kill him. As an indulgence to his wife, Jonah's mother, Mathias chose prison."

"Gee, what a nice guy," Nick said.

"I'm sure Mathias thinks so."

"Sounds like you have more insight into the family than just Jonah."

"I'll be glad to tell you more if you agree to my terms."

"I've already told you I'm not going to work for you. However, I do want to make sure Kennedy stays safe. If that means helping you, then I'll agree to those terms."

"You'll have to move to Dallas."

"Fine. I'll take a leave of absence. Problem is, no one's going to buy that I'm just taking time off. No way in hell will they believe I'm not continuing an investigation of the Slaters."

"Don't worry, a leave of absence won't be necessary. I'll take care of it."

Nick narrowed his eyes at the man across from him. He took nothing on faith these days, especially from a man who was probably just as powerful and well connected as the Slaters. "Take care of it how?"

"I can understand your caution, Gallagher, but it's time to take a stand. I can make things happen, but giving you details is time consuming and pointless. What's it going to be? In or out."

Nick considered all that he had heard. Seemingly content to allow him this time, Justice continued a relaxed pose across from him. The man was as well known for his sexual exploits as he was for his charitable foundations. And yet here he was indicating that he was a hell of a lot more than just a playboy or philanthropist.

"What happens if I say no?"

"Then I'll be on my way."

"Just like that...even though I know this about you?"

"Again, Mr. Gallagher, I don't deal with untrustworthy people. If you say no to my proposal, I have every faith that you will never mention this discussion to anyone."

"But you'll still find a way to use Kennedy."

"By her own actions, Mrs. O'Connell has indicated she wants to be involved in bringing Slater to justice. I intend to make it easier for her."

"How magnanimous of you."

"I make no pretention of my motives." Justice went to his feet. "But from the sound of your comments, it doesn't look like you'll be interested."

"I didn't say that. I would need your guarantee that Kennedy would be protected."

"Protecting the people who work for me is my number one concern."

"Then why is Jonah Slater in prison?"

For the first time since this bizarre conversation started, Nick saw emotion on Justice's face. No matter how unfazed the man pretended to be, Jonah Slater's incarceration had made an impact.

"When the truth comes out, Jonah will receive a new trial and be exonerated."

"You sound very sure of yourself."

"That's because I don't fail, Mr. Gallagher. My methods may take longer than I like, but in the end, there will always be justice."

"Odd how your name fits this mysterious persona of yours."

Without acknowledging the comment, Justice raised a questioning brow, waiting for Nick's answer. And since it had been decided the moment he'd seen Kennedy's picture, he saw no reason to delay the inevitable.

"I'm in. What do I need to do?"

CHAPTER TEN

Slater House Hotels

Dallas, Texas

Rachel Walker peered intently at her computer screen. Crap, that wasn't right. She pulled off her glasses, wiped a couple of smudges from the lenses and returned them to the bridge of her nose. They weren't prescription—just plain, ordinary glass. She didn't wear them to aid her in seeing. Rather, the glasses helped others from seeing the real her. They were the subtlest of the changes she had made to her appearance.

She scanned the spreadsheet until she spotted the mistake. Clicking the backspace key, she typed in the correct numbers, then hit enter. There—her work was finished. What should have taken eight hours had been accomplished in four. Amazing what a properly motivated employee could do. After lunch, while she looked still busy at her job, she would snoop.

Standing, she stretched her back and neck muscles until she heard a small pop. Sitting in one place for a long time wasn't good for her posture or health, but the job was what it was. Boring, but in its own way fulfilling. Right now, she was one tiny cog in the giant Slater machine, but one day she would be much more. This she vowed.

"Hey, Rachel. We're going to lunch. Want to come?"

She glanced over her shoulder at three of her co-workers. They were a friendly group, and despite her desire to stay as isolated as she could, she had blended in well with them. She was just one of the millions of young, single women earning a living in the big city.

Still, going to lunch was out of the question. There were two or three reports she had new access to that she wanted to peruse. She needed privacy for that. Not that she expected to find anything illegal or incriminating in them, but the more she learned about the business the better her chances for promotion.

She gave them a friendly grin. "Thanks, but I brought my lunch."

Throwing her a "see you later," the small, cheerful group of women walked out the door. She turned back to the computer and was about to click onto a new screen when someone called her name.

Startled, she looked up into the smiling face of her supervisor. She had thought the woman had gone to lunch, too.

"Yes?"

"Have you taken your lunch break yet?"

"No, I was just about to."

"I'm going to eat in the break room. Want to join me? I need to talk to you about something."

Refusing wasn't an option. She was finding that her eager-to-please attitude was opening doors earlier than she had ever anticipated.

A shot of fear surged through her that she quickly squelched. If her real identity had been discovered, her supervisor wouldn't be the one dealing with her. It would be someone with more authority and a deadly motive.

The thought giving her ease in its own bizarre way, she nodded eagerly at the woman. Sandra Frost was just one of dozens of supervisors in this huge hotel conglomerate, but that didn't mean she didn't have knowledge to share.

The woman smiled and turned away, never realizing that Rachel had only one thing on her mind—picking the woman's brain of everything she knew about her job and the owners of the company. Rachel was like a sponge, eager to move forward in her new career. She wanted to be known as the most dedicated and ambitious employee the Slaters had ever had. But unlike most ambitious women, her ultimate goal had nothing to do with money or prestige and everything to do with gaining justice.

Seven days later, Kennedy sat in a chair in front of a massive cherry wood desk belonging to Eli Slater. Never had she anticipated that sharing lunch with her supervisor last week would lead her here.

Nerves jumped like manic crickets inside her, and she worked with all her might to get her jitters under control. She crossed her legs, and the instant she saw her leg swinging, she dropped both feet back to the floor. Showing a few nerves was fine—after all, she was interviewing for a new, much-higher-paying position. Revealing that getting this job meant a lot more to her than just a higher salary and some nice perks would have been a major mistake. She was a motivated young woman, eager to move up in the world, nothing more.

When her supervisor had told her about the opening and suggested she try for it, there had been no hesitation in Kennedy's agreement. The closer she could get to the "family", the better for her plans.

As she waited for Eli Slater to arrive, Kennedy reviewed what she had dug up about the man. He was the next to the youngest of Mathias and Eleanor Slater's sons. A thirty-four-old widower with two young daughters, Eli had been in charge of the Slater House Hotels for ten years as chief operating officer. The luxury hotels were in every corner of the world. Eli had run them from the corporate headquarters in London for six years. Four years ago he had moved his family to the U.S.

Known to be tough but fair, it was reported that when he wasn't working, the man was with his children. Rumor was he had been devastated by the death of his wife, Shelley, who had lost her battle with drugs and alcohol only months after giving birth to their second child.

Kennedy had done extensive research on the entire family and had found Eli to be one of the most mysterious—not because she couldn't find any information, but because he seemed so damned normal. An everyday, average man devoted to his family, his job, and his employees. Nothing in his profile suggested that he was involved in anything remotely illegal.

Of course, that kind of cover-up was how the Slaters had stayed out of trouble for so long. They portrayed themselves as a large, loving, and successful family. The only taint was Jonah Slater, who was serving a long prison sentence. And even though she had never met the man, his arrest and conviction had been the beginning of the end for her and Thomas.

The door swung open, and Kennedy twisted her head around as Eli Slater entered. A few inches over six feet tall, the man strode into the room with a surprising grace and lack of sound. For such a large man, he moved with a fluidity she'd only ever seen in a dancer. With thick, blondish hair, an artfully angular face, and warm brown eyes, he could have been the poster boy for All-American good looks. How could evil be so handsomely disguised?

"Ms. Walker, thank you for agreeing to this interview."

Standing, she held out her hand. "It's my pleasure, Mr. Slater. I'm excited for the opportunity."

After shaking her hand with a cool, firm grip, he rounded his desk and dropped gracefully into his chair. The instant she was seated again, he gave her an impersonal but polite smile. "You come highly recommended by all of your supervisors. When I mentioned the need for a new executive assistant in our weekly staff meeting, your name was brought up by several people."

"I'm flattered. I—"

"Don't be. If you're half as good as you're reported to be, then it's hard work that's brought you here."

She nodded and remained quiet.

"This job will challenge you, and at times I'm sure you'll question your sanity and want to quit. However, if you stick with it, I believe you'll find it to be more rewarding than you ever thought possible."

"Can you explain what the job entails?"

"You'll handle my daily calendar and all travel arrangements, organize staff meetings, prepare press announcements. Screen all of my calls—my secretary will give you a list of approved people. You'll also be provided with two assistants and can delegate the more mundane matters to them. Once you're more comfortable with the day-to-day operations, I'll want you take over some of the analytical responsibilities. I understand you're proficient in the most up-to-date analytical software?"

"Yes." She had acquired these skills in previous jobs and had learned even more since moving to Dallas. If she got this job, she would make herself invaluable, indispensible. The more Eli Slater trusted her, the better for her plan.

"Do you have any issues with travel?"

"Travel?"

"Yes, I'll expect you to go with me on business trips and attend various functions."

Even though this was a common duty for an executive assistant, a warning bell went off in her head. She would be in close proximity with this man night and day. Would Eli Slater expect more from her than the normal executive assistant duties? There were a lot of things she would do to gain this man's confidence… sleeping with him would not be one of them.

She took in his expression and demeanor. She saw no indication that he found her even remotely appealing. Though not particularly vain, Kennedy had become accustomed to the gleam of attraction in men's eyes. It was reassuring that Eli Slater didn't appear to even see her as a woman.

"Travel is fine." And because she had to know for sure, she added, "I'm single and am only responsible for myself."

His expression never changing, he stood and rounded his desk once more. "Report here tomorrow morning at nine."

"That's it?" Kennedy inwardly grimaced at her first unguarded moment. But she couldn't believe he was hiring her without even interviewing her beyond those vague questions. And she was supposed to start immediately?

"Was there something more you should have told me or I should have asked?"

"Sorry…no. I just assumed you would have more questions."

"Your reputation got you the job. Our meeting was a formality."

Surprised but pleased, Kennedy stood. "I'll see you tomorrow morning, then. Thank you for the opportunity."

Instead of the cursory nod she expected, a slight gleam came into his eyes. "Thank you for the opportunity, Ms. Walker."

With that enigmatic statement, he opened the door for her, and she walked out.

As she made her way home that night, Kennedy reflected on the grueling and emotional journey she'd taken to get this far.

When she had realized her house was most likely bugged, she had known she had only a finite amount of time before someone came after her. Having lived with so little as a child had trained Kennedy to be a minimalist. She didn't need a lot in the way of material things to survive. Being married and secure with Thomas had blurred that lifestyle, but she had never allowed herself to collect "things" the way regular people did.

With that mindset, she had thrown clothes, shoes, a makeup bag, and her small amount of jewelry into a duffle bag and was ready. Even though a part of her had ached to take some of Thomas's things, she'd forced herself to settle for his leather jacket that still carried his scent and an old Texas A&M sweatshirt he'd practically worn out. On her way out the door, she had weakened and grabbed a framed photo of their wedding day, along with a photo album that chronicled their short life together. Altogether, it had taken her about five minutes.

The only anomaly in her escape had been her middle-of-the-night visit to the ICU ward to visit Nick. Seeing him like that had steeled a resolve in her that nothing and no one could shatter. She had no proof that Slater had been behind Nick's shooting, but it was just too damn coincidental that Thomas had been murdered, and three days later his best friend had been shot.

She had followed Nick's progress as best she could. Through newspapers and by lurking on the Facebook and Twitter accounts of some of his friends, she knew his recovery had been slow and painful. She knew there were days, maybe weeks, when the doctors didn't know if he would survive. But he had. Knowledge of his recovery had helped but hadn't diminished her determination to see this through. Both he and Thomas deserved justice for what had happened to them.

Upon completion of her new identity, she had moved to Dallas. The first couple of months, she had concentrated on getting settled—bought a house, opened a bank account and credit lines at local stores—all the things a new resident might do. And she had continued her research on the Slaters. Having had almost no knowledge of them, other than the few things she had heard, she'd had a lot to learn.

Once she had been reasonably sure of her course, she had applied for a job at Slater House Hotels. At that time, the only opening had been an entry-level position. Even though she had documentation that Rachel Walker had a business management degree, she'd assured the personnel director that she would be quite happy to start at the bottom. Laying it on thick about her admiration for the Slater empire and how much she wanted to work for such an impressive company, she'd never given the man the chance to tell her she was overqualified. Within a week, she had been hired.

Every opportunity for advancement that had come her way, she had applied for and gotten. Yes, they had still been low-level positions, but that hadn't mattered. In each job, she'd learned a little more and earned a reputation for being a motivated, dedicated employee, eager to move up and open for all opportunities.

Today, that reputation had paid off. She would soon be working for Eli Slater himself.

Even though she knew Thomas would never have wanted her to put herself at risk like this, she couldn't help but believe he would be proud of her progress. One day the Slaters would be sorry as hell they had ever heard of the O'Connells of Houston, Texas.

Chapter Eleven

Nick sat in the dark, waiting. Kennedy should be home soon. Breaking into her house had taken him a lot longer than he had anticipated. Not only did she have a quality security system, she had locks that would make most intruders turn around and find an easier target. He wasn't most intruders. He was here on a mission—to talk her out of whatever harebrained scheme she had cooked up. And if that didn't work, then he was going to aid her. Either way, he was here for the duration.

Yesterday he'd followed her from the building where she worked to her house. It had been all he could do not to call out her name when she'd walked to her car. He literally ached to be in her presence but had made himself wait. He was glad he had. As if she knew or feared she was being watched, she had taken an odd, circuitous route home. In fact, he'd almost lost her twice. She was, understandably, skittish as hell.

A week ago he hadn't known what had happened to her or where she was. And now, in mere minutes, she would be close enough to touch. Something he was still trying to process.

He had to give Grey Justice credit. When the man said he would take care of things at the precinct, he'd meant it. The day after their meeting, Nick had gone to work, still struggling with how to take leave without appearing as though he would be pursuing an investigation of the Slaters on his own. He'd barely sat at his desk before his captain had called him into his office. It seemed the governor had requested a special statewide task force be formed to battle inner-city gangs in the major cities. Nick was being asked to join—a six-month commitment, maybe longer. Was he interested?

Oh, hell yeah, he was interested. Nick had never doubted that Justice had somehow created this opportunity. And when he'd gone to his first meeting, his suspicions were confirmed. The meeting had been nothing more than a young man with an envelope with all the information he would need to find Kennedy and a note from Justice saying he would be in touch.

As much as he'd wanted to hop on a plane and go after her immediately, Nick had forced himself to wait. If he were being watched, no way in hell would he lead anyone to Kennedy's door.

In between finishing up as many cases as he could so Margo wouldn't be stuck with them, Nick had spent hours researching. This time, instead of trying to find dirt on the Slaters, he had dug up what he could on Grey Justice. Surprisingly and disturbingly, it wasn't what he had found that concerned him—it was what he couldn't find. The man was a billionaire, several times over, having invented a small computer device that apparently every company in the world decided they needed. Raised in a small town outside London, parents deceased, moved to the States when he was in his early twenties. Single, never been married, dated a variety of women, and had been on several top ten lists of the world's most desirable bachelors.

There were a multitude of articles on Justice, too numerous to count. Problem was, the articles revealed only so much. Without a doubt, someone was controlling the level and quality of information.

It was public knowledge that Justice was heavily involved in his highly touted Grey Justice Victims Advocacy Foundation. The press had labeled him the "white knight" of those in need of a champion. How many knew that the man had a dark side?

Nick had come away from his research with one disturbing conclusion. Grey Justice was a powerful, mysterious man—possibly even more powerful than the Slaters.

Headlights blazed through the front windows. Nick tensed, waiting, anticipating. Seconds later, the front door opened and closed. Footsteps sounded as Kennedy walked into the foyer. He heard beeps as she tapped her security code into the small box beside the front door. Even though she was in another room, he imagined that he could already smell her sweet scent, feel her vitality and essence. For the first time in almost two years, he felt alive.

When he heard the click of a revolver, he smiled. Her instincts were good. She'd detected something off almost immediately. He felt a moment of pride that she was prepared to protect herself. The tension in the room increased. She was only a few feet away from him now. She was silent, but he knew she was there. Alert…waiting.

"Relax, Kennedy. It's me."

"Nick?"

She'd said his name with a slight hitch in her voice, and despite his best intentions, he went hard at the soft, breathless sound.

"Yes."

"How did you find me?"

"Wasn't easy."

"I…" She swallowed. "How are you?"

"Healed. Took awhile."

"I know…I watched the news as much as possible, looking for information on you. I'm so sorry for what happened."

"What do you know about it?"

"I assumed it had to do with the Slaters."

"Why would you assume that?"

"Because of Thomas's murder…and all that happened. Was I wrong?"

"No, you were right on target. I was meeting a man who was going to give me information on them."

"And it almost got you killed. Did you get anything from him?"

"Nope, just a hole in my head."

"I'm glad you can joke about it now."

"I'm not joking…I'm dead serious." He leaned forward, his eyes trying to pierce the dark. "What the hell do you think you're doing here, Kennedy?"

"For right now, I'm holding a gun on you, that's what I'm doing."

Nick's burst of laughter held no humor. "I remember the day Thomas and I took you for your first target practice. You've come a long way from the frightened girl who shook the first time she held a gun in her hands."

"I've come further than you'll ever know. What do you want?"

"A helluva lot of things, kitten, but for right now, I want you to tell me what you've got planned."

Several seconds of silence followed. Was it because of the obvious anger in his voice or because of the endearment that had slipped out? She did remind him of a kitten, wary, untrusting…vulnerable.

"I'm going to make them pay."

"And how are you going to go about doing that?"

"It's not something you need to be involved with. I've got this covered."

Got this covered, my ass. His hands gripped the arms of the chair to keep himself from jumping to his feet and shaking some sense into her. Deciding on a less drastic alternative, he asked mildly, "Mind if we turn the lights on?"

The instant after he said that, light flared in the ceiling fan. Kennedy stood only a couple of feet away from him. Damn, she was beautiful. Not like the old Kennedy, who had been serene in her beauty. This woman was slightly flamboyant and sexy as hell, as if she wanted to attract attention. Something else was different—not in appearance, but demeanor. She'd always had an air of delicacy about her, and after Thomas's death she'd been understandably fragile. Now she had a new awareness, a surprising toughness.

Unable to sit while she stood as if on guard against him, he got to his feet. Just like that, she took a step back. A fist twisted in his gut. Was she afraid of him? Did she think he was somehow in on the shit that had happened to Thomas?

Putting that aside for now, he began walking around the room, picking up small items and setting them back down. Yeah, it was a delaying tactic, but the monumental weight of fear he'd had for the past twenty months had been lifted from him. That was a damn hard thing to adjust to.

The items he could pick up were few and far between. In Houston, her house had been nice and homey, filled with framed photographs and little knickknacks scattered around. By comparison, her house here was Spartan and utilitarian, like she knew she might have to up and leave without taking any belongings with her. He didn't like that. Kennedy deserved to be surrounded by beautiful things.

"Would you stand still already? You're making me nervous."

He turned to face her. Amazing the difference a change of hair color could do to a person.

"In case you're wondering, I checked for intruders when I came in."

Her mouth twitched with a slight smile. "An intruder checking for intruders. That's different. Why would you check?"

"Because you're working for the spawn of Satan, that's why. Even though the Slaters don't seem to know your identity, you're too smart not to be wary."

Kennedy almost gasped at the fury in Nick's eyes. He'd been acting so easygoing, almost unconcerned, that she had let her guard down. But it had all been an illusion. He was furious with her. "How do you know who I'm working for?"

"I've been looking for you for over a year. Do you have any idea what you did to me...to your friends when you left? How worried everyone has been? Dammit, Kennedy, you disappeared without a trace."

Though a part of her acknowledged his right to feel angry, she would not back down. She raised her chin stubbornly, refusing to justify her actions. Hurting her friends had never been her intent, but she'd had no choice. "I did what I had to do. If I'd told anyone, I'd have been putting their lives in danger."

"How the hell did you find out about the hit on Thomas?"

As quickly and succinctly as she could, she explained about finding the safe-deposit key and the packets of information and instructions Thomas had left her.

"What was in them? Did you find something you could use?"

"I don't know."

"What do you mean you don't know?"

"On my way back from the bank, a man ran me off the road. I thought he stopped to help, but when I opened the door, he took the packet I had lying on the seat. He told me if I told anyone about what had happened, I would be killed and so would the person I told. I believed him."

He'd gotten paler as he listened to her story, but what a relief to be able to say it out loud. For so long she'd been too terrified to tell anyone and fearful that if she did reveal what happened, no one would believe such a wild story. But she saw the confirmation in Nick's eyes. He did believe her.

"If the packet was stolen, how do you know about Slater, or what Thomas wanted?"

"There was a letter the man didn't take. I'd stuffed it inside my purse, but the other packet was too large to fit. I'm sure the man thought he got everything."

"Then why run?"

"Because I opened the letter in my house and read it."

"So?"

"Don't you see? How would anyone even know I found the safe-deposit key… that I was going to the bank, unless I was being watched?"

"Someone put cameras in your house."

"That was my only theory. And if he saw me open the letter, he could have seen that Thomas named the Slaters as responsible for his death. I had to leave."

"And you told no one?"

"No. It crossed my mind to go to one of the attorneys I'd worked for and then I decided against it. Thomas said trust no one."

"Did that include me?"

"No, of course not. Thomas wanted me to take the information to you and then disappear. I tried calling you several times. I didn't know you'd been shot. I had no choice but to run."

"I'm not saying you didn't. I'm glad you had the good sense to get away. But my question is, why haven't you tried to contact me since? If you were following my progress, you had to know that as soon as I could, I'd be searching like hell for you."

She shook her head. "It almost got you killed before. I couldn't take the risk of involving you."

"You were protecting me?"

She hadn't thought his eyes could blaze any brighter. "What's wrong with that?"

Once again, he was silent, as if struggling to keep his temper in check. This wasn't a Nick she recognized. She'd often thought about what she would do when she saw him again. She had imagined he'd give her that gentle smile that he seemed to save especially for her. He had been such a good friend, and she'd thought the first thing she would do was throw herself into his arms and hug him. But this Nick wasn't the easygoing, compassionate friend she'd leaned on after Thomas's death. This Nick frightened her a little. So why then was her blood zinging through her veins and her breath quickening? She was mature and self-aware enough to know that it wasn't just fear. This man excited her in a way her friend Nick never had.

"Let me get this straight. I'm a cop, with years of experience in bringing down hardened criminals and murderers. You're a law student...or at least you were."

She straightened her shoulders. "You're the one who got shot. Not me."

Instead of answering with an angry rebuttal, he closed his eyes and rubbed the bridge of his nose. Did he still suffer from headaches because of his injury?

When he raised his head, a glint of amusement had replaced his anger. "You got me there."

Happy to see that some of his good humor still existed, she let the muscles in her body relax slightly.

"If you were afraid for your life, why not just disappear completely? That's apparently what Thomas wanted you to do when he gave you those instructions."

"The Slaters are responsible for his death. I couldn't let them get away with it."

"And what do you intend to do? Make a couple of data-entry mistakes and bring down the empire? Or was your plan more deadly?" His eyes flickered to the gun she now held at her side. "Did you just plan to kill them?"

"Of course not." Pride and anger stiffened her spine. "Mock me all you want, but I do have a plan."

"And it is...?"

She chewed her lip. To a trained professional, her plan would probably seem weak or disorganized. She threw off her doubts. She'd given this plan more than enough thought. It might not be the most direct path, but she had a lifetime to succeed.

"I'm going to get as much information as I can and find a way to destroy them."

Nick stared hard at her for several silent, nerve-racking seconds. She held his gaze, refusing to flinch. He had to see her determination...that she would not back down, no matter what.

Finally, he huffed out a breath and said, "Then I'm in."

"In? What do you mean?"

"I'm going to help you."

Elation warred with panic. Having Nick's expertise and guidance would be a godsend. How she had longed to call on him and ask his advice the last few months. But she couldn't help but worry. She was willing to take this risk because of what she had lost. Putting someone else at risk, especially someone she cared for, didn't feel right.

"I can see you have your reservations. Don't." Guilt darkened his expression. "Despite my lapse in judgment that allowed another man to die and almost got me killed, too, I am quite capable."

"You feel responsible for that man's death?"

"Hell, yes. He came to me, asking for protection. He was my responsibility. I failed. I won't fail you."

"I'm not your responsibility."

"You're a lot of things to me, Kennedy. But for right now, think on this. Thomas was my best friend. I loved him like a brother. On top of that, I almost died because of the Slaters. I have more than enough reasons for wanting to bring those responsible to justice."

She understood his reasoning. And despite her anger at his sarcastic comments about her training, he was right. She wasn't trained for this…she was going on instinct alone.

A disturbing thought came to her. "How did you find me?"

"I'll tell you all of that later." He glanced down at his watch. "But for right now, we're due at a meeting. Do you need to freshen up before we go?"

"What kind of meeting? Where are we going?"

"We can talk on the way."

"I'm not going anywhere until you tell me—"

She gasped as he grabbed her arm and pulled her to him. Cupping her face in his hands, he leaned down till his forehead touched hers. Kennedy's heart pounded, her knees weak. Was he going to kiss her?

The warmth of his breath covered her face as he said in a growly voice that sent an electrical charge zipping up her spine. "Either go freshen up or…"

"Or?"

He took a long, ragged breath and then dropped a kiss on her forehead. "Just go freshen up. Okay?"

Heat spread throughout her body. What the hell was happening here? When had Nick become someone that could turn her on with just the sound of his voice? Why, from the moment she'd seen him, had she wanted to hurl herself into his arms and kiss that firm, unsmiling mouth?

His hands on her felt right…exciting. Was this sexual deprivation? Maybe having had no human contact for so long, these feelings were just a normal reaction. So why didn't she want to hug him as a friend? Tell him how good it was to see him again, like she would if it had been Julie standing here. That wasn't what she felt. The images flashing through her mind had nothing to do with a platonic friendship.

"What's wrong?" He dropped his hands and stepped back...was now looking at her quizzically.

What would he do if he knew her thoughts? Would he be surprised? Maybe embarrassed for her? To him, she was Kennedy, his best friend's widow. She needed to remember that.

"Nothing's wrong. Guess I'm still startled by all of this."

Something gentle, like the old Nick, flashed in his eyes. "Go freshen up. We need to leave soon."

Questions trembled on her lips, but instead of asking them, Kennedy turned to her bedroom. He'd made it clear he wasn't going to tell her anything until they were in the car. The sooner they left, the sooner she could find out how he had found her and, more important, how he planned to help her bring the Slater family to justice. These incredibly odd feelings he invoked in her would have to be explored later.

CHAPTER TWELVE

Nick leaned against the front door, waiting for Kennedy to return. She'd looked so damn good his teeth ached. There was a new maturity about her. After what she'd been through, she had every excuse to be bitter, angry at the world. Instead, he saw a woman sure of herself and her purpose. She had adjusted to her circumstances and was stronger.

He wanted her. Heaven help him…how he wanted her. When she'd been Thomas's wife, he'd forced himself to ignore those feelings. They had been wrong in every way, and he had refused to allow them. Dating a multitude of women hadn't really helped, but it had kept anyone from guessing just how big of a lie he was living.

Even though Thomas had been gone almost two years, that didn't mean he could act on his feelings. She was his best friend's widow and his friend. That was all he was to her.

There had been that one moment, though, when he'd grabbed her and almost shown her how very much he'd missed her. For just an instant he had thought he'd seen something in her expression, her eyes. A spark or something.

He shook his head. Hell, he was crazy. Hadn't he learned long ago that wishful thinking got him nowhere?

"Okay, I'm ready."

She stood before him, dressed entirely in black, from the baseball cap that completely covered her white-blond hair to the black sneakers on her feet.

His mood lightened slightly. "You look like you're ready to break into a bank vault."

She shrugged and headed toward the door. "I've gotten used to being invisible."

He didn't bother to tell her that the change in her appearance made her anything but invisible. She had worked hard to become someone else. She hadn't been recognized so far, so whatever she was doing was working.

Nick opened the door and stuck his head out before allowing her to go through it. He didn't anticipate that he had been followed, but until this was over, the possibility existed. The last thing he intended was to put Kennedy in harm's way.

They were in the car, headed to the warehouse district, when she finally said, "Okay, I've been patient long enough. Tell me where we're going."

"A few days ago, a man broke into my house and offered me a job. I knew his identity but only by reputation. He, however, knew a hell of a lot about me. And about you, too."

"Who was he?"

"Ever heard of Grey Justice?"

"The billionaire?"

"Yes."

"What did he know?"

"Everything, it seems. He knew about Thomas's death. That it was a hit. Knew about my shooting and that you'd disappeared. And he knows the Slaters are responsible."

"How do you know it's not a trap? Maybe he's working with the Slaters to find out what you know. Or to find me."

"I'm sure he has his own agenda and reasons for wanting Slater to go down, but contacting me to aid him makes no sense. If the Slaters were behind this, we'd both be dead. He had photos of you, knows exactly where you live and who you're working for."

"Photos of me?" she said faintly.

"Yeah." He flashed her a sympathetic look. All this time she'd thought no one knew she was here.

"But why would a man like Grey Justice want to help us? Isn't he in the same category wealth-wise as Slater?"

"Yeah. I don't know a lot about his motives. One thing does ring true—he believes Jonah Slater was innocent and was framed by his father. Based on what Thomas told me about the case, I'm inclined to agree with him."

She twisted in her seat to face him. "Thomas's letter said something similar. Not that Mathias Slater framed his son—which seems beyond bizarre—but that his arrest and conviction were just too pat. That's the reason Thomas started investigating the family. I guess he was right. But how is Grey Justice going to help?"

"That's why we're going to meet with him. He says he has a plan."

"You seem to be taking a lot of things on faith these days."

"You have no idea."

So far, Justice had lived up to his end of the bargain, but that didn't mean Nick trusted the man. He'd learned long ago that every person had his or her own agenda. For the time being, their two agendas coincided.

"Where are we going?"

"A warehouse in the Lakeland district. Know it?"

"No. I don't know Dallas that well. I'm mostly just familiar with my neighborhood and the area around Slater House Hotels."

"So what do you do in your job?"

"I started out in data entry, got bumped up to their online reservation department and then moved to their central booking department. A couple of months ago, I was promoted to accounts receivable. And today I got another promotion."

"Seems like you're moving up damn quick."

"That's my plan."

"What plan, Kennedy? You still haven't convinced me you even have one. Do you think making a wrong reservation or data-entry mistake is going to destroy Slater? Are you really that naïve?"

"I'm not naïve…I'm determined."

"Determined to do what?"

"Make them pay."

Cursing softly, Nick pulled to the side of the road.

She looked around curiously. "What are you doing? Why did you stop?"

"Answer my question. Make them pay how? Do you have a plan or not?"

"I thought we had an appointment. Won't we be late?"

"He'll wait. Tell me what kind of plan you had."

She drew in a breath, as if preparing herself for his anger. He promised himself that he wouldn't lose his temper…that he would hear her out. Hell, maybe she had a good plan.

"I'm going to get promoted into a position where I can destroy them from the inside."

He was too stunned to lose his temper. This was her plan? To be a good employee?

"That's it?"

"Okay, I know it sounds vague, but—"

"Vague? Hell, vague would be a compliment."

"I didn't say it was a good plan. I just—"

"It's not a plan, Kennedy. It's a way to get yourself killed." To hell with his promise to not lose his temper. "What were you thinking?"

"I'm thinking that these people took everything from me and they have to pay."

"And how long have you given yourself to bring this plan into fruition?"

"As long as it takes."

"So, basically, you have no set time limit."

She spat out her next words. "I don't give a damn if it takes a year, ten years or a lifetime. I don't care if I'm ninety years old and in a wheelchair. They. Will. Pay."

The streetlight allowed him to see the glittering in her eyes. At first he thought they were tears but reevaluated when he saw the determined set to her mouth and heard the hardness in her voice.

He didn't know whether to pull her into his arms and tell her how damn wonderful he thought she was or shout at her for being so damn self-sacrificing. Since he knew neither one would be the right thing to do, he kept quiet.

Taking Nick's silence as a good thing—at least he wasn't shouting at her—she told him about her latest progress. "Today I interviewed to be Eli Slater's executive assistant. I got the job."

"Are you out of your freaking mind? The minute he recognizes you, you won't live to see the next."

So much for not shouting at her. "He hasn't recognized me…he won't." She leaned forward so the streetlight could show the determination on her face. "I will succeed, Nick."

Long, tense moments passed. She held her breath, sure that he would once again tell her to forget her lame idea. Instead, without saying anything, he checked for traffic and pulled back onto the road.

"What are you going to do?" she asked.

"Like I said. I'm going to help you." His mouth moved up in a small smile. "Hopefully, before you're ninety years old and in a wheelchair."

She had been preparing herself for more arguing. His acceptance took the wind out of her sails.

"Thank you."

"You know that Thomas would die all over again if he knew what you were doing, don't you?"

"I know that. But how could I go on with my life, knowing that whoever was responsible for his death never paid?"

The car turned onto a narrow road and on either side were large, abandoned warehouses. How Nick knew which one to go to she had no idea. The adrenaline rush from seeing him again and their brief argument had dissipated. In its place was a surprising calm. She didn't know what the next few moments would hold, but one thing she did know: She trusted the man beside her.

They pulled to a stop outside the warehouse of what looked to be a former clothing manufacturer. Windows were broken, and weeds grew around the perimeter. No lights indicated there was no one in the building. No cars were visible.

"Are you sure this is the place?"

"Yeah." He leaned toward her, and Kennedy almost gasped, thinking he meant to grab her as he had earlier. She fought the ridiculous disappointment when she realized his focus was on the glove compartment. He opened it and pulled out a Glock. It looked much like Thomas's service weapon.

"You brought your gun with you?" he asked.

"Yes." She held up her purse.

"Good. Keep it hidden but close. Anything goes wrong, don't hesitate to use it to get away."

Her pulse raced. He really wasn't sure about this, but he was doing this to help her.

"Thank you, Nick."

"For what? I haven't done anything yet."

"For wanting to help me."

He gave her one of those enigmatic looks that told her there was so much more behind the handsome face he showed the world. But as usual he wasn't going to reveal anything he didn't want to.

"I want you to stay beside me at all times. Okay?"

She nodded.

"Let's go."

They got out and walked together into the warehouse. Though he wasn't touching her, they were so close she felt the heat of his body. She knew without a doubt that if anything went wrong, Nick would do whatever he had to do to protect her, including putting his own life at risk. What had she gotten herself into? And, most important, what had she gotten Nick into? The last thing she wanted to do was involve someone else in this dangerous game she was playing.

Light flooded the room, and Nick stepped in front of her, shielding her.

A tall, broad-shouldered man emerged from the shadows. "Welcome Mr. Gallagher and Mrs. O'Connell. Please come in."

Instantly recognizing the voice, Kennedy stepped out from behind Nick. "You're the man who took me to the hospital."

Cobalt blue eyes flickered with compassion. "I'm sorry about your child."

Familiar grief tugged at her heart, as it always did when she thought about the baby she had lost. Oddly, even though he had apparently broken into her house, she now felt more secure about meeting the man. If he had wanted her dead—she'd been in the most vulnerable position imaginable—killing her would have been easy. Instead, he had saved her life.

"Thank you. And I appreciate you taking me to the hospital."

"I wish I could have done more." His gaze turned to Nick, who was looking as astonished as she felt. "I'm assuming you didn't know this, Gallagher?"

Nick shook his head. "Had no idea. Kennedy's car was at the entrance to the emergency room. The driver's seat was covered in blood."

"After I dropped Mrs. O'Connell off in my vehicle, I returned to her home and took her car back to the hospital. The blood was mine." He shrugged. "A small sacrifice to make it appear as though she drove herself."

"I almost thought I had imagined you," she said.

"As you might guess, I was in your house, searching."

"For what Thomas had on the Slaters?"

"Yes. I didn't know until later that he kept it locked up in a safe-deposit box."

"You were watching me."

"Again, yes. My apologies. I had hoped to get the information without involving you. When that didn't work, I tried to get to you before Slater's henchman. I was going to ring your doorbell after you returned from the bank and discuss what you found. Unfortunately, Slater's man got to you first."

"He threatened me...said if I told anyone about what happened, he would come back and kill me and whoever I told."

"That's what I figured. I assumed, as I'm sure he did, that he took the only thing your husband had stored in the box. But there was something else, too, wasn't there? Something the man didn't steal?"

"Yes, a letter from Thomas saying that if anything happened to him, it was because of the Slaters. Since Thomas was killed in what looked like a robbery attempt, I probably wouldn't have believed his death had anything to do with them if that man hadn't run me off the road and stolen the packet."

"Where are my manners? Why don't we all sit down…get comfortable?"

"We're here, Justice," Nick said. "Get to talking."

Instead of acting insulted, the man gave a brief nod. "Very well. But Mrs. O'Connell might be more comfortable if she sat down. After all, she's worked all day."

While Nick grabbed one of the folding chairs leaning against the nearby wall and placed it behind her, she took a moment to assess the man across from her. He was about Nick's height and size. He had rich, dark brown hair with a few surprising streaks of gold. It was short, almost military-style length. The lack of hair emphasized his firm, square jaw, high cheekbones, and hawkish nose. His stern, somewhat arrogant expression commanded attention, and for some unknown reason, Kennedy found herself standing straighter.

Nick gently pushed her into the chair he'd gotten for her, making her realize she'd just been standing in one place, staring.

The instant she was seated, Nick said, "Okay. We're comfortable. Talk."

Justice walked forward, and she felt Nick tense. Even though she couldn't see his hand, she knew that it was poised at his side, ready to draw his weapon.

"Let me formally introduce myself, Mrs. O'Connell. My name is Grey Justice." He held out his hand, and Kennedy took it. His grip was strong, his hand large, cool and slightly callused.

"I was an admirer of your husband's and was sad to hear of his death."

"You knew Thomas?"

"Not personally. I knew of him."

"Tell us how you knew of him," Nick said.

"Mind if I sit down? I've had a long day, too."

"It's your meeting." Nick said.

Surprisingly, a dry chuckle came from Grey Justice as he pulled a chair from the wall and seated himself. "I'm glad you recognize that."

Turning his attention back to Kennedy, Justice said, "I heard through certain channels that your husband was investigating Slater on his own. I had hoped to assist him, but circumstances kept me from being able to make contact with him until it was too late."

"Why did you want to help him?"

"For several reasons, but most important because of what Slater is responsible for doing. Your husband had barely scratched the surface of what the family is involved in. They need to be stopped."

"What exactly are they involved in? All I've been able to find so far are a few associations with some shady local politicians and a couple of flamboyant celebrities."

"That's because money can buy a tremendous amount of silence. The Slaters have their fingers in many pies—from money laundering and smuggling to extortion and murder."

"Murder? You mean hiring a hit man?" Nick asked.

"Right. They would never dirty their hands with doing it themselves, not when they can pay others to do the deed. Over the years, we believe the family has been responsible for at least a dozen deaths."

Kennedy could only shake her head. "Why would anyone feel the need to kill that many people? What are their motives?"

"I'm afraid you're trying to make sense of something that's not explainable. They believe they're untouchable and can eliminate problems, if not with money, then in other ways. Unfortunately, your husband found this out too late."

"And how do you propose to help?" Nick asked.

"By helping Mrs. O'Connell—" He stopped abruptly and said, "May I call you Kennedy?"

"Yes."

"By helping Kennedy proceed with her plan."

At the very least, Kennedy expected a snort of disgust from Nick. He had made it clear what he thought about her "non-plan." He did nothing more than say, "And how are you going to do that?"

"I'm not. However, we have a mutual acquaintance that can."

A door squeaked open, and both Kennedy and Nick turned toward the sound. The man who appeared at the door caused Kennedy to spring to her feet. Nick snarled a vicious curse as he stepped in front of Kennedy and pulled his gun.

A solemn expression on his handsome face, her new boss and one of the men Kennedy had planned to destroy strode toward them.

CHAPTER THIRTEEN

His Glock aimed directly at Eli Slater's chest, Nick made sure Kennedy was completely covered. Dammit, he had brought her here, put her life at risk. How the hell could he have been so foolish?

Without taking his eyes off his target, Nick snarled at Justice. "What the hell do you think you're doing? You set us up."

"Lower your gun, Gallagher." Justice said. "It's not what you think."

"No way in hell am I going to lower my gun. You've got exactly one minute before I put a hole through one of you."

Throwing Justice an "I told you so" look, Eli Slater said, "This wasn't exactly how I had planned to meet with you two, but Grey has his own way of doing things."

"We're down to thirty seconds," Nick said. "Somebody better start talking."

"You heard the man," said a shaky but determined voice behind him. Then her voice lowered. "I've got my gun on Justice."

Even though he was furious at himself, he felt a flash of pride at her readiness to help.

"All right, Gallagher," Justice said, "since you've limited me on time, I'll be succinct. Eli is not part of his family's evil empire. For the past three years he's been working with me to destroy their illegal operations."

"What proof do you have?" Nick asked. "How do we know this isn't just a trick to get us to tell you what we know before you kill us?"

"Because both of your deaths could have easily occurred without much effort on my part," Justice said. "We've known who you were from the beginning of your investigation, Mr. Gallagher. And we know you don't have anything against Slater or you would have tried to use it already."

"What about you, Slater? Why would you turn against your father...your family?" Nick asked.

"It would be easier to converse without having a gun pointed at me. If you'll both lower your weapons, perhaps we could sit and I'll tell you everything."

Though still on edge and wary, Nick was beginning to accept this astonishing development. However, he wasn't the only one involved in this. His gun still targeting Eli Slater's chest, he said, "Kennedy? What do you think?"

"As unbelievable as it may seem, I think they're telling the truth."

"Then let's hear them out." Lowering his gun, he added, "Stay sharp, though... just in case."

"Will do."

"Eli, why don't you start? I'll fill in when necessary," Justice said.

A chair scraped against the concrete floor, and Eli Slater settled his large frame into it with a sigh. "Believe it or not, I didn't know about my family's illegal activities until a few years ago."

"How is that possible?" Kennedy asked.

"Money can go a long way in protecting ignorance. I went to university in England and after graduation, stayed there to work for our hotel chain. I married, had children...visited the States only when I had to. My father and I have never been close."

A flicker of sadness crossed his face. "My wife's family moved to New York a few years after our marriage. When she started having health issues, I thought it would be good for her to be closer to them.

"Dallas isn't close to New York, but it's nearer than England. At first I didn't know anything. Everything seemed as normal as always. Then I started hearing whispers, rumors. That's the first I realized that the Slater name had connotations other than wealth and privilege."

"And when you found out, you just joined in," Nick said.

His chin cocked slightly at the insult, but instead of being defensive, he said, "I won't deny that I tried to justify the things I heard. Being wealthy can make you a target. Some people assume that just because you have money, you're somehow corrupt. When it became clear that the rumors might have some truth to them, I had…some personal problems crop up that took my attention away. I didn't do anything until it was too late. Something I'll always regret. When Jonah was arrested, my eyes were opened for good."

"From what I read of his case, no one could dispute that your brother was guilty."

"Yes, thanks to my father."

"Why would a father do that to his own son?" Kennedy asked.

"Mathias discovered Jonah had been digging for incriminating evidence he could take to the attorney general's office. So he set Jonah up," Justice said.

"Your father purposely allowed Jonah to face a twenty-year sentence as punishment?"

Eli nodded. "And there was no 'allowing' to it. Mathias was involved every step of the way."

"How do you know this for sure?" Kennedy asked.

"Because Jonah was the one who made me face facts about the family business."

"Why did it take him getting arrested to open your eyes?" Kennedy asked.

"Jonah is an idealist. Always has been." Sadness darkened his face. "When he first told me about our family's corruption, I didn't believe him. Thought he was rebelling. You know, rich kid feels guilty for all he's been given. Rich is evil, poor is good. Jonah and my father have always had a tumultuous relationship. I just thought it was Jonah's way of sticking it to Mathias."

"What proof do you have that your father was behind his arrest and conviction?" Nick asked.

"Other than I know Jonah would never do anything remotely related to drug smuggling, Mathias admitted as much to me. Said my brother needed to learn a lesson in humility. He made some not-so-subtle threats that I'd better continue to practice the attitude of gratitude myself or something similar would befall me."

"Then how do you know your father isn't on to you, too?" Kennedy said.

"Other than the job I do for Slater Hotels, Mathias has little use for me. He would never consider that I would go against him. That's why I'm in the perfect position to do this." His gaze targeted Kennedy. "And that's where you come in."

"How is Kennedy going to help you?" Nick asked.

"She's going to bait my brother, Adam."

Nick shook his head. "You're not putting her at risk to further your own agenda."

"She'll be perfectly safe," Eli said. "I—"

"Perhaps it would be helpful to explain your reasons for going after Adam," Justice said.

"Sorry, I got ahead of myself. My father is ill. Very few people know he's dying. Adam is my father's lackey…always has been. He does what he's told. And though my brother isn't the savviest of businessmen, he shares certain qualities with my father that will make him a good replacement."

He cut his eyes over to Justice, who picked up the conversation. "Two years ago, Mathias tested Adam. Though things didn't go off as smoothly as they wanted, Adam passed the test, giving his father assurance that if need be, he had what it took to do the job."

Justice gaze went to Kennedy. "Adam was tasked with determining who had leaked incriminating information on the family and eliminating the source. As I said, things didn't go off as smoothly as they'd hoped. Before the source could be dealt with, the information got into your husband's hands, necessitating the elimination of not only the source but your husband as well."

"That means…" Kennedy said.

"Under Adam's direction, your husband was targeted for murder."

Nick felt a shudder go through Kennedy's body and placed a comforting hand on her shoulder. So now they knew who had specifically ordered Thomas's murder. As much as he was relieved to finally know, having Kennedy hear these things cut him in two.

"How do you know all this?" Nick asked.

Justice shrugged. "We may not have been able to get as deep as we want inside their camp, but we do have informants and good intel."

"And…" Eli cleared his throat. "My brother bragged about it."

Fury roared through Nick. "You're telling us the bastard actually bragged about having Thomas killed?"

"Not in those precise words…even Adam isn't that stupid. But it was clear my brother was quite proud of his accomplishment and wanted me to know how successful he had been with a special project Mathias had assigned him. I knew exactly what he was talking about."

Nick glanced down at Kennedy, taking note that though she was slightly paler than before, she was holding up better than he had expected.

"My brother has many flaws," Eli continued, "and his biggest is the one we want to exploit."

"And that is?" Nick asked.

"Greed. The more he has, the more he wants. He can't be satisfied…it's like an obsession. He and I have always had a rivalry of sorts. Anything I have, he wants." He paused for a breath and turned his eyes back to Kennedy. "I need my brother to want you."

"What the hell?" Nick snarled.

Kennedy was already shaking her head. Hearing who had ordered Thomas's murder had been hard, but in an odd way, a relief. Now she knew specifically whom she should hate. But as much as she wanted to destroy the man responsible for Thomas's death, there were certain things she would not do. This was one of them.

"I'm not going to sleep with your brother, no matter what."

"You won't have to." Eli frowned as if trying to come up with the right words. "I don't know how to explain it...my brother...he doesn't like women in that way."

"He's gay?" Kennedy asked.

"No. He doesn't like men either."

"Maybe you'd better tell us what he does like," Nick said.

"He gets off on controlling others...having power over them. Taking what others treasure. He likes to own things and covets what he doesn't have. I guess you could call him a collector."

Nick could smell stink from miles away. This idea was covered in it. "So let's say we agree to this vague and somewhat asinine plan. Your covetous brother wants Kennedy for his very own...what? Executive assistant? Pretend mistress? What then?"

Justice and Slater gave each other a look that sent a sick dread through Nick's body. "What the hell are you asking her to do?"

"She won't be required to do more than she would as my executive assistant," Eli assured him.

"Why doesn't that make me feel any better?" Nick leaned forward so he could catch both men in his gaze. "Look, if you're expecting our help, you damn well better tell us everything."

"My brother's last assistant disappeared under suspicious circumstances."

"Suspicious, how?" Kennedy asked.

"No one has been able to determine the full story. One day she was at work, the next day she wasn't. Adam claims nothing untoward happened the day she disappeared, but there's been no trace of her in the last three months."

The sick feeling of dread within Nick intensified. He glared at Justice. "Was she working for you?"

"No. I'd never even met the woman. She was, however, involved with Jonah."

Eli nodded. "And Jonah believes both Mathias and Adam had something to do with her disappearance."

Nick wrapped his hand around Kennedy's arm to pull her to her feet. "Forget about it, then. Putting Kennedy in the hands of the likes of your brother is out of the question. There's no way—"

"Wait." He felt resistance in her body. "If I become Adam's assistant, what would I have to do to get the information we need?"

Nick couldn't believe she was considering going along with this ridiculous plan. "Hell, Kennedy, this is a helluva lot riskier than what we talked about."

"I know that, Nick, but the man has got to be stopped somehow. If I can do that, then that's what I should do."

"I won't lie," Justice said. "You will be putting yourself at risk, Kennedy. However, we will do everything within our power to ensure your safety."

"So if Adam takes the bait and decides he wants to hire me…or whatever, what then?"

"Adam is our soft target. The more responsibility Mathias gives Adam, the easier it will be to infiltrate and get what we need."

"And would I be attending events and traveling with Adam?"

"Yes to both. My brother likes the limelight. DeAnne, his wife, abhors it. There would be many times that you would go in her stead."

Eli grimaced slightly as he said, "There's one other thing he would expect of you."

Already certain he wouldn't like the "one other thing," Nick tensed even more.

"His assistants have an apartment in his house."

"I would have to live with him?"

Nick shook his head. Oh, hell no, not in his lifetime. About to put an abrupt end to the role they were asking Kennedy to play, he opened his mouth, but Kennedy spoke first, "That means I would have access to his computer, his files. His contacts, too. At his office and home."

"Exactly," Eli said. "I won't say finding incriminating evidence will be easy, but if you play the game right and gain Adam's trust, I believe you'll get what you need."

"Kennedy." Nick paused and drew in a breath, hoping to sound more rational than his gut, which was telling him to throw her over his shoulder and run like hell. "You can't seriously be considering doing this."

She patted his hand, which was still on her shoulder. "Let's hear them out." She turned back to Slater. "How do we ensure that Adam will want me to work for him?"

"Leave that to me. It may take a few weeks for him to get interested, but once he realizes what an asset you are to me, there will be no stopping him from trying to steal you."

Though he had every intention of convincing Kennedy not to take this job, Nick couldn't help but ask, "And what's my role in all of this?"

"You'll be Kennedy's live-in lover."

A frown furrowing her normally smooth brow, Kennedy was shaking her head.

Despite his determination to talk her out of doing this, Nick felt a little stab to his heart at her resistance to him playing her lover. She surprised the hell out of him with her next words.

"Nick's role can't be so minuscule. We're in this together."

"His assistance will be vital, I assure you," Justice said. "As your significant other, he'll live with you, be your protector and tail you wherever you go. If he's caught, he can play the jealous lover, and no one would suspect he's anything else."

Nick shook his head. "That wouldn't work. After my shooting, my photo was all over the news, and not just in Houston. If I'm seen with Kennedy, I'll blow her cover."

"I doubt that either Mathias or Adam are aware of what either of you look like," Eli said.

"Still, I don't want to take the chance."

"No problem," Justice said. "As long as you don't mind some minor alterations to your appearance, we will make sure no one recognizes you."

Hell, he'd have plastic surgery if that would help. That wasn't his biggest concern.

As if she knew he was about to come out with a huge amount of objections, Kennedy grabbed his arm. "If it's okay with you both, Nick and I need to talk about this before we agree."

"That's understandable," Eli said. "Hopefully, while you're making that decision, you'll still come to work for me. Despite my ulterior motives for hiring you, I really do need an assistant."

"Yes, of course," Kennedy said. "I'll be there tomorrow morning."

Nick pulled Kennedy to her feet and pushed her gently to the door. Before he walked out, he turned and addressed both men. "We'll be in touch."

CHAPTER FOURTEEN

Half an hour later, Nick turned into Kennedy's driveway. They'd said little to each other on the drive back, each lost in thought. He put the car in park, wondering exactly where to start to convince her that working directly with Adam Slater would be suicide.

"So, do you want to come in and talk about it?"

"Oh yeah, we're going to talk," Nick assured her.

"No, what you're going to do is try to talk me out of it. That's not going to happen, so if that's the only reason you're coming in, you can leave."

When the hell had she gotten so stubborn and self-sufficient? Or had she always been like this and in self-preservation he had seen only what he wanted to see? Probably—because this confident, self-assured woman was even more of a temptation.

Confident or not, she was going to get herself killed if she agreed to this harebrained scheme. Damned if he would stand around and allow that to happen.

"Either hear me out or I'll take you away right now."

"Like hell you will, Nick. I make decisions for my own life. Not you."

"Fine. Let's go in, and we'll talk like two adults."

She nodded and got out of the car. Nick followed behind her. As she entered the code for the security system, he went through the small house to make sure all was clear.

They met in the center of the living room. The smile she gave him was slightly awkward. He didn't like that. She had always been comfortable around him. He vowed to make himself more agreeable, no matter what.

"So…I could use something to eat. How about you?"

Hell, he'd dragged her out of the house after a long day of work. It was close to ten o'clock. She had to be starving. Here was his chance to show her his agreeable side. "Why don't you sit down and let me fix you something? You must be exhausted."

"Actually, my adrenaline is pumping like I've had five shots of espresso. This is the most optimistic I've been in months."

Before they got into the discussion and the inevitable argument, she needed to eat. "How about we work together?"

"For a meal or the other?"

Turning his back to her, he headed to the kitchen. "Let's start with a meal."

Kennedy bit her lip and then winced, realizing it was sore. This wasn't the first time she had done that tonight to keep herself from saying something she'd end up regretting. Her emotions were all over the place. What an incredible, mind-blowing day it had been.

Nick stuck his head in the doorway. "Where do you keep your skillet?"

Giving herself a sound, mental shake, she joined him in the kitchen. She needed the nourishment to deal with the major argument that would come once he realized nothing could deter her from this new plan.

Barely five minutes later, they sat down to plates of fluffy scrambled eggs and golden-brown toast, washed down with ice-cold milk. Considering that she often had to force herself to eat these days, she was pleased at her healthy appetite.

Nick had cleaned his plate, too, and was leaning back in his chair, his expression much less grim than an hour ago. Maybe they both had needed sustenance to be able to discuss this calmly and rationally.

"I don't want you to do this."

"I know you don't, but this is a much better plan than me trying to dig up something on my own. This will get me into the Slaters' lair much faster, and I'd have access I could never get on my own."

"Your plan is only slightly less asinine than Justice's."

"Do you have a better way? You've been after the Slaters for what…more than a year? And you've gotten zilch."

"No, not yet, but I'm—"

"But you're what, Nick? Hoping that someday they'll get what's coming to them? When? When Mathias Slater dies of his illness and goes to hell? When Adam orders another person's death and someone finally has the guts to bring the bastard down?"

His voice went low and furious. "Just what kind of guts do you think it will take to bring them down? Do you think you're the only one who wants someone to pay? Thomas was my best friend. I miss him every damn day." He leaned forward and locked eyes with her. "I worked for over a year to find enough dirt to bury the Slaters. Their covers can't be penetrated—at least not the normal way. It got to the point where I was chasing my own tail and wondering if the family should be nominated for sainthood instead. They are that good. So don't assume others don't want what you want or haven't tried."

Nick was right. She wasn't the only person hurt by Mathias and Adam Slater. "I'm sorry. You're right."

His hand reached across the table and grasped hers. "We will get them. I promise."

Her eyes dropped to his hand. Large, strong, capable. Just like the man himself. When Thomas had been alive, she'd never given Nick enough credit. She had known he had good points, but his reputation of being a ladies' man had overshadowed them. After Thomas's death, he had been there for her, solid and dependable. Her rock.

"Then let's talk about their idea—me enticing Adam Slater so he'll try to steal me away from his brother. What do you think about it?"

"I think you'll be putting yourself into a dangerous situation that you're not prepared for or trained to handle."

"Such as?"

"What happens when he wants something from you? Like sex?"

"Eli said—"

"Adam Slater might not enjoy sex like a normal human being, but sex can be about more than physical pleasure. It can also be about power. Eli also said his brother was all about power."

She considered him for several seconds. Few people knew about her childhood. Thomas had told her more than once that her ability to survive had made him love her even more. Her past wasn't something she liked to discuss, but if she and Nick were going to trust each other, then he needed to know.

"How much do you know about my background, before I met Thomas?"

The puzzled look on his face confirmed her thoughts. Even the man her husband had trusted most in the world hadn't been given this information.

"Not a lot. I know you lost your parents when you were ten. That you lived in various foster homes. You went to a community college and got a degree in both criminal justice and business management."

"All of that is true. What you don't know is that when I was fifteen years old, one of my foster dads tried to rape me." She took a breath and added, "I killed him."

"Hell," Nick said in a hoarse whisper. "What happened?"

"My foster mother was at work. Gerald, her husband, was on disability. His responsibility was watching us kids. He drank more than he did anything else. I was just developing and apparently caught his eye."

Only by focusing on the facts was she able to block out the absolute terror of that day. "One of my foster sisters had warned me about him, but until that day he'd always kind of ignored me. I didn't give it a lot of thought.

"I was in the laundry room, ironing clothes. He came in and backed me into a corner. Said a bunch of disgusting things, most of which I didn't understand. I kept telling him no. When he grabbed me and threw me on the floor, I started fighting for real. He had one hand wrapped around my throat…I could barely breathe. When he was about to do it, I looked up and saw the cord to the iron dangling in front of my eyes. I grabbed it and pulled the iron down. It landed on his back. He jerked back and when he did, I took the iron and slammed it into his head."

"One blow killed him?"

"Actually, no. He fell back and hit the sharp corner of the counter behind him. Cracked his skull.

"There had been suspicion of sexual abuse before, but when the girls were questioned by social workers, they'd clammed up. Almost before I could get myself together and explain what happened, three of the girls were coming forward. They said Gerald threatened to kill them if they told the truth. With his death, they didn't have to worry about that."

"I'm surprised I didn't run across this information when I was investigating you."

"You investigated me? Why?"

Fury and something else gleamed in his eyes. The look might have once frightened her, but now it only sent warmth throughout her entire body.

"You disappeared completely, Kennedy. The only way someone can vanish like that is if you had professional help. I dug deep into your past, thinking I could find an old friend or distant relative who might have helped you get away."

"What did you find?"

"Two things. That you're a lot more resourceful than I ever believed possible."

"And?"

"You're as alone in the world as I am."

For some reason, that hurt her heart to hear him say those words. The thought of Nick being alone bothered her. Even with the multitude of girlfriends he'd seemed to have, he had been alone.

"And now I've discovered something else. Something I've known for a long time but didn't allow myself to see until now."

"What's that?"

"You are an incredibly strong person."

She smiled. Though it felt like a fractured version of her normal one—she had always been uncomfortable talking about herself. "I'm not that strong…not really. But I am a survivor. I told you that story so you would understand—I will do what I have to do. I've been on my own a long time. I'll admit that when Thomas and I married, I got caught up in the dream. Losing him…losing our baby, made me remember the reality of life. There are pockets of happiness, but for the most part, life can be downright shitty. Stupid me forgot that."

As much as Nick wanted to deny her claim, he wouldn't. She'd fought hard for her self- sufficiency and strength. He damn well wouldn't lessen her accomplishments by spouting platitudes and trite reassurances. She was right. Life could be downright shitty.

"So do you trust Grey Justice and Eli Slater?" Nick asked.

"Yes. As much as I trust anyone, besides you. I know they have their own reasons. I'm not naïve enough to believe they're doing this for me. But if we can achieve the same goal, why not work together?"

"And you believe you can carry this off? Spend hours with the man who ordered Thomas's death? Live with him?"

"Will I hate it? Yes. But I can do it. I don't doubt that."

"Then I'm with you."

He caught his breath at the smile that broke out on her face. He hadn't seen that smile since before Thomas was killed.

"Thank you. I'm hoping I'll play my role so well that Adam Slater will hire me quickly and trust me as fast as possible."

"And what if he doesn't? What if this takes months…or years?"

That determined glint returned to her eyes. "It doesn't matter how long it takes. Like I said before, I'm in this for the long haul. What about you?"

Without hesitation, he answered, "I'm in it for as long as you are. We're a team."

CHAPTER FIFTEEN

Kennedy sat at her new desk and reviewed the list of daily duties Eli's former executive assistant had left for her. The list was substantial, but her mind kept veering to the unbelievable events of the last twenty-four hours. Getting a job with Eli Slater, having Nick reappear in her life, meeting Grey Justice, then learning that her new boss had hired her to help him expose his family's corruption. Each event on its own was stunning. All of them together made for an explosive, mind-boggling day.

Last night after Nick left, she had barely been able to close her eyes. Oddly, the one thing that replayed the most in her mind was Nick's arrival. She hadn't known just how much she missed him until he'd been standing in front of her. What would have happened if she'd gone with her first instinct and thrown herself into his arms?

She shook her head. She knew what would have happened. He would have embraced her as a friend, nothing more. After almost two years of living in a vacuum, with grief and retribution her only companions, she now found herself attracted to another man. But not just any man—Nick Gallagher. During that dark, lonely time, her libido had apparently acquired a twisted sense of humor.

"Rachel, got a minute?"

She jerked her head up to see Eli standing over her desk. Last night, before Nick left, they had called Grey Justice and told him they were both in. He had advised Kennedy to act as if her job with Eli was normal. No discussion of their plan was to be held within the outer office. If, at any time, she felt the need to discuss something secretive, Eli had a small, private office that should be safe. As far as the outside world could see, she was Eli Slater's executive assistant and nothing more.

Reminding herself of those instructions, Rachel pasted on her pleasant smile. "Sure thing."

"Come on into my office, and let's go over my schedule for the week."

Three hours later, Eli finally completed his review of his upcoming week. The morning had zoomed by. He might have been planning the downfall of his father and older brother, but he also had a huge responsibility to the thousands of Slater House employees and their guests. He took his job seriously.

"Once you've finished, give your notes to Helen so she can be updated, too."

Kennedy had met Helen Copeland, Eli's secretary, earlier. As stern and imposing as any four-star general, the woman didn't look as though she had an ounce of softness. As if it was an unimportant piece of trivia, Eli had mentioned in his introduction that Helen had once been Mathias's secretary but had graciously agreed to work for him when he'd moved to Dallas. There had been nothing in his tone to indicate a warning, but Kennedy read between the lines. Helen might appear as though she worked for Eli, but she reported to his father.

"I have a business dinner Friday night. I received the invitation a few days ago but forgot all about it, and now I don't have time to get a date. I'd like for you to attend with me, unless you have other plans."

"I don't have anything planned."

"Excellent. I'll have a car come for you at seven thirty at your house."

"Is this a formal affair?"

"Semiformal. A few business acquaintances are in town for the weekend. Both my father and brother will be in attendance."

An electric surge went through her. "I'll be ready." And she meant the words. At last she would meet the devil and his spawn.

Kennedy stood. "Anything else?"

"As a matter of fact, yes. You have an appointment with a stylist in half an hour. Gunter, my driver, will take you."

The frown on her face caused a gleam of amusement in Eli's eyes. "You'll need something new and elegant for the dinner. All executive assistants are afforded this luxury."

It only made sense that the Slaters' companions, even the fake ones, would need to look their best. And since she planned to attract Adam Slater's attention, having a little help would be welcome.

"What a nice perk. Thank you."

The last year had been all about hiding herself and blending in. From now on, it would be about standing out and making Adam Slater believe he had to have her. She suddenly found herself looking forward to the challenge.

Nick spent the first part of his day becoming Rachel Walker's live-in boyfriend. Figuring they both needed one last gasp of breathing room before they became roommates, he had waited until she left for work before he'd arrived with his things.

In his earlier years as a cop, he'd done a few undercover stints. Most hadn't lasted more than a few days and involved little to no drama. This undercover operation would be the most difficult of his life. He didn't fool himself into believing that living with Kennedy would be easy. They had a job to do, but he had one major issue to get over. His feelings for her weren't the platonic ones of a roommate. There was nothing friendly about the way he'd wanted to devour her luscious lips and feel her body melting into his.

He could do nothing about those feelings, though. Thomas would always stand between them. Kennedy still loved her husband.

Resenting his best friend's presence didn't sit well with him. He'd loved the man like a brother, and if given the option of having Thomas still alive, Nick would have chosen it. He had been the best of men and had made Kennedy happy. And Kennedy's happiness was vitally important to him.

The new cellphone in his jacket buzzed. Earlier today he'd met with a young woman who worked for Justice. She had handed him a packet of various items, including an impressive burner phone that had more bells, whistles and buttons than anything he'd ever seen on a throwaway.

He held the phone to his ear. "Yeah?"

"You get settled?" Justice asked.

"Yes. All moved in."

"Good. Meet me at the Dover Building on Cranston, Suite 712."

"Want to give me a clue why?"

"You said you wanted to know more about Grey Justice. Here's your chance."

Half an hour later, Nick parked in front of a small, shabby-looking building on the outskirts of Dallas. He hadn't misunderstood the address, but this place looked as though it had been abandoned for years. Apparently, once a dry cleaner, the place was now just one of the many dried-up businesses in this part of town.

He shrugged. Wouldn't be the first time Justice had surprised him. With that thought, he strode up to the door and twisted the knob. Locked. He was about to back away and look in the window when a calm, feminine voice announced from an invisible speaker, "Welcome, Mr. Gallagher," and the door clicked open.

Nick walked inside and once again faced what looked like an abandoned business. He heard a soft swishing sound. An opening appeared in the wall, and a middle-age, well-dressed woman appeared. "Grey wanted to be here to meet you, but he received a phone call just before you arrived. He told me to bring you to his office."

Anticipating that he was going to see even more surprising things than a wall magically opening, he followed the woman and then came to an abrupt stop. It was unlike anything he'd ever seen outside a *James Bond* film. Giant screens adorned the walls, showing news reports from all over the world. At least a dozen people sat at computer stations, seemingly involved in whatever was in front of them. Small groups of people sat at conference tables, their expressions earnest and animated. It wasn't quite Mission Control at NASA but still damn impressive.

"This way, sir."

Nick forced his feet to keep moving, the questions coming faster than his mind could comprehend them. How long had Justice been involved in this kind of work? And just what the hell did these people do for him?

He followed the woman up a flight of stairs and then down a carpeted corridor. She knocked on a closed door and then twisted the knob. Grey Justice stood in the middle of the room. "Come on in, Gallagher."

The woman disappeared, and Nick shook his head. "I don't know whether to be impressed or scared shitless. What the hell kind of operation are you running here?"

The other man shrugged. "Nothing too complicated. As I said, I have an unusual hobby of seeing that victims receive justice. This is one of the places where we make those things happen."

"One? How many do you have?"

"Half a dozen spread around the globe."

"What do you do? How does this all work?"

"Let me take you around. I think you'll better understand."

They stood on the second-floor corridor and looked out over the gigantic room filled with computer equipment that would impress any *Fortune* 100 company.

"Every person you see is working on a case." He nodded toward a group sitting at a conference table. "Depending on the degree of complexity, a case might have three to five operatives assigned to it."

"Operatives?"

For a moment, humor glinted in Justice's eyes. "Secret Santa seemed too cliché."

As if he knew all about Nick's reservations, he started down the stairs. "Before you get too overloaded with wild conjectures, let me show you a few cases."

Justice stopped at a workstation where a young Latina woman sat, typing on a keyboard.

"How's it going, Margarita?"

Her dark eyes gleaming, she grinned up at him. "I managed to get the documents to Harris's defense attorney without anyone, even his secretary, seeing me. Now that he knows for certain that his client is innocent and who to call for testimony, the trial should be a short one."

"Excellent. This is Nick, who will be working with us for the next few months. Would you mind telling him how you became involved with us?"

"Sure." Her focus turned to Nick. "Last year, my little brother, Juan, was killed in a car accident. The man responsible had been drinking, but the investigation was shoddy. They made it seem like Juan was at fault...they said he was speeding. When my parents protested that the other driver had been drinking, the sheriff disputed the claim. So instead of the killer of my brother going to jail, he wasn't even fined. To add insult to injury, his insurance company tried to make a claim against my parents' policy, saying my brother was at fault."

"How did you know the other man had been drinking if there was no record of it?" Nick asked.

"The passenger in my brother's car, his girlfriend, said she smelled alcohol on him. She said he was staggering around and cursing at everyone. The sheriff denied her claim...said she was lying." Margarita glanced over at Justice. "We were devastated, sure that nothing could be done. It was our word against everyone else's.

"Then a woman came to see my parents. She said she could help us, but we would have to make sure no one knew where the information came from. My father is a minister, and as much as he wanted justice for Juan, he refused to be a party to breaking the law. She assured him no laws would be broken."

Nick had grave doubts that Margarita had been told the truth about that but continued to listen.

"Two days later, we get a call that the driver had been charged with vehicular manslaughter and driving under the influence."

"And how did that happen?"

"It was discovered that the other driver had paid off the sheriff. The man had a history of driving while intoxicated. If he received another citation, he would go to prison, so he paid the sheriff to lie."

He shot a quick glance at Justice, then returned his gaze to Margarita. "And how was this discovered?"

"The sheriff admitted this."

"I'm sure your parents were relieved."

"You'll never know how much. It didn't bring Juan back, but it gave them peace, and that's all we had asked for."

Thanking Margarita for sharing her story, Nick and Justice walked away.

"I can see your doubts, Gallagher. You don't believe it happened that way?"

"Oh, I believe it, but there seemed to be quite a few lucky breaks."

"If I told you that no laws were broken, would that make you feel better?"

"Look, I'm not so sanctimonious that I believe everything is black and white or certain parameters can't be stretched. I'm just wondering if every one of your cases is so easily and legally resolved."

"The man who killed your mother plea-bargained his sentence down to fifteen years with time served because the prosecutor had a backlog of cases. How did that make you feel?"

Made sense the man would know this...the case was public record. He didn't hesitate in his answer. "Like any son who lost the mother he loved because of a senseless act of violence, I wanted to kill the son of a bitch with my bare hands."

"If you had a way to make sure he got the sentence he deserved, such as a life term or even the death penalty, would you have done it?"

He didn't even have to think about it. "Yes."

"I appreciate your honesty. That's what we're about. We help average citizens... the ones who don't have money, power, or connections, get the justice they seek. Do we sometimes go beyond what's considered legal? Hell yeah, I'll be the first to admit it. And do we occasionally do things that could get us put in jail? If we were caught and convicted, probably so." He gestured to the people working so diligently at their desks. "Every person here has benefited from the Grey Justice Group. And if you ask any of them if they think we went too far, they'll tell you no."

Nick would be a hypocrite if he complained about the organization that was helping Kennedy, but he needed to know one thing. "Just how far do you go?"

Justice's mouth twitched as if he was slightly amused by the question. "As far as we need to but not near as far as we'd like."

"Murder?"

"I have yet to authorize a murder."

Not the definitive answer he was looking for, but he could understand the man's reticence. "You want to tell me how you got the sheriff to confess to a payoff?"

Justice shrugged. "Easy enough. This incident involved a small town in south Texas and not terribly sophisticated criminals. We tracked a deposit the sheriff made to a withdrawal by the driver who killed Margarita's brother. After a little talk with the sheriff, he had a miraculous memory recovery and recalled that the driver had been drinking."

As an officer of the law, Nick was walking a fine line here. He had sworn to uphold the law and took his oath seriously. But as a man who wanted to see punishment come to those responsible for his best friend's death and peace for the woman he loved, he had no choice but to say, "Okay, so I've seen your superhero setup, but where's your cape and fancy car?"

"No cape. And the fancy car is in the shop. However, I do have something we picked especially for you. Follow me."

As Nick followed Justice out the door, leaving behind a world he'd never known existed, optimism began to thrum through his blood. If the Slaters could be nailed any other way, he would have done it in a heartbeat. They couldn't. Despite some lingering reservations, he was damn glad that Grey Justice was on their side. For the first time since his first bizarre meeting with the man, Nick was beginning to believe they could actually carry this off.

CHAPTER SIXTEEN

An exhausted Kennedy let herself into her house. Of all the ways she had envisioned her first day working for Eli, spending the day at an upscale spa had not been on her list. She had been plucked, pruned, and powdered to the nth degree. Vanity had never been one of her flaws, but she had to admit when she'd finally been allowed to look in the mirror, she liked what she saw.

Her skin glowed clear and bright, her hair had an extra sheen to it and her makeup, which had taken almost an hour to apply, made her look like a natural beauty.

Fortunately, she wasn't terribly shy. If she had been, she would've had to get over it quickly. Within minutes of stepping into the exclusive and obviously posh beauty retreat, she'd been stripped bare. The beauty technicians, both women and men, acted as if her nudity was just another day at the office. And she supposed, to them, it had been. For her, it had been a lesson in humility. Every inch of her had been assessed and judged. More than once, Kennedy had wanted to reply sarcastically to their blunt and not-always-kind comments. She hadn't said a word... her reasons for going through the process always at the forefront of her mind. To attract Adam Slater, she needed to look her best. Period.

She stepped into her living room and caught her breath on a startled gasp. A man stood in the middle of the room. Unshaven and scruffy in a sexy "I don't give a damn" kind of way, the best description she could come up with was "badass."

Though she'd always been more attracted to the clean-cut boy-next-door type, she couldn't deny the incredible flush of heat when she took in Nick's new appearance.

"I see you went through your own makeover." She inwardly winced at the breathlessness in her voice.

"Yeah, but I like yours a helluva lot better than mine."

She didn't agree. Nick had always been handsome, but in a cover model kind of way. This Nick reeked of danger, as if with one wrong word, he could take someone apart with his bare hands. Or better yet, rip a woman's clothes off and kiss her into senseless abandon.

Moving closer, she noticed other, more subtle changes. His light hazel eyes that changed colors with his mood were now a solid, piercing green. His brown hair was sun-streaked and disheveled, as if a woman had enjoyed running her fingers through it. A small hoop earring adorned his right ear, and the black T-shirt he wore beneath the black leather jacket gave a teasing glimpse of a vivid tattoo on his left shoulder.

"Nice tat."

"Thanks. I've had it since I was sixteen."

"I can't believe I never noticed before." She leaned forward, her fingers aching to shove his shirt out of the way. "Is it a bird or something?"

"Raven." He pulled the material aside and allowed her to see a beautiful rendering of the wild bird. "We were studying Edgar Allan Poe in lit class. I liked his stuff and thought getting the tat was a nice tribute. My mom didn't agree. Grounded me for a month."

He dropped his hand, and the T-shirt went back into place. Ridiculously disappointed, she took a step back and looked him over again. "So I guess you're my biker boyfriend? Or something like that?"

"Yeah." He grinned, the first carefree one she'd seen on him since he'd come back into her life "That's the one thing I like about this makeover. Gotta sweet ride out of the deal."

She laughed softly. "You get a motorcycle, and I get high-heeled stilts to wear."

His eyes raked up and down her body. The grin disappeared, replaced by a sensual, heated look. If a stranger had looked at her like that, she'd have been insulted. That wasn't how she felt. Instead, she found herself leaning toward him, seeking his approval in a more physical way.

Hard hands gripped her arms. "Whoa. Guess you're not used to standing on those stilts."

Kennedy pulled herself together, thankful Nick had misinterpreted her movements. How embarrassing if he'd realized she had wanted him to touch her, hold her.

One more hot, sweeping gaze from those brilliant green eyes. "This is your new look?"

"Yes." Stepping a few feet from him, she did a slow turn so he could see the full effect. "Apparently, Adam Slater likes his assistants a little on the slutty side."

Nick shook his head. Slutty wasn't the term he would use. There was no way Kennedy could ever look slutty. The short silky black dress clung to her like a second skin, emphasizing soft, beautiful curves. The heels adorning her slender feet showed her long, sleek legs to their best advantage. His mouth went dry. She looked sexy as hell.

"The first time I saw your new hairstyle and color, I thought you looked like a more slender and more beautiful Marilyn Monroe."

"And now?"

"Not anyone who's ever existed. Just what every woman would want to look like."

"Oh…" That little breathy gasp of air did him in every damn time. If those sounds could have been bottled, they'd have given any male-enhancement product a run for its money.

Turning away before she noticed his very inconvenient reaction, he said, "I stopped off at the grocery store and got a few things."

"You brought home groceries on your bike?"

"Actually, no. I had them delivered. All you had in your fridge was yogurt and the makings for a salad."

She grimaced. "I've been meaning to go to the grocery store. Kind of got sidetracked."

Nick shook his head as he headed to the kitchen. "Sidetracked" was a monumental understatement. In the course of two days, her entire life had been upended.

She followed him into the kitchen. "Wow...you did more than grocery shopping."

Nick gazed around at not only the food he'd purchased but a few extra things he'd also had delivered, such as an espresso machine, food processor, blender, and cookware. After opening a few cabinets this morning, he had noticed she had only a few essentials. Back in Houston, her kitchen had been filled with all sorts of gadgets, along with expensive cookware. Stocking her kitchen had pleased him.

"So...you cook?"

He smiled, amused at her slightly worried look. "It was just my mom and me when I was growing up. She worked two jobs and came home dead tired. Figured the very least I could do was feed her, so I learned to cook."

"What about your father? He wasn't in the picture?"

"Barely. He took off when I was two. Being a husband and a father was just not his thing."

"And your mom? She's gone now?"

"We didn't live in the best neighborhood. Drugged-out punk decided to use people as target practice. My mom was one of them."

"Oh my gosh, Nick. How old were you?"

"Eighteen. Was about to start my freshman year at Texas A&M."

"That's why you were so angry."

"How's that?"

"You told me that when you met Thomas, you were one incident away from losing your scholarship, that you were mad at the world. That's why you were having such a rough time. Because you'd just lost your mom."

"Yeah." He opened the fridge and started pulling out food items for dinner. He glanced over his shoulder. "Spaghetti and meat sauce sound okay?"

"Sounds delicious."

He pushed a cutting board and knife, along with a bowl filled with carrots, celery and mushrooms, toward her. "You chop the vegetables for the salad, I'll brown the meat for the sauce."

Pulling out a chair at the table, Kennedy sat down and started chopping. "Did your mom teach you to cook?"

"That and a lot of practice."

"What was she like?"

In the middle of unwrapping the ground beef, he stopped for a moment to remember the woman who had given him life and to this day still influenced him. "She was kind of quiet, had a good heart. Incredibly strong-willed." He smiled and added, "She was strict, too. Determined that I stay out of trouble and do well in school. Make something of myself."

"Did she know you wanted to be a cop?"

"No. Neither did I until after she died." He shrugged. "I wanted to make the world a safer place and thought being a cop was the way to go."

"She would be proud of you."

He went back to preparing the meat sauce. "I'd like to think so."

As Kennedy chopped vegetables, she thought about how lives could change because of one single incident. Nick became a cop because of his mother's death. And now she, who had always planned to go to law school and defend the innocent, was pursuing justice for her husband and their baby.

She glanced over at Nick. "The man you met…the day you were shot. What was his name?"

"Milton Ward."

"How did he have information on the Slaters?"

Nick briefly explained about Ward's job with the accounting firm that did work for the Slaters.

"And he was shot right after he told you?"

He nodded. "About five minutes after implicating the Slaters in Thomas's death."

In the midst of chopping, she almost sliced a finger. "How did he know it was a hit?"

"Careful with that knife."

She returned to her task, this time going slower. "How did he know about the hit?"

"He heard through the grapevine that two hits had been ordered. His and Thomas's. He got out of town, but his conscience got the best of him, and he came back."

"Did he try to contact Thomas…to tell him?"

"I don't think so. I think he got scared and ran."

Kennedy drew in a ragged breath. If only Milton Ward had placed one phone call, Thomas might still be alive.

"So he didn't give you anything?"

"No. We were going together to get the documents." Nick shrugged, the expression on his face one of self-anger. "I was stupid. I offered him protection but didn't take it seriously enough. We were about to get into my car when the shooter passed by. I got hit first…never saw Ward go down."

She still remembered the moment she'd heard Nick had been shot. She had thought herself numb to pain after all she'd been through. She had been wrong. His injury…his possible death, had devastated her.

"I came to see you."

He whirled around. "When? How?"

"The same night you were shot. Well…actually it was about three the next morning. I stole some scrubs, then snuck into ICU."

"I didn't know." A stupid statement. Of course he hadn't. He'd been in a coma. But it was the best he could come up with. She had risked her life to come see him.

"So you'd already left your house? Knew about the Slaters?"

"Yes. I went to see the man Thomas steered me to…the one who helped me disappear. I kept calling, wanting to tell you what was going on. I called Julie… she told me what happened. I had to see you before I left for good."

Emotion clogged his throat. Clearing his voice, he said thickly, "Thank you. You shouldn't have put yourself at risk like that…but thank you for caring."

Their eyes locked. Nick held his breath, afraid he was misinterpreting her expression. Was it just hopeful longing or had he glimpsed something in her eyes? Something besides friendship?

"Kennedy, I—"

An obnoxiously shrill buzzing noise shattered the moment, breaking their eye contact and stopping his words. Hell, he hadn't even known what he was going to say anyway.

"What on earth is that?"

"My new cellphone. Someone apparently thought it was funny to make my ring tone the sound of a chain saw."

Her lips tipped up in a smile. "Chain Saw Gallagher. I like it."

He withdrew his phone from the pocket of his jeans. "Just wait till you hear the name I've been given. Fits me even better."

"Oh, really, what is it?"

"Grimm." Frowning at the identity of the caller, he punched answer and said, "Yeah?"

"Kennedy there with you?" Justice's harsh voice gave a portent of bad news.

Nick glanced over at Kennedy, who was still grinning in delight at his new undercover name. "Yes, she's here."

"Put me on speaker."

Nick pressed the speaker button and mouthed, "Justice" to Kennedy.

"Okay, we can both hear you."

"How did things go today?"

Since he'd spent a good part of the day with Justice, Nick's eyes went to Kennedy, waiting for her to answer.

"Very good. Eli and I had a business meeting this morning. He also introduced me to Helen and indicated she was once Mathias's secretary."

"She's a spy. Stay clear of her."

"Will do."

"And the rest of the day?"

"Was spent turning myself into someone who will hopefully attract Adam Slater. I'll be accompanying Eli to an event Friday night. Both Adam and Mathias will be there."

"There's something you both need to know."

Nick met Kennedy's eyes and said, "What's that?"

"A body was found in a shallow grave in the woods near Tyler, Texas. Authorities found it several days ago but just now identified the remains. The hands and head were missing, took them awhile to do DNA testing on the remains."

Dread clawed at his insides. "Who was it?"

"Teri Burke, Adam Slater's last executive assistant."

CHAPTER SEVENTEEN

State penitentiary

Brownsville, Texas

Eli sat in the glass-enclosed room, waiting for his younger brother, Jonah, to appear. Grey had wanted to be here, to give him the news personally. Since his association with Jonah needed to remain unknown, that hadn't been possible. Didn't matter. Even if secrecy hadn't been necessary, Eli would have declined. This was his responsibility.

Grey believed he had failed Jonah because he hadn't been able to protect him from Mathias. Truth was, Eli was the one who'd failed him first. From the time Jonah was born, Eli had felt a certain kinship with him. As children of a powerful and cruel man, they'd often had only each other. Adam, as the oldest, had received all the attention. Their sister, Lacey, had been an entity unto herself. So it had been Eli and Jonah who'd stuck together.

After graduating high school, Eli had gone off to England and created a new life for himself. Out from under the overpowering influence of the Slater name, he'd felt free for the first time since birth. Problem was, he'd left his younger brother behind.

Oh, he had invited him to come for visits. Had made a few phone calls and had even gone back for a birthday or two. That hadn't been enough. Mathias had seen Jonah as a weakness in the Slater lineage and had taken every opportunity to show his disapproval.

Eli's own problems with his father were numerous, but he had been able to avoid many of them by moving away when he was so young. Getting married right after he'd graduated university and giving Mathias grandchildren had helped some, too. To the outside world, Mathias Slater was all about family. The bastard loved telling people about his grandchildren. To the uninformed eye, the man looked and acted like the doting father and grandfather. Only behind closed doors did Mathias show his true self.

Instead of coming back to the States and checking on his younger brother, Eli had allowed himself to become separated from the entire family. Between his responsibilities as the COO of Slater House, being a dad and seeing to Shelley's treatment, he'd had little energy for anything else.

That was no excuse. Because of his neglect, his brother was serving a prison sentence for a crime he didn't commit. And now Eli was here to tell him news that would make his incarceration a thousand times more painful.

The door opened, and a thin, gaunt man who only vaguely resembled Jonah shuffled into the room. He was dressed in an orange jumpsuit two sizes too large and his hands and feet were shackled like some sort of mass murderer. It was all for psychological effect—Mathias had ordered the harsh treatment. Jonah was no danger to anyone. But this was part of Mathias's punishment for going against the family. And when Mathias Slater wanted something, he got it.

This harsh treatment was supposed to be a lesson for them all—betray the family, suffer the consequences. Eli knew Jonah would have preferred death—which might have been the biggest reason his father hadn't ordered him killed.

"What a great way to cap off another exciting, fulfilling day in the big house—a late-night visit from my big brother. And what do I owe the pleasure of your unexpected company?"

The bitterness in his brother's eyes hid a hurt so deep Eli feared Jonah would never again be the cheerful, goodhearted man he'd once known. No matter what he had to do, he would get his brother freed from this shit hole.

"How are you?"

"Asking about my health? Now that's lame, even for you, Eli. Have you finally run out of platitudes and promises?"

"Mother sends her love."

A hint of emotion gleamed in his dull gaze. Despite her weak, malleable nature, Eleanor Slater loved her children and did what she could to protect them. Unfortunately, up against a man like Mathias, it hadn't been much.

"She still in France?"

"Not yet." Some things in the Slater household never changed. His parents had been spending a month in the south of France for years. That was where Mathias and Eleanor had honeymooned, and everyone outside the family thought it was so romantic that they returned there each year.

"That's not for a couple more weeks."

"Damn, my social calendar must be out of date."

"Has Lacey been by to see you?"

"Yes." His chin cocked up in a defensive tilt. "I refused to see her."

"Why? I know she's worried about you."

"What's the point?"

Their sister fluttered in and out of their lives like a beautiful butterfly. She rarely stayed in one place longer than a week or two. And somehow, in spite of her dysfunctional family and extreme wealth, she was a good kid.

Lacey's good heart and cheerful nature were all due to their mother's influence. Mathias had a tendency to divide women into two categories—a few were to be cosseted and protected as if they were slightly dimwitted, and the rest were trash. Mathias had had almost nothing to do with his daughter's upbringing, which was one of the biggest reasons she'd turned out to be a decent human being.

"She's your sister and she loves you…that's the point."

"And is that why you're here, Eli? You love me?"

"Of course I love you. There's another reason I'm here, though." Eli had never been one to put things off, no matter how distasteful. Drawing in a breath, he opened his mouth to deliver the tragic news when Jonah beat him to it.

"She's dead…isn't she?"

Eli released his breath and said, "Yes."

"Where did they put her?"

Jonah wasn't asking where she was buried. He wanted to know where Teri's killer had left her body.

"In a shallow grave right outside Tyler."

"How was it done?"

"Jonah, there's no need—"

"There's every need." The hard, strained voice barely sounded human.

"Cause of death hasn't been determined."

"What else, Eli? I know you. You're holding something back. Do you think telling me is going to make it worse than it already is? The woman I loved…was going to marry is dead. What else? Tell me, damn you."

Acid roiled in his gut. Jonah wouldn't let up until he knew. And if Eli didn't tell him, he'd find out the truth from someone else. He spit out the distasteful words. "They found her body over a week ago but couldn't identify her." He swallowed hard, continued, "Her head and hands are still missing. That's why it took so long to identify her."

What little light left in his brother's eyes died, leaving a dark nothingness. "Who ordered the hit…Mathias or Adam?"

"I don't know. They both claim to know nothing about it."

"It was Mathias. That's his kind of dirty work." Then, very softly, he added, "I'm going to kill him."

Before Eli could respond, Jonah rolled back in his chair and glared up at the camera stationed in the corner. "Did you hear that, old man?" he shouted. "I'm going to fucking kill you!"

"Jonah…dammit. Stop it!"

"Why?" Eyes wild with grief, he glared at Eli. "We both know he's there. He hears and sees everything." His gaze returned to the camera. "Isn't that right, you sick fuck?"

Two prison guards burst through the door and grabbed Jonah. Instead of fighting them, he stood and walked willingly toward the door. He didn't glance back at Eli...he didn't need to. There was nothing more to be said.

Eli had once again failed his little brother. And if Mathias was watching this, he was doing one of two things—laughing his ass off or hiring someone inside to teach Jonah another lesson.

Dammit, he had to find a way to get his brother out and soon.

CHAPTER EIGHTEEN

Kennedy sat at her desk and stared blankly at the calendar in front of her. She was supposed to be reviewing Eli's schedule for the day, but her mind kept going back to last night with Nick. After Justice called with the news about Adam Slater's assistant, the atmosphere had been as solemn as a funeral. Once again, a Slater had destroyed someone's life.

As they ate dinner, Nick had described his meeting with Grey earlier that day. From the way it sounded, the man had been helping people gain justice for quite some time. Even though the Slaters were apparently tougher to pin down than other criminals had been, Grey Justice believed it could be done.

She and Nick had discussed their roles. They had agreed that while she was within the confines of the Slater House offices, she would be safe. Actually, Nick hadn't necessarily felt this way, but since he couldn't very well enter the building to keep an eye on her, he had conceded that Eli Slater could ensure her safety. When she went outside, Nick would either be with her or close-by.

The independent part of her rebelled at the thought of a 24/7 bodyguard. Other than her few short years with Thomas, Kennedy had relied on herself. And while she knew she could protect herself with her gun and had taken some self-defense courses, defending herself against a hired killer was beyond her expertise. So, dislike it as she might, she would go along with the extra protection.

While she was at work, Nick had said he would delve deeper into the Slaters' financials, hoping to find a link between the family and anything that looked remotely questionable. Grey had mentioned last night that new computer equipment would be delivered to her house today. So while she worked within the Slater ranks, Nick would work from the outside.

"I don't give a damn what you think!" a harsh male voice shouted.

Kennedy's head popped up. When she'd arrived this morning, Helen had told her that Eli was in a private meeting and under no circumstances was he to be disturbed. She'd been at her desk for two hours, so whoever his visitor was, they'd had a lot to discuss. From the shouting, the conversation wasn't pleasant.

The door to Eli's office was flung open, and a tall, blond-haired man stormed out. Breath seized in her lungs as her heart went into an immediate gallop. She'd seen enough photos to recognize Adam Slater, Eli's brother.

Her mind had replayed this scenario a thousand times. Knowing that at some point she would come face-to-face with her enemy, she had thought about all the things she could say to him, all the ways she would act. Not once did she doubt that she could handle herself. Until now.

The instant he noticed her, she dropped her gaze to her desk. Footsteps sounded as he came closer. Her heart raced, and a light, floaty feeling fuzzed her brain. She knew he was standing at her desk, looking down on her. She could hear his breathing. What if he recognized her? What if she screamed that he was a murderer? What if—

"And you are?"

She released the breath she had been holding, raised her head and stared up at the face of the man responsible for Thomas's death. Why didn't he look like a monster? How could he look so human and ordinary?

"Do you have a speech problem?"

"No...I—" *Get it together, Kennedy!* "My...uh...my name is Rachel Walker. I'm, um, I'm Mr. Slater's assistant."

"Since when?"

"I hired her a few days ago." Eli stood at the door to his office. The mild look on his face belied the anger gleaming in his eyes. He was furious and trying not to show it. She'd learned a few of his tells over the last couple of days. As if to confirm her thoughts, he added in a hard, cold voice, "Leave her alone."

Adam returned his attention to Kennedy and for the first time she noticed his eyes—muted shades of brown and blue blended together to create a murky, dead-looking color. They were the eeriest shade she'd ever seen. She wondered if anyone had ever suggested he wear colored lenses because his eyes were probably his most unattractive feature. They were downright evil looking.

"Where are you from?"

Every cell in her body froze. Was the interest gleaming in his weird eyes because he was merely nosy or for another reason? Did he recognize her?

"Is she hearing impaired, Eli? How noble of you to hire the disabled. Once again, your halo is glowing."

"That's enough, Adam. Get out."

Kennedy forced her frozen lips to open. "Amarillo. I'm from Amarillo." When he continued to stare at her, she added, "That's just on the other side of—"

"I'm aware of my Texas geography, my dear."

Feeling like a dunce on top of everything else, Kennedy dropped her gaze back to the papers on her desk.

"Is that a blush I see? My, my. I don't think I've seen anyone blush in ages. What did you say your name was again?"

Furious at herself, she raised her gaze and this time spoke clearly. "Rachel Walker."

He looked her up and down as if she were a prize horse he was considering. "I'm in need of a new assistant." Without looking away, he addressed his brother. "Where'd you get her?"

"She's been an employee of Slater House for a while. And don't even think about trying to steal her from me. Your assistants seem to have a habit of leaving, one way or another."

Thin, male lips tilted with a mocking amusement. "Not my fault they turned out to be…incompetent."

Though stunned by the sheer callousness of the man, Kennedy forced herself to maintain a neutral expression.

"I believe I told you to leave." The dangerous raspy whisper barely sounded like it came from Eli.

Finally pulling his creepy gaze away from Kennedy, Adam faced his brother. "Perfection can be such a bore, Eli. Perhaps that's why Shelley checked out on you."

Eli took a step toward his brother, the threat in his face apparent. "Get the hell out of here. Now."

Adam gave a little wink to Kennedy. "Hope to see you again soon." He then strode out the door with a slow, insolent arrogance.

"Ms. Walker, are you all right?" Eli's voice finally brought her back to herself.

"Yes…I'm fine." She swallowed back bile. No, she really wasn't, but Helen's eagle eye saw everything.

She managed a fractured smile. "Just a slight headache." A lame excuse, but the last thing she needed was for the woman to report to Mathias that Eli's new assistant acted strangely the first time she met Adam.

She also needed to convince Eli that she could handle this situation. Practically falling apart at Adam Slater's feet was not the way to prove that, though. The next time she would be better prepared. She swore she would.

Eli stood in front of her desk. "I'm headed to a meeting downtown. I'd like you to accompany me."

"What meeting?" Helen asked. "I don't have anything on your itinerary."

"I made the appointment on my way into work," he answered smoothly. His eyes targeted Kennedy. "Can you leave now?"

"Yes, of course. I'll just get my coat."

"I'll get your coat. Meet me in the lobby."

Eli's expression never changed. If she hadn't known the real reason behind his "meeting" she would have assumed it was authentic. Unfortunately, she did know. She appreciated him covering for her but was infuriated at herself that it was necessary.

So grateful to have some alone time to compose herself, Kennedy barely glanced at Helen as she passed by her. She stepped into the elevator and stared at the closed doors. Twenty-five floors later, the doors slid open, and she had no better excuse than she'd had before. She had behaved like an imbecile. There was no way Adam Slater would want to hire her as a message person much less his executive assistant.

The cellphone in her suit jacket chimed. Since exactly three people knew her number, she braced herself for Grey's or Eli's voice telling her to forget about being involved in bringing the Slaters down.

"Hello." She grimaced at the timidity of her voice.

"What's wrong? You look like you lost your best friend."

The husky male voice with its slight edge of amusement sent equal parts relief and warmth throughout her body. Then Nick's words penetrated her brain.

"You can see me? Where are you?"

"I'm at your house. The tech person that Justice sent over with the equipment is a whiz. He just hacked into the cameras there. I can see you standing in the lobby."

"Did you happen to see how I screwed up a few minutes ago?" she asked wryly.

"No. We're still working on getting feed inside the executive offices, but I heard from Justice that you met Adam. Why do you think you screwed up?"

"Because I acted like an idiot. I should have—"

"Don't beat yourself up. He caught you off guard. You'll do better next time."

"If there is a next time."

"There will be. No one expects you to be an expert at undercover."

"Maybe not, but I expect better of myself."

"You ready?"

Kennedy turned. Eli stood behind her, holding her coat. Again, not by any flicker of emotion did he show his disappointment in how she had reacted to Adam.

"Eli's here. I have to go," she said to Nick.

"Okay. See you tonight."

His words gave her a much-needed boost. Nick would be outside the building when she walked out the door this evening. He would follow her back home and would be spending the night.

Dropping the phone back into her pocket, she went to take the coat from Eli, but he held it up, indicating he would help her put it on. Smiling her thanks, she slid her arms into the sleeves. With him so close, he was able to speak low without fear of being heard. "You okay?"

"I'm fine. I'm sorry about how it went."

"Let's get out of here."

Fully expecting to be told that she couldn't act her way out of a paper bag much less entice Adam Slater, Kennedy walked out the door. The minute they were on the street, Eli placed a hand at the small of her back and gently guided her toward a black limo waiting at the curb. The back door was opened, and a tall, massively built man stood waiting to help her inside.

Kennedy slid inside, Eli followed, and the instant he sat across from her, she blurted, "I'll do better next time."

His brow furrowed in what looked like real confusion. "Are you under the impression that you're going to be fired?"

"You can't be thrilled with the way I handled myself with your brother."

"Hell, you did better than I did. I wanted to punch the fucker." He grimaced. "Sorry. My language deteriorates when I'm around my family. And I never planned for you to meet him that way. He surprised me this morning…was waiting in my office when I walked in the door."

"How can I make sure the next time I meet him that I'll make a good impression?"

"That's exactly what we're going to talk about with Grey. We're meeting him at his office."

"That's not a problem? For us to be seen with him?"

"Grey's a business associate. And you're my executive assistant who has accompanied me to a business meeting. No one will consider it strange."

Kennedy glanced nervously at the open window that should have separated them from the driver. She was beginning to realize that there was a lot more to covert work than just pretending to be someone else.

"Don't worry. Gunter has been with me for years. He's loyal to our cause."

She was glad to hear that, but she shouldn't have just started talking without being sure. She hated being green.

"Gallagher mentioned that you'd do your damnedest to be perfect. Relax. There's nothing you need to concentrate on now other than attracting my brother's attention. Once you do, we'll take it to the next step."

"And what step is that?"

The limo stopped in front of a large office building. His hand on the door handle, Eli gave Kennedy a brilliant smile. "The one where we upend any and every illegal activity my father and brother are involved with and put an end to them forever."

For so long the enormity of what she wanted to do had weighed heavily on her shoulders. She'd felt so alone and isolated. And now, she had Eli Slater and Grey Justice in her corner. And she had Nick. Suddenly, she felt confident of their success. They were going to get justice for Thomas…for her baby, and the other countless people Mathias and Adam Slater had destroyed.

Feeling as though she could take on a grizzly and win, she walked into the office complex of Grey Justice Enterprises with a self-assured air. A solemn young man greeted them in the lobby and ushered them into the elevator, where they traveled to the seventieth floor. The doors opened, and Kennedy stepped into luxury. The setting was starkly beautiful. Paintings on the soft cream-colored walls were clearly originals. The gigantic area rugs, covering rich hardwood floors, were thick and cushiony beneath her feet. The semicircle of floor-to-ceiling windows in front of her revealed the most spectacular view of Dallas she'd ever seen. The setting was meant to impress and intimidate and did both quite well.

"Welcome, Eli. Good to see you again."

As if he'd come out of the walls, Grey Justice materialized before them. Startled by his sudden appearance, Kennedy took a step back, right onto Eli's shiny Italian leather shoe. She heard a slight indrawn breath and inwardly winced. The sharp spike of her heel had to have hurt. She turned to apologize and stumbled. Fortunately, Eli caught her shoulders before she could fall at his feet.

Her confidence threatened to disintegrate, but Kennedy pushed her doubts aside. Okay, so she wasn't the most graceful person in the world. That didn't mean she couldn't do this job.

As if he hadn't just witnessed her less-than-elegant entrance, Grey gave her a warm look as he held out his hand. "And you must be Eli's new assistant."

"Yes, I'm Rachel Walker. It's so nice to meet you, Mr. Justice."

Grey released her hand and then turned slightly, revealing a woman behind him—quite possibly the most beautiful woman Kennedy had ever seen. Thick, silky hair the color of blackest midnight flowed over her slender shoulders. With dusky, honey-gold skin as flawless as a marble statue; eyes a startling, clear gray; classic, high cheekbones; and a full, mobile mouth, the woman was so breathtaking it was impossible not to stare. At a little over average height, she had a slender, feminine curviness that any woman might envy. The expression on her lovely face said she was more than aware of her appeal. In fact, Kennedy didn't believe she'd ever seen anyone quite so confident and sure of herself.

"Let me introduce you to my assistant. This is Irelyn Raine. Irelyn, you know Eli, of course. And this is Rachel Walker, Eli's new executive assistant."

Irelyn gave a brief nod of acknowledgment to Eli, but her eyes were focused solely on Kennedy. A small, enigmatic smile lifted her mouth as she said in an elegant British accent, "Lovely to meet you, Rachel. Please follow me."

Apparently expecting no argument, she turned her back and walked with a brisk, feminine stride to an open door. When she reached it, she turned and arched a questioning brow.

"This is your first lesson," Eli murmured softly. "Don't worry. She doesn't bite."

Not quite sure she was ready for whatever lesson this woman had planned for her, Kennedy forced her legs to move forward. Irelyn made no attempt to disguise that she was carefully assessing her, making Kennedy feel as awkward as a toddler just learning to walk. The confidence she'd had when she had entered the office was now completely gone.

She entered the room and the door clicked close.

"Okay, bitch," the woman behind her snarled, "tell me the truth. Are you screwing my man?"

Completely taken off guard by the verbal attack, Kennedy whirled on a gasp of air. A camera clicked in her face. *What the hell?*

"Now see, sugar." Irelyn said with an authentic Texas drawl. "That's the look we gotta get rid of. You look like some stranger just smacked your fanny and pinched your boob."

No longer looking as though ice wouldn't melt in her mouth, Irelyn's smile was one of sweet sincerity. Her lovely face animated with friendliness, she winked at Kennedy. "Don't worry, darlin'. We'll whip you into shape. By the time I'm finished with you, you'll be able to stare down a cobra, much less a slimy maggot like Adam Slater."

Returning the smile with a relieved one of her own, Kennedy felt that, despite their unbelievably odd beginning, she'd just made a lifelong friend.

CHAPTER NINETEEN

Beneath half-closed eyes, Mathias Slater leaned back in his chair and watched his son Adam putter around the room like a lovesick possum. One would think that out of three boys, one of them would've been worth a damn.

The only one who'd showed any gumption whatsoever was now rotting in prison. Boys had to be punished when they were bad. The young upstart should have been happy he hadn't done more to him than arrange a little prison stay. He'd deserved a helluva lot more.

"How's that contract on the Beechmont property coming? Construction on the mall still set to begin in May?"

His mind obviously a million miles away, Adam gave an absentminded nod.

"Boy, get your head out of your ass and focus on business."

Even though Mathias's voice no longer sounded like the crack of a whip, he could still get attention when he wanted. Adam jumped slightly and turned to him. "Sorry, Daddy. I'm just restless, I guess. The Beechmont contract went off like a dream. We might even be able to start construction a couple of weeks early, depending on the damn lawyers. You know how they love to hold things up."

Couldn't argue with him there. Damn lawyers almost bled him dry every year. But you get what you pay for, and Mathias paid millions to make sure life ran smoothly.

"What's got you so restless? It ain't another woman again, is it?"

"No, nothing like that. And despite what you think, I wasn't having an affair with Teri Burke."

Mathias snorted. "Hell, son. I know that. You think I got rid of her because of that? You got into lots of women's panties before, and I didn't say nothing. That cold fish of a wife don't satisfy you, and a man has his needs. I got rid of that woman because she and Jonah had something going."

Adam stumbled in the midst of his roaming. "That's not possible. I would've known."

He didn't bother to say the obvious. If a situation didn't involve him and his needs, Adam could be as oblivious as a hibernating turtle. "They were discreet, but I knew all about it. My boys don't do anything without their father finding out. Besides, you didn't need to know. You focus on what I tell you to focus on. I'll take care of the other stuff. If I need you for something else, you'll know it."

"What's going to happen when you die?"

Despite himself, Mathias flinched. He'd been pissed since the day he got the diagnosis. Not because he feared death. He'd been through too much to fear anything, even his last breath. No, what infuriated him was he wouldn't be around to oversee his empire. He'd scraped, scrambled, and fought for every cent he had. To think that others would be making all the decisions galled him like nothing ever had before. That old saying "you can't take it with you" was just so damn unfair.

"I'm going to have to leave most of it to you. You up for the challenge?"

"I'll do my best."

"I'm not asking you to do your best," Mathias snapped. "You damn well better do better than your best. You got that?"

"Yes, sir." As if he'd exhausted himself with his prowling, Adam collapsed into a chair and let out a long, dramatic breath.

"What the hell is your problem, boy? That spiteful little wife causing problems again?"

"No. She's been kind of quiet lately."

That was one blessing. Even though he'd encouraged Adam to marry into the Swenson family, it'd been all about business. The family was comfortably wealthy, but most of all, they had powerful connections. Being related to them had been a beneficial arrangement, but he sure as hell would hate to go home to that cold bitch every night.

"I wanted to talk to you about a new investment," Adam said.

Mathias's heart clicked up a beat. Nothing made him happier than to talk about investments and making more money. He didn't care what other people said. If there was one thing a man could never have too much of, it was money.

Adam wasn't the sharpest fish in the tank, but Mathias had been working on him for years, trying his damnedest to make him into something. The boy rarely wanted to talk about business, so maybe his lectures were finally getting through. "Tell me about it."

"That vacant building over on Pine and Fourth Street, you know where that strip mall used to be."

Mathias nodded, not even needing that much detail. No one knew this city better than he did. It was his home, and a man should know every square inch of where he hung his hat.

"I want to open a restaurant, specializing in cuisine from all parts of the world."

"How so?"

"The restaurant would be divided into five different areas. Each area would focus on a particular type of cuisine."

"So it would actually be five different restaurants?"

"Yes. Each one would be small but elegant."

He had to hand it to the boy…the idea was a different spin on dining. Didn't do much to crank his motor, but since his appetite had been off for the last few months, opening a restaurant held little appeal. Still, if the idea was successful, he wouldn't mind profiting from it.

"I talked to Eli about it this morning. He thinks it's a lame idea."

"You talked to your brother before coming to me?"

The panicked look on his son's face would have been comical if Mathias had been in a laughing mood. To think that his spineless, least-useful son had heard about the venture first put him sour on the entire plan. However, if Eli thought the idea stank, then Mathias definitely wanted it to succeed.

"How much do you need?"

"You mean you—" Adam broke off and regrouped. "Just two and a half million."

Mathias leaned forward, feeling better than he had in months. He'd show his good-for-nothing son, who disapproved of everything he did, a thing or two about being a good business manager and investor.

"Tell me everything about it." And remembering that depending on what happened in the next few weeks, he might well have an expiration date in the not-too-distant future, he added, "And let's make sure we can get it open by June."

Grey stood at the door to his office and watched an exhausted Kennedy almost fall into Nick Gallagher's arms. She had been what his people called "Rained out." There was no one quite like Irelyn Raine.

"I like her. She's tough."

Irelyn glided toward him as if she were on some kind of invisible skates. He had yet to find a flaw, at least physically, in his beautiful partner.

"How will she handle the event Friday night?"

"By the time Friday rolls around, she'll be exactly what she needs to be. She might be terrified on the inside, but she'll be irresistible on the outside."

Her lilting Irish voice washed over him like the finest brandy. There wasn't an accent or dialect that Irelyn couldn't imitate. With him, she always used her native one.

"You'll attend the event with me. She'll feel more confident if she sees you. And if something happens, you can smooth it over."

Not by a flicker or change of expression did she indicate the order bothered her, yet he knew her well. She didn't like being told what to do and definitely didn't want to attend a dinner hosted by the Slaters. Didn't matter. They'd come to an agreement long ago. She would do as he said.

Giving him the mysterious, satisfied smile of a contented feline, she said, "I'll leave you to your work."

"Headed to the gym?"

She stopped mid-stride. "Yes. Why?"

"No reason. Just wondered."

The flicker in her eyes said she knew he was lying. She knew better than anyone that Grey never did or said anything without reason. But just like she had so many times before, she accepted his answer without argument and walked away.

Grey watched until she disappeared into the elevator and the doors closed, hiding her beautiful face from view. No, there was no one like Irelyn Raine. And he was damn glad there wasn't. One Irelyn was more than enough for this world.

Chapter Twenty

"Better?"

"Yes, thank you." Feet up, a warm cloth on her forehead, Kennedy lay back in the recliner, feeling like a big, giant wuss. She also felt as if a sledgehammer had been systematically pounded into her body. Less than five minutes after she'd made the assessment that she had found a friend in Irelyn Raine, she had been reassessing her opinion. The woman was a demon, no doubt about it.

By the time she'd walked out of that room nine hours later, she had shed tears, said curse words she'd never believed she could utter and had even thrown her shoe at the woman. The only reaction Irelyn revealed was a slight maneuver to avoid being hit.

Kennedy had been so surprised and relieved to see Nick waiting at the elevator, she'd thrown herself into his arms as if he were her rescuer. And that's exactly how she'd seen him. Her head was splitting open, and her stomach was a huge knot of nerves.

Though the alarm in his eyes had been obvious, to his credit, he hadn't asked any questions other than did she want to be carried. Even though every part of her body was saying yes, she had refused. Damned if the beautiful demon woman would see her act like a complete wimp.

Nick had brought her home, given her a cup of hot tea and then a warm compress for her head. He'd even dimmed the lights and turned on soft music.

"Want to talk about it?"

She took a moment, breathed in and out, imperceptible breaths, as she had been taught, and answered with absolute sincerity. "Without a doubt, today was one of the most valuable learning experiences of my life."

"Really? You looked like—"

He broke off, most likely because his description wouldn't have been a compliment. She laughed softly, surprised and pleased she could find humor in the situation. She knew exactly what she had looked like—having been surrounded by mirrors the whole day. There wasn't any angle she hadn't seen of herself or a facial expression she hadn't studied.

She gave herself a few more seconds to answer—something else she had learned. Think fast but carefully. "I learned how to be someone else on the outside."

"You mean like acting?"

"In a way, but not. Acting can sometimes look fake. I need to be Rachel Walker in every way possible. Before, I was Kennedy pretending to be Rachel."

"And now you're no longer Kennedy?"

"Actually, I'm more Kennedy than I ever was before."

A furrow appeared on his brow. "You know that makes no sense. Right?"

"Yeah, I know."

How could she describe something that had no reasonable explanation? Somehow, within that nine-hour time frame, she had learned how to compartmentalize. She could still be Kennedy with all of her insecurities and doubts, but when the time came to be Rachel, without a doubt she could be the sophisticated, self-assured executive assistant. She also knew that the next time she encountered Adam Slater, he'd be a lot more impressed than he had been today.

"How about some dinner?"

"Sounds wonderful, but I'm too exhausted to cook, and it's not fair to ask you to do that again."

"No worries. There's a Chinese restaurant two blocks down the street that delivers. Sound okay to you?"

If she'd had any extra energy, she would have thrown herself into his arms again.

"Sounds perfect."

"Still like lo mein and spring rolls?"

"There's so much you know about me, isn't there?"

"Not nearly enough." Before she could ask him what he meant, he dropped a kiss on her forehead and got to his feet. "I'll go place the order."

Kennedy watched him go with an odd yearning inside her. For so long she had wanted to see her friend Nick. To talk to him, ask his advice. But now that he was here, there was something more than friendship between them. Did he feel it, too, or was it just her hopeful imagination that she'd seen attraction spark in his eyes? The thought was both thrilling and scary.

He was in serious trouble. Only by reminding himself that Kennedy was exhausted and vulnerable had Nick been able to keep from pulling her into his arms for a soul-deep, devouring kiss.

When she'd practically collapsed in his arms earlier, it had been all he could do not to carry her away someplace safe. He wanted justice for Thomas's murder as much as she did, but his overprotective instinct was telling him to get her out. It was too late for that. She believed she could do this and win. And even though Justice and Eli Slater believed it, too, after seeing her exhaustion today, his doubts had returned. The plan was iffy at best. But what he was one hundred percent sure of was his need to protect Kennedy at all cost.

Nick placed the order for their food and then returned to the living room. He had planned to ask Kennedy if she wanted a foot rub or massage. Yeah, a lame excuse to touch her but what the hell? Before he could say a word, he heard a soft, shallow breath of sleep.

Taking the decorative throw she'd draped on the back of the sofa, he covered her and then sat down to watch. There were a lot of things he could be doing, but for the life of him, he couldn't think of anything more important than this. In all the time they'd known each other, he had never seen her sleep. She looked peaceful, delicate…so damned beautiful his entire body ached with need.

When she and Thomas had married, Nick had forced himself not to think of her in any other light but as his friend's wife. Hadn't been easy. Seeing her happy and thriving had helped. Knowing Thomas was good to her and obviously adored her lessened his pain. He had dated voraciously, specifically seeking out women who looked nothing like Kennedy. He had developed a reputation and was envied by many men. Little did they know that he would have given all of that up to be with the woman he loved.

Thomas might be gone, but in a way he was still here, his presence almost as strong as if he were in the room with them. They were doing this job to seek justice for his death. When that was over, what was next? He would go back to being a cop, but what about Kennedy? Would Thomas always stand between them?

"You look so serious."

Her voice, soft and drowsy, stirred the deep cauldron of emotions he fought on a daily basis. Calling himself a fool didn't stop him from standing and going to her. Her eyes were only half open, but as he sat on the arm of the recliner, they went wide. His heart thudding like a violent drummer, Nick leaned forward and placed his mouth over hers. She tasted better than any fantasy he'd ever allowed himself. He heard a slight gasp and tensed, waiting for her to pull away and demand to know what he was doing. Instead, she raised her head slightly to allow for a deeper connection. He didn't question why or how. He didn't think at all. For the first time in his life, he was kissing the woman he loved.

As much as he wanted to hold her, make love to that luscious mouth, he kept the kiss light, allowing Kennedy to set the pace. When he felt her stiffen slightly, he fought every instinct within him to keep her close, and backed away. And waited. Had it been a mistake? Would there be regret in her eyes?

"What's happening here, Nick?"

That wasn't regret he saw...more like confusion. Maybe a hint of wonder? He took that as a good sign but didn't push. It was way too early to admit his feelings. Hell, he didn't even know if he'd ever be able to do that.

He shrugged, as casual as possible. "Just felt right."

"It did, didn't it? I—"

Whatever she'd been about to say was cut off by the loud blast outside her door. Surging to his feet, Nick pulled his gun from the holster at his waist. "Where's your gun?"

She frowned up at him. "In my purse, in the bedroom. But why? Wasn't that—"

"Get it and lock your bedroom door. If I'm not back in five minutes, call 911."

Though he could still see questions in her eyes, he was grateful she came to her feet immediately and ran to the bedroom.

He waited until he heard the door click before striding to the window. A lone car sat in the driveway, puffing out fumes like a frenzied smoker. The roof of the car held a sign, advertising the Chinese restaurant he'd ordered from. A kid holding a large brown paper bag meandered up the sidewalk toward the house.

Nick blew out a ragged sigh. The loud blast had been nothing more than the kid's car backfiring. At least he hadn't dropped to his knees and hid the way he had the first few months after he'd gotten out of the hospital. Still, he'd thought he was through with that shit.

The doorbell rang. Even though he was positive about the noise and was sure the kid was just delivering their food, Nick took nothing for granted anymore. Shoving the gun in the small of his back, he covered it with his T-shirt and opened the door.

A brown bag was shoved toward him. "That's $34.30."

Handing him the money and tip, Nick accepted the bag and closed the door. He turned and saw Kennedy's face peeking around a corner. "Everything okay?"

He held up the bag of food. "Just the food delivery. Apparently, the kid needs a new carburetor for his old car. Car backfired."

"I thought that's what it was." Frowning, she asked, "Are you all right?"

"Yeah." He grimaced an apology. "Just residual damage from the shooting. Hadn't had that reaction in a while. Sorry I scared you."

"Totally understandable. Besides, we're not exactly living carefree lives these days."

"You got that right. Come on, let's eat and forget about it for a while."

Kennedy followed him into the kitchen. Now that the excitement of that moment had passed, the memory of what happened right before returned full force. Nick had kissed her. Not only that, she had kissed him back. It had been soft, sweet…absolutely delicious. And she had wanted more.

While Nick unpacked the food, Kennedy went about getting plates and silverware. When they were settled at the table, sitting across from each other, she lifted her gaze to his and asked quietly, "Are we just going to pretend the kiss didn't happen?"

"What do you want? Do you want to forget it happened?"

The question was unexpected but more than reasonable. Yet how could she explain what she was feeling when she really didn't know herself? For so long, he had been Nick, Thomas's best friend and occasional poker buddy. The guy who came over on Saturdays to watch football games or dropped by unexpectedly with pizza, a six-pack, and a movie. Now, he was gorgeous, sexy, considerate, protective, surprisingly mysterious Nick.

For the first time in almost two years, Kennedy felt alive. But also incredibly confused.

Taking the easy way out wasn't her usual preference…in this, she had no choice. She simply couldn't face these new feelings right now on top of everything else.

"I wouldn't want to ruin our friendship."

Nick wasn't one for taking the easy route, either. "Is that all you want? Friendship?"

"Do I have to answer that right now?"

His eyes blazed with a thousand questions, and her emotions churned. Would he challenge her? She might not be able to say for sure what she was feeling, but one thing she knew for certain—she didn't want to lose Nick.

"Sorry." He gave her a grimacing smile. "Didn't mean to push."

Their earlier camaraderie now shattered, they ate in a tense, uncomfortable silence.

Hoping to return to a neutral, less complicated subject, she said, "Why do you think Grey Justice does what he does?"

Having just taken a giant bite of an eggroll, Nick took a minute to chew and swallow before answering. His slightly halting words gave her the idea that he'd been wondering the same thing. "I think something must have happened... to make him want to see others get their justice. Maybe he didn't get justice himself." He shrugged. "That's the only explanation I've been able to come up with. Doubt we'll ever know unless he wants to tell us."

"I did some research on him the night we met with him. Even though there's a ton of press about him, his past is very sketchy."

"I noticed that, too."

"You dug into his past, too?"

"I wasn't about to get you involved with him without checking him out."

She dropped her gaze to the food on her plate, touched by his concern. From the moment she'd lost Thomas, Nick had been looking out for her.

Raising her eyes back to his face, she gave him something she should have done the first time she'd seen him again—an apology. "I'm sorry I didn't contact you. I know you must have worried about me."

A hot light blazed in his eyes, searing, thrilling...mesmerizing. Suddenly breathless, she sat transfixed, speechless, as hidden depths she'd never known existed came to life in his eyes. Who was this man?

Seconds later, as if the moment never happened, he said, "My first thought was that Slater's people had gotten to you and dumped your body somewhere. The longer I searched for you, saw the diversionary tactics you used, the more I realized you had disappeared on purpose. Even though I worried, I was glad to know it had been your choice to leave."

"Thomas left me explicit instructions on who to contact and what I needed to do to disappear and get a new identity. Without that, I doubt I would've been so resourceful."

"I'm glad he did, but as I said before, you're a strong woman. You would have figured it out."

"After you recovered, I thought about contacting you but couldn't make myself do it. You'd almost been killed. I hated to put you at risk again."

A pained smile twisted at his mouth. "I'm the one who's supposed to be protecting you."

"How about we watch each other's backs from now on?"

"Deal."

They ate in silence for several more minutes. Kennedy was glad that the earlier tension had eased. She would have to face what was happening between them eventually, but for right now, she couldn't deal with the whirl of emotions that had gone through her at Nick's kiss. And that hot stare had almost melted her. She'd never had anyone look at her like that.

"So you met Adam Slater today?"

She jerked her attention back to the present. "Yes." She grimaced, remembering the babbling, blushing, awkwardly painful event. "It wasn't my finest moment. I blushed and stammered like a schoolgirl. I even tried to explain to him where Amarillo was. I'm sure he thinks I would be useless as an assistant."

"Eli seemed to think his brother was quite taken with you."

"If that's the case, then he's right in his assessment that Adam covets whatever Eli has, because my conversational skills wouldn't have impressed a five-year-old."

"The dinner party on Friday night…you going to be ready to handle that or should we wait for another opportunity?"

"No, I can handle myself now."

"Just by spending an afternoon with Justice's assistant?"

"I'll be seeing her every day until Friday. And, yes, without a doubt, I will be ready." Still unable to explain the phenomenal experience with Irelyn Raine, she said a quiet but confident, "Don't worry. I'll do great."

His gaze admiring, he sat back in his chair. "Anyone ever tell you that you're one hell of a woman, Kennedy O'Connell?"

Like a flash wildfire igniting, heat rushed through Kennedy. She told herself it was simply pleasure at Nick's compliment that was making her glow, but she knew it was much more. Nick's approval was becoming more important to her every day.

"Are you finished?"

"What?"

"Your meal? Do you want more?"

"No...I mean, yes, I'm finished."

Apparently thinking exhaustion had finally caught up with her, he stood and began to gather the half-empty boxes of food. "Why don't you go on to bed...I'll clean up the kitchen."

Kennedy stood, whispered a soft good-night, and sped out of the kitchen. Maybe she was exhausted, not thinking clearly, because her first instinct when he'd told her to go on to bed was to hold out her hand and ask him to join her.

CHAPTER TWENTY-ONE

Nick stared at the monitor, captivated by the beauty on the screen. Wearing an ice-blue cocktail dress with some kind of silver sparkles that glittered when she moved, Kennedy stood out in the horde of people like a small exotic bird among a gathering of crows. She took his breath away. Even though he had seen her leave the house looking like a sexy angel, seeing her on camera was still a shock to his senses. He'd tapped into the security cameras in the hotel ballroom to observe the crowd around her, but his eyes were drawn back to her again and again.

A limo had come by to pick her up, and Nick had been ready to demand an explanation of why she would be unprotected. When he'd seen Eli's driver, Gunter, he'd been slightly reassured. The man was well over six feet tall and built like an army tank. After a few pertinent questions, Nick felt even better, learning that Gunter's résumé included a U.S. Army Special Forces stint and two black belts. If this man couldn't protect Kennedy, no one could.

Still, watching her leave, knowing she would be in the presence of evil, had been damned hard. Only by reminding himself that she would be surrounded by dozens of other people was he able to let her go. He had mentioned his concern to Justice and was reassured to learn that two bodyguards, Justice's employees, would also be attending with the sole purpose of watching Kennedy's back.

Nick scanned the crowd of people once more, noting several familiar faces, both politicians and local celebrities. Looked like most of the Dallas elite was in attendance, but still no sign of Mathias or Adam.

If Kennedy was nervous, it didn't show. Maybe the camera didn't pick up the nuances of emotions like the naked eye, but somehow he didn't believe that was the explanation. She simply had become someone else the moment she'd walked into the ballroom. He didn't know what the hell Irelyn Raine was teaching her, but whatever it was had an amazing effect on Kennedy's personality. The transformation was fascinating.

A movement at the edge of the screen drew his eyes away from Kennedy again. Like a small parting of the Red Sea, people began to back away. And then he saw the reason—Mathias and Eleanor Slater had arrived. Apparently, they were considered the VIPs of the VIPs. The deference being shown to Mathias was sickening.

Nick tried to look at him objectively, as if he didn't know about the man's evil deeds. Mathias might be pushing seventy and, according to Eli, in poor health, but he was still a striking man. Though only about five-feet-ten, his erect, rigid posture made him appear much taller. With thick silver hair and an amazingly unlined face, he could have passed for a man twenty years younger. His complexion looked healthy, but Nick figured he owed that to makeup. Having investors know about his illness would have been bad for business.

Eleanor Slater stood beside her husband as the less flamboyant of the two. Though she also didn't look her age, her too-smooth features hinted at a skilled plastic surgeon. Small and slight, she had a fragility about her that seemed incongruent with the man she had married.

Research revealed that Mathias had been flat broke when he'd married his wife. She'd been the one with the money, but Slater had been the one with the pedigree dating back centuries. And Mathias had turned her millions into billions.

Behind Mathias and Eleanor were Adam and his wife, DeAnne. If not for expensive clothing and a general air of arrogance, neither would stand out in a crowd. Wealth had enabled them to be something they wouldn't ordinarily be—interesting.

Nick's eyes darted back to Kennedy. She had just spotted the entourage. He waited to see if her demeanor would change. Even though she had assured him she was prepared, he worried that once she saw Adam and Mathias together, her composure would shatter. He was astonished that she did change, but not in the way he feared. A confident assurance swept over her. Maybe because he knew her so well, he was the only one who noticed. Before she had been quietly beautiful, now she glowed with an inner light.

Instead of waiting to be introduced to the Slaters, she did something he was sure the family hadn't had done to them in forever. She snubbed them. With barely a nod of acknowledgment, she turned her back on them as if they didn't matter in the least.

Chuckling, Nick sat back in his chair and watched, fascinated, as Kennedy/ Rachel made a lasting impression on one of the most powerful and influential families in the world.

As if another person possessed her body, Kennedy had done the unthinkable. She had just treated the Slaters as if they were nothing to her. While others moved toward them in droves, as if they were rock stars, she headed in the opposite direction. Eli had assured her that treating them this way was a surefire method to gain Adam's attention.

After spending her afternoons with Irelyn, Kennedy now possessed a confidence she had never imagined. She was half-convinced that the beautiful tyrant was actually some sort of sorcerer or witch who'd cast a magical spell.

"I believe we've already met."

Recognizing the voice immediately, Kennedy turned a cool, inquiring gaze up to Adam Slater. Her brows arched in haughty confusion. "Have we?"

"Yes, the other day…in my brother's office." His smile smug, condescending, he added, "Don't tell me you don't remember. I believe you tried to give me directions to Amarillo."

When she had told Irelyn what an idiot she'd made of herself on meeting Adam, Irelyn had offered her maybe one of her wisest pieces of advice on handling a man like Adam Slater—barely veiled insults.

"Oh yes, now I remember." She gave him a small, frozen smile. "I wasn't sure you would know."

"Honey, there's nothing I don't know about this state."

"How nice for you." She turned away, her disinterest more than apparent.

Any normal person would have felt the insult and either left or at the very least responded with something equally rude. Not Adam, who moved to stand in front of her, his ugly eyes gleaming with interest.

Kennedy arched another brow, vaguely wondering if her forehead would be sore tomorrow.

"Are you enjoying your new job?"

"It has its challenges."

His forehead furrowed, revealing his confusion. "Do you know who I am?"

The look she gave him was almost pitying. "I thought we established we met the other day."

"Yes…but—"

If he had been anyone else, Kennedy might have felt sorry for him. He was clearly out of his element.

"But?" she questioned.

Shaking his head, Adam backed away, muttering something unintelligible.

As if uncaring of his plight, Kennedy turned her back to him and continued a slow, steady walk through the crowd. She made herself stop from time to time at different clumps of people, pretend to listen, smile vaguely, and move on. She refused to allow herself to think that she might have overplayed her "ice queen" demeanor and Adam had lost interest. He had to take the bait.

"Very well done, my dear. I do believe you have a new admirer." Stunning in an off-the-shoulder black evening gown that lovingly hugged every slender curve, Irelyn Raine gave her a nod of approval.

Though glowing at the rare praise, Kennedy reached for some reassurance. "You don't think I overdid it?"

"Absolutely not. However, you must remember you are the icy bitch. You are not playacting. Understand?"

"But of course, my dear. Who else could I be other than who I am?"

The woman was as hard to read as a closed book yet Kennedy could swear she saw a glimmer of pride in her beautiful gray eyes.

"Oh my…I do believe he's back for more mistreatment," Irelyn murmured. "Should be an easy kill, but don't flaunt the victory."

Taking a delicate bite of a pâté-covered cracker, Kennedy tapped her foot to the music playing softly in the background and waited. Acknowledging that she knew he was coming toward her would have given him an advantage. She didn't intend this man to ever get the upper hand with her on anything.

"Would you like another drink?"

Deciding to throw him a bone, she said, "Champagne," and waited to see if he took orders well.

He grinned as if delighted to be of service. "Be right back."

Taking an inner, invisible breath, she released it slowly, relieving the tension in her spine. As she waited for Adam to return, her gaze scanned the crowd. The giant chandeliers above made the glittering jewels draped around the necks and wrists of Dallas's wealthiest women sparkle like moonbeams. Men in dark suits and tuxedoes stood in circles, nodding and munching their way through lavish and artistically prepared hors d'oeuvres.

She had never attended anything quite so elaborate. Though she and Thomas had gone to a couple of Christmas parties for the law firms she had freelanced for, both had agreed that fancy shindigs just weren't their thing. Those parties had been nothing compared to this event. If she had been Kennedy and not Ice

Queen Rachel Walker tonight, she'd have felt as out of place as an opera singer at a rodeo. Oddly enough, she felt very much at home here.

"You look lovely tonight, Rachel. Are you enjoying yourself?"

She twisted around at the sound of Eli's voice. She had seen him standing in various groups but had talked to him only once, when she had first arrived. Dressed in a tuxedo, Eli had turned many women's heads as he'd made his rounds. With his looks and wealth, she was surprised that he didn't have several women hanging on his arm, vying for his attention.

"Thank you. You look quite dapper yourself. And, yes, I'm having a lovely time."

He lowered his voice. "Hope you're not enjoying yourself too much, because it's time to leave."

She replied in an equally quite tone, "Are you sure? Adam's coming back with a glass of champagne for me."

"I'm following Irelyn's orders."

Since the woman knew more about men than Kennedy thought there was to know, she wasn't about to question Irelyn's decision. With a cool nod of approval, she allowed Eli to take her arm and lead her through the throng of people.

Halfway to the door, Adam appeared at her side. "Where are you going? I have your drink."

"I want to see Sophia and Violet before they go to bed," Eli said.

"Hell, isn't that why you have a nanny?"

"Yet another reason why I'm thankful you never had children."

"Yeah, you'll be voted father of the year, I'm sure." Adam swung his gaze to Kennedy. "I can take you home. There's no reason for you to leave."

"She's with me, Adam. I will see her home. Why don't you go pay attention to DeAnne? She looks a bit lonely."

"I don't believe I need you telling me to pay attention to my own wife. At least mine didn't swallow a bottle of pills to get away from me."

Before Eli could respond to his brother's incredibly cruel jibe, Kennedy said icily, "Gentlemen, if you're going to act like spoiled children fighting over a favorite toy, I believe I can find my own way home."

Eli grabbed her arm and pushed her forward. "You're going home with me."

Before she could respond or even gauge Adam's reaction, she was out the door. They walked through the lobby of the hotel in silence. Though he still gripped her arm firmly, thankfully he had loosened his hold a little. She could feel the tension in his body and knew that Adam's last words had hit him where he was the most vulnerable. What kind of man, much less a brother, made that kind of comment about a man's dead wife?

The instant they were seated in the car, Eli released her and then slumped back into his seat. "I'm sorry about that. You'd think I'd be immune to Adam's barbs."

"It's hard to be immune when he strikes cruelly at something so incredibly painful. I'm sure you miss her terribly."

"Shelley's been gone a long time."

"That doesn't mean you stopped loving her or missing her. Death doesn't destroy love."

Sadness and something like bitterness darkened his eyes. Kennedy knew almost nothing about Eli's relationship with his wife, but she got the feeling it had been complicated.

"You still love Thomas?"

The abrupt question surprised her. About to say absolutely, she stopped herself and thought about the question. The answer was yes, of course, but was it that simple? Thomas would always be in her heart and mind. He had been her first love, and for so long, she'd believed her heart could never consider taking the risk again. Now she wasn't so sure.

"I will always love Thomas."

A fleeting, bleak expression crossed his face. "I'm glad to know that kind of love really exists." Then, as if they hadn't discussed anything so intensely personal, he became all business. "How do you think it went tonight?"

"Good…at least, I think so. He seemed rattled at my lack of awe."

"Irelyn read him perfectly. Adam is so used to having women fawn all over him, a woman who doesn't intrigues him. Add that to the fact that you look sexier than any woman there tonight." He grinned in a boyish, charming way. "The man is probably in tears."

Proving that sophisticated Ice Queen Rachel had definitely left the building, she blushed to the tips of her toes. Sexy?

Clearing her throat, she touched on a topic that still worried her. "You said that Adam wouldn't be interested in sleeping with me."

"He won't. Oh, he thinks he will, but when it comes down to it, he'll want to conquer you, not have sex with you."

"And what exactly does conquering mean?"

"Having you behave exactly as all the other women he's met. You keep up the attitude, and I guarantee you, you'll receive an offer to work for him."

"How long do you think it will take?"

"Neither discipline nor patience is Adam's strong suits. When he sees something he wants, it's hard for him to rest until he has it. I would expect him to approach you within the next few weeks."

Weeks. The thought both excited and scared her. The possibility that very soon she would be offered an opportunity she'd thought she might have to wait years for was stunning. Thank God for Irelyn's training.

"I didn't meet your father. Our eyes met briefly, and that was it."

"Staying off Mathias's radar for right now is a good thing. He's not the one who'll bring you into the Slater fold. Adam's our target."

Eli glanced down at his watch. "Would you mind very much if we went to my house first before I drop you off? I really did promise my daughters I'd tuck them in tonight."

"That's no problem. In fact, I'll call Nick, and he can pick me up at your house. That way, Gunter won't have to go out again."

She didn't add that she simply wanted to see Nick as soon as possible. She knew he had tapped into the cameras at the party and looked forward to hearing what he thought of her performance.

A disturbing thought flitted through her mind. Would he prefer the coolly elegant Rachel to the slightly awkward Kennedy? As much as she enjoyed the playacting, she could never be Rachel Walker all the time. But Rachel was more the type that Nick dated in the past. The thought depressing her, she sighed unconsciously.

"You okay?"

"Yes." She grimaced to make her excuse seem more real. "These shoes are becoming more uncomfortable by the moment."

"Why don't you give Nick a call then? That way he can be there not long after we arrive."

Taking the cellphone from her purse, she punched the speed dial for Nick. When he answered, she heard the concern in his voice. "You okay?"

"I'm fine. But would you mind picking me up at Eli's house?" She recited the address Eli gave her.

"Be there in ten minutes."

She was about to thank him and hang up, but he surprised her by saying softly, "Great job tonight. And you looked just as beautiful on camera."

Glowing at the compliment, she dropped the phone back into her purse. It wasn't until Eli spoke that she realized she'd been staring into space, smiling like a lovesick teenager.

"You have a close relationship with Gallagher."

"He's been a good friend, and he was my husband's best friend. They went to school together."

"He seems to care a lot about you."

Since she was only discovering that the feelings she and Nick had were moving into a realm beyond friendship, Kennedy didn't respond. How could she talk about something that she could barely comprehend herself?

They remained silent the rest of the trip to Eli's house. A giant gate opened just as the car approached, and they traveled several hundred yards along a winding drive before stopping. Kennedy didn't know what she had expected but certainly not this fairytale, castle-like mansion, including turrets and a door that looked large enough to admit a giant.

"A bit pretentious, isn't it?" The wry tone of Eli's statement cut into what she was sure looked like wide-eyed amazement.

"I think it's beautiful…perfect. Every fairy princess's dream."

"That's what my daughters think, too. My wife had it built after falling in love with a similar one in England."

"You had no say in the matter?"

She had meant to tease him, but the bleak look returned to his eyes. "I was otherwise occupied."

She didn't ask what had kept him from being involved in building their home. Whatever the reason, it pained him to remember.

They were halfway up the steps when an older, heavyset woman opened the enormous door. "The girls were just about to get into bed. I assured them you would be home to tuck them in."

"Thank you, Teresa." He glanced down at Kennedy. "Rachel, this is the children's nanny and our housekeeper, the completely indispensable Teresa Longview."

"It's nice to meet you, Teresa."

"Thank you, ma'am." Teresa beamed at them, her expression easy to read. She thought Eli had brought a date home for a romantic evening. Her words confirmed this. "I'm so happy to make the acquaintance of such a lovely young woman. Can I get you something while you wait for Mr. Eli to return?"

"Thank you. But I can't stay."

"Nonsense. Mr. Eli won't be long. I'll just light the fireplace in the family room."

"No, really… You see, I'm not—"

Eli interrupted. "Teresa, would you mind making some of your famous apple pancakes for breakfast in the morning?"

The woman's face went even brighter. "That would be my pleasure, Mr. Eli. Let me double-check and make sure I have the right apples." She scurried away as if on an important mission.

"Sorry," Eli said when she was out of sight. "Thought it would be easier not to explain and disappoint her. Teresa's been after me to find my children a mother."

"So I take it you don't date often?"

His mouth took on a bitter twist. "You know what they say, once burned and all that." His eyes darted to the stairway. "Hope you don't mind, but I want to catch the girls before they fall asleep. And if I know Gallagher, he'll be here before I get back."

"You go on up. I'll see you in the morning."

She watched him run up the grand staircase with an energy and eagerness she hadn't seen in him before. Whatever problems Eli had, one thing was certain: He adored his children.

"Would you care for tea while you wait?"

Kennedy turned back to see Teresa's disappointed face. She'd obviously realized that Kennedy wasn't here on a date with Eli. "Thank you, no. My friend should be here soon to pick me up."

"You're not Mr. Eli's girlfriend?"

"No. I'm his executive assistant."

"I see."

And because she was curious about Eli and his deceased wife, she couldn't help but ask, "Did you know Shelley, Eli's wife?"

"Yes. Poor dear girl. So troubled. Mr. Eli did everything he could for her. You would think those sweet, precious babies would have been enough to keep her happy. She seemed to be getting better, and then one day Mr. Eli found her on the floor in her bedroom. She'd been gone a couple of hours by then. Nothing could save her."

"How sad." She had read the newspaper reports. Shelley had died from an overdose of sedatives and alcohol after struggling with addiction for years.

Headlights from a car flooded the room. Though she would have liked to know more about Eli and his family, she breathed out a happy, relieved breath. *Nick.*

CHAPTER TWENTY-TWO

Nick barely paid attention to the mansion as he waited for the door to open. Ever since Kennedy had called him, he'd been focused on one thing only—assuring himself that she was okay. He'd watched her on camera, and though he hadn't been able to hear her, her facial expressions had been priceless. And so had Adam Slater's. The man couldn't have been more obvious that he was enamored of the beautiful and standoffish Rachel Walker.

He was surprised when Kennedy opened the door. Her smile was bright, but her eyes revealed the stress she'd been under.

"Thanks for coming to get me. I hated for Gunter to have to bring me home."

Nick led her to the car, wanting with all his might to gather her into his arms and tell her how damn glad he was to see her. Instead, he allowed her to make small talk until they were both in the car and back on the road.

"Want to talk about it?"

"You saw everything that happened. How do you think it went?"

"I think you'll have Adam Slater begging you to work for him within a matter of days."

"Eli agrees, though he said it might be weeks."

"Were you nervous?"

"Yes and no. Having already met him helped. Even though that first meeting was a big flop, at least I had gotten over the initial shock. Seeing Mathias was a little more daunting."

"Didn't look like you two spoke to one another."

"We didn't. Eli said that was a good thing. Getting Adam's attention is our focus, not Mathias."

"You did a damn good job of that. Hard to believe this was your first outing."

"Thanks, but that's the key word, isn't it? *First*. Even though you and Eli think it will happen quickly, who really knows how long it will take Adam to decide he has to have me as his assistant? If he ever does."

"Then we'll find another way."

She shot him an amused look. "Optimism? From you?"

"Maybe I still have some left."

"After what you've been through, it would be impossible to not be changed in some way."

He didn't bother to tell her that her disappearance had been a lot harder on him than the bullet that had almost killed him. It'd taken awhile and a lot of work, but he had recovered from his injury. He hadn't been sure he'd ever get over Kennedy's complete absence from his life.

Wanting to forget that hellish time, he moved on to a more pleasant topic. "Hungry?"

"Starving. How did you know?"

"Remember, I watched you at the party. You ate exactly half a cracker with some nasty-looking goop spread over it and a few swigs of water."

Her eyes danced with laughter. "That goop probably cost more than my first car."

"Hope it tasted better than it looked."

"Actually, it didn't. I've always been more of a cheese-and-crackers kind of girl."

"How about something more substantial than cheese and crackers? Want to have dinner with me?"

Her expression was almost comical. "Dinner? With you? In a restaurant?"

"Yeah. Dinner, with me in a restaurant. Why is that such a shock?"

"I don't know. Guess I haven't been to dinner at a restaurant in so long, it surprised me."

"Is that a yes or no?"

"Yes. Definitely, yes." And then she smiled.

His breath hitched. That was the smile he'd missed, the one he'd fallen in love with years ago and hadn't seen in too damned long.

Ten minutes later, Kennedy and Nick were sitting in an elegant Italian restaurant discussing wine selection. Nick had asked for a table close to the fireplace, and despite the fact that the restaurant was crowded, they were seated within minutes close to a cozy, romantic fire. The ease with which he had gotten what he asked for reminded her that he had dated numerous women and probably knew every trick imaginable to get a table.

The thought punched a big hole in her bubble of happiness. When he'd asked if she wanted to have dinner with him, she'd been startled but excited, too—almost as if they were going out on a date. But remembering that Nick dated and discarded women as casually as one changed shoes, her excitement quickly ebbed.

"What's wrong?"

"Why do you think something's wrong?"

"Because I know you."

Uncomfortable that he'd read her so correctly, she blurted out the words before filtering them. "Going undercover like this has probably put a serious crimp in your social life."

She hadn't meant to sound so flippant or ungrateful. Instead of calling her out for her catty remark, his response stunned her. "I haven't dated anyone since Thomas was killed."

"No one? But I—"

He leaned forward and spoke with an intensity that sent goose bumps all over her body. "Did you actually think I could date anyone, have any kind of normal life, until I found you?"

Momentarily stunned, Kennedy could think of nothing to say. The pain in his eyes was unlike any emotion she'd seen in him, and her heart ached. She should have found a way to let him know she was okay. She had been thinking only of herself, her needs. She touched his hand. "I'm so very sorry. Forgive me…please?"

With mercurial speed, his intense look disappeared. "I've found you and you're safe. That's all that matters." He dropped his gaze to the wine list. "What sounds good to you?"

Disappointed in the shift in conversation—she felt as if she'd been on the edge of a major discovery—Kennedy made a couple of suggestions. Nick knew much more about wines than she did. He made the choice and ordered for them. Once that was done, they talked about ordinary things, like weather forecasts and whether the Cowboys would make the playoffs this year. They were munching on their salads when things turned serious again.

"Do you see Julie very often?"

He shook his head. "Not really. After I woke up in the hospital and they told me you were missing, we saw each other almost every day. I think when she realized you weren't coming back, we sort of lost touch. Last time I saw Hank, he told me she was getting even more involved with her charity work than she had before. Even got elected to some state boards. Said staying busy helped."

Tears welled in her eyes. "I can only imagine how much she hates me for leaving like that."

"I'm sure she doesn't hate you. When this is over, she'll be very happy to see you."

"I hope you're right…and I hope I get to see her again. I'd love to think I could go back to my old life…my old friends."

"You'd want to go back?"

"Yes, of course. I—" She stopped herself. For so long it had been her dream to find the people responsible for Thomas's death, bring them to justice and return to her old life. Resume her old friendships, go back to law school…be Kennedy once more. Now, she realized that might not be possible. That life was the one she had built with Thomas. Her circumstances and appearance weren't the only things that had changed. She wasn't the same person she'd once been. Did she even want the same things as before?

"You okay?"

"Yes, I guess I just haven't given much thought to what happens once this is over. Maybe because I never thought it would be over."

"It will be one day. I promise you."

"I hope so."

They ate in silence for several more minutes, and then Nick asked a question she hadn't thought about in a long time.

"Were you angry with Thomas, once you learned everything?"

She nodded. Nick would understand her anger better than anyone. "I was furious for a while, but finally forgave him. He never meant for any of this to happen."

"Yeah, I felt the same way. He didn't know what that family was capable of. Hell, I doubt anyone knows except for those who've tried to go up against them."

"I still talk to him from time to time…though not as much as I did when he first died. I think that's one of the ways I finally forgave him—by telling him exactly what I thought." She grimaced at the confession. "Guess you think that's silly."

"Not at all. I think that's all part of recovery. After my mom died, I did the same thing. I don't think you can go from having a person in your life one day and then not having them the next without doing something like that. Takes time…talking helps."

"So you talked to Thomas, too?"

Something like guilt flickered in his eyes. "No."

His answer was uncharacteristically abrupt, telling her the conversation had made him uncomfortable. She made one final statement. "This is the first time I've been able to talk about this to anyone."

His hand covered hers. "Thomas would be proud of you."

"You think so?"

"After he stopped yelling at you for putting yourself at risk…yeah, I think he would be damn proud."

She smiled at that. Thomas hadn't really had a temper, but he'd had a way of getting his point across that left few questions on how he felt about a matter. Without a doubt, he would have had some issues with her decisions, but she did like to think he would be proud, too.

"I think he would be happy we're working together. Don't you?"

"I promised him I would take care of you."

His answer had the same effect as an ice pick on an overinflated balloon. How could she let herself forget the real reason Nick was helping her?

"Ravioli for the lady?"

They both jerked at the voice of their server with their food, and Nick released her hand.

The rest of the meal passed uneventfully. And when they went home, she to her bedroom and Nick to his, nothing happened other than a soft exchange of good-nights.

After such an eventful evening, Kennedy figured the instant her head touched her pillow, she would be out like a light. But sleeplessness plagued her. Nick was here to watch over her because of his promise to Thomas. Wishing for something more or different was pointless.

When sleep finally claimed her, the last thought on her mind was the intensity in his eyes and his words, *Do you think I could have any kind of life until I found you?*

Was that just a promise to a friend?

CHAPTER TWENTY-THREE

Mathias swallowed his blood pressure medicine, knowing he would need it in the next few minutes. He'd been told about the video of Jonah and Eli but had yet to see it. Contrary to what his ungrateful sons thought, he didn't stay in front of a television screen 24/7 watching them screw up their lives. He controlled thousands of lives, billions of dollars. His sons were barely worth the trouble of having someone monitor them weekly, much less hourly.

"You ready?"

Mathias glared up at the hulking, pug-nosed man standing beside him. Cyrus handled the more unpleasant aspects of keeping Mathias the most powerful man in America. Having been with him for years, the man knew every Slater secret.

As efficient as he was deadly, Cyrus rarely messed up. That little incident in Houston a couple of years ago was probably the first screw-up he'd had since their early days together. Of course, that was due in large part to the ineptitude of his oldest son. Adam's first independent action as a Slater leader had been a near disaster.

Even though Mathias ended up having to do some major cleanup to ensure all leaks were plugged, the matter had been resolved satisfactorily. That damn busybody cop and good-for-nothing accounting clerk had gotten what they deserved. The other cop...Gallagher something or other, had gotten off easy, with a valuable lesson learned: Never tangle with a Slater and expect to win.

And that cop's widow? She'd learned her lesson, done the smart thing and disappeared completely.

"Would you like to wait until later…when you're feeling better?"

Mathias's blood pressure shot through the roof. Sometimes he wondered if Cyrus enjoyed these kinds of things a little too much. How many times had he caught a gleam in his eyes or a slight smirk on his ugly, wrinkled face? If Mathias hadn't trusted him more than anyone else, he'd have had the giant killed. Problem was, he'd have had to find someone to do the deed. How ironic that the only man he could have trusted to kill Cyrus was the man himself.

"Mr. Slater…sir?"

"I'm ready," Mathias snapped. "Turn it on."

Without another word, the screen blinked bright. At first the images were so blurred it was hard to tell that the two men sitting across from each other were his sons. Then the image cleared, and he saw them. Eli, with his ever-present holier-than-thou expression, and sitting across from him, separated by a glass partition, was Jonah, his youngest son. The boy looked ill, like he'd lost weight. Good. He needed to suffer. Defiance and lack of loyalty had put him where he was. Mathias wasn't a man to feel pity or regret—they weakened the mind. Looking at the dull, almost-dead eyes of his son, he felt none of that now. A man reaps what he sows, and Jonah was reaping a whole mess of bad stuff.

The voices were lower than he liked. He waved an irritable hand at Cyrus. Since they'd done this a thousand times over the years, Cyrus knew exactly what he wanted. The volume increased, and Jonah's voice came through loud and clear.

"She's dead, isn't she?" Jonah said.

Oh yeah, they were talking about the harlot Jonah had hooked up with. If not for her, his youngest son might've never started digging where he hadn't belonged. Any time a man got led around by his pecker, trouble always followed. The woman had gotten off lucky. He'd wanted to see her suffer, but Cyrus had persuaded him to move on. A bullet in the head had been too good for her, but he comforted himself with the knowledge that her head and hands would never be reunited with the rest of her body. That was something.

The minute Eli confirmed Jonah's statement, the kid's eyes blazed with a life Mathias had never seen in the boy. Was he finally getting through to him? Maybe now his youngest realized how serious his daddy was about teaching him a lesson. Could this be the turnaround he'd been hoping for?

Jonah's chair rolled back, and he stared straight up at the camera. Little pipsqueak knew his daddy would see this. When the vile contempt spewed from Jonah's mouth, Mathias had a small moment of pride. The little shit could spit out venom with the best of them. He liked seeing that fire. Neither of his other boys had it.

But as quickly as it came, the pride vanished and a fiery wrath replaced it. How dare he talk like that to his daddy? Did he actually think he was going to get away with such behavior? The disrespect wasn't something any father would stand for, much less Mathias Slater.

The brat ignored Eli's hushed urgings to stay quiet. Mathias ignored Eli…he'd given up on him long ago. He might do an adequate job with Slater House Hotels, but he was too weak and mealymouthed to be the kind of man that Mathias could be proud of. Eli's poor choice of wife had been the last straw.

But Jonah. Oh, his dear boy Jonah. He might actually grieve because the boy was going to have to be punished again. This time in a more substantial way than just a prison sentence. He'd had it too easy.

The screen went blank, then dark. Mathias drew in a breath and then expelled it, along with a harsh, rasping cough. Damned lungs. They were going to give out on him before he could get done all the things that were necessary to carry on his legacy. Dammit, he didn't have time to take care of this matter. Wasn't it just like his children to be so blasted inconsiderate? He refused to think what was going to happen when he did finally kick the bucket.

Cyrus still stood beside him, waiting. He knew Mathias wasn't going to just sit back and let his good name be defiled.

"He needs a stronger lesson," Mathias finally said.

"Yes, sir."

"You'll handle it?"

"Of course. How severe shall I get?"

Jonah's vile, rebellious words reverberated in his brain, and the decision clicked. Mathias barely took a moment to consider the consequences. A powerful man had to make quick decisions without regret or sentimentality getting in the way. The kid was a hopeless case…was never going to come around.

This would be a good lesson for the two other boys. Their daddy only had so much patience.

Pulling himself to his feet, Mathias winced at the sound of popping joints. He wasn't that old, dammit. Taking another breath, making sure this one was shallower, he said, "Make it the last punishment he'll need."

For the first time in a long while, Mathias saw a glimmer of surprise in Cyrus's face. Maybe the lesson wasn't going to be just for his children. Maybe this man needed to see it, too. No one, but no one, defied Mathias or defiled the Slater name without severe repercussions. Time for the piper to be paid. Too bad Jonah hadn't realized that before.

Feeling older than when he'd come into the room, Mathias shuffled out the door. Now he had to figure out how to deal with what would follow. Eleanor, Jonah's mama, would have to be protected at all costs. By keeping his Nora from the harsher truths of life, they'd had forty-one happy, peaceful years together. Losing her son would be difficult for her, but he would be there to comfort and console her, as any good husband should.

The press, on the other hand, would eat this up, and while it wasn't necessarily the best publicity, he would do what he had so many times before—make lemonade out of lemons. Perhaps a donation to a prison library—The Jonah Slater Memorial Library had a nice ring to it.

The idea gave him a boost of energy. The matter was closed.

Kennedy stood in front of the floor-length mirror in what she had come to call her "torture chamber." From one in the afternoon until six in the evening, she trained with surely the most devilishly devious, physically beautiful, and extraordinarily irritating woman on the planet.

She made a sudden move and winced as a sore muscle reminded her of yesterday's new torture routine. Irelyn had taken her into another room in Grey's vast office complex filled with weight machines, free weights, exercise mats, and yet even more mirrors. Admittedly, Kennedy hadn't been able to exercise as she would have liked the last couple of years, but she had still felt she was in reasonably good shape. Irelyn had proved that theory wrong.

Next week they were to begin self-defense classes. Even though her body might resent the training, Kennedy was grateful for all the time and energy being spent on her. She hoped to be able to pay back their investment in her with what they all wanted—Adam and Mathias Slater in prison where they belonged.

"You look as though you've got a fire ant between your toes. What's wrong?"

Shifting to take the weight off one foot, Kennedy explained, "These shoes are too tight."

"They're the perfect size. You're just not used to wearing four-inch heels. You'll get used to them."

She shot an envious glance down at Irelyn's low-heeled pumps. "Easy for you to say."

"Take your shoes off."

Relieved that she was being given a reprieve, she quickly complied and almost cried at the instant relief to her poor feet and ankles.

Instead of going on to another part of her lesson, Irelyn surprised her by slipping out of her own shoes and sliding her long, narrow feet into Kennedy's stilettos. She watched in awe as Irelyn walked up and down the room with the cocky assurance of a supremely confident woman. There were no glitches in her graceful steps and no painful grimaces on her lovely face.

"How long did it take you to learn how to do that?"

"I don't measure time. It's wasteful and useless."

Kennedy eyed the other woman carefully. She'd given up on trying to read her, learning quickly that Irelyn could be anyone, with any emotion, within the blink of her beautiful gray eyes. But just for an instant, she'd seen beyond the impenetrable façade to a woman of churning and volatile emotions.

"So, are you ready to try it again? This time without the whining?"

The mask was firmly back in place, but to Kennedy the last few moments had been a revelation. This woman was as human as anyone, but whatever had happened in her past had created the Irelyn Raine of today. Seeing that little bit of vulnerability gave her confidence that she could do it, too.

Sliding back into the shoes Irelyn handed her, Kennedy put everything into being the woman she needed to be to trap and ensnare a snake. When she was finished with him, Adam Slater wouldn't know what hit him.

"Excellent."

Irelyn's word of praise made her proud. They were few and far between and therefore all the more treasured.

"Grey wants a meeting. Let's go."

How the woman knew what Grey wanted wasn't something she wondered about anymore. Once she'd almost jokingly asked if they had some sort of psychic connection, since Irelyn seemed to know what Grey Justice wanted without any indication that he had told her. Then one day Irelyn had pushed her silky black hair behind her ear and Kennedy had seen the earbud. The revelation came quickly. Was he in touch with her constantly? The thought made her uncomfortable. Not for her sake, but for Irelyn's. Grey Justice was the most intense and focused person she'd ever met. That kind of constant attention had to be exhausting. She had it only for a short time each day, and then she got to go home to Nick. At that thought, her spirits lifted. What would she do without him?

"The idea of seeing Grey today seems to have pleased you."

Another crack in Irelyn's armor? That remark had held a distinct hint of jealousy. Did she have romantic feelings for Grey? When Kennedy saw them together, they acted as impersonal as any employer/employee.

Since the last thing she wanted was to get on this woman's bad side, she shook her head. "I was just thinking of Nick."

"Ah, Mr. Gallagher." Her expression became dreamy. "Now there's a man who can curl a girl's toes."

She should have been used to remarks like that about Nick. All of her friends, married or single, had carried a crush for him. A man didn't look like Nick Gallagher without attracting many admirers. Irelyn's comment should have slid off her back as easily as any others she'd ever heard. But it didn't. This was said by a woman who, if she set her sights on someone, could get her man.

"Something wrong?" Irelyn asked.

"No...I...uh...no."

"How eloquent." She opened the door. "Why don't you deal with the green-eyed monster later? Now it's time to face a real monster."

And with those astonishing words, she walked out of the room.

CHAPTER TWENTY-FOUR

Grey stood beside the window in his office. He'd heard Irelyn's remark about Gallagher and her less-than-flattering comment about him. Odd how he could still feel the barbs after all this time. It wasn't as if he didn't deserve them. Some would have been horrified by his arrangement with Irelyn. Others might have applauded his ingenuity. He didn't care what others thought. Their relationship was no one's business, and as long as it remained beneficial, nothing would change. That had taken Irelyn a long time to accept, but she had finally come around. However, every now and then, the bitterness seeped through.

Noting the frown on Kennedy's face as she came closer, he said, "You're looking a bit stressed. Everything okay?"

"Yes." Then, as if she remembered her lessons from Irelyn, she gave him a brilliant smile and added, "Irelyn is an excellent teacher."

"Yes, she is, in more ways than one."

Her accent as authentic as any born and bred Texan's, Irelyn waved her hand in a self-deprecating way. "Well, bless both your hearts. You'll have me blushing like a schoolgirl with such praise."

Grey could only shake his head in admiration. Despite the darkness that had caused their lives to intersect, this woman had fascinated and enthralled him from the moment he met her.

Kennedy pulled him back into the present. "Irelyn said you wanted to talk to me."

"Yes. Eli's on his way up. We want to talk with you about a slight deviation to our plan."

"Should I give Nick a call or is he already on his way, too?"

His admiration for Kennedy O'Connell was already high, but it just soared. She was loyal to a fault and was determined not to leave Gallagher out of anything. She trusted the man implicitly. It'd been a long time since he had felt anything as human as envy, but he recognized the symptoms.

"Gallagher will be here soon. However, I wanted to talk with you first. Your influence will be instrumental in getting him to go along with our plan."

Doubt flickered on her face, but to her credit, she just said, "Okay. I'm listening."

"Irelyn has a relationship with someone within Slater's inner circle. He won't tell her who or when, but someone has been targeted for termination. We'd like to prevent another death, if possible."

"Are you sure he's not talking about me? Maybe they've found out who I am." Panic hit her face. "Or Nick? Could it be Nick?"

"No. If your identity had been discovered, there would be no need to plan or even inform Mathias. You would be dead within minutes."

Her laugh held no humor. "Small comfort."

Grey shrugged. He wasn't much into sugarcoating the truth. "Someone has been targeted, that's all we know. Who and why are unknown."

Irelyn seated herself across the room from Grey and Kennedy, the separation a normal thing for her. "My contact will share only so much. I feed him useless information from time to time. In return, he gives me tidbits."

"How do you know they're not useless, too?"

"Because they've proven to be true. He's the one who told me—"

"That's enough, Irelyn."

Though she shot him a small glare at his hard tone, she closed her mouth.

"What do you mean by a deviation?"

Eli entered just as Kennedy was asking the question and answered for Grey. "He means that you're going to have to become irresistible to Adam a lot sooner than we'd planned."

Grey took in Kennedy's reaction and was damn impressed that he couldn't read her. He saw no panic or fear. In fact, if she revealed any emotion at all, it was a glimmer of excitement.

"How are we going to do that?"

"We can discuss the how in a minute. What I want to know from you is, are you ready to go as deep as you need and do what's necessary to bring down the bastards responsible for your husband's death?"

Without hesitation, she answered, "I believe I've proven that by being here. You don't need to question my commitment. I'm ready to do what it takes."

"That's all I needed to know." Grey glanced over his shoulder at the door to his private bathroom. "Why don't you go freshen up?"

"Why?"

He liked that she wasn't intimidated. He had way too many people in his life who did what he told them to do without question. Most times, that was a convenience he enjoyed. But when he was asking someone to put her life on the line, then that person had every right to question him. And every right to expect an honest answer.

"I'd like to gauge Gallagher's reaction without your influence."

Body stiff with indignation, her reaction was as easy to read as a first-grade primer. "You don't trust him? I assure you, Mr. Justice, Nick Gallagher is the most honorable man I know."

"Don't get your tail feathers ruffled, Kennedy. I do trust Mr. Gallagher. If I didn't, believe me, he wouldn't be involved in this case. However, I need to know how he will react to our change of plan without having you influence him."

She stood, her look of stubbornness telling him she would do what he asked, but she still didn't like his request. He didn't have any issues with that. Few people liked what he asked them to do.

He waited until she'd left the room before he said to Irelyn, "Can she do this?"

"Yes. But only with Gallagher's full approval. They're *true* partners…she won't do it if he asks her not to."

Ignoring the obvious reference to their own strange partnership, Grey nodded. "That's my opinion as well."

The room went silent as they waited for Gallagher to join them. He had told Kennedy the truth—he did trust Gallagher. Problem was, the man had a tendency to soften his reaction when Kennedy was in the room. He was protective of her…a good thing. However, there was a fine line between protective and overprotective. Grey wanted to see Gallagher's reaction before bringing Kennedy back.

As soon as the man entered the room, a new tension developed. Gallagher's instincts were good. He knew this wasn't a typical meeting.

Grey made a low-key start. "How do you think she's doing?"

As Grey asked the question, he took note of both Eli's and Gallagher's expressions. Depending upon their responses, he would know how they would take to his new plan.

"Based on what I saw the other night with Adam, I think she's doing damn well."

Gallagher's response was no surprise. The man was so head-over-ass in love, he couldn't see straight. And that might be Grey's biggest problem of all. His plan was going to put Kennedy right in the middle of the lion's den. The way things were escalating, though, he didn't think they had a choice. Time was running out. If they didn't act soon, someone else was going to die.

"I agree," Eli concurred. "Adam didn't know which end was up."

"How about we up the ante?"

"Up the ante how?" Gallagher said.

"Make her even more irresistible."

"That might pose a problem unless we make some changes," Eli said. "I don't see Adam moving faster than we anticipated. He's not naïve. If he suspects she's being pushed on him, he'll back off completely."

As was often his way, Grey approached his explanation with a question. "When you first brought your family to the U.S., besides Shelley's illness, what was your biggest problem?"

Comprehension came almost immediately to Eli's face. "Adam."

"How so?" Gallagher asked.

"He wouldn't leave Shelley alone. It was like he couldn't bear that I had a wife and a family. I finally had to tell him to either back off or I'd kick his ass. That worked. Adam isn't one to risk getting a bruise if he can prevent it."

"So you think if Kennedy, I mean Rachel, is in a relationship with Eli, that will make Adam want her more?" Gallagher asked.

"More and faster," Grey said.

Gallagher shook his head, his resistance obvious. "How would a romantic relationship with Eli make Adam want her more? You both said he's not into women that way."

Eli nodded. "You're right, he's not. But me having something…anything better than what he has is going to eat at him. He won't rest until he's stolen her away from me."

"I want this asshole taken down as much as anyone, but why are we rushing things? What's changed?"

Grey shot a glance at the woman who'd been sitting quietly, absorbing the nuances of their discussion. Irelyn only spoke when she had something to say. Since they'd begun their partnership so many years ago, he had learned that and many more things, such as her ability to pull a splinter out of a bear's paw without him knowing it.

Responding to Grey's look, Irelyn said, "I have it on good authority that something big is about to go down."

"What exactly does that mean?" Gallagher asked.

"Someone is going to die." Elegant shoulders lifted in a slight shrug. "That's all my contact knows so far. He's not always told his target until the last minute. I'll try to get more later tonight, but he's proven himself sound on several occasions."

"Who is your source?"

"Mr. Gallagher, I trust you as much as I trust any man."

Correctly interpreting Irelyn's statement, a crack appeared in Gallagher's stern expression, showing an amused appreciation. Grey fought his own smile. Irelyn always spoke her mind in such a way that few people had doubts about her opinions.

Quick as lightning, Gallagher's amusement disappeared. "Putting Kennedy at more risk than she's already at based upon an unidentified source who has a feeling something's about to go down isn't something I'm willing to risk."

"Maybe you should let her make that decision for herself." Irelyn said.

Shit. Nick went to his feet. The minute he'd walked into the room, he had known something was going down. There had been an electrical energy in the air, supercharged and tense. These people might have the same goals as he did, but Kennedy's safety was his first priority. About to tell them exactly where they could put their asinine ideas, he swallowed his words when the person he most wanted to protect entered the room.

Justice waved a hand at Kennedy. "Come on in. We were just discussing our new strategy."

She gave Nick a fleeting, encouraging smile, and he knew the truth. She had already agreed. "What the hell did you call me here for if you've already coerced her into doing this?"

"They didn't coerce me, Nick. When Grey told me we needed to make some changes, I agreed. If we can get this done faster, then that's what we need to do."

"Not at your expense we don't." Nick gave everyone in the room with the exception of Kennedy a hard look. They'd damn well known how he would react. "Getting blindsided doesn't exactly make me a team player."

Justice nodded. "I understand your concerns. Why don't you sit down again and let us tell you how this can work? If you don't agree after you hear us out, we'll consider going in another direction."

Nick watched Kennedy come toward him. Moving with her natural grace, she also had the confident air of a woman comfortable with herself and the direction she was headed. Even though she'd never seemed to lack confidence before, she had a new assurance about her. She really believed she could do this. He could feel his resistance crumbling in the face of her assurance. Still, he wanted details. This bullshit of vagueness was unacceptable.

She settled beside him and gave him another quick smile. She probably meant the smile to reassure him, but all it did was remind him how damn vulnerable she was. His gut was beginning to get that feeling when things were about to turn to shit.

"Here's where we are."

As Nick listened to the plan, he carefully watched everyone's expressions. Each one of them had their own agenda and reason for wanting to see Mathias and Adam Slater go down. He had one, too. However, his agenda was twofold, and at the top of that list was making sure that Kennedy stayed safe. If that delayed justice for Thomas, then so be it.

After Justice laid out their plan and each person's role, the room went silent. If they thought he'd jump on board immediately, they were going to be disappointed. Even though he saw some merit to making changes, there were parts of the plan that clawed at his gut.

"What do you think?" Kennedy asked.

He took in her hopeful expression and the trust in her eyes. If he said no, would she go along with his decision?

"I'd like to discuss this with you in private." His gaze roamed around the room. "Anybody got a problem with that?" His tone indicated he didn't give a shit if they did or not.

Justice glanced down at his watch. "No problem. It's getting late, and I have an appointment across town. Why don't we pick this back up tomorrow after you and Kennedy have had a chance to talk?"

No one objected and within seconds, Nick and Kennedy were alone in Justice's office.

"Nick, I really think—"

He held up his hand. "Let's discuss it when we get home."

Nick followed her into the elevator, struggling with how he was going to talk her out of doing something so damned dangerous when he knew without a doubt she had already decided to take the risk.

CHAPTER TWENTY-FIVE

Kennedy went into the house, Nick right behind her. As was his usual habit, he went through each room, searching. Even though she was tired and hungry, even though she still wore the damn stilettos that were killing her feet, she stood in the middle of the living room, unsure how to handle the situation. Nick was furious with her. He didn't have to shout for her to know that. His grim silence all the way back from Grey's office had been more than enough proof.

Okay, she should have waited for him before she agreed. They were in this together. Partners didn't make a decision of this magnitude without getting input from the other. But the palpable sense of urgency after Grey had explained his reasons for altering their plans had made agreeing seem so necessary.

The instant he returned to the living room, she apologized. "I'm sorry, Nick. I should have waited to discuss it with you first."

He stopped so abruptly she could tell she had startled him with her apology. Hopefully, they could now discuss it without anger. And hopefully she could convince him that this was the right thing to do.

He released a ragged sigh. "I should've expected Justice would try something like this. He's ruthless."

"I'm sure he can be, but his reasoning—at least on this—is sound."

"How so?"

His tone said he disagreed, but at least he gave her an opportunity to explain further. Before she could answer, a giant rumble came from her stomach. She grabbed her belly, embarrassed by the noise.

Nick grinned. "How about we talk while we eat?" Then his eyes dropped to her feet. "And why don't you take those off and get into something comfortable?"

Even though she knew he meant nothing by it, she felt a blush start from her feet, spreading all the way up to her face. Silly didn't even begin to describe her thoughts. Nick would probably blush, too, if he knew what she had been thinking.

"Sounds good. Why don't you order in?"

"Chinese okay again?"

"Perfect. You know what I like."

"In food, yeah. But not in everything."

She really must be tired because every time he said something, she imagined there was a hidden meaning. Before she could completely embarrass herself and reply with what would be a blatant come-on, she said, "Okay…well, I think I'll take a quick shower and then—"

"It'll be at least a half hour before the food arrives. Why don't you take a long, hot bath? Relieve those aching muscles."

She gulped. "Good idea." Spinning around, she strode as fast her shoes would allow her to move.

Wanting her so badly he could taste her, Nick watched Kennedy leave the room. His subtle innuendoes hadn't gone unnoticed, and her blushes made him want to cover her pink skin in kisses. No matter how much he wanted her, that wasn't going to happen tonight, if ever. They had some major decisions to make.

He grabbed his cellphone from his pocket and placed the order for their food. Then, because thinking about Kennedy all slick and wet lying in the bathtub had him hurting in places he didn't like to hurt, he headed to his room for a quick, intense workout.

Changing into sweats and a T-shirt, he grabbed the weights and got to work. With each lift of his barbells, he renewed his determination to talk her out of this scheme. He had been reluctant to get her involved with Justice in the first place but had consented because he knew he could protect her. This new game put them on a different playing field, and it was far from even. How the hell was he going to keep an eye on her if she was sleeping in the lion's den, with the beast only a few yards away? What was going to happen if the bastard tried something and she couldn't get away from him?

The doorbell rang. Sweating with exertion, his mind swirling with all the dire ways this new plan could implode, Nick dropped the weights onto the mat. He grabbed a towel and swiped at his face as he headed to the door. After paying the deliveryman with cash, he knocked on Kennedy's bedroom door. "Dinner's here."

"Be right out."

Nick busied himself by setting the table. He poured Kennedy a glass of her favorite wine and grabbed a beer for himself.

"Smells delicious."

He caught his breath at the beautiful and glowing woman at the door. Her hair curled around her face in damp tendrils, and Nick clenched his fists to keep from reaching out and smoothing them away. Dressed in a long-sleeved T-shirt and jeans, with thick socks and an old pair of house shoes she had confessed to having since college covering her bare feet, she shouldn't have looked sexy. But, dammit to hell, she did.

Turning away before he could embarrass himself, he nodded toward the table. "Have a seat. Everything's ready."

They dug into their meal, each of them quiet as they satisfied their hunger. A few minutes later, Kennedy collapsed back into her chair. "That was wonderful, and I'm feeling tons better."

He knew this was her cue to talk about the new plan. Determined to hold his temper since he was sure they were both on different planes right now, he eased into the discussion. "Adam might not be a genius, but he's been around the block enough to know when he's being snowed. You change your attitude toward him too quick, chances are he'll catch on."

"You're right. But pretending to date Eli shouldn't put him on alert. The man is obviously intrigued by me. If he sees me dating his brother, that'll just make him move faster."

"Yeah. Intrigued is a good start. Mess with that…move too fast…" Nick shrugged. "Who knows what he'll do? The plan is to get into his office, not his bed."

"Getting into his bed will never happen. But we have to do something."

"Why? Because of that bullshit Justice was throwing at you?"

"Why would he tell us that if it's not true?"

"Because the man's got a helluva lot of other reasons to want Mathias and Adam to go down. We've got just one—Thomas."

"Like what?"

"I don't know what they are, but they exist."

"Okay, maybe you're right. But…what if it's not bullshit? What if we don't do something soon and someone else dies?"

"A lot of someones have already died, Kennedy. I don't want you to be the next one."

"But if—"

Nick got to his feet. He wasn't convincing her of anything.

"Where are you going?"

"Need to show you something I found the other day."

While he was gone, Kennedy went about clearing the table. The discussion wasn't going well. She had no clue how to persuade him to change his mind but already knew she wasn't going to change hers. Maybe altering their plan would make no difference. But if she didn't do it and another person died? Could she live with that?

Nick returned with several sheets of paper and handed them to her. "I was doing some research the other day and stumbled on this."

"What is it?"

"Newspaper articles."

Puzzled, Kennedy glanced down at the headline: *Body Found Floating in Thames*

Still not understanding, she looked up at Nick again. "Why am I looking at a *London Times* article, dated…" She glanced back down again. "Seventeen years ago?"

"Read the article. Then we'll talk."

She dropped into a kitchen chair and quickly scanned the brief story. No identification had been found on the middle-age man, and his only distinguishing mark had been a tattoo of the scales of justice on the inside of his right wrist. The article ended with a request to contact the London police if anyone had any information on the man's identity.

More confused than ever, she looked up at Nick. "Okay. So what? An unidentified dead man in London seventeen years ago."

"Read the second article."

Kennedy shuffled the pages and found the second article, dated a couple of years later. An unidentified woman had been found dead in a burnt car outside Dublin, Ireland. Though the body was burned badly, there had been a tattoo on the inside of her wrist. A photograph of what remained of the tattoo was included in the article. Kennedy had to squint to make out the image, but she could see a resemblance to the tattoo of the man two years before in London.

"Neither the man nor woman was ever identified, and they both had similar tattoos." She shook her head. "Connect the dots for me, Nick, because I'm completely lost."

"Justice and I worked out in his gym last week. He has a tattoo on the inside of his wrist, identical to these tattoos."

"Did you ask him about it?"

"No. I didn't think anything of it at first. His last name is Justice. And the little I know about him made having those scales seem right. When I got home, I did some research on the tat and found these articles."

"It still doesn't mean he was involved."

"Kennedy? Seriously? You think this is just a coincidence?"

"Grey can't be more than thirty-five. Seventeen years ago, he was barely out of high school."

"And we know zip about what he was involved in back then."

"So, what are you saying? That we can't trust him? That we need to just forget seeking justice for Thomas?"

"That's not what I'm saying at all. But giving him your blind trust, putting your life on the line, based on some kind of vague bullshit that they *think* something is going to happen is damn stupid."

She shot up from her chair. "The only man I've given my blind faith to is you, so don't you dare stand there and call me stupid. Or maybe I am stupid for thinking you actually wanted to get Thomas's killer."

"Damn you, Kennedy. You know that's not what this is about."

"Well, then, what is it about? You accuse Grey of being vague…what about you? You're keeping something back from me. I know you are. How the hell am I supposed to trust you completely when you won't tell me everything you know?"

"I've told you everything."

"Have you?"

His eyes burned with an intensity she had never seen in them before. The tick in his jaw, his tell she'd learned long ago, said he was keeping something back. Dammit, she could tell he wanted to say something. "Tell me, Nick. Just tell me!"

His eyes blazing fiercely, he shouted, "Fine! You want to know the truth? Here it is. The thought of that bastard getting his hands on you sickens me. The thought of anyone but me touching you sickens me. I love you, dammit! So there. Satisfied?"

All breath left her body. Her legs so shaky they felt as if they might collapse at any moment, she dropped back into the chair she'd just left.

"You love me?" She stared up at him in wonder. "How? When?"

He was looking away from her, almost as if he was ashamed. "Almost from the moment I met you."

She shook her head as tears filled her eyes. "Oh, no…Nick…"

"Don't look at me like that. I don't need or want your pity."

She didn't know how else to look at him. All this time… All the time she'd been married to Thomas, Nick had loved her. And she had never suspected. He had never let on that he saw her as anyone other than his best friend's wife.

"It's not pity… I just…" She shrugged, feeling incredibly helpless and out of her depth. "I just never knew."

His hard gaze zeroed in on her again. "You were never meant to know. But that's not what we should be talking about. My point is, both Justice and Eli have their own reasons for wanting to bring Mathias and Adam down. Hell, for all I know, Irelyn probably does, too. I want the bastards as bad as they do but not at your expense."

Kennedy pushed herself to her feet and walked slowly toward him. Nick had that earnest, intense expression on his face. At one time she had believed it was his angry look. Now she knew it was something entirely different. She could barely believe the truth, but it was staring her in the face. Nick Gallagher actually loved her.

Stopping within inches of him, she softly said, "Kiss me."

"What?"

She went closer, put her hands on his upper arms, stood on her toes and said, "Kiss me, Nick."

For a moment she thought he would refuse. She felt the resistance, the battle within him. Then, with a groan she barely recognized as being human, he jerked her forward and covered her mouth with his.

The shock of his firm lips stunned her. Nick kept his mouth steady, the pressure undemanding yet unrelenting. Heat swept through her, and with a soft sigh of acceptance…of surrender, Kennedy sank into his warm, hard embrace, opened for him and let him take the kiss even deeper.

Coherent thought disappeared as she allowed herself to feel for the first time in almost two years. A whirling vortex of emotions swirled through her. Nick's arms felt wonderful, strong yet tender. She felt cherished, special…so incredibly safe, as if all the problems of the world could be solved within his embrace. A wave of intense longing surged through her, and Kennedy arched up against his hard body, following along willingly. Wanting, needing…giving herself up totally.

His conscience pounded…Nick refused to listen. He couldn't. It would tell him that this was all wrong. That she was responding only because of what he had revealed. That she was allowing this only because she was lonely and missed her husband. That the kiss meant nothing to her. All he allowed himself to think about was the here and now—the heaven of Kennedy's arms, the delicious taste of her mouth. The soft, feminine body moving sensuously against him was the one he'd dreamed about for years. Her arms, her body, her lips were telling him she wanted this. Nick was prepared to give her everything.

When her mouth opened beneath his, he smothered a groan, pulled her closer, his tongue devouring her sweetness. His arousal, hard and aching, pushed into the softness of her sex. Would that scare her? Would she pull away from him? She released a small sound, and he wanted to snarl in anger. No…too soon. He didn't want to let her go. But that wasn't what she did.

Instead of pulling out of his arms, she grabbed his hips, pressed him deeper into her softness and began a slow, sensuous dance that almost blew his head off. Holy hell!

Lifting her against him for a better hold, his mouth still on hers, Nick moved swiftly from the kitchen. The bedrooms were too far away…the sofa in the living room was his target. He walked blindly, thankful he knew this house so well, and was next to the sofa in seconds. Laying her on the cushions, Nick did what he had forced himself to believe could never happen. With his mouth, his hands and his body, he seduced Kennedy. Reassured her with words he'd always longed to say, his hands and mouth aroused her…petted and played with her. Allowing her no time to think, to regret…to wonder if this was a good idea, his hands slid beneath her shirt, pulled at her jeans, stripping her bare.

For too long he had wanted this to happen. He had forced himself to give up thinking about her when she and Thomas married. His feelings hadn't been right. Even though the knowledge that she slept in another man's arms every night tore at his soul, he had been at peace because he'd known that Thomas loved her. And she had been happy.

But now...now she was his. Nick could wait no longer...he'd loved this woman forever. Telling himself that he was selfish in taking what he desperately wanted would do no good. He had to have her.

Her clothes lay on the floor, and Kennedy lay before him, all soft, womanly loveliness. He had imagined what she looked like naked. His dreams could never have matched the reality. *Perfection.* Creamy silken skin, soft and giving, invited... enticed. His hands skimmed up and down her body, adoring, cherishing, loving every inch of the sexy, beautiful woman before him.

Her breath came in pants, the scent of her arousal so intoxicating he called on every ounce of willpower to slow down and savor. The ravenous beast within him snarled that he'd waited too damn long, urged him to unzip and bury himself deep into her sweet heat. No. After years of dreaming and then forcing himself to squelch those dreams when they'd appeared, he would not rush this. Tonight Kennedy was his, and he would show her how very special she was to him.

His hands glided down her satin body. His mouth followed, trailing kisses, licking, nibbling, sucking. He delighted in her shivers when he licked certain sweet areas, like the tender spot between her neck and shoulder, the hollow at the base of her throat. Swirling his tongue around a taut, brown nipple, he lost himself in her taste. His teeth scraped the tight bud and then nipped slightly, and she responded with a gasp and an arch of her body. So responsive, so incredibly sweet.

Going to her other breast, he cupped it in his hand, loving the silken heaviness. Unable to hold back, he lowered his head and suckled deep, drawing her breast into his mouth. Once again, he bit her tender nipple, only a little harder this time. A cry escaped her as she arched, coming completely off the sofa, and held his head at her breast. He delighted in learning what she liked, discovering her needs... what turned her on.

Nick trailed kisses down her silken torso to her stomach, bathing her with his tongue. He smiled at the little hitches in her breathing, the soft moans and whispered, "Yes," when he did something she really liked. Going lower, he took a moment to inhale and savor her scent. He'd never smelled anything more delicious or satisfying than Kennedy's arousal.

Burying his face in the soft, mahogany curls covering her sex, he inhaled again. Then he pulled away a little and took in the incredible beauty before him. Kennedy's entire body was flushed. Nipples, tight and distended, called out for his mouth again. Her body quivered, shook with desire. Her eyes were closed, her soft mouth slightly open as she moaned with need.

He wanted to go back and revisit every inch of the delicious flesh he'd just tasted, but later. For now, there was only one place he had to go...had to taste. He propped her right leg onto the back of the couch, and shifting her left leg, let her foot drop to the floor. And then she was open, exposed...her delicate scent calling to him. The sweet, moist flesh he glimpsed beneath her curls enticed, invited. His mouth watered in anticipation. Kneeling before her, he cupped her bottom with his hands, buried his face between her legs and claimed her.

Kennedy opened her mouth on a silent scream of ecstasy, wanting to cry, to shout the incredible magic of the moment...she was too busy flying, soaring into an unknown, never-before-experienced event she never wanted to end. Too delicious, too decadent. Nick seemed to know her body better than she did. His kisses tasted unlike anything she'd ever had. Everywhere he touched, everywhere his mouth went, he brought fire.

She had been frozen for so long, and she wanted to bask in his warmth. His touch made her feel alive. Her entire body burned with renewal. When his tongue delved deeply inside her, she knew she couldn't stop the avalanche of orgasm if she tried. Losing all sense of who she was, where she was, Kennedy gave herself up to the incredible ecstasy and beauty of the most delicious feeling in the world. Nothing mattered except reaching the ultimate pleasure. At the pinnacle, she found her voice and screamed, the sound echoing throughout the house.

For several long seconds, she could do nothing but try to catch her breath and savor what had to have been the most explosive orgasm in the history of orgasms.

If a person could have an out-of-body experience and survive, she'd just had one. At last, floating back to earth, she managed a gasping, "Nick...I..."

His mouth covered hers, stealing her breath, stopping her words. She tasted herself on him, and a new wave of arousal hit her. Pulling at his shoulders, she felt mild, distant surprise that he had stripped. When had that happened? As her hands touched hard, naked skin, she forgot all questions as she explored his beautiful hard male body. He felt wonderful, velvet smooth, masculine and warmth, heat and desire. *Nick.*

When he whispered, "Open for me, Kennedy," she didn't question his meaning. Arching her body upward, she opened her legs wide and almost sobbed as he slid smoothly inside her, going deep, filling her completely. Her arms wrapped around him tight, Kennedy allowed Nick to take her away from every worry, every care. She felt freer than she had in a long time...reborn, renewed.

Rhythmically thrusting and retreating, Nick drove into her at a dizzying pace. Kennedy had no time to think, barely had enough time to breathe before she gained a new height of pleasure. She heard distant gasping, sighs, cries for more. Then she heard her voice calling for Nick, screaming his name, begging for release, begging for more, telling him what she wanted, needed. Soaring through a velvet cloud of pleasure, she reached a new, higher pinnacle and then toppled over the edge to oblivion, landing softly, safely back into Nick's arms.

Breath shuddered through Nick's body as he worked to control his need. He'd just had her and wanted her again. With the knowledge that no matter how many times he made love to Kennedy, it would never be enough, Nick forced himself to pull from the wet, hot heat still pulsing around him. He was too heavy for her delicate body but couldn't bring himself to completely release her. What if he looked into her eyes and saw regret?

"Nick?" she whispered.

"Yeah?"

"Could you carry me to bed and make love to me again?"

Humbled by the softly worded request, emotion clogged his throat. "Hold on," he said thickly.

Standing, he lifted her in his arms. Her face dreamy and sated, she wrapped her arms around his neck. The trust in that gesture tightened his chest.

He pushed opened his bedroom door, dropped her gently onto the bed and then followed her down. Giving her no time to think, to question the rightness or rationality of "them," he kissed and caressed her back into arousal.

Every gasp, sigh, hitch of her breath, was something he'd remember to his grave. Nick cherished her as he had wanted to for so long. When taking him became uncomfortable, he brought her to climax again with his fingers and then again with his mouth. When she was close to dozing off, he would wake her arousal again, not wanting sleep to rob them of this night. He never wanted it to end.

Just before dawn, when he knew he could no longer keep her awake, he allowed her to settle beside him. As she snuggled up against his side, her breathing still slightly heavy from her last explosive release, he whispered into her hair, "Sleep, sweetheart."

She smiled vaguely, more asleep than awake.

Nick tightened his arms around her. Though exhausted, he refused to sleep. What if he woke and realized this had been a dream? No way in hell would he take that chance.

Chapter Twenty-six

Kennedy woke with great reluctance. Her eyelids felt heavy, weighted from lack of sleep. Why was she so tired? Yawning, she rubbed her face sleepily, tried to bring clarity to her blurred mind…decided that could wait till later. A few more minutes of sleep couldn't hurt. Rolling to her side, she snuggled deeper into her pillow. Cool sheets met bare skin. She froze, her heart stalling in her chest. Why was she nude? She hadn't slept without clothes since Thomas…

Her eyes popped opened. Memories, lush and decadent, flooded her mind. Oh sweet mercy! She jackknifed to a sitting position, her panicked gaze taking in the empty bedroom. She was in the guest room. How had she not known that? She hadn't known it because she hadn't cared. She had been so wrapped up in Nick, lost in the way he made her feel. Lost in a sweet, glorious bliss she'd never experienced before.

Swinging her legs around, she dropped her feet to the floor and covered her face with her hands. He had told her—actually shouted that he loved her. And the way he had treated her, the care he had taken with her… A hot wave of heat flooded her as she remembered all he had done, the sexy, erotic things he'd said. He'd been tender, passionate, deliciously inventive.

Every part of her body felt sore, used, achy. Without a doubt, he had given her the kind of pleasure she'd only ever read about in steamy romance novels. She honestly hadn't believed she was capable of those kinds of physical responses. He had taken her, challenged her, and made her feel things that she'd never…

No, no. That wasn't right. She and Thomas had enjoyed a wonderful sex life. It had been filled with passion and tenderness. He had satisfied her in every way.

She looked around the room. Where were her clothes? A memory washed over her, and a blush burned through her entire body. They were on the floor of the living room. Nick had stripped them from her, while she lay on the couch.

Kennedy jumped from the bed, dashed out the door and ran down the hall to the master bedroom. Her knees touched the edge of the bed and then she sat down abruptly.

She needed to see Nick, find out what he was thinking. Had last night meant as much to him as it had to her? Where did they go from here? A giddy sort of hope filled her.

But before that happened…before she had a conversation that could well change her life, she had someone else she needed to speak with first.

She began, softly, shakily, "Hi, Thomas, it's me…Kennedy."

Nick carried the heavy-laden tray down the hallway. The thought of waking up a sleepy and sex-exhausted Kennedy made his movements faster than was safe for two glasses of orange juice, two mugs and a large carafe of coffee.

It was Saturday morning, and Nick wanted to do something he never thought he'd have the chance to do—share a late-morning breakfast with Kennedy as they read the newspaper to each other. Most times, when fantasies about Kennedy arose, he had beaten them into submission, but when one had slipped through occasionally, this was one of the most prevalent.

Some men fantasized about sex, some about football. Nick's fantasies involved him and Kennedy sharing the mundane as well as the spectacular. And no doubt about it, the sex had been spectacular…beyond anything he could have ever imagined. But now, he wanted to show her that he wanted much more than sex.

Of course, his big secret was out now. He sure as hell had never envisioned shouting that he was in love with her. Actually, he'd never allowed himself to even dream about that possibility. Still, he couldn't deny that her response to his less-than-romantic declaration had been more than he ever could have hoped.

He veered right to go to the guest bedroom he had been using. A slight, muffled sound stopped him. Looking over his shoulder, he noticed that the door to the master bedroom was half open.

Nick turned around and headed that way. Had she woken and decided to get dressed? He stopped at the door, was about to push it open farther when he heard a sniffle. Sticking his head inside, he spotted Kennedy sitting on the bed, her back to him. About to ask her what was wrong, he heard her mumble something. Was she talking to herself? He strained to hear and then stopped breathing. A hammer slamming full force into his chest couldn't have been more painful when he finally made out some of her words, "I'm sorry, Thomas."

Silent and grim, Nick backed away and headed back to the kitchen. Stupid as it may seem, he didn't eavesdrop on private conversations between husband and wife. And what the hell had he expected? That Kennedy would suddenly be in love with him just because he could make her scream when she came?

He placed the tray on the kitchen counter and removed the items. She didn't need to know he had overheard her.

Pouring himself a cup of coffee, he pulled in a breath and faced facts. She had apologized to Thomas. What had been the best night of his life, bar none, Kennedy apparently considered a huge mistake.

Did he feel guilt? Hell yeah. He'd been living with that for years. A man didn't fall in love with his best friend's wife and not stay eaten up with it. And even though he still felt the guilt, it was, as usual, intermingled with an unending want.

Hearing Kennedy's steps heading toward the kitchen, Nick pushed away the pain. Being hurt over something you couldn't change accomplished shit.

"Good morning," she said softly.

Game face on, Nick turned. "Morning. Want some coffee?"

"Yes, please." She flicked a nervous look at him. "How are you feeling?"

"Good. You?"

She jerked slightly, as if surprised at his abrupt tone. "I'm fine." She smiled shyly. "Maybe a little sore."

"Take a shower…that'll help."

"Yes, I suppose it will."

She bit her lip and then winced. He didn't have to wonder why. Her mouth was swollen from his kisses. He poured a cup from the carafe and handed it to her.

"Thanks." She took a small sip and then said, "So, I guess we should talk."

Drawing on his ability to shield his thoughts, Nick shot her a blank, questioning look. "About what?"

"About last night. We—"

"What about last night? We had sex. It was good." His smile was as cocky as he could muster. "Damn good."

"But—"

"I've got to get going."

"Where are you going?"

"Thought I'd do some recon around Adam Slater's estate. If you're going to be staying there soon, I want to know as much about the property as possible."

"So we're going to go along with the new plan?"

"Of course. Isn't that what you want?"

"Yes…but last night…you—"

"Last night I did and said a lot of things. It's a new day."

"Wait. Is something wrong? I thought—"

"Can't think of a thing that's wrong." He swallowed the last of his coffee. "See you later."

Frozen in shock, so hurt and stunned she could barely catch her breath, Kennedy watched Nick stalk out of the kitchen. Seconds later, she heard the front door slam shut, and then the roar of his motorcycle told her he was gone.

What the hell...? Of all the things she'd thought they would say to each other this morning, this hadn't hit her radar. He had told her he loved her. Had that been a lie? Had he said that to get her to sleep with him? No, she couldn't... wouldn't believe something like that. But if it wasn't that, what had happened?

The cold, remote man of this morning had been the total opposite of what he had been last night. Could he just turn his feelings on and off like that? Her mind whispered an insidious thought: Of course he could. He was Nick Gallagher, playboy extraordinaire. How many times had Thomas told her about Nick's sexual escapades? Not the actual details, but enough to know that the man could sleep with a multitude of women and have no permanent feelings for them. He rarely dated the same woman for more than a month. How in the hell had she thought she was any different?

Had one of the most incredible nights of her life meant nothing more to him than scratching an itch?

Kennedy refilled her coffee cup and headed upstairs. She felt achy and out of sorts. Every time she moved, another memory of last night washed over her. She'd never been so immersed in another person, dominated, controlled or felt so incredibly safe.

She shook her head. She had to stop thinking of him. What happened had happened...there was nothing she could do to change it. She needed to adopt Nick's attitude. It'd been damn good but was in the past.

With that thought in mind, Kennedy practically ripped her clothes off and jumped into the shower. Getting Nick's scent off of her body, as well as easing the aches of overexcess, was a priority. Then she would set her sights on the future. She needed to contact Grey and let him know she was definitely in on their new plan.

Hot water gushed over her, and she found herself lingering over her breasts, the soreness of her nipples, the small, slightly achy bite mark Nick had left on her shoulder when he'd taken her from behind. No, no, no. Shaking her head, she opened her eyes and concentrated on getting clean. As she washed between her legs, she ground her teeth together and focused on everything but the delicious soreness in her sex. She had been used and used well, she needed to remember that.

Grey couldn't say he was surprised to see Gallagher at the door of his penthouse. His home address was a well-guarded secret, known to only a few. Wasn't the first time Gallagher had proved himself resourceful.

The expression on the man's face kept Grey from making any sarcastic remarks. He knew that look. Gallagher had the appearance of a man who'd had his balls doused with hot pepper sauce and then handed to him on a platter. Nothing could destroy a man quite so well as having his heart ripped from his chest by the woman he loved.

Maybe if they'd known each other longer, Grey would've asked him what had happened…invite him to share. But a man wouldn't spill his guts to just anyone. An enormous amount of trust was involved—something Gallagher had in short supply.

Grey did nothing more than lead him into his living room and nod toward the coffee service on the table. He waited until the other man had poured a cup and downed half of it. Yeah, a guy who could swallow that hot, bitter brew without flinching had a lot on his mind.

"Since it's a little early for social visits, I'm assuming you've come for another reason?"

Gallagher took another swallow and then gave him a glare that would probably have made most people back up and look for an escape. "I think we need to get a few things straight."

"And that would be?"

"First, if you use Kennedy, you're a dead man."

"Use her? In what manner?"

"You know what I'm talking about. If this is all a game to you, then you need to cut her loose. I'll continue to work with you, but she can't be a party to this."

"So you believe I'm in this for myself?"

"Don't bullshit a bullshitter, Justice. I recognize the signs of a man who wants vengeance. I agreed to our arrangement because it worked for both of us, but I made it clear that using Kennedy to further your own agenda is out of the question. That hasn't changed."

"My issues with Slater have nothing to do with this. We agreed that—"

"We agreed as long as it benefitted both of us. Getting Kennedy killed wasn't part of it."

"What makes you think she's in danger more than she was before?"

"Changing the rules in the middle of the game is a sure way to cause havoc. If Adam Slater suspects any kind of setup, the first person he'll get rid of is Kennedy."

There was something else on Gallagher's mind. A distrust that wasn't totally coming from this proposed change.

"What else is bothering you?"

"Your tattoo…the one on your wrist. Where'd you get it? What does it mean?"

"The scales of justice? Surely you can put two and two together."

"Yeah, but it's not adding up to what it should. Two people were found dead with that same tattoo."

He kept his expression careful, indifferent. "When did this happen? And where?"

"England and Ireland. About seventeen years ago."

So no new ones. Grey eased a breath from his body and arched a brow. "You think I had something to do with their deaths when I was barely seventeen? Not sure if I should be insulted or complimented."

"I learned long ago that coincidences are about as rare as unicorns. Don't tell me those deaths aren't related to you. I'm not buying it."

"Contrary to popular opinion, I don't own everything…including exclusive rights to my tattoo. I'm sure there are many people who have it—and some of them have probably died."

Gallagher's eyes frosted over. "Forget it. The deal's off. If you can't trust me enough to tell the truth, I'll damn well not trust you with Kennedy's life."

As Gallagher headed toward the door, Grey knew he could stop him with another bullshit story. Lying had been a way of life from birth. So why wasn't he speaking, preventing the man from leaving? Maybe he was tired of lying, but he sure wouldn't tell him the truth. They'd just have to find another way to get to Slater.

"You want to know the truth about the tattoo, Mr. Gallagher?" a soft, lilting voice asked.

Grey closed his eyes on a silent sigh. Of course, Irelyn had been listening to every word.

Gallagher halted and turned to the beautiful woman standing just outside the bedroom door. "The truth would be a nice change."

"The man and woman who were found dead, one in England, the other in Ireland, were my parents. They were murdered because of their work for an organization they joined before they were married. The tattoo was a mark each member of the organization wore. Then a man…a very evil man…went through the organization, systematically eliminating each member. Grey was an orphan… my parents took him in and raised him as their own. We grew up together, and when he was old enough to make a decision, he joined the group. When the assassin came, Grey and I barely escaped with our lives."

Grey could only stand and stare in awe at the story Irelyn had just weaved. Her words carried just enough truth to make the story seem plausible, but she'd left out some very important details.

"What was the organization?" Gallagher asked.

"The name is unimportant, but their goals were similar to what we do now. They brought justice to people who had been wronged. When Grey and I came to the States, we had to lie low for a while. I was still a teenager. Grey concentrated on amassing a fortune while I grew up. Only within the last few years have we been able to start again."

Gallagher's narrow-eyed gaze swung toward Grey. "Why wouldn't you tell me the truth?"

"Because the story is mine to tell…not Grey's. He promised he would never tell anyone. Think what you want about him, Mr. Gallagher, but above all, Grey is a man of his word."

Grey kept his silence. Anything he added would only muck it up. Besides, the deep stab to his chest at her words would have probably affected his voice. She hadn't been complimenting him when she'd said he was a man of his word. The promises he'd made to her hadn't been exactly what any woman would want to hear.

"Fine," Gallagher growled, "but remember this, Justice. If anything happens… if Kennedy even gets a paper cut, no one, nowhere, will be able to protect you from me." With those words, he strode out the door.

Turning to the woman who'd just saved his ass, he gave her an admiring look. "Once again, you've managed to earn my admiration."

"Maybe one day I'll earn my freedom."

Holding out his hand to her, he watched her glide elegantly toward him. When she placed her hand in his, he brought it to his mouth, savoring the soft, delicacy of her skin. Then, knowing she wouldn't refuse, he pulled her back to the bedroom for another few hours of bliss in Irelyn's arms.

Chapter Twenty-seven

Kennedy went about her day as if Nick's cold rejection hadn't crushed her. A chaotic childhood had created an adult who craved routine. Today, despite her bruised heart, was no exception. Saturdays were housecleaning days.

She and Thomas had made a game of it. Each of them had chores of their own, and the one who finished first got to pick the movie they would rent or go see that night. That had worked fine until the day she caught him stuffing clothes under the bed so he could win. The expression on his face had been priceless—like a little boy who'd been caught in a lie. Even now she could smile at the memory.

Thomas. This morning she'd had her last conversation with him. Maybe it was silly, but she'd felt the need to say goodbye again. Last night had been a turning point for her. She would always love Thomas, and he would be forever in her heart as her first love. But she'd felt that her night with Nick had been closure in a way and a new beginning.

Too bad Nick hadn't felt the same way.

Shaking her head at the mystery of the man she'd thought she knew, Kennedy put away the vacuum cleaner and turned back to take stock. There was really nothing left to do. This house was half the size of the one she and Thomas had shared, with probably less than a fourth of the belongings she'd once had.

When she had moved here, setting up a home had been for appearance's sake only. It was the place she slept, ate and did her private research on the

Slaters. Now, maybe because of Nick, she realized how incredibly barren her life had become.

She shook off the odd sense of emptiness. She still had a purpose, and until her goal was accomplished, this was her life.

A stomach rumble reminded her that coffee and juice were all she'd had since dinner last night. She headed to the kitchen, pulled open the pantry door and stared, undecided. She needed to eat, but the thought of making something just for one held no attraction. Her hand on a box of cereal, she heard the key in the front door and froze. Nick was home.

Refusing to run to greet him in the hopes that he'd lost his disagreeable mood, Kennedy stayed put. She told herself that standing and staring at the open pantry was a good, "normal" look for her. Nick didn't need to know that she was looking at nothing.

"Hey."

She turned and faced him, holding her breath. He did look less forbidding, but not by much.

"Hey yourself," she said.

He held up a pizza box. "I brought lunch…if you're interested."

"Sounds delicious. I was just contemplating a bowl of cereal."

In silence, as if they'd done this a thousand times, she went about setting the table with plates and forks while Nick poured each of them a glass of soda. They sat at the table and began to eat. She was halfway through her second slice when she took the time to note that her favorite toppings were on one side and what were apparently his favorites on the other.

"How did you know that mushrooms, black olives, and ham were my favorite toppings?"

His broad shoulder lifted in a shrug. "Have a good memory."

She couldn't name the number of times she and Thomas might have shared a pizza with Nick in the past. However, for him to remember something so insignificant was incredibly sweet.

"Thank you. It's delicious."

That earned her an acknowledging grunt but not much more. Subtle attempts at getting him to talk were apparently not going to work. Fine. Before her mind had been blown by his admission of love last night and the incredible events afterward, they had been discussing Grey Justice's past. Their argument had yet to be settled.

"I've given a lot of thought to those articles you found, and I'm still not convinced there could be any connection between them and Grey."

"That right?"

"Yes. He wouldn't have been much more than a teenager. It's ridiculous that—"

"I've already talked to him about it. He confirmed my suspicions."

The thought that he might not have told her anything if she hadn't brought it up was disturbing. Tabling that for later, she said, "How did he know them?"

Instead of answering her question, he shot her a quizzical look. "You're not shocked…appalled that Justice is connected to two murder victims?"

"Not much shocks me anymore. And appalled? That would mean that I thought Grey ruthlessly murdered them. I don't."

"You don't think the man is ruthless?"

"I have no doubt he's ruthless. I don't, however, believe he's a ruthless murderer."

"Why? Because he's helping you?"

"I've told you before that I know he has his reasons for wanting to get Mathias and Adam. But he could do that on his own. He didn't need to involve me."

He considered her for several more seconds and then said, "I admire your faith in people, especially after what you've gone through." Before she could respond, he went on, "But I'm not willing to gamble on your safety."

"And what does that mean?"

"Simply that Justice knows you're the only one I care about in this project. No matter what happens, you stay safe. End of story."

How could he say that…look at her in that piercing, intense way of his, and act the way he had this morning? It made no sense.

"So Grey knew these people. How?"

"Apparently, they were Irelyn's parents, who worked for an organization similar to the one Justice has now. They were killed, Justice and Irelyn came to the U.S."

"How sad for Irelyn. I didn't realize she and Grey had been together that long."

"I told him we had agreed to their new plan."

"I'm glad you said yes. If this will get me inside Adam's place faster, then it's what we need to do."

Nick dropped a half-eaten slice of pizza on his plate and stood. "I'm going out for a while. Need anything?"

Apparently, their talk was over. Unable to stop herself, she asked a question for which she wasn't sure she wanted an answer. "About last night. Can we talk about what happened?"

"There's nothing to talk about. We had sex."

"And that's all it was to you? Sex?"

"Look. We got carried away. It was good…even great. But we need to keep our minds on the reason we're here. This is for Thomas. Remember?"

"Don't patronize me, Nick. I know damn well why we're here." She stood and said with as much dignity as possible, "You're right. It was just sex. And people say things they don't mean all the time. It meant nothing."

She turned her back and began to wash out her plate in the sink. She knew he was still there…knew he was staring at her back. She willed him to say something… say anything that would indicate that last night had meant more to him than just sex.

"I'll call you before I come home…see if you need anything."

She closed her eyes against threatening tears. She shouldn't have expected more.

"And you're wrong, Kennedy. It wasn't just sex. And everything I said last night, I meant."

She whirled and faced an empty room. Seconds later, the roar of his motorcycle told her he was gone once more.

CHAPTER TWENTY-EIGHT

"What's your problem, O'Connell?"

Kennedy jerked her attention back to the woman in front of her. She'd been less than attentive this afternoon and had tried Irelyn's patience more than once.

"Sorry. Just have a lot on my mind."

"Oh, really? Gee, sorry if finding justice for your husband's murder is getting in the way of your other social obligations."

The stinging barb went deep. Kennedy opened her mouth to defend herself and then stopped. Irelyn was right. Pining over a man who obviously didn't know the meaning of love and commitment was a useless thing to do. This and only this should be her priority.

"You're right. I'm sorry. Can we go over that one more time?"

She had to hand it to the woman. Irelyn wasn't one to hold a grudge. She simply nodded and repeated what she had said earlier, "The evening will begin at seven with cocktails in the grand parlor." She pointed to a large area on the diagram. "Dinner will be served at eight here in the formal dining room." Again, she pointed to the dining room on the diagram.

The entire floor plan for Adam Slater's twenty-six-room mansion lay before them. After almost two weeks of absolutely no progress, things were finally about to heat up. Two days after they'd made the decision to up the ante on enticing Adam, he and his wife, along with Mathias and Eleanor Slater, had left the country.

Mathias and his wife took a trip each year at this time, but Eli had said this was the first time Adam and his wife had accompanied them. The news of their departure had put a considerable damper on their plans.

Not wanting the weeks to be a total waste, she and Eli had officially become "an item." And even though the aim was only to establish themselves as a twosome, she discovered that she was enjoying herself. Pretend dating didn't have the pressures of real dating. There was no need to worry about whether he would kiss her or expect something from her. Anything remotely romantic was done in front of as many people as possible to make an impression. So far, that had been only some hand-holding, and once he'd kissed her cheek in front of some Slater House employees. Eli said nothing got the rumor mill going faster than a little office romance.

One thing she hadn't expected was how much she had come to genuinely like Eli Slater. Despite his wealth and evil relatives, he was a kind, considerate man with a surprisingly down to earth take on life. If she hadn't been so hung up on Mr. Tall, Dark and Grimm, she might have wished for something deeper.

Things were about to get even grimmer. Adam was now home and had called Eli with an invitation to a formal dinner for some business associates from Italy. And not just any associates. From what Grey had said, these men were Mafia, through and through, and would have made Tony Soprano look like a choirboy.

"How long will the dinner last?"

"The main meal…at least two hours. The evening is designed to impress. My source says there are twelve courses. Adam is flying in a chef and his staff from a restaurant in New York to prepare the meal."

Twelve courses. That kind of meal was beyond Kennedy's knowledge. Fortunately, once they finished reviewing the house plans, Irelyn would go over what would occur during dinner. Heaven forbid she picked up the wrong fork.

"So the dinner will be over at ten or so. What's after that?"

Irelyn pointed to another room. "This is the formal parlor, where after-dinner drinks will be served. Women will congregate in one part of the room, men in the other."

"That seems very archaic. Even if these men are little more than thugs, are wives always pushed aside?"

"Probably. Machismo is alive and well in the Mafia. However, these women aren't wives, they're mistresses. The men rarely bring their spouses. The business trips are thinly veiled opportunities to travel with their insignificant others, while their wives and children stay oblivious and at home."

Correctly interpreting Kennedy's look of disapproval, Irelyn laughed softly. "You'll soon learn that mistresses can be much more valuable when gathering information. A powerful man will say certain things to his lover that he would never tell his wife."

Having the opportunity to be separated from the men was a good thing, then. While she was listening to the women chatter, hopefully she could pick up something useful. And Eli would be doing the same with the men.

The reason behind the dinner was unclear, as was Adam's invitation to Eli. The brothers rarely saw each other socially. Everyone agreed on one thing—Adam was up to no good. Was he about to enter into something illegal with the Mafia? If so, could they discover something worthwhile that would finally put a stop to the bastard?

"And there are eighteen guests coming?"

"Yes. Not including you and Eli, along with Adam and his wife."

"What about Nick? When will he arrive?"

"As soon as everyone is seated for dinner."

According to Eli, any proof that Adam had ordered Thomas's death or documentation of any other illegal activities he was involved in would be in his house. Eli hadn't added, but had made it clear, that someone had already conducted a thorough search of his brother's office and found nothing.

While she and Eli were listening to idle chatter with the hope of picking up something they could use, Nick would be breaking into the mansion and searching Adam's office. If caught—she shivered at the thought—he would play Rachel Walker's jealous ex-lover and demand to see her. When she protested that no one would believe such a lame excuse, she was told it was up to her and Nick to be convincing enough to make it plausible.

Since she and Nick were now barely talking to each other, convincing others that they were ex-lovers might well prove the easiest part of the job.

"You've wandered off again, O'Connell."

"No, I haven't. I was just thinking how, if it becomes necessary, Nick and I are going to convince people we're ex-lovers."

"Why? Because you are lovers and you're concerned you can't pretend he's your ex?"

"It wouldn't be pretend…not really."

"So he is no longer your lover?"

Without any idea it was about to happen, her lips trembled and tears pooled in Kennedy's eyes. She missed talking to other women. If Julie were here, she'd spill her guts. With Irelyn, she wasn't sure what to say. Even though she had glimpsed the occasional vulnerability behind her beautiful façade, she still wasn't convinced that Irelyn felt emotions like other women.

Kennedy took a chance and confessed, "Nick is barely speaking to me."

"Why?"

"That's the thing. I don't know. We made love for the first time a couple of weeks ago. And it was beyond spectacular. He even told me he loved me… had loved me for years. The next morning, he acted like it had meant nothing. Later, he said he meant everything he said, but he still acts so angry and cold. When I try to talk to him, he says we need to concentrate on this job, nothing more."

An unusual, awkward expression appeared on Irelyn's face. "Just so you know, I'm not the kind who's going to hug your neck and tell you everything's going to be okay. Got it?"

"I don't need a hug or trite reassurances. Tell me what you would do." As soon as she said the words, she knew the request was foolish. There wasn't a man alive who could sleep with this beautiful woman and act like it meant nothing.

Surprising the hell out of her, Irelyn's gaze went distant and unfocused as she said softly, "You act as if it meant even less to you. You pretend there's nothing he can do or say that can hurt you. You become impenetrable to pain. He never has to know that each harsh word or uncaring act cuts so deep you feel as though you're bleeding out."

Kennedy was wise enough to know they were no longer talking about her and Nick. Who had hurt this woman so badly that she had to pretend to be impenetrable to pain? Grey? Or someone from her past?

As if she was aware of her exposure, she smiled slightly and her slender shoulders lifted in an elegant, dismissive shrug. "If that doesn't work, toss him aside. If he's too stubborn to see that you love him, that's his problem."

"But I don't—" She swallowed the words, realizing she was about to deny something that she wasn't sure about. Was she in love with Nick? Is that why his cold behavior had hurt so much?

"I need to run an errand, and from the look on your face, you need some time alone. Just be sure you're comfortable with the layout of the mansion. You need to know every nook and cranny if something goes wrong. When I return, we'll review the menu and utensils."

Kennedy nodded, barely aware when Irelyn left the room. Yes, she would memorize the layout and be ready. For right now, she needed to consider the monumental realization she'd just experienced. She was in love with Nick.

How and when had it happened? When she'd fallen in love with Thomas, it had been a quiet knowledge…a gentle awareness that he was the man she was meant to be with. But now, with Nick, it wasn't a calm, serene knowing. Her feelings were explosive, mind-boggling… absolutely astonishing. She wanted to sing, shout, cry, laugh and dance. And she wanted to get in his face and find out just what the hell was wrong. Then she wanted him to kiss her until they were both breathless with need.

"You're either remarkably excited about your upcoming evening at Adam's house, or something else is going on."

Grey stood at the door, only a few feet away. When he wanted, he could be as quiet as a ghost.

"Just have a lot on my mind." She winced. She'd said the same words to Irelyn. She really needed to come up with some better excuses.

"I'm sure you do. I wanted to reassure you that our team will be right outside the mansion, and infrared cameras will pinpoint each person. Once Nick begins his search, we can follow his progress. If anyone is coming his way, he'll have a few seconds' notice to either hide or get out."

A few seconds didn't sound like a lot, but she was grateful for any advanced warning. The thought of Nick being caught by Adam's guards worried her a lot more than being in the presence of evil men.

"Can I ask you a question, Grey?"

"Certainly."

"As grateful as I am to be involved in going after the Slaters, I can't help but wonder why you allowed an amateur like me to do this. Nick told me about all the people working for you. I'm sure there're others who could do what I'm doing… probably with their eyes closed."

"That's true…though maybe not with their eyes closed." He shrugged as if unsure how to explain. "What happened to you was immensely personal. I believe every person has a right to gain their own justice, if possible. You deserve your pound of flesh. And don't underestimate yourself. You've done an exceptional job capturing Adam's attention."

"Thank you. And thank you for allowing me to be a part of this. You're right. Being personally involved in gaining justice is enormously rewarding."

He nodded solemnly and started to back out of the room. Kennedy couldn't help but make sure he knew how grateful she was to someone else. "I couldn't have done any of this without Irelyn, either. She's a remarkable woman."

"Yes, she is."

"Now she could have done this with her eyes closed."

Something like sadness flickered in his eyes. "I agree. There's nothing that Irelyn can't do."

"How long have you two been together?"

As if he feared she'd be asking even more inappropriate questions soon, he gave her his signature enigmatic smile, said, "Not nearly long enough," and retreated.

Kennedy returned her attention to the diagram in front of her. She would complete this job and make sure the people responsible for Thomas's murder paid for their sins. Then she wanted to move on with her life. The question was—would Nick want to move on with her?

"Okay, move around the room one more time. The feed was a little blurry, but I think we've got it fixed."

Holding the phone to her ear, Kennedy made her way around her bedroom once more and without thought, sang softly to herself, "August Mendoza had a problem and asked Stuart Singleton to help him out. Then Omar Delucci told Stefano Denzi—"

"How's that?"

Kennedy grimaced, feeling silly. She was no great composer or singer. "Sorry, I made up a song to help me remember the men's names."

There was the slightest pause on the other end, telling her she'd surprised Grey. "Well, that's…different."

"So is the picture clearer?"

"Yes. Perfect."

"That's good. I don't think I could find another place to put this thing." And she wasn't exaggerating. The short, sleeveless, backless cocktail dress had precious little material, much less a place to pin a jeweled brooch. Fortunately, the shoulder straps were wide enough to accommodate matching jeweled brooches, one of which held the tiniest camera she'd ever seen.

"Eli is headed your way…ETA, five minutes."

"Okay. Thanks."

"Talk to you when you get home. And don't worry, we've got your back," Grey said.

Her back wasn't what she was worried about. What if Nick got caught and someone hurt him? Even if they believed his excuse for breaking in, that didn't mean they wouldn't do something to him. A stalking ex-lover might make them angry, give them incentive to teach him a lesson. What if she couldn't stop them? What if they—

"You look...amazing."

She turned to see Nick standing at her bedroom doorway. His gaze swept up and down her body, hot enough to melt her clothes off. Kennedy shivered at the look. This was the first time since the night they'd made love that he had shown her anything but polite indifference.

"I can't figure you out."

A small smile lifted his mouth, but his eyes remained solemn. "It's not worth your time to try. Just wanted to reassure you that everything will be fine. I should have no trouble getting inside. Justice has assured me anyone headed my way should be no problem to detect."

She nodded. They'd gone over this a dozen times. Adam's people would disarm the security alarms while the guests arrived. This would enable Grey's team to hack into the alarm company, override their system and show a false reactivation. Nick would be able to enter without alerting anyone to his presence. Everything should go fine as long as he didn't get caught.

"And you'll just be searching Adam's office, nothing more."

"Yes. Eli is certain any damning files that exist will be there. By the time your meal is finished, I should have the entire room searched."

"If you get caught—"

He shook his head. "Stop worrying about me. You've got enough to deal with."

The doorbell rang, alerting her that Eli had arrived. She wanted to say more... so much more. Instead, she turned to grab a small, jeweled purse from the dresser. When she turned back, she was surprised to see the worry in Nick's expression.

Moving toward the door, she mustered a reassuring smile. "Don't look like that. You're the one taking the risk. I'll be enjoying a twelve-course feast and listening to scintillating conversation."

She was about to slip by him when he grabbed her elbow and pulled her into his arms. Warm masculine lips pressed a soft kiss on her forehead as he whispered gruffly, "If anything happens to you, I'll never forgive myself."

Kennedy closed her eyes, drawing strength from his hard, strong body. She didn't know what Nick's issues were…she might never know. However, she didn't doubt that he cared.

"I'll be fine." And before she did something crazy, like drawing his face down to her and kissing that beautiful, unsmiling mouth, she pulled out of his arms. "See you in a few hours."

She could feel his eyes follow her as she stopped at the hall closet for her coat and then made her way to the front door. Before she opened it, she stopped for a quick second, took the small, silent breath that Irelyn insisted as an imperative, and then pulled the door open to reveal an equally bleak-looking Eli. Refusing to allow the doubts that were apparently shared by both Nick and Eli, she greeted him with a cheerful, "Let's get this party started."

CHAPTER TWENTY-NINE

Nick kept one eye on the clock and the other on the large monitor revealing Adam's dinner guests. Not being able to hear the conversations was frustrating, but they'd had no choice. Knowing that strict screening would be applied to everyone, including the use of bug-detection devices, they'd eschewed everything but the small camera attached to Kennedy's dress. It was doing a good job of showing faces. And Grey had two expert lip-readers who were carefully watching as well. Between the five of them, surely to hell they could get something incriminating to work with.

Everything was going as planned, and yet nothing felt right. Maybe it was his own shitty attitude that was souring his opinion. He and Kennedy were acting like strangers with each other. His fault, not hers.

She had said she couldn't figure him out. He couldn't blame her for feeling that way. One minute he was telling her he was in love with her, the next he was treating her like she meant nothing. And she meant everything.

His behavior was both ridiculous and juvenile. So she'd felt guilty for screwing her husband's best friend. So what? He felt guilty, too. Had lived with that feeling for years. There were certain rules in friendship, and he'd broken a cardinal one. An honorable man didn't fall in love with his best friend's wife. And now he'd slept with the widow of his best friend. You didn't get much scummier than that.

Kennedy's guilt was understandable, too. She'd told Nick that she still talked to

Thomas...meaning she still saw him as her husband. Walking in on their one-sided conversation after a night of no-holds-barred passionate sex with him had been jarring. Well...so the hell what? Had he expected something else? A declaration of love? He knew that was never going to happen. And just because she'd responded with an explosive passion meant nothing. Kennedy was a healthy young woman who'd been alone for almost two years. The need for physical intimacy was as natural as taking a breath. It only made sense that she would turn to a man she trusted. But her heart would always belong to Thomas.

And now he was treating her like a stranger, barely speaking to her, and when he did, he was unfailingly polite. It was a testament to her patience that she hadn't picked up the nearest hard object and slammed the thing into his thick skull.

The hole he had created was a deep one. How could he explain his behavior without telling her what he had overheard? Part of his reluctance was pride— he freely admitted that. Stupid him had been so damn happy about what had happened, he hadn't allowed himself to think how Kennedy might have felt. And now they had a crevice between them he wasn't sure could ever be breached.

He heard Justice behind him. "Looks like they're getting ready to go into dinner. You ready?"

Nick didn't bother to turn. "Yeah."

"With everyone congregated in the dining room, the majority of guards will be there. If you think you're about to be detected, don't engage. The last thing we need is for Adam to get suspicious and wary."

This time Nick shot a glare over his shoulder. "I know the drill, Justice."

As if he hadn't spoken, the man went on, "If you can't get away without detection, alert us and we'll create a diversion. If that's not possible, you'll play the jealous ex-lover...demand to see Rachel."

About to give another sarcastic reply, he stopped when an inner voice that sounded amazingly like Thomas's told him to get his head out of his ass and into the game. Straightening his shoulders, he did exactly that.

"I'll be in and out as quickly and quietly as possible."

The other man slapped him on the back and opened the back door of the van. Nick jumped out. Dressed in a long-sleeved black T-shirt and black cargo pants that held several necessary tools, Nick strode to the gate surrounding the property and was up and over it in a matter of seconds. Other than his daily workouts, it'd been awhile since he had done anything physically challenging. A healthy dose of adrenaline surged through him.

Only by focusing on the job before him was he able to forget that Kennedy was inside the house in the midst of some of the most corrupt people in the world. Once they'd learned the names of the guests, Nick, along with a couple of Justice's top researchers, had dug up tons of information about what he had come to think of as The Nasty Nine. Apparently, there wasn't anything these men hadn't done or wouldn't do. If a man is judged by the company he keeps, then Adam was proving he was a dirty, rotten scumbag.

The reason for the meeting was more speculative than fact. Eli mentioned that Adam had come to him a few weeks ago touting an idea for a new kind of restaurant. He'd been looking for investors. Eli had not only declined but had relished telling his brother that it was a stupid idea. Rumors were that Mathias had offered his son a substantial amount of money, but for some unknown reason had recently pulled his funding.

Adam was now in deep debt and looking for more money. Did the prick know that he was getting in bed with the kind of men who wouldn't hesitate to kill him if he disappointed them? The Slater name might have been synonymous with wealth and power, but nothing trumped betrayal. Did Adam not realize they could cover up a murder just as easily as he could?

Nick kept low as he ran through the back area of the estate. Fortunately, giant oaks and elms made hiding easy. Within a hundred yards of the house, he lost all coverage and made a mad dash to the back of the mansion. In seconds he was standing at the cellar door. After careful study of the blueprints, everyone had agreed that the cellar was the most vulnerable entrance and the easiest to breach. Using the handy little tools he'd been given for the job, Nick proved the theory right and was inside the cellar in less than thirty seconds.

The instant the lock clicked and Nick pushed open the door, he had the thought that this was an oddly defining moment in his life. He'd just committed his first B&E—breaking and entering. Earlier today, he'd taken steps to ensure he brought no shame to the police department if he was caught, but still the experience was a strange one.

The dank smell of old earth and damp concrete put him in mind of a grave. Sweeping his flashlight over the surprisingly roomy interior, he located the stairway leading up to the first floor. This should put him in a hallway on the west side of the mansion. The dinner party was on the opposite end. Adam's office was on the north side.

The door was unlocked and opened easily, quietly. He listened for a few seconds to make sure he heard no one and then stepped into the hallway, closing the door behind him.

And now to find what he needed and get out without being caught.

Could a face crack from never changing expressions? Kennedy didn't know but had the feeling she'd find out before the night was over. The perpetual smile felt frozen on her face.

Even though she hadn't looked forward to this evening, she had thought being in the presence of hardened, heartless criminals might prove, at the very least, interesting. She had been wrong. These bloated, middle-age men were rude, crude and altogether unpleasant creatures. They treated their mistresses like bizarre pets, patting their bottoms or uttering the occasional sexual innuendo that, despite the language barrier, no one could misunderstand.

Her Italian was barely passable. She had worried that would be a problem, but now she was exceedingly happy she didn't understand everything. The ribald laughter was clear enough.

So far the only enjoyable part of the evening was the meal. Her stomach might be tied up in knots, but she could still appreciate excellent food.

As the conversation flowed around her, Kennedy kept her ears open for anything she felt might be useful. So far the talk had covered golfing and gambling, and one beefy gentleman, Franco Bellini, kept talking about wanting to attend his first rodeo.

Their mistresses, some beautiful and exotic, others fairly ordinary looking, sat beside them. Kennedy couldn't help but notice that their faces looked as frozen as hers felt.

Eli sat to her right, Adam her left. When she'd sat down, she had thought this would be her opportunity to talk with Adam a little more. She had been wrong. The man may have wanted to sit beside her, but with his wife on the other side, his behavior was surprisingly impersonal and cordial. She had worried that he'd lost his attraction for her but was reassured, if repulsed, when in the midst of a new course being served, he took the opportunity to lean close to her and whisper, "You smell delicious."

By that time, her smile was already permanently fixed, so she was sure he felt confident his compliment was well received. She felt fortunate that during the rest of the meal, his wife and other dinner companions required his attention.

Eli was the least surprising of the night, staying firmly ensconced in his disapproval of his brother by barely acknowledging his existence. To keep up appearances of their romantic relationship, he frequently whispered in her ear. To the rest of the guests, they probably looked like two lovers sharing an intimate conversation. Little did anyone know that Eli spent most of those moments regaling her with news about his daughters. Violet had lost a baby tooth, they suspected Sophia was lactose intolerant, and both girls were showing signs of having artistic talent. So far, the tidbits he shared of his children were the most interesting things she'd heard.

Where was Nick right now? They had been at the dinner table for well over an hour, so she at least felt certain he hadn't been caught breaking in. Had he found any files or information? Was he almost finished? Maybe he had already left. She would love to think he'd be waiting for her at the house when she returned home. That he would be safe and sound. If anything happened to him, she would never forgive herself.

"Is the lemon ice too tart?" Eli murmured in her ear.

She glanced down at her plate, barely aware that they were now eating dessert. Based on the amount in her dish, she'd apparently eaten half of it without even realizing it. Inwardly cursing herself for her inattention, she shook her head. "It's delicious. Why do you ask?"

"Because you lost that vague smile you've had on your face for the past three hours."

Her mouth moved up in a genuine smile this time. "And here I thought no would notice if I kept the same look on my face."

"Don't worry. It was an exceedingly pleasant look."

"I guess I was just thinking of something else."

Keeping his voice low, he said, "Everything will be fine."

"I know. I—"

She broke off when she caught a snippet of conversation Adam was having with one of his guests.

"I have it in my office on my wall. After dinner, I'll show you."

Everything inside her went still. What if Nick was still in Adam's office? What if he were caught? The excuse of a jealous ex-lover breaking into the house had never worked for her.

"Steady," Eli murmured.

She leaned close to Eli, ensuring no one else could hear, and whispered, "I have to warn him."

"That's not the plan."

"Then we need to deviate from the plan. He's going to be caught for sure. I have to let him know."

"And if you're caught before you get to him?"

"I'll just say I was looking for the restroom and got lost."

He considered her for several seconds and then said, "Go. I'll cover for you."

Without giving herself time to think about all the ways this could go wrong, Kennedy placed her napkin beside her plate. Eli stood and pulled out her chair, allowing her to stand. Of course, that got everyone's attention.

Trusting Eli to make an appropriate excuse to the sea of curious faces now staring at her, Kennedy said a soft, "Excuse me," and fled. As she exited the room, she heard Eli say something, and the room exploded with male laughter. Whatever he'd said obviously worked.

Thankful that Irelyn had insisted she memorize the layout of the mansion, Kennedy zipped through hallways as if she'd lived here all of her life. A couple of minutes later she stood at the closed door of Adam's office. Was Nick inside? Had Grey and his team alerted him that someone was headed his way? Maybe he had already left.

She turned the knob and was disappointed to find it unlocked, indicating that Nick was most likely still inside. Pushing the door open, she whispered, "Nick?"

CHAPTER THIRTY

What the hell?

Nick stood inside the small supply closet. When Grey alerted him of impending company, along with the astonishing news that it appeared to be Kennedy, he'd stepped inside to hide, sure that he must be mistaken.

Emerging from the closet, he whispered harshly, "What's wrong? What are you doing here?"

"Adam is bringing a group of men back here in the next few minutes to show them something. You need to get out."

About to snarl at her that she'd just put herself at risk for nothing, he stopped. She looked so earnest and worried he couldn't bring himself to say anything other than, "Thank you. Now go. I'll be fine."

"Did you find anything?"

"I—"

"Damn, Gallagher," Justice growled in his ear, "You got a party going on in there? At least five more people are headed your way. ETA thirty seconds."

"Shit."

"What's wrong?" Kennedy asked.

"They're on their way. Does anyone know you're gone?"

"Yes. But Eli covered for me."

Nick eyed the closet. It'd be a close fit but— He whirled around. "What's Adam going to show off?"

"A boar's head. He said it was mounted on the wall in his office."

The thing was across the room, hanging over the mantel. "Okay, get in the closet with me. We'll just have to wait them out."

Despite the glaring awareness of Kennedy's inexperience, he had to admit she was thinking more clearly than he was, since she remembered to lock the door before heading his way. All he'd been thinking about was getting her hidden.

The closet was barely big enough for his large frame, much less two people. Flattening himself against the shelves, he pulled her inside, her back to his front, and then closed the folding doors. The top of her head barely grazed his chin, and when he breathed in, he caught the scent of something delicate and feminine.

"Can you breathe?" he asked.

"Yes." To prove it, she breathed out and pressed even deeper into him.

Nick ground his teeth together. Of all the freaking times to get turned on, this ranked right up there with the worst. But there it was, with a mind of its own. They already didn't have enough room, but the damn thing between his legs was making it even more crowded.

"Nick?"

Of course she felt him against her. Hard not to notice a steel pole pressing against your back. Her body softened against him, and he bit his tongue to keep from groaning.

His voice almost soundless, he said, "Stay still. They're—"

The sound of the office door opening stopped him. They both tensed, barely breathing…waiting.

"My guide said he almost never had anyone bag a boar their first time out. This one was so large we had to call for a bigger truck to haul his gigantic ass out of the woods."

Male laughter rang out, followed by even more bragging from Adam. Then, as inevitable as a sunset, came the sharing and bragging of hunting triumphs from the other men.

Nick paid little attention to their words. The slats in the door were blessedly narrow, but he was able to see four men, Adam in the middle, gazing up at the mounted head. If they turned and looked closely enough, they'd probably see him and Kennedy. He just had to hope that wasn't going to happen.

Kennedy shifted slightly, and Nick went cross-eyed. Oh hell and hell again. Her firm ass was pressed against his thighs, and all he could think about was the need to grab her hips and lift her up until he could fit himself inside her.

She moved again. Dammit…if she didn't keep still… To keep himself sane, his hands slid to her hips and held her slightly away from him. As long as she wasn't touching him, he would get through this.

Silent as a whisper, she pushed back against him. Cursing his weakness, his hands slid around to her stomach and pressed her even harder. He felt her take a swift inward breath. Bending his head, he nuzzled the petal-soft nape of her neck, inhaling a delicate scent that was only Kennedy.

They stayed like that for who knows how long. The voices across the room continued on, more hunting stories, laughter. The woman in his arms held his total attention. He was hot, aching, so damn hard, and if he could have gotten away with it, he would have lifted her dress and taken everything he needed.

Kennedy was burning from the inside out. Nick's rigid penis throbbed against her…all she had to do was move her hand up slightly and she could have touched him. The men outside the door were forgotten. Her blurred mind dimly conceived that if they were caught in each other's arms, the alibi that Nick was a jealous ex-lover could probably work quite well. She could just say she succumbed to him in a moment of weakness. And that's exactly what she wanted to do—succumb.

With that thought, she allowed herself to feel Nick's body, absorb his clean, male scent, appreciate his hardness against her softness. His mouth was pressed to the back of her neck, not moving, just there, soft but hot, causing shivers throughout her body.

As heat slid through her, Kennedy closed her eyes and let her fantasies take flight. She imagined Nick turning her around and covering her mouth with his, plunging his tongue again and again. The desire was so real, she could almost taste him…their kiss was a wild, untamed mating of tongues. He whispered sexy, intimate things in her ear. The pulse between her legs throbbed with need and Nick's finger would be there, easing inside her, causing her to burn hotter, brighter. Then she would tear off her clothes and let him cover her with kisses. She wanted to lick and nibble every part of his gorgeous, muscular body until they both burst into flames. She wanted to take him in her hands and taste—

"They're gone." Nick's gruff whisper crashed-landed her back to earth.

"What?"

"They're gone."

She opened her eyes and squinted to peer through the slats. He was right. The room was empty. How silly to be disappointed.

"We need to get out of here." Even to her ears, her whispered words sounded disappointed.

"I know." His voice was thick.

Forcing herself to take the initiative, she pushed the door open and took a step out.

"Wait." Before she could guess his intent, he grabbed her shoulders, spun her around and slammed his mouth over hers.

With a small whimper of gratitude, Kennedy opened for him and let those fantasies she'd just had become reality. Plastering her body against his, her hands roamed his body, loving the feel of him, the heat of his skin beneath his clothes burned hot, almost scorching her fingers.

Without warning, he pulled away abruptly, looked down at her. Was he going to end this so soon? Would he go cold on her again? No, she wouldn't allow it.

Breathless with need, she asked, "What's wrong?"

"I… Nothing. Not a damn thing."

He covered her mouth again. This time he kept a steady pressure, not moving. It wasn't so much a kiss as much as it was a gentle drawing, as if he were taking her essence into him. She wanted more…the fire, the heat. She had to taste him completely. Her tongue flicked out, licking his mouth. The catch she heard in his breathing told her he liked what she'd done.

Taking another chance, she licked again. A groan came from deep within his chest as he covered her mouth and plunged deep.

Yes…she had to have him. Here. Now. Her hands went to the zipper of his jeans. Cupping him, she stroked, loving the feel of him, delighting that he grew even harder, longer. Her fingers grabbed the tab of his zipper, but before she could go further, he covered her hand. "Not here."

She froze. Good heavens, he was right. What was she thinking? And now she had the difficult task of going back to the party looking normal when all she wanted to do was strip naked and let Nick have her here, on the floor, on the desk. It didn't matter. She wanted, had to have him.

Any second, this would be over. Her eyes closed, dreading the end of this intimacy that had told her so much more than he probably even realized.

His body shifted, and Kennedy tensed, waiting for it to end. Instead, he whispered, "Just one more taste." This time he gave her the kiss she wanted, needed. Delicious, decadent, thrilling. His tongue plunged, retreated…he traced her lips with the tip of his tongue and then kissed her once more. His body ground against hers, and when she moaned at the lack of friction on the place she needed him most, he dropped one hand to her bottom, lifted her up and fit himself into her. Yes, this was it…what her body needed. Arousal, sharp and wild, zinged through her, and Kennedy found herself on the edge of orgasm. She never wanted him to stop moving into her. She—

"Excuse me, but I think it's time for Kennedy to return to the party."

They were in close enough proximity that she clearly heard Grey's voice in Nick's ear. A blush almost consumed her. While they'd been making out, practically having sex and most likely panting like two out-of-control animals, Grey and his team had heard every sound. And, oh dear heavens, she had a camera on her shoulder. What had they seen?

Mortified, Kennedy backed out of the closet.

Nick's eyes, burning with a fierce light, held hers captive as he put a finger to his ear. "Be out in a minute. Kennedy's headed back to the party." He dropped his hand from his ear and then correctly interpreting her look, reassured her, "The mic was off. And I had my hand on your shoulder most of the time. They couldn't hear or see anything."

Relieved, she nodded. That still didn't excuse her behavior. Here she was in the middle of the most important job of her life, and she couldn't control her hormones. "I'd better get back. I'm sure Eli's run out of excuses for me." She gazed around the office. "Did you get anything we can use?"

"I don't know. Based on what's here, you'd never know the guy was even in charge of the family budget much less multimillion-dollar companies."

Disappointed, she sighed. There had to be something somewhere.

"I'll see you when you get home."

Nick's words sounded like a promise. She hoped so, because she wasn't about to allow him to return to his coolness of the last few weeks. She gave him a heated look that in no way could be misinterpreted and then hurried out of the office. On her way back to the party, she made a brief but necessary stop at the powder room to make sure she didn't look as hot and needy as she felt. Surprisingly, though her cheeks were flushed and her swollen mouth no longer held a trace of lipstick, she looked almost normal. Way more normal than she felt inside.

She returned to the parlor, knowing that everyone had congregated there as Irelyn had described. Sure enough, the men were on one side, the women on the other. Though they eyed her speculatively when she seated herself, no one mentioned her absence. She listened as they chatted among themselves, once again a polite smile frozen on her face. If any of them talked of something she could use, she never caught on. For the most part, they chatted about fashion, where their lover was taking them after they left Texas and the jewelry they'd been unable to bring when they were traveling.

When they finally reconnected with the men, she was glad to hear Eli tell his brother that they must leave. What would happen when she opened the door to her house? Would Nick, the passionate man she'd just made out with, be there? Or would it be the cool, polite Nick who barely looked at her anymore? She didn't care which one greeted her. Whether he knew it or not, he'd opened something inside her. She wanted him unlike anyone she'd ever wanted in her life. No matter what excuse he gave, he would not be able to deny he wanted her. And he was going to have her, as she was going to have him.

Nick stood in the middle of the living room, waiting for Kennedy. He knew she and Eli had left Slater's house, that they were on their way home. How would she react when she saw him? Would she be embarrassed or as hot and needy as she'd been inside that closet?

For the first time in his life, he'd almost lost complete control. The men in the room, only a few feet away, had stopped being anything but a small, irritating noise in his head. The only thing that had mattered was Kennedy in his arms, all soft, warm, and so damn ready for him. It had been good that the closet had been so small, because if there'd been any way he could have unzipped his pants and had her...nothing would have stopped him. The need to drive into her had been the only thing on his mind.

Justice's voice in his ear had been a freezing splash of reality. He hadn't mentioned to Kennedy that the man might not have been able to hear or see them, but the infrared camera would have shown their two bodies glued together. Hopefully she wouldn't realize that, because he knew she was already embarrassed by what happened.

But no matter how she was feeling when she got home, embarrassed or not, he was going to have her tonight. Regrets and recriminations would wait until tomorrow. Tonight, she would be his.

The flood of headlights shone through the window. Seconds later, the door opened and she was there. A litany of words crossed his mind. Apologies for acting like a jerk for the past few weeks, excuses for his lack of control in the closet, reasons he would go insane if he didn't kiss her within the next second. Nick did none of those. He simply held out his arms.

Happiness flooding through her, Kennedy didn't hesitate. She threw herself at him, almost sobbing in relief as his arms closed around her. He held her close for several long seconds and then pulled away slightly. She looked up at him, wanting to see his face this time, needing to see the desire she'd only been able to feel earlier. Yes, it was there. Need, heat, desire, but most of all love.

She'd been burning for what seemed like hours. "I need you right now."

He grinned. "Yes, ma'am." Lifting her off her feet, he walked a few steps forward and pressed her against the wall. "Tell me what you want."

Any other time, she might have been hesitant or shy. Not tonight. With urgent hands, she tugged at his T-shirt, and he helped her by raising his arms, allowing her to pull the shirt over his head. When he was bare, she buried her face against his chest, licking, nibbling. Yes, this was her dream, her fantasy. He tasted incredible…salty, musky, sexy…. *Hers.*

Nick was vaguely aware of dropping his pants and flinging them behind him, his total focus on the woman whose tongue was licking his bare chest, driving him to insanity.

"Oh hell, Kennedy. I don't think…" He sucked in his breath when her teeth scraped his nipple.

"I love the way you taste."

Those sexy words almost ruined his plans to let her take what she wanted. Only by filling his hands with her clothes was he able to keep from laying her on the floor and devouring her like candy. As if her dress had been made of paper, the material practically disintegrated as he pulled it from her body. His fingers dipped beneath her throng underwear and ripped them away. At last she was completely nude. Nick stepped back to take in the sight and groaned at the beauty before him.

"Nick?" She was breathing heavily, looking up at him, beautiful whiskey-colored eyes dark with desire.

His voice guttural, he gave her an ultimatum. "Here...now."

Thank sweet heaven, she whispered, "Yes," because he knew for a fact he couldn't last another second.

Placing her arms around his shoulders, he muttered, "Hang on." The instant she complied, he lifted her legs, wrapped them around his waist and buried himself deep inside her heat. She climaxed on his first thrust, and Nick followed her with his second.

Panting, gasping, his forehead against hers, he growled, "Not enough. Need more."

"Me, too."

"Don't want to move...can't let go."

"Then don't...so good." She pressed soft frantic kisses to his face, his neck and chest.

"Yes," he breathed and then drove into her again. She gasped out a sob, and he set his mouth over hers, swallowing the sound. His hands grabbed her hips and held her still as he hammered into her softness, thrust, retreat, thrust. Never enough...would never be enough.

A distant sound buzzed in his head. Nick ignored it...couldn't think of anything other than the woman in his arms, sobbing his name, asking for more. An electric tingle zipping up his spine told him he was within seconds of another release. Wanting to make sure Kennedy came first, he pressed deep into her, pinning her to the wall and grinding. Sure that she would be screaming in ecstasy in seconds, instead he heard her gasp out, "What's that sound?"

He thrust...nipped at her neck, muttered, "Hmm?"

"I hear something."

"Cat...probably. Ignore it."

"I don't have a cat."

"Dog, then."

She laughed softly. "I don't have a dog, either. I think it's coming from your pants."

His pants? His pants were on the floor. Why would— Oh hell, she was right. With a ragged sigh of deepest regret, he pulled from her warmth and lowered her legs until her feet hit the floor. When he was assured she could stand on her own, he twisted round and snagged his jeans that somehow were almost halfway across the room.

Phone to his ear, he barked, "What?"

"I need to see you and Kennedy immediately," Justice said tersely.

"Your office?"

"No, my apartment."

Nick shot a quick glance over at a naked, glistening Kennedy, still slumped against the wall, her breathing slowly returning to normal, a dazed look on her beautiful face. He ground his teeth and turned away from temptation. Any other time, he might've told the man whatever it was could wait until tomorrow. The stark urgency in Justice's voice told him this wasn't something that could be put off.

Closing his eyes, Nick took in a ragged breath and said, "Be there in ten."

Chapter Thirty-one

For the first time in years, Grey wanted to kill someone. The violent life he'd left behind usually sickened him to remember, but right now he would have taken great pleasure in beating the ever-living shit out of Mathias Slater until the man lay bloodied and dying. Even then he doubted he'd feel any better, but at least the world would be cleaner.

Irelyn sat several feet away from him, the look on her face one he hadn't seen in a long while. He didn't like seeing it now but could do nothing but play the cards he had been dealt.

"I didn't know, Grey."

"I know you didn't."

"Do you want me to leave?"

The dull, emotionless voice sounded nothing like the self-assured woman Irelyn had become. Once again, she sounded like the scared young girl who had learned the fate of her many sins.

"No. Both Kennedy and Gallagher should know. It's time to come clean with your source."

"Are you going to kill him?"

Though her voice sounded only slightly curious, he knew better. Gathering up all the fury he had stored away for days like this, Grey said coolly, "No. You are."

"What?" Shock flared in her eyes. She shook her head. "No, Grey…you can't ask me to do that. You can't."

"I can, and you will. You knew this day would come."

"But he can still be useful to us. There's no need to—"

"There's every need. He's outlived his usefulness. We should have done away with him years ago. This time we have no choice."

"Do you hate me that much?"

"I feel many things for you, Irelyn. Hate is too mild a word for what I'm feeling right now."

"I—" She broke off at the sound of the buzzer announcing the arrival of Kennedy and Gallagher. Since Eli was otherwise occupied, Grey had asked them to come to his penthouse. If anyone saw them, they'd have to come up with a feasible excuse. Maybe he was getting soft, but he just didn't want to deliver this news in a damn warehouse.

"Do you want me to tell Kennedy what I know about her husband's death?"

"I'm leaving that up to you." ,

"How thoughtful."

Though the sarcasm was mild, he was glad to hear it. Despite his words and uncompromising position, he did have sympathy for what Irelyn faced. And the last thing he wanted to do was destroy her. However, she had known this time would come. If he'd had any inkling it would have come down to this, he would have had the man killed long ago. But then again, there were plenty of other hired killers more than happy to take his place. If there was one thing this world didn't lack, it was assholes willing to destroy lives for money.

Kennedy and Gallagher entered, both looking as grim as he felt. Of course being called out of bed at one o'clock in the morning for a meeting was rarely a good-tidings event. And considering what he had seen on the infrared when they'd been in the closet, neither of them had been sleeping.

"Would either of you like coffee?"

Kennedy shook her head, but Gallagher went to the coffee service and poured two cups of coffee, liberally sweetening one of the cups. Yeah, he'd been around this block before…he knew bad news was coming.

Grey waited until Kennedy was holding her coffee mug and Gallagher had taken a seat beside her. He looked at them and said the words that twisted his insides. "Jonah Slater was murdered tonight."

Nick breathed out a curse, knowing without having to ask what had happened. He caught Kennedy's expression. She looked sad but slightly confused, too. Despite all that she'd been through, she was still an innocent about so many things. When this was over, just how much of that innocence would she retain?

"I'm so sorry to hear that," she said softly. "I know you thought a lot of him, Grey. I'm sure Eli must be devastated."

"Yes, he is."

"Do they know what happened? Who did it? Another prisoner?"

Surprise and then a hint of compassion crossed the other man's face. He gave Nick a quick glance, as if to ask him if he'd like to explain.

"Either his father or brother were responsible, Kennedy," Nick said.

"What?" She moved her gaze from each person to the next as if to verify his words. "No, that's not possible. No father or brother would have a family member killed like that, no matter how much they hated him."

"Oh, get a clue, girl," Irelyn snapped. "Are you really so naïve that you don't know that families kill each other every damn day? It's the world we live in, and if you're going to survive, you'd better get used to it. You can't bury your head—"

"That's enough, Irelyn." Justice's hard voice slashed like a knife. "Kennedy doesn't need a life lesson from you."

"She needs it from someone."

"No, she's right to tell me that, Grey. If Mathias or Adam were responsible for this, then I am stupidly naïve. I just cannot fathom such evil."

"How's Eli taking it?" Nick asked.

"About the way you'd expect. He feels like he failed his little brother."

"So where do we go from here?" Kennedy asked.

"This changes nothing," Justice said. "I'm sure Adam will approach you soon for a job. When he does, express your sympathy for his brother's death but don't go overboard. Adam has you pegged as an ambitious, cold-hearted bitch. Showing too much compassion—something he can't comprehend anyway—might make him reconsider his opinion of you."

"Should I go to the funeral?"

"Yes. That would be expected. And Eli needs all the support he can get right now. I'm sure he'd appreciate your help.

"There's something else you need to know," Justice went on. "As you're aware, Irelyn has a source."

Comprehension came quicker this time. "This is the hit your source told you about," Kennedy said. "But why couldn't he tell you it was going to be Jonah?"

"He didn't know who it was at the time," Irelyn said. "By the time he learned the name, things were already in motion. I had no chance to talk to him before it was done."

"So does this source work for the Slaters in some way?"

"Yes and no," Justice said, then shot a glance at Irelyn.

Nick was surprised at the glimpse of vulnerability in the woman's eyes. Even though she was as beautiful as a porcelain doll and he'd occasionally seen evidence of a real person beneath her careful façade, he'd sure as hell never thought to see her looking so fragile.

"My source is a contract killer," Irelyn said.

"A hit man?" Nick asked.

"Yes, he does that, too, but his specialty is orchestrating murders. I knew he was going to set one up for the Slaters, but as I said, he often doesn't get told the target until the last minute. Since I can't let on that I'm fishing for information, I have to be as subtle as possible. Jonah's murder took place before I knew it was going to happen."

"He's the one who arranged Thomas's murder, isn't he?" Kennedy's voice, soft and without inflection, brought immediate silence to the room.

"Yes," Irelyn answered in an equally soft voice.

"Did you know he was going to have him killed?"

"Not until it was too late."

"How did he set it up to look like a robbery?"

"Do you really want to know?"

"Yes…I think I need to."

"I don't know all the details. He learned about the young man's release from prison."

"His name was Miguel Ruiz."

"Very well. He learned about Ruiz and how close he was to his family. He told him to follow your husband. That he would be stopping at a grocery store in the evening. Your husband wasn't to come out alive. He threatened Ruiz's family."

"I don't understand. Why wouldn't he go to the police…tell someone?"

"My source…he's incredibly adept at discovering his mark's weaknesses and using them to achieve his goals. Perhaps he knew Ruiz didn't trust the police." Slender shoulders lifted in a slight shrug. "I don't know."

Nick narrowed his eyes on Irelyn. "How the hell would he know Thomas would be going to a grocery store?"

Irelyn shook her head. "Again, I don't—"

"It's my fault," Kennedy said.

"How was it your fault?" Nick asked.

"Almost from the moment I learned I was pregnant, I started having these wild cravings. Thomas stopped by the grocery store almost every night to pick up whatever I was craving that day. It became our little joke." She swallowed a small sob. "Some joke. It got him killed."

Before Nick could dispute that, Irelyn beat him to it. "Don't be ridiculous. If it hadn't happened in a grocery store, it would have happened somewhere else.

Your husband was marked for death the moment he launched his investigation into the Slaters."

"But how did anyone know about his investigation?" Kennedy asked. "He never even told me or Nick what he was doing."

"The Slaters have eyes and ears everywhere. If he did research on his computer, made phone calls at the station…" Justice shrugged. "That's one of the ways they've been able to keep their nose clean for so long. They have a lot of people looking out for their interests."

"And now they've gone so far as to kill a family member." Kennedy shook her head. "Just how screwed up do you have to be to do something like that?" She turned to Irelyn. "This source you have. What good is he if he doesn't tell you anything in time?"

Justice leaned forward, blocking Irelyn from view as if protecting her. "Irelyn was doing her best to find his target. Even though Mathias is as cold and heartless as death, I don't think any of us even considered Jonah. The thought of a father arranging his son's murder…" Justice shook his head as if still trying to wrap his mind around the concept.

"Why now?" Nick asked. "Jonah has been in prison for almost three years. And from what Eli said, neither Mathias nor Adam has visited him in all that time. What did he do to piss them off?"

"I'm responsible for that."

They all whirled at the sound of Eli's voice. If a person could remain alive after getting the life knocked out of him, that man was Eli Slater. His face had lost all color, and his eyes were sunk into his head.

"It's not your fault, Eli," Justice said. "Jonah was a grown man. He made his own decisions."

"I should have found another way to tell him about Teri."

"What happened?" Nick asked.

With zombie-like movements, Eli moved farther into the room. The instant he reached a chair, he dropped into it as if his legs could no longer hold him.

"He insisted on knowing the details of her death. Like any sane man who learned that the woman he loved had been killed and in such a sadistically vile way, he went ballistic. We both knew Mathias had eyes on him at all times. He screamed into the cameras that he was going to kill the old man."

He shook his head. "The thought even went through my mind that Mathias would do something, but I convinced myself that even my father wouldn't go so far as to kill his own child. I thought he might have him beaten to teach him a lesson. I forgot who I was dealing with…should have known…should have done something."

"What could you have done?" Kennedy asked.

"Hell if I know. Found some protection for him. Supplied him with a weapon." His hand made a weary swipe down his face. "Help him escape. Anything other than just sitting on my ass and letting him get killed."

The room grew silent again. Kennedy looked around at all the sad, serious faces. This was wrong…so very wrong. How could one man be responsible for so much destruction and get away with it for so long? And not just get away with it, but also thrive. He was evil incarnate and had to be stopped.

A new resolve swept through her. "The only thing to do is continue what we're doing. Once I start working for Adam…move into his house, have access to his computer, if there's anything to be found, I'll find it."

"And what if you find nothing?" Nick asked.

Though surprised at the vehemence in his voice, she gave him the only answer she could. "Then we'll have to find another way to get what we need."

Nick surged to his feet and began pacing. She wasn't the only one who noticed his odd behavior. Grey was watching him curiously, too.

Finally stopping in front of Kennedy, Nick said softly, "Don't do this, Kennedy. We'll find another way. I got a couple of leads from his office we can check out. Let's work with what we've got. I swear to you…on my life, I will not rest until both Mathias and Adam are behind bars. But you working for him… That isn't the way to get to them."

"What are you talking about, Gallagher?" Eli asked. "You got a few names from his office…basically you got jack shit. This is the only way. Without Kennedy, we've got nothing."

"I don't accept that."

She took Nick's hand and asked softly, "What is it? Why have you changed your mind?"

"Isn't it obvious?" His arm swung out in a wild gesture. "Hell, Mathias had his own son killed. Do you know what he would do with you? He wouldn't give ordering your death any more thought than he would in ordering a takeout meal."

"Aren't you the one who didn't like changing the rules in the middle of the game?" Irelyn asked.

"Mathias Slater changed the damn rules when he had his son murdered."

Kennedy dragged her gaze from Nick's worried face and took in everyone else's expressions. There was anger and sadness but also determination. They believed this was the best way and that she could do it. She had to believe it, too.

She got to her feet. "Nick and I need to talk. I'll go into the office as usual tomorrow." She glanced down at her watch. "Or rather today. Eli, if you need me to do anything—help with the funeral arrangements, make calls, whatever you need--just let me know."

Taking Nick's hand once again, she pulled him to the door. They were in the car, headed back to her house, when he let out a long, ragged sigh and said gruffly, "You're still going to do this, aren't you?"

"Yes."

"I can't lose you, Kennedy. Not again."

A strong surge of love swept through her. When all of this was over, they would explore their feelings and desire for each other to their hearts' content, but until then she needed him to understand one thing.

"I don't want to lose you either."

His smile was oddly sad. "Then we're in this together, no matter what."

"No matter what."

CHAPTER THIRTY-TWO

Kennedy typed the last word of the cover letter for the quarterly financial report. Finishing it was the most productive thing she had accomplished in days.

Eli had been absent most of the week. Two days after his brother's funeral, his daughter Violet had fallen on the playground at school, bumping her head. They'd been in the middle of a meeting when he'd received the phone call. If anyone had ever doubted his love for his children, the stark look of fear on the man's face would have dispelled even the most cynical.

Violet had been diagnosed with a slight concussion, and Eli had opted to work from home.

The death of Jonah Slater had been a major news story for several days. As expected, Mathias Slater had made the most of the tragedy. He'd held a news conference, and with tears streaming down his face, demanded justice for his son. The irony would have been laughable if it weren't so incredibly horrific.

Other than her appearance at the funeral, looking like a thin, pale wraith, Eleanor Slater had been strikingly absent from all press coverage. She was reportedly in seclusion, devastated by the loss of her youngest son.

The funeral had been a sad, odd event. With Eli on one side of the room, the rest of the Slater family on the other side, and Jonah Slater's flower-draped casket in the middle.

Eli had made no concessions. Even the press had mentioned that there seemed to be strife inside the powerful family. Of course, none of the articles said anything negative about the Slaters, even Jonah, who to most of the world was a convicted criminal. Which made Kennedy wonder about the sheer gullibility of the average citizen. The lack of bad press for such a powerful family should have been a clue that someone with too much money and power pulled strings behind the scenes.

She admitted that she had once been a member of the gullible club. Before Thomas's death, she had never noticed the lack of scandal or negative press on the Slaters. In a world where reporters seemed to claw like voracious buzzards for the most salacious and scandalous information, the lack of negative media coverage was a glaring anomaly.

Her plan to entice Adam had stalled out for the time being. She had seen him at the funeral and caught a glimpse of him at the televised press conference but nowhere else. Attending social gatherings where she could flaunt her relationship with Eli had understandably been put on the back burner. Their plans were in a holding pattern until life could get back to the semi-normal one they had been living.

She and Nick had reached a strangely, easy relationship. There was no mention of the future, their feelings for each other, or those deliciously hot moments up against the wall of her living room. But there was something there—an invisible yet powerful hope. For now, that was enough to sustain her.

"Well hello there."

She'd been so lost in thought, she'd forgotten where she was. Jerking to attention, she looked up into evil, ugly eyes. Moving her gaze slightly, she noticed something else alarming. Helen, the woman who'd been watching her for days as if she thought she would steal something, had disappeared. And now Kennedy was alone with Adam Slater.

Panic threatened, and Kennedy battled it down with a fierceness that would have done Irelyn proud. How many times had she gone over this scenario with the woman? There was nothing this man could say or do she wasn't prepared to handle. And she had Nick. He was looking out for her, had his eyes on her at all times. Even now, he was watching and waiting, ready to intervene if necessary.

"Hello," Kennedy said coolly. "May I help you?"

Again, that disconcerted look came over his face. If she hadn't despised this man with a deep abiding hatred, she might have enjoyed this little game. Unfortunately, this was deadly serious.

"I…uh." His eyes darted to the closed door of Eli's office. "I came to see my brother. Is he in?"

She frowned up at him as if he were an imbecile. "Surely you know about your niece's accident. Your brother has been with her all week."

"Oh yes, of course. I just thought he might've come in today."

Dismissing him in silence, she turned her attention back to the paperwork on her desk. She knew he wouldn't walk away. He had come to see her, of that she had no doubt. Why, was another issue.

"Have lunch with me."

The words were blurted out with the finesse of an awkward teenager. Raising her head, she gave him another cool smile. "I can't leave the office unattended."

"No worries." He pulled his iPhone from his pocket and pressed a key. "Helen will be back in just a moment."

So he had been the one to get Helen out of the office. Apparently, she worked for both Adam and Mathias. Good to know.

Since spending more time with him was something she had to do, no matter how distasteful, she said, "All right."

She withdrew her purse from a drawer and then pulled out her keys to lock her desk. On returning them to her purse, she palmed her cellphone, hit a button on the side and then dropped it into her jacket pocket. Nick might not be able to get to the office in time to follow them, but the microphone she'd enabled would ensure he heard their conversation.

As she passed under the camera, her only link with Nick right now, she looked up and gave him a look that he hopefully interpreted correctly. She was fine.

Everything was going as planned—at least from her perspective. Question was: What were Adam Slater's plans?

Nick weaved in and out of traffic, his focus on Slater's silver Bentley two car lengths ahead of him. Kennedy had looked confident when she'd walked out of her office, but he knew her better than anyone. The vulnerability had been there, too. She had no experience in handling snakes like Slater. If the bastard put one hand on her, Nick would be there.

When Justice had suggested that Nick play Rachel Walker's boyfriend, he'd been doubtful. Then when she'd supposedly begun a relationship with Eli, they'd had to cast him in the role of a jealous ex-lover, which he had liked even less. Now he was glad for the role. A jealous ex-boyfriend would work well for this cover, because Adam Slater needed to know of his existence. Even though Nick would have to refrain from beating the crap out of him, getting in his face with some well-chosen threats would be gratifying and useful.

Earbud in place, he listened as Slater strived to be charming to an obviously unimpressed and underwhelmed Rachel.

"I've made reservations for us at Mitch's. You've probably never been there, but—"

"Why would you assume I've never been there?"

"Have you?"

"No. But your assumption seems odd."

"Just a turn of phrase. That's all. So tell me about yourself, Rachel."

"What is it you want to know?"

"Everything."

"Why?"

"Because you interest me."

"How so?"

There was a long pause, and Nick could just imagine the discomfiture on Slater's face. The man finally gave a surprisingly honest answer. "Because you're not scared of me. Instilling fear in people has its advantages but can grow old and tiresome."

"People fear you?" She sounded insultingly surprised.

Confident male laughter and then, "The whole world fears the Slaters."

"I don't."

"And that's why I have to have you."

"You're married. Or did that conveniently slip your mind?"

Nick grinned. Kennedy wasn't allowing him any leeway.

"Yes, I'm married," Slater said. "Not happily, though."

"Why don't you leave her?"

"Unfortunately, there are many reasons to get and stay married. Love is rarely one of them." A long pause followed, and then Adam said, "Here we are. How about we leave off the discussion of my unhappy marriage and talk of more pleasant things?"

"All right. Perhaps you can start by telling me what you want from me."

Kennedy held her breath as she waited for Adam's response. Was she being too bitchy? Since this wasn't a normal personality trait for her, she worried she was going a bit overboard.

Instead of the disconcerted look he often had with her, he gave her a heat-filled glance. "That, my dear, is exactly what I want us to talk about."

Even though she wanted him interested in her enough to take the bait, his look sent shivers down her spine. She allowed him to help her out of the car and then fell into step beside him as they headed toward the restaurant. Right before she walked inside, her eyes darted around and found what she was hoping to see. Nick sat on his motorcycle about ten yards back. Though he wore sunglasses, she had no trouble seeing the determined expression on his face. If anything happened, he would be there for her.

With that reassurance, Kennedy entered the elegant restaurant with a renewed confidence. She could do this…she was sure of it.

The instant she and Adam were spotted, the maître d' rushed toward them as if royalty had arrived. If everyone treated them like this, no wonder the Slaters believed they were above everyone else. As soon as they were seated in a secluded alcove, Adam ordered a bottle of wine and, the instant they were alone, went into full Lothario mode. A charming smile stretched his mouth, but the predatory look in his eyes never faded as he took her hand and pulled it to his lips.

Kennedy jerked her hand away. "You're moving a bit fast, don't you think?"

"No faster than my brother did."

"What are you talking about?"

"Don't be coy. I know you and Eli are seeing each other socially."

"What of it? He's single, and so I am. And, as we've established, you are not."

"Maybe so, but Eli can't give you what I can."

"And that would be…"

"Power, prestige. You would be the envy of every woman."

She had trouble holding back laughter. "You certainly have a high opinion of yourself."

"Nothing undeserved, I assure you."

Kennedy pushed back her chair to stand. "My ambitions don't include sleeping around to get what I want."

Instead of the anger she expected, his eyes gleamed with amusement. "You think I want to sleep with you? My dear, that's the furthest thing from my mind."

Kennedy didn't know whether to be insulted—which would have been a stupid reaction—or intrigued. "That's certainly not the impression I'm getting from you."

"My apologies. I just find you so delightfully unexpected." He nodded his head at her empty seat. "Please, sit down again and let's chat. No more touching, I promise."

Her expression wary but interested, Kennedy seated herself again. "All right. I'm listening."

"I want you to come work for me."

"Why?"

"Because I think we would work well together. Wealth and power obviously don't impress you. I need someone like that in my camp."

Yeah. And the fact that he would be stealing her right from beneath his brother's nose had nothing to do with it. Eli and Grey had this man pegged to a T. Adam's attraction to her had nothing to do with sex and everything to do with greed. He simply didn't want his brother to have something he didn't.

"Why would I leave Eli?"

"You may be sleeping with him, but he's a means to an end, nothing more."

She gave him a frosty glare. "Once again, you insult me with your assumptions."

"My apologies. So you do care for my brother?"

"I believe we've established that my relationship with your brother is none of your business."

"Fine. But you have to admit that working for Eli is a mere stepping stone to where you really want to go."

"And you're supposed to be the next step up?"

"Oh no. I'm far above the next step up. I can do things no ordinary man could get away with."

His sheer arrogance made her insides threaten to explode. Showing no outward sign of her inner fury, she asked coolly, "Oh, really. Like what?"

"Come work with me, and you'll find out."

No other words could have enticed her more. This was exactly what she wanted. Still, she couldn't seem too eager. "I don't know. Leaving Eli in the lurch wouldn't be fair."

"You let me deal with Eli. You don't ever have to see him again if you don't want to."

"And I would be performing the same duties for you as I do for Eli?"

"With a few notable exceptions." Before she could say anything to his obvious reference to sex, he held up his hand. "My bad. Yes, you would be performing the same duties, but I'm a mover and shaker in the state. Eli is nothing more than an ordinary businessman."

Deciding to play on his ego a bit, she nodded. "You do have a cutthroat reputation that Eli doesn't have. I find that strangely appealing."

"You can have some of that power, too. Just say yes."

"The temptation is strong."

His smile smug, he took a long swallow of wine and leaned back in his chair as if his mission was accomplished. "I have to admit, I'm surprised you're agreeing to it already. I thought I would have to coerce you a little more."

"Who said I was agreeing to it?"

"I can see the answer in your eyes. I'm good at reading people. That's why I know we'd work well together."

Kennedy took a moment to think about her next move. One of the many things she'd learned from Irelyn was that giving yourself time before responding served two purposes. You wouldn't speak words you would later regret, and the other person would know they weren't in total control. Speaking without thinking gave power to others. And, in this case especially, she refused to allow this man to believe he could control her. She was in charge of this situation.

"So, what's it to be?"

With her slow response, the doubt had returned to his eyes. Allowing him to sweat a little more, Kennedy took time to really look at the man who had destroyed her life. He was so very ordinary looking. His thick blondish hair was probably his best feature. The rest of him was a mishmash of Mathias's and Eleanor's features and, unfortunately for Adam, he hadn't gotten their best. In fact, it was hard to see any resemblance between Adam and Eli. Where Adam had gotten shortchanged on looks, Eli was quite handsome.

Seeing the impatient flicker in his dark eyes, Kennedy took a breath and then said in a calm, almost bored voice, "You're right. I do think we would work well together."

"Excellent!"

Before he could gloat in his triumph, their food arrived. Taking the interruption as a brief reprieve, Kennedy stayed quiet. Small talk was something you did to fill an uncomfortable silence or when you felt at ease with your companion. For this situation, silence was just another power play.

She focused on the food in front of her. When she did look up, she was pleased to see the uncertainty in his gaze again.

"How is your meal?"

"Delicious. Thank you." Though she could have been eating dirt for all the pleasure she derived from it, her taste buds did acknowledge that the food was good.

"I come here maybe once or twice a week. All I have to do is walk in the door, and they have a table for me."

Adam had told her earlier that he'd made reservations. He was still trying to impress her and proved that even more by suddenly filling the silence with a long, babbling string about his influence within the city and state. Kennedy was more than pleased to let him. The more he talked, the less she had to say. And while much of the chatter was hot air, she listened intently, looking for information that could later be used against him.

They were in the middle of dessert when things became uncomfortable again.

"You know Eli won't marry you, don't you?"

Even if she hadn't been playing the role of ice queen, the question would have offended her. "As we've established, my relationship with your brother, or anyone else for that matter, is not your concern."

"It is if I'm to trust you."

"How so?"

"My brother and I don't see eye to eye on most things. Even though he's in charge of Slater House Hotels, he's not involved with certain other aspects of the family business." He shrugged. "Eli's a selfish, self-absorbed asshole. Always has been. He looks out for number one."

She was glad she wasn't drinking anything or she would have spewed liquid all over the most self-absorbed asshole she'd ever met.

"I see." Deciding to play on his ego again, she nodded. "I've observed a little of that, but he is quite charming."

Belying the description of Eli being selfish and self-absorbed, Adam said, "Those brats of his are his biggest concern. No woman is going to come before them."

"You're probably right."

"Of course I am." His smile one of triumph, he continued, "As my executive assistant, you'll enjoy all the perks of such a prestigious position without having to contend with any other distractions."

"That's good to know." And then because she simply wanted to see his reaction, she said, "By the way, my condolences on the loss of your brother, Jonah."

For the first time in their brief acquaintance, she thought she glimpsed some humanity in the man. A look that could have been sadness crossed his face, and even though the emotion disappeared almost immediately, she did believe it confirmed Eli's contention that Mathias was responsible for Jonah's death, not Adam.

As if he'd revealed no emotion, he said, "Thank you, but every family has a bad seed or two. Jonah made his bed a long time ago."

Unable to offer more sympathy and certainly resistant to agreeing with him, she took a sip from her glass and said, "This wine is delicious."

"Come work for me, and I'll see to it that—"

He broke off, distracted by loud voices coming from the front of the restaurant. Kennedy twisted her head around and swallowed hard at the man striding toward them. Dressed in faded jeans, scuffed boots, a white T-shirt and black leather jacket, Nick moved like a giant panther, graceful, dangerous...predatory. Green eyes glittering with a fierce jealousy, he swept his hot gaze over her before targeting Adam.

This was a scenario they had discussed many times. Nick needed to make his presence known in her life in case he ever had to intervene when she needed him. Still, that couldn't have prepared her for the impact of his appearance. He was like a fierce, untamed warrior—the ultrasexy, badass biker kind.

Even though Nick had heard every word of their conversation, seeing Kennedy sitting there looking so calm and in control stilled the fear inside him. Sitting outside, listening to the garbage Adam spewed had been difficult, but Kennedy was behaving like she'd done this her entire life. He was so damn proud of her.

"What the hell are you doing here?" Nick growled. His eyes darted to Adam as he added with scathing disdain, "With him?"

Her eyes wide with both anger and embarrassment, Kennedy shook her head and whispered in a loud, hushed voice, "You shouldn't be here. This is a business luncheon."

He shot another glare at Adam. "Yeah. I'll bet."

"Rachel, I'm assuming you know this heathen?" The tone of Adam's voice was as insulting as his words.

"Yes. Grimm is my ex-boyfriend."

"I see." His expression amused, contemptuous, Adam said, "Would you like to join us? Mr....uh, Grimm, is it?"

Nick ignored Slater, turned to Kennedy again. "We need to talk."

"No, we don't. We've said everything we have to say to each other."

"No, we haven't, and you know it."

"I can't do this right now, Grimm. You need to leave. As I told you, this is a business luncheon...with my new boss."

"I thought Eli Slater was your boss."

"It's complicated and really none of your business."

"I'm not leaving until you agree to talk to me."

"Fine. Call me later. Now leave before the maître d' has you thrown out."

Giving both of them a warning look, with an extra vicious glare at Slater, Nick nodded and growled, "Fine."

Backing away, he strode out of the restaurant, his purpose complete. Now Adam knew that Rachel Walker had a jealous ex-boyfriend who would have no issues with beating his ass, Slater or not.

CHAPTER THIRTY-THREE

The instant Nick left the restaurant, all life seemed to have been sucked out of their surroundings. Soft music and muted conversation flowed around them, but everything was bland and lacking without his electric presence.

"So he's your ex-boyfriend?"

"Yes." She shrugged and grimaced. "He has an overpossessive streak that drove me crazy."

"Don't worry. Once you move in with me, you won't have to worry about stalker ex-boyfriends."

Even though she knew this had been coming, the thought of living under this man's roof nauseated her. Still, if she were to get the information she needed, this was an important move.

"Move in with you? Why would I do that?"

"All my assistants live with me. Your job is a 24/7 position. You'll receive a generous salary and benefits, ample vacation time and many perks. However, when you're not on vacation, you'll be at my beck and call."

She could tell he expected resistance. Commonsense told her to express a certain amount, but she wasn't going to delay the process by telling him she would have to consider it. With that in mind, she frowned and said, "That seems extreme. Couldn't you call me at home if you need me?"

"No. There are times that I'll need you at a moment's notice. Living in my house will make it easier for both of us."

"Then maybe you'd better tell me exactly how much money and vacation we're talking about."

He named a salary double the amount Eli had offered when she'd gotten the job with him. The vacation time was also generous. If she hadn't known she was going to work with the devil, she could almost have believed that Adam was a generous, thoughtful employer. But she did know and was therefore as wary as hell.

"Why so much? The money Eli is paying is at the top tier for executive assistants."

"For one…I want to make sure no one tries to steal you away from me. Also, forgive the slur, my dear, but making sure you have more than enough money should ensure you won't sell information to my competitors."

Excitement sang through her blood. Knowing she would have access to information that could ruin him almost made her forget her role. Suppressing her glee, she nodded calmly. "I see."

"So, what's it to be? You ready to work for a real mover and shaker?"

Taking a breath to steady her voice, Kennedy gave him her first genuine smile since she'd met him. "I believe I am, Adam."

Mathias hung up the phone and took a moment to savor the victory. Wasn't every day a man cheated death. The damn doctors here in the U.S. had been all set to sign his death certificate. Good thing he'd had the wherewithal to seek out alternative solutions. Once again, it all came back to the money. He could afford whatever it took to get the job done. He had controlled people's lives with it, paid to have them killed when they pissed him off, and could make a man do any damn thing he wanted. And now, thanks to that money, he'd just told the Grim Reaper to go to hell.

His personal physician was calling it a miracle. No sign of disease, as if he'd never been sick at all. Mathias didn't believe in miracles. He believed in money. Wealth was the ultimate problem solver.

And now, the way he was feeling, he could live to be a hundred…if not more. No one could stop him…nothing could hold him back.

The buzzer on his desk went off. Mathias growled into the intercom, "Yes?"

"You son Adam is here, sir."

"Send him in. And make sure we're not disturbed."

Seconds later, Adam strode into the office like a cocky rooster. Mathias sighed. The boy had learned nothing from their last tangle. Why couldn't he have had at least one son who acted in a manner befitting a Slater? This little pissant should have been slinking in with his tail between his legs, crawling to his daddy, asking forgiveness. What did the little shit have to be smug about?

Adam had always been the most arrogant of his sons, and Jonah, his youngest, had been the exact opposite, mild-mannered and humble. Eli had been in the middle, never seeming to need his father for anything. Of course, thanks to Mathias and his stern treatment, Jonah had finally grown a backbone. Too bad it'd gotten him killed. Should've been tougher on the little twit.

Adam threw himself into a chair and sprawled out like a giant, lazy hound. As much as it galled Mathias, he refrained from berating his son. Right now, Adam was his only familial ally. And even though the kid held on to his daddy's coattail like a terrified kitten, alienating him might do more harm than good. The idiot had yet to figure out that he was Mathias's tool, to be used or discarded at will.

"Get your feet off the furniture, son, and tell me what's got you looking like you just hit your first home run?"

Grinning like a fool, Adam said, "I just stole Eli's assistant right out from under his nose."

"You did what?"

"You've seen her, Daddy. She's that sexy number that Eli's been sporting around town to all the functions. Stupid of him to think he could hold on to something so fine. Barely took any coaxing at all for her to come work for me."

"What are you talking about? Why would you want to steal your brother's assistant?"

"Well, for one thing, you did away with mine, and I haven't been able to find an adequate replacement."

Mathias let that little chastisement slide. Picking and choosing his battles had gotten him this far. Still, it didn't keep him from looking forward to slapping the shit out of the boy one day very soon.

"Surely there are other young women you could get to fetch and carry for you. Why's this one so special?"

"Because she's gorgeous, and Eli always acts so smug when he's with her, like he's got something I can't have."

Mathias barely refrained from rolling his eyes. Of all his sons, Adam had always been the most covetous. Whenever one of his brothers or friends got something new, they'd had to watch out, 'cause Adam would find a way to either destroy it or take it away.

"How do you know you can trust the girl? You know as well as I do that Eli doesn't give a rat's ass hair about the family. He'd love to destroy both of us and take over everything. For all you know, this bitch is a spy."

Adam let loose a guffaw that would've done a donkey proud. "Don't be silly, Daddy. She's ambitious and seems moderately intelligent, but she's no brain surgeon. There's no way in hell she'd have the smarts to spy on us."

"Maybe so, but how do you know you can trust her? Just because you think she's not smart enough to spy, how do you know she's not going to spit out some family secrets? Your last assistant sure as hell didn't know when to keep her mouth shut."

Adam waved away the objections. "I know, but Teri was doing all of that for Jonah. She probably thought he'd take over the family business someday. Rachel is different. She's got no loyalties to Eli."

"What do you know about her?"

"Everything there is to know. It's not like I was born yesterday… I had her thoroughly investigated. She's from Amarillo, has no family, and never been married. Never been arrested—not even a speeding ticket."

"How do you know she's smart enough to handle the job?"

"She's got a college degree, and she got promoted several times at Slater House before Eli scooped her up for his assistant. She's been working for him for several weeks, and you know he's not one to put up with foolishness. Besides, I'm a good judge of people."

Good judge of people, his ass. No, Adam had seen something shiny and new that belonged to his brother and decided he had to have it.

"You'd better be right, boy, 'cause I'm not going to pull your ass out of the fire if she's not on the up-and-up."

"You won't need to, Daddy."

Mathias raised himself up and glared at his son, ready to talk about the real reason he'd told the boy to come see him. "You want to tell me what the hell you're doing having that Italian Mafia group over at your house for dinner?"

Adam's face went three shades lighter, and then he swallowed so hard that Mathias saw his throat convulse. "I… It's not what you think, Daddy. It was… it was Eli's idea."

His eyes narrowed on the boy. "That right?"

"Yes, sir." Adam nodded like an eager puppy. "See…Eli knew I needed more funding for the restaurant. And since you'd made it clear you weren't going to give me more, he suggested I call them. It wasn't until later that I realized how dangerous they were. I didn't take anything from them. Honest."

He hated when one of his children lied to him. "That's good to know, son. And you know exactly why I didn't give you more money. That place is a money pit. That's two and a half million of hard-earned Slater dollars I'll never see again. You know how stuff like that riles me."

"Yes, sir. But I'll get that money back for you someday. I promise."

Even though that was about as likely as a July snowstorm on the sun, Mathias nodded his head as if he really believed it. Adam, the jackass, looked both relieved and jubilant. Yeah, he thought he'd pulled one over on his old man.

"Get on out of here, boy. I got work to do. And don't forget to go by and see your mama. She's still hurting over losing Jonah."

Huffing out a breath like a snotty, teenage brat, Adam stomped out the door. The instant it closed, Mathias pressed the intercom. "Round up Cyrus. Get him in here."

"Yes, sir."

Mathias blew out an explosive sigh. He'd always known Adam was the dumbest of his kids, which had worked well for many years. That was going to have to change. Not only had he lost a mountain of money on that dumbass idea of a restaurant, he'd gone and gotten in bed with some hoodlums. Those Italian boys were in the big leagues. Not as powerful as a Slater, but still, they could do some damage if they wanted. When Adam disappointed them, as was inevitable, his son was going to pay big-time. And that meant it could come back and bite Mathias on the ass, too.

He had covered for the idiot for the last time. To the rest of the world, Adam Slater was a brilliant businessman. To his father, who had created the illusion, he was a fool who could barely count to a hundred without help. Every dime the world believed Adam had earned had been carefully orchestrated by Mathias.

Didn't matter that Adam was his own blood. When a man made a mistake, blood couldn't count. Mathias was a man who believed in survival. If that meant standing on the fallen bodies of others to stay alive, then that's what he'd do, kin or no kin.

Lying to a parent was about as big a sin as one could commit. It was time for a hard lesson for another of his boys.

And no matter what Adam had said about the woman he'd stolen from Eli, Mathias wouldn't rest easy until he'd had her thoroughly researched. He'd come too far and sacrificed too much to have some little bitch from Amarillo ruin it for him. And if she was up to no good? Well, then, she'd end up in the same position as Adam's last assistant. Dead and in pieces.

CHAPTER THIRTY-FOUR

The transition from Slater House to Slater Enterprises had been much easier than she anticipated. One day she'd left work after a full workday as Eli's assistant. The next day, she'd traveled to another office building ten miles in the other direction and reported to his brother.

Adam wasted no time introducing her as the assistant he'd stolen from his younger brother. The speculative and knowing looks she received from his upper management bounced off her like a rubber ball against concrete. If they wanted to believe she was here to fulfill some sort of sexual depravity with Adam Slater, let them. She had a purpose far beyond what they could imagine. Her reputation as an executive assistant was the least of her worries.

After the round of introductions, she was shown to her new office. Most people would have been thrilled to have their own office, filled with nice furniture and even a semi-decent view out her window. She wasn't one of those people. The fact that she had an office disturbed her. She had liked being out in the open when she worked for Eli. In an office, she couldn't see what was going on, who came to visit Adam, or hear what someone might say in an unguarded moment.

Since the appropriate response should have been gratitude and awe at her new surroundings, Kennedy did just that, along with the proper amount of arrogance, of course. She found herself walking a fine line between cold, ambitious bitch and subordinate. She was sure Irelyn would have had no problem carrying off such a role, but she was no Irelyn.

She had seen the woman only once since learning that Jonah had been killed. Though Irelyn had behaved as coolly confident as always, there had been something different about her, too. Maybe it was because she'd learned about Irelyn's relationship with the man who had arranged Thomas's death. While Kennedy had been anticipating and planning her future with Thomas and their baby, Irelyn had known none of that was possible. That lay between them. And though she couldn't say the time she spent with Irelyn had ever been comfortable, their meetings had become easier. The last one had held the awkwardness of their earlier sessions.

The last few minutes of that session had been the most surprising and revealing time Kennedy had ever spent with the woman. She'd been gathering up her purse and coat when Irelyn put a hand on her arm and said quietly, "I know you must hate me."

Kennedy shook her head. "I don't understand you, but I certainly don't hate you. I believe you would have tried to prevent Thomas's death if you had learned about it in time."

Kennedy thought she saw a gleam of appreciation in her eyes. "Thank you for that." And then a hardness crossed her features as she'd leaned closer and whispered, "If you get in trouble…if anything happens, don't depend on anyone but yourself. Not Nick, Eli…certainly not Grey. Save yourself…don't wait on someone to do it for you. Be your own hero."

Then, as if nothing unusual had been said, she drew back and gave her usual jaunty smile. "See you next time."

Kennedy had left that meeting more confused and intrigued than ever about Irelyn Raine.

A buzzer ripped her back to reality. Pressing the intercom key, she said, "Yes?"

"Come in to my office and let's go over this month's agenda."

"Be right there."

Gathering her calendar, along with her cellphone, which she slipped into her suit jacket, Kennedy left her office and headed to meet with her new employer, eager to take her next step toward destroying him.

Grey eyed the man across from him. He was usually excellent at reading people, but he had to admit that Nick Gallagher was a challenge. For the first time in a while, Grey had no idea how the man was going to respond to his offer and request.

"I understand you resigned your position with the Houston Police Department."

Gallagher shrugged. "Thought it best since I was breaking into a prominent citizen's home."

"I imagine that would be difficult to explain to your superiors. You have any plans for the future?"

"Beyond destroying Mathias and Adam Slater? No, can't say that I do."

"I offered you a job when we first met. Now that you've seen the private side of our victims advocate operation, any interest in joining us?"

"Possibly. Once the Slaters get locked away, I'll make a decision for the future."

"Fair enough." His gaze dropped to the phone Gallagher held in his hand. "How's she doing?"

"From what I can tell, things are going smoothly. Adam might be proud of his newest acquisition and smug that he one-upped his brother, but he apparently intends for Rachel to do her job."

"Excellent. The more responsibilities he gives her, the more she will gain his trust." Grey stood and headed to the large bar across the room. "Want more coffee?" Though he ran his corporations in one of the largest skyscrapers in downtown Dallas, Grey was more comfortable discussing certain issues within the privacy of his penthouse.

Gallagher shook his head. "So why else am I here?"

"As I mentioned when we first met, you have excellent instincts, Gallagher."

Grey hesitated a moment before he made the request. It'd been years since he had been so conflicted over a decision. Even though the stage was set, with everything in place, the ramifications would be long-lasting, possibly permanent. This upcoming event had been years in the making, and while one part of him hesitated to carry it through, another, stronger part of him was infuriated that he was even vacillating.

Permitting the memories to reemerge for only a moment, he allowed the familiar wrath full reign. Yes, this had to be done.

Nick watched Justice curiously, intrigued and surprised at the conflict he saw in the man's eyes. Having observed his strength and arrogance firsthand, this obvious inner struggle was definitely out of character.

Justice took a breath, the arrogance firmly back in place. "Irelyn has a difficult assignment coming up…one that will change the dynamics of her relationship with me. For some inexplicable reason, I've noticed that she doesn't have the normal antipathy toward you as she has for most men. If you come to work with us, I'd like you to partner with her on future assignments. I think you would complement each other."

Of all the odd and obscure things Justice had said since Nick had met him, this statement was at the top of the list. Justice and Irelyn lived together. Though they didn't flaunt their affair, he was quite sure their relationship wasn't platonic. And while he had been around the block enough to know that love wasn't a requirement for sex, he'd seen the admiration on Justice's face when he thought no one was looking. The man had strong feelings for the woman and yet was willing to jeopardize their relationship to get a job done. Nick didn't know if that made Grey Justice heroic or a fool.

"I would have no problems working with Irelyn. She's a remarkable woman."

"Yes, she is."

Sensing that Justice had said all he intended about the matter, Nick went to his feet. "Kennedy will be going to lunch soon. I want to be at the building in case she decides to go outside."

Justice nodded in an absent manner, his forehead furled as his attention was diverted by something he was reading on his phone.

Figuring the man had another fire to put out, Nick let himself out of the penthouse. His focus was on his own phone, watching Kennedy working at her computer in her office. Because of that, Nick barely noticed he was out on the street until he heard the roar of traffic. He raised his head to get his bearings.

Halfway to his bike he had parked across the street, the squeal of tires behind him had him looking over his shoulder. A limousine shuddered to a stop on the street, the back door swung open, and Eli Slater shot out like a missile. Looking neither left nor right, the man barely missed plowing into a streetlamp as he charged inside the building and disappeared.

Hell, what now?

Chapter Thirty-Five

Kennedy gazed around her sparse bedroom. In less than an hour, Adam Slater's limo would arrive at her door and whisk her away to live in his mansion. She couldn't help but wonder when she would be able to return to this little house that was beginning to feel more like home. Return to Nick and hopefully a future with him.

"Your gun. Where is it?"

She turned back to Nick, who'd been pacing between the hallway and her bedroom for the last half hour, his eyes dark with worry.

She opened a plastic box that resembled a makeup kit. Holding up a pink canister that looked like shaving gel, she unscrewed it and out slid the cylinder of a gun. "Every item inside this box has a secret compartment hiding a part."

"And you're comfortable with the assembly?"

"Yes," she said with the utmost confidence. As was usual, unless Kennedy practiced something fifty times or so, Irelyn didn't feel she was prepared. With this particular task, she'd assembled and broke apart the gun close to a hundred times before the other woman had been satisfied. This was definitely something Kennedy could do with her eyes closed.

"You carry it with you at all times. Even to the bathroom...and to bed. Understand?"

"I will," she assured him. "I even have a thigh holster for my suits, as well as an ankle holster for when I wear pants." Hoping to lighten his mood, she teased, "The thigh holster is very sexy, if I do say so myself."

"A thigh holster, huh?"

The gleam in Nick's eyes sent heat throughout her body. The past few days they'd become more comfortable expressing their attraction for one another. Nothing overt—just caressing touches, light kisses. Once, she'd patted his ass, and he'd jumped a foot off the floor, but the look he'd given her had been satisfyingly electric.

Even though a part of her wanted the wild, frenzied Nick who'd pushed her against the wall and had her screaming with ecstasy in seconds, she found herself enjoying the simple pleasures of sexual attraction.

"Don't suppose you'd want to try that holster on…model it? You know, just to make sure the fit is right or it doesn't show through your clothing?"

She laughed softly, loving that once again she could. "Adam's chauffeur is picking me up in twenty minutes. Otherwise, I might just take you up on your offer."

She wished she hadn't mentioned Adam, because the light went out in Nick's eyes, and the worry returned. "It pisses me off that you're not able to take your own car."

"I don't like it either, but since he's made a couple of concessions for me already, I didn't want to push this one."

"Yeah, real big of him to let you borrow his driver and limo one day a week to go to a beauty spa. The bastard wants to keep tabs on you even when you're off the clock."

She couldn't help but agree. Adam Slater's behavior was borderline obsessive. Since being in his house and having access to his secrets was what they'd been working so hard for, objecting to his possessiveness would have been counterproductive.

Conveniently owned by Grey, the spa was the ideal location for their meetings. She would be able to give a weekly report of her progress without anyone the wiser.

And though far from ideal, at least she would be able to see Nick once a week, too. Maybe not as privately as she would like, but still something she would anticipate.

Knowing Nick's dislike of the situation had more to do with his concern for her than anything else, she skillfully switched subjects. "Did you ever find out why Eli rushed into Grey's office the other day?"

"No. When I mentioned it to Justice, he said it concerned another matter. Since we have more than enough to deal with, I didn't push."

"Eli seems different lately...don't you think?"

"Different...how?"

She couldn't put her finger on it...maybe it was just her imagination. "I don't know. Maybe less sad or something."

"Maybe he's found a woman. I've heard that can do remarkable things for a man's attitude."

"Is that right?" Standing on her tiptoes, she pressed her body firmly against his. "Then I think you could use an attitude adjustment."

His erection rose hard and thick, grinding into her softness. Kennedy hummed her approval of the deliciously delicate heat slowly spreading through her body. Moving her hips deliberately and provocatively against him, she caught her breath as arousal thrummed in her sex.

With the hope that he would lower his head so she could reach his mouth, she pressed soft kisses to his neck and then his chin. When he didn't move, she said softly, "Kiss me, Nick."

He grabbed her hands, dropping them to her sides and then backed up out of her reach.

She frowned, hurt at his obvious rejection. "What's wrong?"

"Nothing. I just don't think we need to start something we can't finish."

"Does it always have to have a finish? Is there anything wrong with just playing?"

"Is that what you want...to play?"

"No, of course I want more, but playing can be fun, too."

"We don't have time for fun. Slater's driver will be here any minute."

"It's not lack of time, and you know it."

"What are you talking about?"

"Why do you do this, Nick?"

"Do what?"

She wanted to stomp her foot in frustration. "I know you want me." Her gaze dropped to the bulge pressing against his zipper. "That's pretty damn obvious. You told me you love me. Have you changed your mind?"

"That's never going to change."

"Why do I sense a big fat 'but' at the end of that sentence?"

He stared at her for several seconds. The conflict in his eyes told her he had a war going on inside him. "Nick? What? You know you can tell me anything. What's holding you back? Why can't you just let go with me?"

As if the answer was wrenched out of him, he answered in a ravaged voice, "I heard you, Kennedy...the night after we had sex that first time. I heard you talking to Thomas. Apologizing."

Confused, she could only stare at him. Yes, she had talked to Thomas when she'd woken up that morning, but when had she apologized? Why would she— Then she remembered. Unable to stop herself, she let out a little giggle.

"You think it's funny?"

"No, not really. Just..." She sighed. "Do you know why I was apologizing to Thomas?"

"Because you felt guilty...like you had betrayed him."

Had she? "Maybe a little at first. You were the first man I'd even been attracted to since Thomas. But the apology had nothing to do with betrayal. It had to do with the realization that while Thomas and I had a great sex life and I loved him deeply, what you made me feel that night wasn't something I'd ever experienced before." She could feel a blush crimson her cheeks at the confession.

"Yeah, right. Tell that to someone who didn't see your marriage up close and personal." He turned and walked out of the bedroom.

Now furious, she stalked after him. "You don't believe me?"

He stopped in the middle of the living room. "You don't have to lie to make me feel better. I know Thomas was the love of your life."

"I will love Thomas for as long as I live. He was a wonderful man, and I was incredibly blessed to share those few precious years with him. That doesn't mean I can't love again."

His face set as if etched in granite, he shook his head. "You'll never get over him."

She opened her mouth to argue and then stopped as realization hit. "Wait a minute. It's not me who can't get over Thomas...it's you. You're the one who feels guilty. You said you loved me for years...even when I was married to Thomas. You felt guilty about that. And now that you've slept with his widow, you feel even guiltier."

A knock on the door had them both turning. Dammit. Not now. This was the first open, honest conversation they'd had about their relationship. She felt as if she were on the edge of a major breakthrough. With just a few more minutes, they might have worked through this and finally settled this battle. But what choice did she have? She had to leave.

With only seconds to spare, she needed to be as succinct and direct as possible. Pulling in every bit of emotional strength she had left, she gave him an ultimatum: "You need to decide if you ever really loved me, Nick, or if you just loved the idea of me. If you knew Thomas at all, then you know damn well he'd be happy that the two people he loved most in this world had found each other. But you need to make a decision." Emotion clogging her throat, she swallowed and continued huskily, "Am I Thomas's widow or the woman you love? I can't be both."

She turned away from him and opened the front door. Allowing the driver to take her bags, she followed him out, refusing to glance back to see what effect her words might have had. As she made her way to the limo, she gave herself a lecture. It was time to get her head back in the game. This was for Thomas...she would do whatever it took to get justice for him.

When this was over, would Nick be waiting for her or would he let his misplaced sense of guilt destroy their chance at happiness together?

CHAPTER THIRTY-SIX

From inside a van that touted a twenty-four-hour plumbing service, Grey watched the monitor. As his one concession to Irelyn, he had agreed to no audio. He didn't like it but knew when to push and when to let go. He would see everything unfold. Hearing the camaraderie between the two wasn't something he'd been looking forward to anyway.

The doorbell must have rung, because Irelyn rose gracefully from her seat on the sofa and headed to the door. Her usual elegant stride was a bit off tonight, but that was understandable. Fortunately, he was probably the only person who would have noticed the difference.

She opened the door and greeted her guest as she always did—with a kiss on both cheeks and a warm embrace. Seeing their affection with each other always twisted through his gut like a knife skewering his insides.

They chatted back and forth for several moments, looking as easy with each other as only two old friends could. Considering they saw one another only a few times each year, the man's trust in Irelyn was admirable. Very soon he would realize the blind trust he'd given her had been misplaced. Irelyn had switched her loyalties years ago.

The first time Grey had seen the man who had caused heartbreak for so many, he remembered being surprised at how very ordinary and uninteresting he looked. Evil could be disguised in many forms and faces. Still, one would think there would have been something to indicate the wickedness that resided behind that average-looking exterior. Of course, that was how the man had been able to hide for so many years. Medium height, medium build, non-descript features. When he wasn't causing destruction and heartache, he was just a face in the crowd.

Their meetings always included a meal—one that Irelyn cooked. The man didn't trust restaurant food prepared by strangers…for good reason. There must have been countless people who would have loved to kill the bastard.

In previous encounters, Grey would listen intently during their dinner conversation, hoping to pick up clues or nuances of upcoming events the man might care to discuss. He was always very careful in his language, but if one listened closely, there was usually a gem or two that could be used. This time Grey's inability to hear was of no real consequence…after all, this meeting wasn't meant to elicit information. This would be the last conversation the man ever had with anyone.

Their easy camaraderie was something Grey had never been able to understand or comprehend. Intellectually he could, but deep within him, knowing what this creature had done, it was hard to swallow. Irelyn saw something in the man that Grey couldn't. She saw safety and affection. Grey saw a cold-blooded killer.

Irelyn laughed, and Grey caught his breath. Even though he couldn't hear the sound, he was mesmerized by the animation on her beautiful face. Joy filled her eyes—something she never had with him. He'd heard her laugh from time to time, but that had been when they were out in public and, as always, she had been acting a role. Laughter when they were alone was non-existent—not that he'd ever given her a reason.

At last the dinner ended. As was their custom, the man seated himself on the sofa while Irelyn went to the bar across the room and poured cognac into two snifters. Though he couldn't see the deed, Grey knew she had added an additional ingredient to one of the drinks.

She carried the glasses to the sofa, handed one to her companion and then sat across from him. Grey kept his eyes on the glass in the man's hand, watched as he swirled the liquid around, staring down into its depths. Hell, what was taking him so long? Why wasn't he drinking? Did he detect something off? Being in the death business for most of his life, the man had to have good instincts.

Grey put his hand on the door lever. If this went sour, he would have to act fast.

The man raised his glass in some kind of toast to Irelyn, then at last tilted it to his mouth and took a long drink. The instant he swallowed, Grey released a heavy sigh tinged with both relief and sadness. In the next few moments, two lives would change forever, and one would end.

Grey waited. He could do nothing until the event was over. The two people on the screen continued to talk for several more minutes. The poison wasn't the fastest-acting, but it was unidentifiable in blood tests and the most effective for the desired result—death.

Without warning, Irelyn did something extraordinary. She shot up from the sofa and stared directly at the camera, which was inside the small clock on the mantel. Fear like he'd never seen before was flashing in her eyes. What the hell?

A movement to her right caught his attention. The man on the sofa clutched his chest, his face a deep red. He keeled over, landing in a heap on the hardwood floor. Irelyn tore her eyes away from the camera and dropped to her knees beside the man. She loosened his tie, pulled a pillow from the sofa and shoved it under his feet.

None of those actions were part of the plan. She was supposed to leave immediately. A cleanup crew would be there in minutes to erase all evidence of her presence. So why the hell was she repositioning the body and giving CPR to the bastard?

Grey jumped from the van that had been parked half a block from the luxury apartments. If the man revived and realized Irelyn's betrayal, what she had done, she would be dead in seconds.

Dammit, he would never forgive her if she went and got herself killed.

Cursing every floor of the thirty-story building, he sprang from the elevator the moment it shuddered to a stop. Inserting the key into the lock, Grey pushed the door open, ready to kill the bastard with his bare hands if he'd put even one finger on Irelyn.

He heard soft, rasping sobs and huffs of labored breath. He ran toward the sounds and found what he had seen on the screen. Irelyn was on her knees, giving CPR to the man on the floor. Only, it was apparent the lifesaving act was a useless endeavor. The bastard was most definitely dead.

Aware that she was as dangerous as she was volatile, Grey sat on the sofa a few feet away from her and said in a calm, firm voice, "It's over, Irelyn. He's gone."

The ravaged face of a stranger, eyes wild with horror, looked up at him. "He didn't do it. He had nothing to do with Jonah's death. He said he was in the process of arranging the hit when another inmate jumped Jonah and killed him."

When Grey said nothing—hell, what could he say—she leaned forward and grasped his knee, clawing into his skin with her nails. Inches from his face, she shouted, "He didn't fucking kill him, Grey!"

"It doesn't matter anymore. He's dead. There's nothing to be done."

"Yes, there is. We can call an ambulance. They can revive him. Help me with the CPR. We can save him."

"No. He was never meant to survive this night, Irelyn. It's what we agreed on."

"That was when we thought he was responsible for Jonah's death."

"He might not have killed Jonah, but how many others has he killed? How many lives has he destroyed? He had to die."

The truth finally hit her. She collapsed back onto the floor and stared down at the body of one of the most ruthless and heartless contract killers in the world. "I loved him."

"I know you did."

Hearing a noise at the door, Grey sat up. The cleanup crew had arrived. He needed to get Irelyn out of the apartment so they could do their job.

He went to her, pulled gently on her shoulder to help her stand. "Come on. Let's go."

Instead of resisting him, she surprised the hell out of him by falling into his arms. A wave of tenderness threatened…Grey shoved it aside. It was an emotion he didn't allow in his life anymore. Still, he was extraordinarily gentle as he picked her up and cradled her in his arms.

Eyes closed, skin ashen, she pressed her face against his neck and said softly, "I hate you for this."

"I know."

"I'll never forgive you."

"I know that, too."

And with that settled between them, Grey carried Irelyn from the room.

CHAPTER THIRTY-SEVEN

Kennedy wasn't sure what she had expected when she entered Adam Slater's home, but it certainly wasn't DeAnne Slater screeching at the top of her lungs in an argument with her husband.

Kennedy stood in the doorway, hesitant to move forward. The couple stood on the second-floor landing. A giant foyer separated them from her, but she had no trouble hearing their heated exchange.

Adam's butler stood behind her, holding her luggage. She didn't know what the butler was doing, but she had a feeling he was staring in open-mouthed amazement, as was she.

"I don't care what you told her. I will not allow another woman to live in this house again. You call her and tell her she's not going to live here or so help me, Adam Slater, I'll make you regret it for the rest of your life."

"Now, DeAnne, you know that's not going to happen. You go to your room and sulk if you like, but I make the rules around here."

"You don't make the rules, and you damn well know it. You can barely wipe your ass without your daddy's permission."

"That's enough. I'm assuming we won't see you for dinner."

"You'll be lucky if you ever see me again. I—"

Apparently realizing she had an audience, the woman glared down at Kennedy. "Looks like your *houseguest* has arrived."

Even though her words dripped with bitterness, Kennedy heard the hurt behind them. When Adam remained silent, DeAnne turned on her heel and disappeared. Seconds later, the hard slam of a door was her final comment.

"Rachel, welcome."

Adam came down the stairs toward her with a broad smile, giving no indication that only seconds before he had been engaged in a shouting match with his wife.

"I've come at a bad time."

"Absolutely not. We're both thrilled to have you here. DeAnne can be a bit dramatic, but when you get to know her, I know you'll love her as much as I do."

Kennedy chose to ignore the double meaning of those words.

He raised his eyes to the man standing so patiently behind Kennedy. "Take Ms. Walker's bags to her rooms."

Wordlessly, the man headed up the stairs.

"I know you've seen this wing of the house, but let me show you the rest."

Kennedy made appreciative remarks as they traveled from one elegant room to another. Adam reminded her of a teenager doing everything he could to impress a girl. He pointed out priceless artifacts, sharing little stories of how he'd obtained them. The thought came to her that if he lost all his money and didn't go to prison as she wanted, he might make an excellent tour guide.

An hour and a half later, they had finally finished the tour. Between her nerves and the need for the perpetual smile etched on her face, she was exhausted and wanted nothing more than to go to her assigned quarters and fall into bed. Adam's next words banished her exhaustion and put her on high alert.

"Dinner should now be ready. We'll dine in the small dining room. DeAnne won't be joining us, so it'll be just us two." His smile grew smarmy as he added, "Give us a chance to get to know each other better."

Already ragged nerves shot straight to her stomach and developed into full-blown nausea. Had his insistence that he didn't want to sleep with her been another one of his lies? Before she could come up with a proper excuse to skip dinner, she heard a throat being cleared behind them.

Adam glanced over his shoulder, impatient arrogance on his face. "Yes, Stanley?"

"You have a call, sir."

Returning his attention back to Kennedy, he lifted his hand, as if waving away an irritating insect. "As you can well see, I'm in the middle of something. Take a message or tell them to call back."

"But, sir, I believe you will want to talk with this caller."

"Okay. Fine. Ring it to my cellphone."

"I think you'll want to take this call in private."

"Oh." Adam's eyes went wide as he turned back and gave Stanley his full attention. "Send it to my office. I'll get it in a—"

"Sir." This time Stanley's voice held a tinge of exasperation. "I believe you'll want to take this one in the secure room."

Though she could see only Adam's profile, the instant tension in his body indicated the caller was vitally important to him. What really caught her attention were Stanley's words: "secure room."

They had been over the diagram of the mansion numerous times—she knew this place as well as she knew her own home. And other than his private rooms he shared with his wife, Adam had shown her the entire house, top to bottom. Not once had he mentioned a "secure room."

Could he have a special room in his private quarters? Or was there another room not on the blueprints? Maybe one that Adam had added on after the mansion was completed? Was that why Nick had been unable to find anything incriminating or useful in his office?

With an absentminded glance, Adam said, "Excuse me, Rachel, I need to take this. I doubt that I'll be free for dinner after all. Your meal will be delivered to your quarters. Good night."

Gone was the charming gentleman eager to impress. This was a man worried about an impending phone call. Dammit, she really wanted to know what that call was about.

Her smile was polite, cool. "Thank you. I'll see you in the morning."

With a vague nod of acknowledgment in her general vicinity, he headed in the direction of his office. Kennedy took a step to follow him. A voice behind her said, "This way, Ms. Walker."

Knowing she could do nothing right now, Kennedy followed Stanley out the door. Was this the break they had been looking for? The place where Adam kept his secret files?

She intended to find out.

Nick sat in the dark. The only light was from the monitor on the desk in front of him, which revealed a sleeping Kennedy. As before, they had opted for video over sound. Justice had offered a new bug just on the market that was known to be undetectable, but with Adam's paranoia, they chose not to take the chance. The travel alarm clock Kennedy brought with her served as their camera. It wasn't much—giving him access to only a small part of her bedroom, but at least each night when she lay down to sleep he knew she was safe for one more day.

The Friday meetings they had scheduled at a salon Grey owned would be their only communication. The lack of contact with her would drive him crazy, but he had known going in that this could be a long-term commitment. Kennedy would have to earn Adam's trust before any further progress could be made.

Nick rubbed his grit-filled eyes. Sleep wouldn't come for a long time. How could he rest when her last words to him continued to slam into him with the force of a jackhammer? She had seen straight through him. The excuse he'd thrown at her—that she would never get over Thomas—had been a coward's attempt to hide his own guilt.

She had once asked him if he had talked with Thomas after his death. He'd thought about it a lot. When he was a kid missing his mother so much he'd wanted to smash the world to bits, talking things out with her had helped. Self-therapy? Some people might have laughed, but he knew to his soul that talking to her had helped him survive.

Something else that had helped him survive had been Thomas. Without his friendship... his persistent, unending cheerfulness, Nick figured he'd have been dead or in prison by now. If for no other reason than what Thomas had meant to him...done for him, he owed him this.

Taking a shaky, determined breath, he stared into the darkness and said, "Thomas... I—"

He rolled his eyes. Damn, he felt stupid. What he'd done as an eighteen-year-old kid was a lot harder at thirty-three. But if he didn't get this said and out of his system, there was no way in hell he was ever going to find any peace.

"I..." Rubbing his hand down his face, he blew out an angry, desperate breath. "Guess you know by now that I'm in love with Kennedy. Have been for a long time."

He paused, trying to come up with the right words. Then, as if a dam burst, they exploded, "Thomas, I'm sorry. So damn sorry. I never meant this to happen. When you started dating Kennedy, I was happy for you. You guys were great together. You loved each other so much. Then the longer I knew her, the more I realized that I couldn't stop thinking about her. She was sweet and beautiful...so incredibly kind. She could light up a room just by walking into it. And her smile is like—" He stopped, shook his head. "You already know all that."

He took a breath. "Remember the summer before you guys got married... right after you announced your engagement? Remember I disappeared for a few days? Told you I had some family business up north I needed to take care of? That wasn't what happened. I stayed in my apartment, forced myself to come to terms with the truth—you and Kennedy were meant to be together. You made her happy, and I know she made you happy.

"Then everything blew up. You got killed. Believe me, I would have done anything to prevent that. Not only because it hurt Kennedy so much, but because... well, I loved you, too, man. You were the best friend a guy could ask for."

He swallowed hard, cleared his throat. "The thing is, Thomas. I still love her...I always will. That year and a half that she disappeared was about the worst time of my life. I'd lost you and then got shot. That was bad...real bad. But Kennedy...

not knowing where she was, if she was okay." He shook his head. "That's a hell I'll never get over."

"So…here's the thing. I love her…want to be with her for the rest of my life, and I really need you to be okay with that. I promise to cherish and protect her." He let out an abrupt laugh. "That is if she'll have me after I've been such an asshole the last few weeks."

He cleared his throat again. "So…uh…that's it. That's where I am."

Nick sat there for several more minutes. He didn't know what he'd thought would happen. A lightning bolt? Some kind of vision of Thomas giving him a thumbs-up? Of course, nothing like that occurred. He still felt silly and foolish.

The longer he sat there, the more he realized that he felt something else, too. A lightness, a lessening of guilt…an increasing feeling of relief as if he'd just gotten something major accomplished. And he guessed he had. Thomas was up in heaven, he had no doubt about that. And he'd heard Nick's confession. Everything was out in the open. He hadn't felt this free in years.

Wiping tears from his face he hadn't even been aware of, Nick turned his gaze back to the monitor. Expecting to see the woman he loved sleeping peacefully, he jerked upright at the sight of an empty bed. Where was she?

He leaned forward, trying for all he was worth to see beyond the limited view of the camera. Then he saw her. The camera's angle caught a small section of the mirror, giving him a minuscule view of her bedroom door, showing Kennedy, dressed in black, creeping out her bedroom.

Dammit, no. This wasn't their plan. Where the hell was she going?

CHAPTER THIRTY-EIGHT

Blood pumping with adrenaline, a jubilant Kennedy returned to her room. When she'd left half an hour ago, she'd had little hope of finding the room on her first try. She had been set on eliminating a small area each night, believing her search would take days, if not weeks. If she hadn't been specifically looking, though, it would have been easy to miss.

The door to Adam's office was so large that the eye saw that and nothing else. Unless you were looking for something else. To the left of the door was a small alcove with a security pad. To a casual observer, the pad appeared to be a thermostat control. She'd examined the device thoroughly and was convinced it was a keypad to get inside. Did a door slide open or the wall push in? She didn't know...that would have to be discovered later. Her goal for the night had been accomplished, and she was quite pleased with herself.

Of course, if Nick could see her, he would most likely want to spank her. Her only comfort was that at three in the morning, he would be asleep. He'd told her he wouldn't sleep until he saw her get into her bed and turn off her lights. Then he would rest. When he woke in a few hours, he would have no idea that she had made a major find.

She stifled a giant yawn as she practically ripped off her clothes and fell into bed. Her last thought before she drifted into a sound sleep was how impressed everyone would be when she told them what she had found.

Nick was at Eli's office just after dawn. He knew Kennedy was safe—he'd seen her come back less than half an hour after she'd left her bedroom. That didn't lessen his worry or anger. In fact, seeing her saunter back in like nothing had happened had pissed him off mightily. Just like the night of the dinner party, she had gone off-script and disobeyed a direct order.

The instant he had seen her sneak out of her room, he had called Justice. Though the man had shared Nick's concern, he had urged caution. Showing up at Adam's mansion in the middle of the night as Grimm, her asshole ex-boyfriend, demanding to see her, might have caused more harm than good. However, he'd been disturbed enough to get Eli on the phone. They'd been in the middle of a conference call discussing a possible extraction plan when Kennedy's bedroom door had opened and she'd returned.

Just where the hell had she been sneaking around at three in the morning and who had seen her?

A security guard had been waiting at the front door of the Slater House building and had sent him up to Eli's office. He sat in the outer office, waiting for Justice and Eli to show. He didn't want to gang up on Kennedy, but she needed to know the risk she had taken was unacceptable. She was there to listen and report back, not to go out on her own and get herself killed.

The elevator doors opened, and both men walked out. They looked only slightly less disturbed than he felt.

"Did you talk to her?" Nick asked.

Eli shook his head. "I called Adam and told him we were having trouble with a project that Rachel had headed up. He agreed to let her come to the office to iron things out. I don't like asking favors from him but didn't feel we had a choice."

"I agree," Nick said. "I'd like to talk to her alone."

Justice nodded. "No problem, but before you do that, something happened last night that both of you should know about."

Nick was about to ask what when the elevator doors opened again, and there was Kennedy, safe, secure and looking only mildly curious. When she saw all three of them together, she rushed forward, her eyes wide with worry. "What's wrong? Did something happen?"

"Why don't we go into my private office?" Eli said.

The instant the door was closed, Kennedy whirled around. "What's happened?"

"Before Gallagher has his say," Justice said, "I need you to know something, Kennedy. The man directly responsible for Thomas's death…the man who arranged everything, is dead."

Her legs suddenly weak, Kennedy found the closest chair and sat down abruptly. Nick came to stand beside her and placed a comforting hand on her shoulder.

"How do you know…how did it happen?"

"We received a report last night." Justice said.

"Did someone shoot him or something?"

"No, he had a heart attack."

That seemed so unfair. This evil man had arranged for innocent people to be murdered, but he got to die of natural causes.

"This was Irelyn's source," Kennedy said. "Is that going to cause any problems in our plans?"

"No. He hadn't been useful to us in a while."

Grey stooped down in front of her, his expression sincere, compassionate. "I wanted you to know so you can decide if this is enough."

She stared at him blankly. "Enough?"

"Do you want to stop pursuing the Slaters? I know you wanted the man responsible for Thomas's death to pay. Now that he's gone, I wanted to give you an opportunity to withdraw. We will continue to go after them, but if you choose not to, I understand."

She was shaking her head before he finished his sentence. "That man might have arranged the murder, but he was hired by the Slaters. They still need to pay."

"And you want…?"

"I want to continue. We've come too far to back out. It won't bring Thomas back but Adam and Mathias are responsible for his death and need to pay for their crimes."

He nodded and then stood to face Nick. "And Mr. Gallagher?"

She just realized how quiet Nick had been. Glancing up at him, she was stunned at the decidedly unfriendly look he was giving Grey.

"Kennedy and I need to talk. Then you and I will discuss the matter and a few others."

"As you wish." A slight amusement entered his eyes. "I look forward to that discussion."

His gaze dropped back to Kennedy, the compassion she'd glimpsed before now gone, replaced by a hardness he rarely showed her. "You need to know something else. I stand by whatever decision Mr. Gallagher makes. Understand?"

No, she really didn't. Of all the bizarre ways to start her day. She'd been woken from a sound sleep by Adam's voice coming over the intercom like some kind of otherworldly entity. He had mentioned the ability to contact her this way, but waking up to his voice had been jarring. When he'd told her that Eli needed help with a project she had headed up and could she get to his office immediately, she'd sprung out of bed like a slingshot. Something major must have happened for them to arrange a meeting.

And now this announcement, along with everyone's odd behavior. Eli was standing in the background, silent but as solemn as the other two men.

"Is that agreeable to you, Mrs. O'Connell?"

Grey's hard voice shook her out of her stupor. Why was he suddenly acting so harsh with her and speaking so formally?

"That's enough, Justice," Nick growled. "Kennedy and I will talk and decide together how we'll proceed."

"Very well." He glanced at his watch. "I have several issues I need to attend to, so I'll take off now."

He strode toward the door and was almost out of the room when Nick called after him, "We'll talk soon, Justice."

Without turning back, Grey said, "I'm sure we will," and closed the door.

"Well, I guess while I'm here, I'll get some work done." Eli headed toward his formal office. "If you need me, let me know."

Somehow, Kennedy got the idea he was talking directly to Nick.

The instant the door closed, leaving her alone with Nick, she jumped to her feet and whirled to face him. "What on earth is going on here?"

Nick battled within himself. At first all he'd wanted to do was shake Kennedy until her teeth rattled. But now, seeing her safe and sound, his first instinct was to hold her close. He chose a combination of the two. Cupping her face with his hands, he covered her mouth with his, savoring the soft, sweetness of her lips, swallowing her gasp of surprise.

Before she could respond, he pulled away, grabbed her shoulders and shook her slightly. "What the hell were you thinking?"

"What on earth are you talking about? Will you please tell me what's going on?"

"Why don't you tell me where you were at three this morning?"

"What? I don't..." Comprehension came quick. "I was going to tell you about that. I—"

"What's the number one thing I told you not to do?"

"You told me not to take any chances, but I had to do this, Nick."

"Dammit, you still don't get it. What would have happened if Adam or one of his staff had caught you?"

"I was going to tell them that I'd lost my earring and was looking for it. I even had one in my hand to show them."

She looked so damned proud of herself he wanted to kiss her and then shake her all over again.

"Did you ever consider that Adam might have people watching you just to make sure you're not out to betray him?"

She huffed out an exasperated breath. "So this meeting...this overreaction, is all because I went searching? Nick, I—"

"Overreaction? Just what kind of reaction was I supposed to have when one moment you're asleep and the next you're sneaking out of your room? Do you honestly think that Adam wouldn't have you killed at the first sign that you're not who you say you are?"

"I know exactly what he's capable of, but how am I supposed to just sit back and wait when I know I have a viable lead?"

"Because that was our agreement. We're a team…remember? If you get some intel, you find a way to let me know, and then we'll decide how to proceed together. Going off on your own isn't going to accomplish anything other than get you killed."

The conflict was there in her beautiful eyes. She was so damned independent and stubborn. How ironic that he found those qualities so attractive and yet they might end up getting her killed.

She released a ragged breath, and he knew he'd finally gotten through to her.

"Fine. I'm sorry. I won't do it again."

"You had to know I'd have my eyes on you."

She grimaced, guilt shadowing her face. "I thought you would be asleep. That I could be gone and back before you noticed."

He struggled not to explode again. "You knew I'd be pissed."

"Yes." She sighed again. "I admit, it was stupid. Okay?"

Before the discussion ended, Nick needed her to know where he stood. "Do that again, or anything remotely similar, and you're off the case. Understand?"

Temper flared in her eyes, but thankfully she decided not to argue the point. Instead, he saw a slight smile curve her lips as she said, "So now can I tell you what I found out?"

"Yes, as long as you promise you won't do it again."

"I promise. Okay?"

He nodded, satisfied. "Okay, what did you find out?"

Even though a part of her still smarted from the lecture, she was mature enough to know that Nick was right. She'd acted impulsively, and if she'd been caught, it might've destroyed their entire plan.

Still, she hadn't been caught, and she did have something to share. "When Adam was showing me around the mansion, his butler interrupted us to tell him he had a call and suggested he take it in the 'secure room.'"

"Secure room?"

"Yes. That room was definitely not on the tour and isn't on the blueprints of the mansion."

"I'll be damned, the bastard's got a secret room."

Smiling brilliantly, she added, "And I found it."

"Where?"

"Right next to his office is a keypad. It's designed to look like a thermostat, but on closer inspection I realized it's a security keypad. I felt around the area, and there was a long, narrow indent in the wall that I believe is an opening."

"I'm not even going to think about what would have happened if anyone had seen you feeling around the wall."

"They didn't, so let's get past that and talk about how we're going to get into the room."

"I'll talk with Justice and Eli. We'll discuss scenarios during your spa day on Friday. Sound good?"

"Yes." She glanced down at her watch. "I guess I'd better go. Adam's driver is waiting outside to take me back to the house."

Kennedy forced herself to head to the door. If she stayed any longer, she would bring up issues he wasn't ready to deal with yet. Her hand was on the door when he called out, "I had a long talk with Thomas last night."

She turned back to him. A lump of emotion jumped to her throat. She knew that had been hard for him...and maybe even harder to admit. "Did it help?"

"Yeah...a lot."

"And?"

His eyes locked with hers, he walked slowly toward, saying softly, "When this is over, I want to take you to a tropical island and make love to you for days on end."

Happiness bloomed throughout her body. "Sounds perfect," she whispered.

Standing before her, he continued in that soft, growling voice she loved "And I'd like to talk to you about another kind of partnership. A permanent one."

"Sounds even more perfect."

Lowering his head, his breath warm and sweet on her face, he placed a soft kiss on her forehead, her nose and then her lips. "I love you Kennedy. Forever, for always."

Before she could respond, he kissed her with a reverence and tenderness that brought tears to her eyes and made her heart swell with emotion. Kennedy let him set the pace for the kiss, understanding that Nick was finally letting go of the guilt and pain he'd felt for so long.

When he raised his head, he gave her the brightest, most beautiful smile he'd ever given her. "I'll see you Friday."

Her heart so full she felt it might burst, she nodded and walked out the door as if she were walking on clouds. The battle to gain justice for Thomas was still on, but at last, she had won the war over Nick's heart.

CHAPTER THIRTY-NINE

The minute Grey walked into his penthouse, he knew she was gone. There was a feeling of emptiness about the place, and though he'd been in his home many times without Irelyn there, this time was different.

Last night, he had undressed her and helped her put on a nightgown. She had been silent, her face blank. He knew she had still been in shock. He had offered her a cup of tea, laced with a mild sedative. She had shaken her head when he'd put the cup to her lips, and he had set the drink aside, allowing the small defiance. After carrying her to bed and covering her with a light blanket, he had stayed to watch her sleep. In his gut, he had known it might be the last time.

Refusing to put off the inevitable, he went directly to her bedroom and shoved open the door. Irelyn's delicate scent, jasmine with a hint of spice, lingered in the room. A fragrance he'd had developed especially for her. Though everything still looked the same, including the glass cabinet in the corner filled with porcelain clowns she had collected on their travels, the atmosphere was cold and barren. Without Irelyn's dynamic personality, the room was a beautiful, empty shell.

Even though he already knew the answer, he crossed over to the walk-in closet. The instant he opened the doors, his suspicions were confirmed. Suits, dresses, jackets, slacks, and evening wear, color coordinated and neatly hung, filled the spacious area. One entire wall was devoted to her love of shoes. Irelyn was a clotheshorse…looked phenomenal in anything. With her generous salary, she had been able to purchase whatever she wanted. And while the full closet should have reassured him, he was immediately aware of one telling exception.

The cubbyhole where she kept her "go bag" was empty. When she had created the space years ago, he had been amused. She had done it to taunt him with the knowledge that she could leave anytime she liked. They had moved around the world, and wherever they ended up, she had found a prominent place to store the reminder of her independence. Years had passed before he had realized she did this not only to taunt him, but as a reminder to herself that she wasn't a prisoner. That it was her choice to stay and not because he wouldn't let her go.

Grey turned away from the evidence of her defection. A familiar, unwanted ache of abandonment threatened, but he pushed the feeling away with a lifetime of discipline. He searched for the fury and rage he'd expected to feel and knew it was no longer there. It had been years since he'd felt those things for her. The job Irelyn performed last night had been her last payment to him. A stupid, insane part of him had hoped she would stay for other reasons.

Pushing aside all emotions, he pulled his cellphone out and pressed a key. The sooner he had her things removed, the better. As he'd learned a lifetime ago—one went on, no matter what.

Nick eyed Justice as he walked into the living room of the penthouse. Eli would be along shortly. Before he arrived, some things needed to be cleared up.

Nothing showed in the other man's face, but there was something different about him. Pinpointing it would have been a useless endeavor. Justice would go only so far in his trust of others. Nick could identify with that personality trait. What concerned him right now was just how far this man would go with another issue.

"You want to tell me what happened to Irelyn's informant?"

Not a flicker of guilt or secrecy showed in the other man's eyes. "I believe I mentioned he died of heart failure. Many do…even soulless, merciless killers."

"Damn convenient."

"Not for him, it wasn't. I'm sure he was quite put out."

"Cut the bullshit, Justice. Did you have anything to do with his death?"

"Are you asking as an officer of the law or as a member of the Justice Group?"

"You know full well I'm no longer a cop."

"But you're not a member of my team?"

Instead of answering, Nick said, "You told me once that your group didn't murder to achieve justice. Has that changed?"

"Despite what you may think, what happened to Irelyn's contact has nothing to do with you."

"He was responsible for Thomas's death, wasn't he?"

"He was guilty of many other things unconnected to Thomas O'Connell's death."

"So you did kill him? Or have him killed?"

"I don't intend to answer the question, Gallagher, no matter how many times you ask. If you're a member of my team, certain information is on a need-to-know basis. If you're not a member, then the matter is definitely none of your business."

Nick knew he had a choice to make. Justice could cover this up as well as the Slaters could conceal their own sins. And how many lives had been saved by ending this bastard's life?

"Let's get one thing clear. If I become a permanent member of the team, getting involved in vigilante justice is out for me. I'll do what I have to do to help others, but I draw the line at murder."

"Contrary to what you apparently believe, so do I. As I said, this man's death had nothing to do with you or the O'Connell case."

Eli came through the door, and Nick let the matter drop. As a cop, he'd been walking a fine line since he had become acquainted with Justice. But he was no longer a cop, and the man who'd arranged Thomas's death was gone. Try as he might, he couldn't work up an ounce of outrage that a sleazy contract killer had gotten what was coming to him.

"So what's this new information?" Eli asked.

As Nick explained what Kennedy had uncovered on her unauthorized search, Eli's eyes lit up like he'd been given an early Christmas present. "I've been in that house a thousand times and not once knew about a secure room."

Justice looked almost as pleased as Eli. If Kennedy had been here, she'd have been patting herself on the back, making him doubly glad she wasn't. The last thing she needed to see was their approval.

"With nothing incriminating in either his work or home office, makes sense that this is where he's keeping his private files," Nick said. "Question is, how are we going to get inside?"

"How about Irelyn?" Eli asked. "She was able to bypass security and search his office at work. Think she can do the same at his house?" He glanced over at Nick. "I know you can pick locks and break into his house but Irelyn's got the kind of skills to break into Fort Knox."

"Irelyn is no longer on this operation. She has chosen to terminate her employment."

"Damn, I hate like hell to hear that," Eli said.

By not even the slightest flicker did Justice indicate that Irelyn Raine leaving his employment disturbed him. His very lack of emotion or regret told Nick that it bothered the man a hell of a lot.

"We'll find a way in," Justice said. "We'll meet with Kennedy on Friday. In the meantime, work on some scenarios you think might work."

Nick stood. "The sooner we can get inside and obtain whatever information Adam has, the sooner Kennedy can get away from him." Before walking out the door, he glanced back at Justice. "And if that job offer is still open, I'll take it."

CHAPTER FORTY

The days passed in an agonizingly slow pace for Kennedy. Even though Adam kept her busy with his daily schedule, sometimes they seemed to be running around in circles. Luncheons, cocktail parties, impromptu business meetings. Thankfully, she didn't have to attend most of them, but keeping up with his schedule was a challenge. When she'd worked for Eli, he had spent most of his time in his office. When he did go out, his destinations revolved around business. There had been little socializing.

She was beginning to see the many differences between the two brothers and found herself continually surprised that they were even related. Working with Eli had been interesting because she'd had the opportunity to observe the various aspects of running a large company. She had liked Eli's business style—tough but fair, with a sense of humor thrown in.

Adam was supposed to be in charge of several different interests for Slater Enterprises, but she'd seen little of his business skills. From the few reports she'd been permitted to see, others managed those interests. Which begged the question: Just what the hell did Adam Slater do?

Eli had said that Adam was the weakest link, and she could definitely see his reasoning. The prestige and power behind the Slater name were there, but without intelligence to back them up, the man was an empty suit.

Living in the same house with him hadn't created the headache she'd feared. Other than riding to work with him in the mornings and returning home with him in the evenings, she saw little of him outside the office. Was his absence a concession to his wife? Or, now that he had achieved his goal of stealing her from Eli, had his interest waned? Either way, Kennedy was grateful. Unless he was ready to reveal secrets that would help achieve her goals, she was quite happy to stay off his radar.

The puzzle of how to get inside the secure room continued to hound her. On Friday, she would meet with Nick, Grey and Eli, and she imagined this would be their main topic of discussion. Her goal was to arrive at that meeting with a plan.

She was overcompensating but couldn't stop herself. Even though she had discovered a major piece of information, Kennedy recognized that she had been foolish. If she had been caught in her search, even with the lame excuse of looking for her earring, there might have been suspicion. Adam might not be the brightest star in the sky, but he had good instincts when it came to self-preservation. If he had been suspicious of her at all, everything could have fallen apart. Nick's anger had been justified.

Nick. How she wished she could have spent more time with him. His confession that he'd talked with Thomas had stunned her and his declaration of love was more than she could ever have hoped to hear from him.

"Rachel, is something wrong with your hearing?"

She jerked to attention. Adam was standing in front of her desk, the glare in his eyes an indication that he'd been there awhile.

"Sorry, I was concentrating on something and didn't hear you come in."

"You were staring out the window. Should I get you an office without one?"

Only by reminding herself that she needed to stay on his good side was she able to refrain from telling him exactly where he could stuff the damn window. Instead, using the same attitude she'd had since meeting him, she raised a cool, arrogant brow and remained silent.

His breath puffed out, telling her he'd had onions in his breakfast this morning. "Sorry. I'm just put out about a few things. My lunch with Maxwell Greene got canceled."

She opened her day calendar. "What day did you reschedule?"

"I didn't."

That explained the sour mood. For the past few days, she'd seen a marked agitation in Adam and had a feeling the lack of support and funding on some new projects were the reasons. The amount of information he allowed her to know was limited. He didn't quite trust her yet, which was another reason her middle-of-the-night search had been foolish.

Hoping the suggestion she was about to make wouldn't come back and bite her in the ass, she casually said, "When I was working with Eli, I became acquainted with Grey Justice. Have you considered approaching him as an investor?"

His eye gleamed with interest. "How close did you two get?"

For a man who didn't seem all that interested in sex, Adam had a surprising one-track mind when it came to relationships between men and women. "Not that close," she drawled. "I did hear him mention to Eli that he was looking to expand his portfolio beyond his current investments. Perhaps your ideas would be of interest to him."

"That's an excellent idea. Give the man a call. I've tried to approach him in the past, but he never seemed interested."

"I'll be glad to."

When he continued to stand there, she realized he wanted her to make the call in front of him. Hoping that Grey would back her up, she checked her cellphone for contact information and placed the call.

Adam mouthed, "Put it on speaker."

Less than a minute after she'd identified herself and asked to speak with Grey, he came on the line. "Hello, Ms. Walker," Grey said warmly. "What can I do for you?"

Relieved he had accepted the call, Kennedy said, "Sorry to bother you, Mr. Justice. I'm now working for Adam Slater, and he has some interesting investment opportunities coming up. When I was working for Eli, I heard you mention that you wanted to expand your investment portfolio and thought you might be interested in some of Adam's projects."

"What an intriguing idea. I'll give Adam a call. Thanks for thinking of me, Rachel."

"My pleasure, Mr. Justice."

"Good day."

Kennedy released a silent, relieved breath and looked up at Adam. He was beaming at her as if she'd just split the atom. "I knew hiring you was a good decision. Sometimes my daddy doesn't know his ass from a hole in the ground."

Meaning Mathias hadn't wanted Adam to hire her. Why? Was it because she had worked for Eli, who made no secret that he despised his father and brother, or was there another reason?

"Glad I could be of some help to you. I—" She halted when her intercom buzzer sounded and Adam's secretary said, "Rachel, would you tell Adam that I have Grey Justice on the phone for him?"

His eyes wide with wonder at how fast Grey had called him, Adam flew out of her office. Smiling her satisfaction, she leaned back in her chair. Even though it might cost him some upfront money, she hoped that Grey would go along with at least one of Adam's ideas. She needed to gain Adam's trust. Bringing him an investor of Grey Justice's ilk would go a long way to helping her achieve that trust.

She'd barely had that thought when Adam burst through the door, excitement dancing in his eyes. "He's interested! I pitched an idea to him, and he wants to meet."

She had no doubt that if she had been standing, the man would have hugged her. "That's wonderful, Adam."

"This has got to work out. If it does…if he'll give me what I need, I'll be able to get out from under the slime I'm dealing with now."

Afraid to appear too interested in who and what he meant by slime, Kennedy said, "With a man like Grey Justice behind you, other well-known, strong investors will be interested, too."

"Exactly. I'll be able to go completely legit."

Before she could even consider coming up with an appropriate response, Adam dashed toward the door again. "I'm gonna call Daddy and tell him who I'm having lunch with. He'll shit his pants for sure." He turned back before going out the door. "Grey wanted to make sure you came with me. I'll get Barbara to make reservations. Be ready at noon. Oh, and I realized I forgot to tell you why I came in here before. There's a fundraiser for some charity next Tuesday night at the civic center. DeAnne can't attend, so I'll need you. Be ready at six. We'll have cocktails before."

Feeling as though she'd made major inroads in gaining Adam's trust, she turned her mind to her other dilemma—how to get inside his secure room and find something that would nail the son of a bitch for good.

The solution to getting inside the secure room came from the one person she never thought would be remotely helpful—Adam's wife. Thursday morning, Adam left for an early breakfast meeting, leaving Kennedy to ride into the office alone. She had just stepped into the giant marble foyer when a shaky but determined female voice stopped her. "I suppose you think you're something special to him."

Turning, she faced DeAnne Slater. Since moving in, this was the closest she'd been to Adam's wife. She'd gotten occasional glimpses of her going from room to room like a sad, ghostly apparition. Standing slim and erect, makeup and hair perfect, shoulders so stiff they looked close to breaking, the woman held herself with a proud but fragile dignity.

Kennedy shook her head, easily recognizing the other woman's jealousy and hurt. "I'm nothing to him but an executive assistant…an employee. That's all."

DeAnne mouth twisted in a bitter smile. "That's what they all say at first, but they're lying, just like you are. He won't leave me for you." Her mouth twisted even tighter as she added, "He needs my money too much."

"I assure you, Mrs. Slater. I am not interested in your husband beyond my duties as an assistant."

As if she hadn't heard her, DeAnne nodded to something behind Kennedy. "He'll replace you as easily as I replace those flowers. Every three days a florist brings in new flowers and throws the old ones away. That's what will happen to you…he'll throw you away, too."

Knowing she wouldn't convince the woman, Kennedy murmured a soft, "You're worrying for nothing, Mrs. Slater," and walked out the door.

As she slid into the backseat of the limo, she couldn't help but feel sorry for the woman. Her husband was a slimeball, but it was obvious that she loved him.

She was in the elevator, headed up to her office, when the solution struck her. Could it be done? If there was anyone who had the ability to arrange such a thing, it was Grey Justice.

Friday morning, Kennedy arrived for her meeting at the spa, confident she had the perfect plan. She had thought of little else the last twenty-four hours and was certain this was the easiest and quickest way inside.

Nick had greeted her with a hug and a quick kiss, bringing color to her cheeks. This was the first public display of affection he'd ever given her. Not that this was exactly public. They were meeting in a small, private room at the back of the spa with only Nick, herself and Grey in attendance. Eli hadn't been able to get away.

"Let me get this straight," Grey said. "You want me to send one of my people into Adam's house as a florist employee, break into his secure room, and copy incriminating documents?"

Hearing Grey put her idea into actual words made her plan sound much less brilliant.

"I know that it might be difficult to find someone like that." She shrugged, deflated that her idea hadn't panned out.

"I have at least a half-dozen someones like that."

"Really? So you think—"

He flashed a quick, approving look her way. "I think it's a damn solid idea."

Nick was shaking his head, apparently not agreeing.

"You don't think it's a good idea, Gallagher?"

"Actually, I think it's a great idea, and I have no doubt you have an arsenal of people who could break into the room."

A smile tugged at Grey's mouth. "Not an arsenal but enough. So what don't you like?"

"Any evidence we gather on Adam won't be obtained legally and could be inadmissible in court. Our goal is to nail the bastards for good. The Slaters have their own arsenal, all attorneys, whose number one goal is to make sure they keep their clients out of trouble."

As if a little thing like "inadmissible in court" was barely worth mentioning, Grey said, "You let me worry about that. Let's just get something."

CHAPTER FORTY-ONE

Monday morning, a florist van pulled up in front of Adam Slater's residence, and four people emerged. As was usual, two went inside to dispose of the old flowers and clean up any residue. While this took place, two others would begin the process of bringing in vases of artfully arranged fresh flowers.

Since this same florist had been performing these duties every three days for six years without any issues, the Slater staff paid little attention as they went about their own duties. No one noticed the slender young woman with a large bouquet in her hands disappear down a hallway in the direction of the owner's private office. If anyone had seen her, nothing would have been said. After all, there was a long, narrow table only a few yards from that location, so this was perfectly normal behavior.

Setting the flowers on the table, she took a moment to shift the vase to show the flowers in their best light and then took another second to sniff appreciatively at a perfect rose. Satisfied, she nimbly took the few necessary steps to the keypad she'd been told to look for. Sure enough, there it was. Expert eyes assessed the make, model and style. The realization of its type caused her to huff out a disappointed breath. She had been told to expect anything, but this was beyond a bummer.

She shrugged philosophically…a job was a job. Maybe what was behind the door would offer more of a challenge. With that cheerful thought, she plugged a small device into the top of the pad and in an instant the numbers popped up on the screen. She keyed in the numbers and heard a click. With a slight push, the wall smoothly opened, and she stepped inside.

A quick glance at her watch told her she had seventeen minutes. Plenty of time to find this guy's secrets. With the tune of the theme from the old *Batman* show humming in her mind, she set to work. Within minutes she was huffing her disappointment again. This dude really was kind of pathetic. Apparently, he thought the keypad and concealed door were enough, because he hid nothing away. No locked desk drawers or cabinets, no secret safes to offer any kind of challenge. Heck, the guy didn't even have his computer files password protected.

As a flash drive copied his computer files, her little camera whirred like a dervish as it rapidly photographed page after page of paper files. She paid no attention to what she was copying. Her job was to get everything she could and bring it to her boss. This Slater guy was making it too easy for her to do just that.

She closed the last drawer just as the flash drive indicated all files had been copied. Depositing the small device into her smock pocket, she took a moment to ensure her initial assessment was correct and there were no cleverly hidden safes or compartments. The room was boring and empty…just blah. Still slightly disappointed but comforting herself that she had achieved her assigned task, she pulled back on the wall opening and listened. Assured she was safe, she stepped back into the hallway and closed the panel behind her.

Taking another moment to give the flowers on the hallway table one last sniff, she then strode down the hallway toward the front of the house. She took a deep breath and smiled at the scent of fresh flowers that filled the air. She might live in a dumpy apartment with only an ornery cat as company but she could still appreciate the finer things of life.

The sound of the old *Mission: Impossible* theme now reverberating in her head, she walked out the front door. Pleased that her co-workers had taken up the slack, and their work was done, she slid into the front seat. Turning to her partners, she flashed a sassy grin. "Mission definitely not impossible."

A stack of papers flew across the room, scattering across the expensive Persian rug in Grey's private office. Three grim faces glared down at the pages, all wishing to see something that simply did not exist in them—proof that Adam Slater was neck-deep in corruption and murder.

"Son of a bitch," Gallagher growled as he surged to his feet. "He's going to get away with it."

"We don't know that for sure," Grey said.

Gallagher paced around the room again, something all three of them had taken turns doing over the last couple of hours.

"There's got to be something she missed," Eli said. "There's no way in hell my brother is innocent of all the shit that my family's responsible for. No way in hell. I know to my soul that he ordered the hit on Thomas O'Connell and Milton Ward. The asshole even bragged about it."

"She didn't miss anything, Eli. If anything had been there, Charlie would have found it."

"Then it's over," Gallagher said. "We might as well pull Kennedy out now. The longer she's there, the more dangerous for her."

Not known to be a cheerleader in any form or fashion, Grey searched for uplifting words to boost morale. He pointed to photocopies from a notebook Charlie had found in Adam's desk. "We've got his notes about hiring a hit man. They were made a week before O'Connell was murdered."

Gallagher shook his head. "Take that to the Dallas police, and they'll laugh you out of the building. Hell, he could claim he was writing a book. Other than Adam, everyone we know who was involved in the hit is now dead."

Regretting the death of that bastard killer wasn't something Grey would ever do. "Maybe we can get a confession from Adam. Confront him with these notes. We could record him admitting he did it. There's nothing he likes better than to brag."

Eli shook his head. "Whatever Adam says or does, Mathias will find a way to get him out of trouble. That's one of the reasons I thought getting into his private files was so vital. With a shitload of documents proving his corruption, we might've had a chance. The vague ramblings of a hit man for hire wouldn't raise an eyebrow."

"Then we'll just have to go after Mathias," Grey said. "We always knew Adam was our soft target."

With that statement, what little optimism remaining in the room flatlined. No one believed that the wily, sly Mathias Slater could be caught and prosecuted.

"Kennedy will be at the spa at one o'clock," Grey said. "We need to make some decisions."

"It's not Friday. How'd she get away?" Gallagher asked.

"She and Adam are going to a charity benefit tonight. I had lunch with them yesterday to discuss some of Adam's projects. She made a point of asking for time off in front of me, saying she wanted to get a manicure. He agreed to let her have a few hours off."

His expression back to its usual grimness, Gallagher said, "I'd like to go see her alone, unless either of you have something encouraging to tell her."

Grey shook his head, the hopelessness of their campaign against Adam and Mathias hitting him hard. It was heroic of Gallagher to be the one to tell Kennedy that all the work she'd done was going to be for nothing.

"Tell her we'll keep trying. All is not lost."

"I'll tell her, but understand this." His eyes targeted both Grey and Eli. "Kennedy's part in all of this is officially over. We're not going to use her to come at Adam from a different angle. After today, she's out."

Grey couldn't argue. Their last hope had been breaching Adam's secret office and finding evidence to back up their suspicions. With nothing viable to incriminate him, there was no point in pursuing a dead end.

"Please let her know that her contributions were outstanding. Without her, we never would have gotten this far."

"I'll do that."

Gallagher gave one last look around the room filled with paper files strewn all over the floor and every piece of furniture. "Amazing. Out of all this shit and not one shred of evidence to condemn him. Who knows? Maybe we've got it wrong and Adam is actually one smart bastard."

The instant the door closed, Eli said, "I'm going to confront Mathias tonight."

"You think the time is right?"

"What's the point in waiting?"

"What do you hope to accomplish?"

An unusual bitterness crossed Eli's face. "My hope is the SOB has a heart attack and keels over dead. Barring that, I just want to see his face when he finds out the truth. Mathias isn't used to failure, and this will be the biggest one he's ever had. That, if nothing else, will give both of us a small amount of peace."

Kennedy had never looked so forward to a manicure in all her life. She knew by the wink Grey had given her during lunch yesterday that his people had been able to get inside Adam's secret room. So when she had asked for time off for a manicure in front of him, without a doubt he'd known what she meant. She had to find out what evidence they had uncovered.

Jumping out of the limo, she raced into the spa. The calm atmosphere and soothing music were in complete contrast to the excitement racing through her. Within the next few minutes she would find out if all of this was over. The thought of being able to wake up tomorrow in her own bed, in Nick's arms, had her practically dancing into the small back room where the meetings took place.

"Hey," Nick said.

Unable to control her exuberance, Kennedy launched herself at him. Nick's arms closed around her, held her tight. She took a moment to absorb the delicious feeling of being with the man she loved. Then, unable to stop herself, she pulled away to beam up at him. "So, is it done…is it over? Did we get what we needed?"

If she had been a little less enthusiastic and a little more perceptive, she might have sensed that something hadn't been right the moment she ran into the room. The tenderness on Nick's face melted her heart, but the sadness in his eyes told her something was terribly wrong.

Refusing to panic, she said, "What's wrong?"

"Before I tell you anything, I want you to know you did a great job. No one has been able to get this close to Adam before. I'm proud of you."

"Thanks, but why don't I feel any better? Tell me."

"There was nothing in the office, Kennedy. Not a damn thing other than some vague notes about hiring a hit man. No names were even mentioned."

"That's it?"

"Yes. The young woman who broke in went through his computer files and every paper file. She copied everything he had."

"But there's got to be some kind of proof, Nick. I mean, if he's been in cahoots with his father all these years. All the drug trafficking, money laundering, and murders for hire have got to have some kind of paper trail."

"If it exists, Mathias has it all."

She felt as deflated as a blowout on a worn tire. After all the time and energy they had put into digging up dirt on Adam and now they were back to where they had started—with absolutely nothing.

"What about Adam's notes about a hit man? Aren't they worth something?"

"Justice mentioned he would discuss the matter with a friend at the DA's office. But we agreed that all it would take to make any suspicion disappear is a call from Mathias."

She stumbled backward, grateful that a chair happened to be behind her, though she wasn't sure she would have noticed. She felt numb inside.

Nick went to his knees before her. "Don't look like that, sweetheart. We won't give up. I meant to tell you this the other day and got sidetracked. I quit my job with the Houston PD. I'm going to work for Justice full time, and I won't rest until I get what we need to nail those bastards. I swear I won't."

As she looked into his beautiful face, full of so much love and caring, an odd sort of peace swept over her. Thomas never would have wanted this. He had wanted her to go on with her life, find happiness again. But she hadn't been able to let go...her need to make the people responsible for his death pay for their crimes had

NOTHING TO LOSE | 345

been too strong. And now, even though she hadn't achieved her goal, she didn't regret the decisions she had made. She was a much stronger person than she had been before. She had proved that she could weather any storm.

Someday Mathias and Adam would get in over their heads and not be able to buy their way out or they would die and the devil would take care of their sins. Either way, it was time to let this go.

Taking Nick's face between her hands, she leaned down and pressed a soft kiss to that grim, unsmiling mouth she loved so much. "Thank you, Nick, for being Thomas's best friend and mine."

"What are you saying?"

"I'm saying this is over."

A punch in the gut couldn't have had more impact. What the hell did she mean? "What's over?"

"This need for revenge…for justice. It's time to let go and move on with our lives."

"But I—"

"This clandestine, undercover stuff isn't for me." She grinned. "I think I've proved that."

"You've done a damn good job. Don't sell yourself short."

"I'm not. Even though it didn't turn out as I'd hoped, I'm proud of what I accomplished. But this isn't what I want for my life."

"What do you want?"

"I want what Thomas would have wanted me to have. A normal life, a normal job. I want a family…a marriage, children." She paused and then added breathlessly, "I want those things with you."

He swallowed hard. "With me?"

"Yes, I love you. More than I can ever say…more than I ever believed was possible."

Nick stood, pulled her up with him, and just held her. He had never allowed himself this dream, but oh, how he wanted it.

Releasing her slightly, he pressed a soft kiss to her smiling mouth, savoring her taste. "I'm going to make you so happy...I swear I will."

"You've already started," she whispered softly.

His mouth settled over hers again, and for once in his life Nick let himself believe there really were such things as happy endings.

CHAPTER FORTY-TWO

Would this night never end? Kennedy shifted from one foot to the other, trying to find a comfortable position. The room was overcrowded, the noise almost deafening, and if Adam leaned over and whispered one more time with his bacon-scented breath coating her ear, she was going to explode.

She should have made an excuse and refused to attend tonight's function. If she had gone along with Nick's suggestion of just not returning to her job, she could have been at home, in his arms right now. But she hadn't wanted to raise Adam's suspicions, so she had forced herself to attend. Thankfully, this would be her last event with this man at her side.

"Did I tell you that you look especially enchanting tonight?"

"Yes."

Seeming not to notice her less-than-enthusiastic response to his compliment, he let his eyes roam up and down her body. "There's something different about you. You're practically glowing."

If she responded with the truth and told him that she was in love with a wonderful man and that in just a few hours she would be in his arms where she planned to stay a lifetime, she doubted the news would go over well.

"The spa does wonders for a girl."

"I'll have to tell DeAnne to get over there, then. They'd probably have to keep her a week or two, though."

Why DeAnne Slater loved her husband was a mystery. Instead of appreciating what he had, Adam couldn't stop himself from wanting something new and different. Well aware she might end up walking home, Kennedy couldn't have stopped herself from stating her opinion if she'd wanted. "You're a damn lucky man to have a woman like DeAnne love you."

His eyes wide with insult, he reared back as if she'd slapped him. "I don't believe I need some little nobody from Amarillo telling me anything about my wife."

Nick had been right. She should have refused to come tonight.

"I believe it's time for me to go. I'll get a taxi."

"Don't be ridiculous. Look…I'm sorry I snapped at you. I guess I'm just overly sensitive." He grabbed her hand and squeezed. "Don't be mad."

"I'm not mad. Nevertheless, I would like to go home. I'm getting a headache."

"Okay, fine. I'll call for our car." His lower lip puffed out in an actual pout, reminding her of a five-year-old child. For the first time ever, she felt sorry for this man. He really was a child in a man's body. Unfortunately, he was a very evil child.

"I'll get my coat."

His ear to his cellphone, he didn't bother to acknowledge her comment.

Blowing out a long sigh, Kennedy set her sights on the coat-check counter across the room. Though at least a hundred people separated her from her goal, she comforted herself that the end was in sight. The minute they pulled into Adam's drive, Nick would be behind them. She was already packed. All she needed to do was grab her things, and she would be gone. She planned to tell Adam that she no longer felt suited to be his executive assistant. The little argument they'd just had would actually be helpful.

She grabbed her coat and was on her way to the door when everything blew up in her face.

"Kennedy? My God, Kennedy…is that you?"

Startled, she whirled and faced the woman. Even though almost two years had passed, she looked the same. Dark brown hair pulled into an elegant knot, lively, light green eyes, and the perky little nose that she'd said she hated because it didn't fit her face. She was even wearing the cocktail dress Kennedy had gone shopping with her to buy. Kennedy remembered her grumbling, saying it was a week's salary, but then she had caved, promising to wear it to every social event for the next ten years. Apparently, Julie had kept that promise.

What was she even doing here, in Dallas, at this event? And what was Kennedy supposed to do now?

Panicked, Kennedy turned without a word and started toward the front door again. A hand wrapped around her upper arm and swung her back around.

Going into full Rachel mode, she snapped, "I beg your pardon. Please unhand me."

"Kennedy…it's you." Julie's smooth brow furrowed with confusion, doubt. "Isn't it?"

"I don't know what you're talking about. Now, please, I have to go." Jerking her arm away, she took half a step and ran straight into a frowning, curious Adam.

"Do you know that woman?" he asked.

"No, never saw her before in my life." She rubbed her forehead. "I'm really getting the most horrendous headache. Can we please go?"

Thankfully, Adam's expression was one of irritation, not suspicion. "Yes. The car's outside waiting on us. Let's get out of here."

Weaving in and out of the crowd, they finally made it outside. The limo's back door was already open, and Kennedy practically dived into the dark interior. She couldn't trust that Julie wouldn't follow. Adam slid in across from her and didn't appear to see anything amiss. She was suddenly thankful for the dimwittedness she'd been feeling sorry about only moments before. That could have been a disaster.

As they drove through the darkness, she leaned her head against the cushioned backseat, just wanting to get this night over with and get home to Nick. She glanced out the window and sat up, an awful kind of dread washing over her. "Your driver missed the turn."

"No, he didn't. I need to make a quick stop at my office."

"But I thought we were going home."

"It'll only take a minute. You can stay in the car. What's your problem anyway?"

Get a hold of yourself, Kennedy! "Sorry. My head is pounding." She managed a strained smile. Nick was following behind them. He would see them stop and would wait on them. Nothing had changed. She was just stressed about seeing Julie…that was all.

The fifteen-minute drive to the Slater building seemed interminable. Kennedy kept her head turned, looking out the window. She could see Adam's reflection as he looked out on his side, seemingly lost in thought. They were a mile from the office when she noticed the change. First, he stiffened, and then he turned. She knew what he was going to say before the words came out of his mouth.

"Kennedy. That woman called you Kennedy."

"I don't know what she called me." She shrugged in the careless, arrogant manner she'd seen in Irelyn a hundred times. "I don't know the woman, so it really doesn't matter."

He turned back to the window again. Kennedy couldn't breathe. She knew he was putting things together, and for the life of her, she couldn't come up with a way to stop him.

He turned back to her again. "That cop's wife was named Kennedy."

"What cop?"

"You know exactly who I'm talking about. You're not Rachel Walker. You're that bastard cop's wife."

"I have no idea what you're talking about."

Shaking his head, his hand reached into a small compartment beside him and returned with a gun. "I knew this would come back and bite us in the ass. Cyrus was supposed to kill you and messed up."

Keeping the gun pointed at her, he muttered something to his driver. The man nodded and put a cellphone to his ear.

"Adam, I don't know what—"

"Save it," he snapped.

A thousand thoughts went through her mind, none of them included the solution for how to get out of this without getting shot or killed. She had a gun in her thigh holster. Problem was, she needed to divert Adam's attention so she could retrieve it. Her cellphone was in her coat pocket, but since she hadn't taken the time to put it on, the coat lay beside her. If she could get to her phone, she could press the speed-dial key for Nick.

"I'm cold. Mind if I put my coat on?"

"Jack," Adam shouted. "Turn up the damn heat. Our passenger is cold."

"But I—"

Adam brought the gun within an inch of her face and snarled, "Shut up or I'll do you here."

Kennedy sank back against the seat. What now?

Chapter Forty-three

Eli let himself into his boyhood home. If he'd rung the bell, the butler would have opened the door. If he had called ahead, his mother would have greeted him. He did intend to see his mother before he left, but for right now, he wanted to go in unnoticed.

He stood in the middle of the foyer and took in the familiar fragrances of home. Most people who saw where one of the wealthiest families in the country lived were surprised at its simplicity. The house was half the size of his own home. There was nothing pretentious about Mathias and Eleanor's house. His father was not a collector of anything other than money.

Though their mother had worked hard to make the house a beautiful place to live, the memories here weren't particularly warm or good. Yes, there had been some fun times, but they'd been few and too far between the bad times to make any real impression. For the most part, all he remembered were cold looks and hateful comments, along with the occasional ass-whupping when his father was particularly displeased.

Then his mother would come along and try to soothe everyone's feelings by making excuses for Mathias. The three he remembered the most:

"He's had a hard day at the office."

"You know how riled he gets when you defy him."

"He loves you. He just has a hard time showing his affection."

What a weird pairing his parents had made.

"What are you doing here, boy?"

Eli turned to see his father standing in the doorway of the family room. Not very tall, a little on the thin side, but always larger than life—that was Mathias Slater.

"I wanted to see how Mama's doing."

"Your mama's just fine."

"She didn't seem fine a few weeks ago when she attended the funeral of her youngest son."

Mathias glared. "You'd better not bring that up. I just now got her settled down about it."

"Settled down? You think the death of a child—one who was murdered—is something you can just 'settle down'?" Eli snorted a humorless laugh. "You really are a piece of work, old man."

"You don't come into my home and insult me, boy. Did you not learn your lessons growing up?"

"I learned many lessons, Mathias. One of the most valuable ones was how not to be a lousy father."

"Yeah, you've done so well with your life, haven't you? Married a woman who barely knew her name because of all the shit she poured into her body. Who knows what those children would have been like if she had lived."

"Shelley was ill."

Mathias snorted. "You make excuses for her all you want. She didn't love her children or you either."

"My children are none of your business."

"They're my grandchildren. I've got a right to have a say in how they're raised."

"Like hell you do."

Mathias pointed his finger at him—a gesture Eli remembered all too well from the hundreds of lectures he'd received as a child. "Mark my words, someday you'll come running to me, asking for help, and I won't give a damn."

"You don't give a damn now."

"That's not true, but then again, that was always your problem, Eli. You never wanted to face the truth."

Fury filled Eli, and unable to wait any longer, he shouted, "You sanctimonious asshole. You want to face a truth? Here's one for you." Turning back to the door, he swung it wide and looked out. "Come on in."

The scathing words Mathias had planned froze on his mouth. He watched in horror as a ghost from his past stepped back into his life.

"Hello, old man," Jonah said. "Remember me?"

"Jonah?" a female voice screeched behind them. "Jonah... Is it really you?"

Too shocked to speak, Mathias watched as his wife rushed forward and fell, weeping, into her youngest son's arms.

Mathias gripped the door. He always had a contingency plan. Nothing ever took him by surprise. How the hell had this happened?

Keeping an arm around his weeping mother, Jonah gave Mathias the meanest smile he could ever imagine. Now this was the man Mathias had always wanted to see. For the first time ever, he saw himself in the boy. If he weren't so flabbergasted and speechless, he'd have been laughing his ass off in glee. Finally, the kid had turned into somebody he could be proud to call his own.

Mathias had always prided himself on being flexible when necessary. His smile bright, he said in a booming voice, "Welcome home, son. I can't tell you how happy I am to see you."

"Is that right?" Jonah said. "You look a little shell-shocked to me."

"I gotta admit, I'm surprised, too." Mathias shot a hard look at Eli. "Did you arrange this?"

"Wish I could take credit, but I can't. I didn't know he was alive until several days after his funeral."

"Well then...who...how...?" Dammit, he hated that he was sputtering, but he really didn't understand how this had happened. When he gave orders, they were carried out immediately, to his specifications.

"The day before I was to be…" Jonah frowned. "What's the terminology you people use? Terminated? I had a visit from an old friend of yours—Cyrus Denton."

"Cyrus?" Even to Mathias's ears, his voice sounded strained. The one man he'd trusted for years to take care of his problems had betrayed him in the worst way possible. He was going to have the bastard drawn and quartered and then have him blasted six ways to Sunday.

Jonah went on, still wearing that mean-looking grin. "Yes, Cyrus. He explained what was supposed to go down, but said he couldn't let it happen. He even admitted to being responsible for carrying out several executions, but the thought of setting up the termination of a family member wasn't something he could condone. He arranged for a replacement body—some poor sucker, a John Doe, who'd been killed in a hit-and-run a couple of days before. Since I believe you indicated you wanted me to learn a very harsh lesson, the guy's mutilated corpse worked well."

"Mathias? What on earth is he talking about?"

Eleanor was looking at him in horror, like he was some kind of freak. Mathias forced a smile to his stiff lips. "Now, Nora, you know these boys are just pranking us. Don't tell me you believe any of these ridiculous allegations."

A fiery glare took in both of his sons. "You boys tell your mama that you're just fooling."

His arm around his mother, Jonah looked down, shaking his head. "I'm sorry as I can be, Mama, but you can't keep your head in the sand any longer. You're married to a monster."

"Stop it!" Mathias shouted. "You hush your mouth this instant." He softened his voice when he looked at his wife. "Nora, honey. Why don't you go lie down? Somehow or other, these boys have got it in their heads that their father is guilty of all sorts of terrible stuff. I'll get it straightened out…I promise."

Giving him the sweet smile he'd fallen in love with years ago, she nodded. "I think I will lie down for a while." She hugged Jonah again. "I'm so happy to see you, son."

The room went silent. Mathias saw the pitying look the boys gave their mama as she left the room. They thought there was something wrong with her, loving a man like him. Neither one of them knew what love even meant.

The instant he knew Nora was out of earshot, Mathias snarled, "You've gone and done it now. The one thing I've tried all my married life to prevent is your mama from being hurt. Sometimes a man has to handle messy details of business, but I've always tried to protect Nora from the hard stuff. There's no telling what kind of damage you've done to her."

Jonah shook his head. "You are such a piece of work. Acting like you love her when the only thing that's ever mattered to you is the almighty dollar."

"That almighty dollar paid for braces for your teeth, a snazzy car at fifteen, and a college degree from that fancy university you just had to attend. I sure didn't hear you complaining about those dollars then."

"If I had known about the backs of good men you had to step on and destroy to earn that money, I damn well wouldn't have accepted a dime from you."

"You don't get it, do you, Jonah? This is life. You provide for your family, you protect the woman you love, and you raise your children to survive and succeed. That's what my daddy did… That's what I did. And when you finally find somebody worthy of you, that's what you'll do."

Jonah took a step toward him, fire in his eyes. "Don't you ever…ever talk to me about Teri. I know you had her killed, you son of a bitch."

"You think I'm going to deny that? That piece of trash was good for only one thing and—"

Jonah lunged toward him. Eli tackled the boy, keeping him from making a major mistake. "You'd better thank your lucky stars your candy-assed brother stopped you, son. Around here, we don't disrespect our elders like that."

A wild-eyed Eli snarled, "Shut the hell up, Mathias, or I'll let him beat the shit out of you."

Laughter bubbled in his chest. "Oh…so my boy Eli's finally got a backbone, too. Maybe getting rid of Shelley actually did help you grow up."

Eli froze. Had Mathias just said what Eli thought he'd said? Dropping his arms from his brother, he turned and faced his father. He was barely aware that Jonah was now holding on to him.

"What did you say?" Eli whispered.

Biting his pursed lip, Mathias shrugged. "Guess the cat's out of the bag now." He shook his head. "She had to go, son. Surely you knew that. She wasn't Slater material. So damn sickly and weak... The woman never could've raised those girls right."

Still not fully comprehending the awfulness of Mathias's words, Eli asked hoarsely, "What did you do?"

"Nothing really. I just sent Adam over there with a bottle of booze and some sedatives. He was supposed to offer them to her, to prove to you that she loved them more than she loved you or her children. Next thing I know, he's calling me, squalling like a baby because she was deader than a doornail."

Mathias shrugged as if it didn't matter...as if he'd run a stop sign, committed some minor traffic offense, instead of having commissioned a cold-blooded murder. He'd had his own daughter-in-law killed.

A blinding red haze washed over Eli's vision. He knew his feet were moving, but all he could focus on was the need to purge the world of the sick son of a bitch standing before him.

Large hands grabbed him, pulled at him. Eli shrugged them off, kept moving forward.

"No, Eli, you can't."

Recognizing Jonah's voice, Eli shook his head, tried to pull away. "It's time he dies, Jonah."

"I know that, but you can't do it, and neither can I. We'll make him pay somehow but not this way. Damned if either of us are going to prison for putting the son of a bitch away."

"Nora...what the hell are you doing? Put that thing away."

Eli and Jonah turned simultaneously. Eleanor Slater stood several feet away, a pistol firmly clutched in her hands.

"Mama! No!" Jonah shouted.

Eli tried to reach her...too late. The gun exploded. Mathias's face was one of shocked dismay as he clutched his chest and then slammed backward onto the floor.

Life went into surreal slow motion. Eli reached his mother, took the gun from her shaking hands and held her tight against his chest. He looked over at Jonah who was holding a limp Mathias in his arms. The look on his brother's face confirmed his fears. Their father was dead.

He might have wanted to see the bastard die, but never like this.

His mother buried her face against Eli's chest. Her words broke his heart as in a voice that was soft, low and incredibly sad, she said, "All these years I've made excuses for him. I just couldn't do it anymore."

Holding her close, Eli rocked her in his arms, whispered reassurances, and tried to figure out just what the hell they were going to do now.

CHAPTER FORTY-FOUR

Nick switched off the engine on his motorcycle and coasted in silence for several yards. For whatever reason, the limo had detoured and gone to the Slater building, parking at the front door. Kennedy had said nothing about plans to go there after she and Adam left the fundraiser. So what the hell was going on?

Powerful streetlamps lit up the entire parking lot, so finding a shadowy area to hide wasn't easy. He parked his bike then ducked behind a large bush. The driver's door of the limo swung open, but no one exited. Then the back passenger door came open, and Nick saw the top of Kennedy's head as she got out. Adam followed close behind her.

Cursing himself for not bringing binoculars with him, he squinted, trying to see the expression on Kennedy's face. It was too damn far and dark. Both she and Adam entered the building, disappearing from his view.

This wasn't right. There was no good reason for Adam and Kennedy to be at this place and so late. He stepped out from behind the bush. Time to put his Grimm persona to good use.

He halted as another car swung into the parking lot and parked right beside the limo. A tall, thickly built man emerged, took a moment to say something to the limo driver and then strode into the building. The limo drove slowly away.

Shit. Nick took off toward the building, his heart in his throat. This was no ordinary stop…Kennedy was in trouble. Reaching the front door, Nick went inside, thankful no one had locked the door. Just as he entered, the cellphone in his jacket vibrated. A look at the screen showed him it was Kennedy calling.

Hoping that was a good sign, Nick activated his earbud, was about ask her what the hell was going on, when he heard his worst nightmare already in progress.

Thankful that Adam hadn't objected to her bringing her coat, Kennedy had been able to slip her hand in the pocket and press the key for Nick.

Adam pushed her forward, and she stumbled, only halfway acting. Running in stilettos hadn't been in Irelyn's lesson plans. Wanting to alert Nick to what was happening, she snapped, "Adam, holding a gun on me is totally unacceptable behavior. I demand to know what the hell is going on."

His hand swung out, slapped her hard across the face. "Shut up or I swear I'll kill you here."

Only by sheer luck was she able to stay upright. The blow to her face stung, but Adam gave her no time to recover. He pushed her into the elevator and pressed the button for the forty-second floor.

"Why are we going to your office on the forty-second floor?" She winced inwardly. Had that been too obvious?

She was once again grateful for Adam's lack of intelligence as he answered her without any hesitation. "We're going to wait there till someone comes to take care of you."

In what seemed like only seconds, they had arrived at Adam's office, and he was pushing her into the lobby. Nodding at a chair in the plush waiting area, he said, "Sit down. Get comfortable."

Kennedy dropped into a chair and looked around at her empty, elegant surroundings. She turned back to Adam, who had seated himself across from her. Everything seemed so calm and normal. They could've been two people conversing about business or world politics. The only anomaly was the pistol pointed directly at her head.

She'd love to get to her gun. Strapped to her outer thigh, its weight was reassuring but frustrating. So far, whipping the weapon out from beneath her dress without attracting his attention had been impossible. His eyes had been locked on her since he'd pulled his gun. So for right now, she could only continue to play his game until he took his eyes off her.

She huffed out an angry breath. "Adam, for the last time, I don't care who you think I am. My name is Rachel Walker, and I'm from Amarillo."

"Problems?"

Both she and Adam turned at the sound of a male voice. A tall, heavy-set man strode toward them, the gun in his bear-claw hand twice the size of Adam's. Her heart dropped. She might have been able to disarm Adam, but no way could she handle this man.

"You must've been in the area," Adam said.

"I'm never far away," the man said. "You should know that by now."

"Who are you?" Kennedy asked the question, already knowing the answer—hard to forget the voice of a man who had tried to kill her. She was surprised she had the ability to speak at all. And though she sounded a little shaky, she was encouraged to hear the steel behind the words.

"Cyrus Denton." He shook his head, real regret in his eyes. "Mrs. O'Connell… it is you. You look very different at a distance, but up close, I can definitely see the resemblance."

Seeing no reason to continue to deny her identity—even if they decided they'd made a mistake, neither of them intended for her to leave the building alive.

"You're the man who ran me off the road and stole the packet Thomas left me."

Adam released a weird crowing sound. "I knew it!"

As if Adam wasn't there, Cyrus kept his focus on Kennedy. "Why didn't you just forget about it like I told you? If you had, none of this would be happening now."

Fury overriding her fear, she sprang to her feet and glared up at him. "My husband was murdered. I lost my child. You think those are things I could just forget?"

"Out of all the jobs I've handled for the Slaters, killing you was one of the most unpleasant tasks I'd ever been assigned. That's why I let you go. I admire your courage and devotion to your late husband and child. Unfortunately, they're going to get you killed."

"Wait a minute," Adam said. "You told me the wreck was so bad, you thought she was dead. If you let her go, then you knew she wasn't hurt. This is all your fault."

Denton turned to Adam. "Shut up, idiot. It was your screw-up to begin with. Ever wonder why that was the first and last termination Mathias assigned to you? Because everything you touch turns to shit."

Eyes and mouth both gaped open in astonishment. "You can't talk to me that way. My daddy—"

"Your daddy knows exactly what happened. If you had let me handle things when we first learned about those stolen papers, none of this would have been necessary."

"I didn't have enough facts."

"One of these days you'll learn that if you wait till you have all the facts, you've missed your chance. Course, by then, it'll probably be too late again."

Cyrus pointed to the elevator with his gun. "Let's go, Mrs. O'Connell."

"Where are you taking her?"

"What does it matter? I'm taking care of your problems like I always have."

"So…like…are you going to shoot her or what?"

As if he were explaining a complicated matter to a child, he said, "First, I need to find out who's involved in this with her."

"How are you going to do that?"

"You want details?"

"No…I guess not."

"You stay here. I'll be back—" His eyes narrowed, focusing on something behind her.

Kennedy turned and almost cried out. The security monitor on the receptionist's desk showed the front lobby, where Nick was standing at the bank of elevators, violently punching numbers with one hand, his Glock in his other hand.

"Good thing I disabled all but one freight elevator." His eyes swung back to Kennedy. "Looks like we know of at least one other person involved."

"That's her ex-boyfriend," Adam explained. "Grimm something or other. I had him checked out. He's evil looking but fairly harmless."

"Just like you had Rachel Walker checked out?" Cyrus taunted.

Throwing him a hateful glare, Adam slammed his mouth shut.

"There are a whole lot more than two people involved," she assured him. "Just you wait. An entire arsenal of people will be here soon."

"Then I guess I'd better take care of the two of you real fast. Adam, keep your gun on her at all times. I'm going to take care of her friend, then I'll be back to get the girl."

"You don't think you should just go ahead and shoot her here?"

"You want to explain the blood to your employees tomorrow?"

"No."

"Then keep her here till I get back." And because he obviously thought his employer's son was an imbecile, he nodded toward the gun in Adam's hand. "You have bullets in there, right?"

"Of course," he snapped. "At least I think so."

Rolling his eyes, Cyrus pulled another gun from his pocket, unlocked the safety, and handed it to Adam. "Put yours away and use this one. Just don't shoot yourself."

He turned and strode toward the freight elevator in the corner.

Only by reminding herself that Nick was a trained professional was she able to sit still and watch the man walk away. If she tried to go after him, she had no doubt he would kill her and wouldn't even have to use his gun. She closed her eyes and prayed with all her might for Nick's safety. She could not bear to lose him…she couldn't.

"Sit down," Adam said. "Looks like we're going to be here awhile longer."

Kennedy turned her attention back to the man who had ordered Thomas's death. A sudden, inexplicable calm swept through her. Earlier today, she had accepted that the lack of incriminating evidence against Adam meant he would never pay for Thomas's death. But she had a chance to change that. Her cellphone had a microphone. A recorded confession, along with Adam's notes bragging about hiring a hit man, would be impossible to dispute.

Nick would have heard that Denton was on his way down. He would know what to do. Now it was her turn.

Returning to her chair, a shiver, only partially an act, visibly swept through her. Gathering the coat in her lap closer to her, she slipped her hand in her pocket and hit the record button on the side of the phone.

She took an imperceptible, bracing breath to steady herself and faced the man who had destroyed her life. "You won't get away with killing me."

"Of course I will."

"How many people have you killed?"

"Me?" He looked slightly amused. "No one personally. I mean, it's not like I have a six-shooter and go around shooting people. I run several multibillion-dollar companies. My time is limited."

Actually other people ran the companies for him. From what she could tell, Adam went around making bad investments, losing money and then schmoozing people hoping to recoup his losses. She held her tongue. Telling him what she thought about his business skills would have only put him on the defensive. The boastful side of Adam would get her what she needed.

"So you just have other people kill for you."

"Something like that. Your husband and that sleazy mole from our accounting firm were actually my first termination assignment."

Yes, this is where she wanted him to go. "You're the one who ordered my husband's death?"

"Yes. Quite an empowering moment, if I do say so myself."

Fighting the urge to hurl herself at him and pummel his face into a bloody mess, she asked, "How did you know about Thomas's investigation?"

He made a casual wave of his gun. "We've got informants everywhere. When we first heard about O'Connell, we weren't really worried. The man could find nothing. Then that sleazebag snitch Milton Ward contacted your husband. We had no choice but to take both of them out. And despite Cyrus's opinion, everything worked out just fine. With the exception of you dying, that is. But that was his fault, not mine."

She had what she needed. Now it was time to escape and find Nick. Calling on one of the more amusing acting lessons Irelyn had given her, Kennedy whispered truthfully, "I hate you," then covered her face with her hands and began to sob uncontrollably. The noise sounded authentic to her, but was Adam buying it? She dared a peek through her fingers. Irelyn had told her tears made men uncomfortable, and sure enough, Adam was squirming in his seat, looking lost, helpless and completely out of his element. Apparently, this trick worked even on conscienceless criminals.

"Could you get me some tissue?"

"There's some right behind you."

Kennedy turned. He was right. There was a box of tissues behind her, along with a wooden statue of Venus. She bent down but instead of the tissue, she grabbed the statue, whirled and slammed it against the gun in his hand, knocking it to the floor.

Adam cursed, grabbing for the gun. Kennedy dashed toward the stairway door, cringing when bullets whizzed by her. He had recovered the gun sooner than she'd expected. Another bullet whooshed by, inches from her face, and slammed into the wall beside her.

Kennedy jerked the door open and dove. Soaring through the air, she landed on her side, halfway down the stairs. Ignoring the pain of her bruised hip, she took a second to pull the gun from her thigh holster and slip out of her shoes.

Springing to her now bare feet, she took off down the stairway.

CHAPTER FORTY-FIVE

Hidden behind the giant desk in the foyer, Nick tried to suppress his rising panic as he waited for Cyrus Denton to arrive. In the middle of Kennedy's conversation with Adam, which included him admitting he'd ordered the hit on Thomas, there had been some kind of scuffle. Nick had heard a man grunt and rapid footsteps. The terrifying sound of several shots being fired. And then nothing. No words, no sounds. Had Kennedy been shot? Was she lying on the floor somewhere, bleeding out, while he waited for this asshole to show up?

A voice rumbled behind him. "Okay, slowly stand up, drop your gun. Put your hands in the air."

Jaw locked with frustration and fear for Kennedy, Nick stood and put the gun beside him on the desk.

"Now, don't be stupid. Take your left hand and push the gun toward me."

When Nick complied, he added, "Bend down and with your left hand, take the gun from your ankle holster."

"I don't have a gun at my ankle."

"Lift your pant legs, let me see."

Nick pulled at his pant legs to show he had no hidden weapons at his ankles.

"Huh…I'm surprised. I figured you for a guy who would've been better prepared. Okay, let's head over to the elevators. There's a little lady I think you'll be happy to see…at least for a few minutes until I have to kill you both."

Nick kept his hands up, but instead of moving forward, he slowly turned to face the man.

"Dammit, I told you—" Denton's eyes went wide. "Well, I'll be damned... you're that cop I shot."

Of all the things he'd thought the guy would say, this hadn't been one of them.

"Thanks for telling me." Nick gave an arrogant nod. "That'll just make me doubly glad when I kill you."

The big man grinned his approval. "I like a man with confidence." He jerked his head toward the long bank of elevators. "Let's get going...they're working now."

Denton was a professional killer. Nick wasn't about to underestimate him, but neither was he going to follow the guy's commands. This ended here.

Hands still in the air, Nick twisted sideways and went for his gun on the counter. Denton got there first, grabbed the gun. Nick landed on the other side of the counter. Squatted down, he waited for his opportunity.

"Now that was a damn stupid move. Get up asshole...it's time for you to die."

Pulling the gun he'd tucked underneath his jacket at the small of his back, Nick surged to his feet. "You first." Firing, he put one round in Denton's forehead, one in his chest. The man fell back like a giant oak.

He grabbed the dead man's gun, retrieved his weapon from the floor and then made a mad dash to the elevators. His fist pounded the Up button as he whispered urgently, "Come on...come on..."

Pulling out his cellphone, he pressed speed-dial for Justice. The instant the man answered, Nick said quickly, urgently, "I need backup at Slater Enterprises."

"Sending help now."

Nick pocketed his phone, glared up at the elevator lights. Why the hell did the elevator have to take so long? Should he go ahead and just try for the stairs? He could—

Rapid gunfire sounded. He whirled. The stairs! It was coming from the stairs. Taking off like a madman, Nick skidded to a stop at the entrance to the stairs. He jerked open the door and took off up the stairway. More gunfire erupted, and then the most horrifying sound of all spiraled down to him: a blood-curdling scream of agony.

Kennedy raced down the hallway, grabbed hold of a door, twisted the knob. Locked, dammit. She took off again. She was now on the thirty-fifth floor, having made it seven floors down before Adam caught up with her. He'd shot at her three times, missed twice. That gun she'd been so proud to have in her hand had flipped from her fingers the instant she'd been shot. She had managed to get away from him, but fire burned in her right shoulder, blood trickled down her arm, which was becoming increasingly useless. And she had no weapon.

She came to another door, jiggled the handle. Locked again. Dammit, didn't anyone leave their door open in this place?

A squeak sounded from behind her, and she glanced over her shoulder, saw the stairway door opening. He'd found her. She turned a corner, saw another door, said a prayer and reached for the door handle, which twisted and came open. Closing the door softly behind her, she had little time to explore her surroundings. Though the room was dark, she noticed the small light of a soda dispenser. No wonder she had been able to get inside...this was a break room. She fitted herself between a cabinet and a vending machine, stooped down and waited.

Adam's quick footsteps sounded in the hallway. His voice, loud and wheedling, sent shudders through her body. "Ken...na...dy! Where are you? Come on out, hon, and let's settle this once and for all. I know you're dying to see your wimp of a husband and that little baby you lost. Just think, all you have to do is walk out into the hallway, and it'll all be over. Then you can live happily ever after." Laughter rang out. "Oops, I mean die happily ever after."

She knew the taunts were supposed to enrage her so she would make a mistake. Nothing the evil bastard said could hurt her. She had been through hell...lost everything she held most dear, but she had survived, found life again and a wonderful man to share it with. This loathsome creature would not steal anything more from her.

So she waited…held her breath. She tried not to think about Nick. He was trained and fit. He knew how to handle himself. He would survive—there was no other option. She just needed to find a way to get away from Adam, and then Nick would take care of him.

Footsteps were right outside the door. Kennedy froze in place, barely breathing.

Adam paused for an instant, and then he moved away. Seconds later, she heard his loud sigh and then, "Well, I guess she's on another floor," and then footsteps again as if he were moving farther away. She heard the slam of the stairway door.

His actions reminded her of a child playing hide-and-go-seek, trying to make a playmate believe he had given up and moved on. So she waited.

Dizziness assailed her…she had to get something on her shoulder to stop the bleeding or she would pass out. Grateful her eyes had adjusted to the dim lighting, she spotted a stack of napkins on one of the tables. She crawled to the table, grabbed the napkins and tucked a wad under her sleeve.

Nausea threatened, but she fought it for all she was worth. The pain was nothing compared to losing Nick…she needed to get to him. Adam had to have gone to another floor by now. She could wait no longer.

Cautiously, she opened the door and peeked out. No sound. Quickly, quietly, she targeted the exit sign above the stairway door. If Adam was on the stairs, waiting for her, she'd have to duck back out quickly, but she had no choice but to move.

She opened the door, listened intently…still no sounds. Taking a chance, she ran down the stairs. Her head spun, the steps blurred before her, but she made herself continue. To keep herself focused on staying upright, she ticked off the floor number with each level she reached—twenty-five, twenty-four.

Where was Adam? Was he searching each floor? She could only hope. Sixteen… fifteen… Had Nick taken care of Denton yet? Was he on the elevator, headed up to Adam's office? How long ago had he called for help?

Tenth floor…nine more to go. She could do this. Her arm was bleeding profusely now…she'd lost the napkins somewhere. The blurred red of an exit sign danced over her head, taunting her…inviting her to go inside, rest for a bit. Not yet, not yet.

Fifth floor, four more to go. She could do this, she could do this. Think of Nick. He was waiting for her…he loved her…

Fourth floor…three more to go.

On the third-floor landing, the door surged open. Adam stood at the entrance, his mouth stretched in an evil, devilish grin. Creepy, dead-like eyes gleamed with an inhuman malevolence. "Ha…ha…ha…caught ya!" He raised the gun slowly as if savoring the final moment.

Oh hell no. She had come too far, lost too much, to let this bastard win. She caught sight of a fire extinguisher hanging from the wall. With superhuman strength and the roar of a furious woman who would not be defeated, Kennedy grabbed the cylinder and swung it around. She wasn't aiming at anything in particular but managed to knock the gun from his hand.

Adam yelped and dove for the gun. Kennedy swung again, aiming for his head, only hit his chest but managed to keep him from the gun. With a growling curse, he lunged toward her. She swung again, caught his shoulder in a glancing blow. He stumbled back and then surged forward once more.

Aware that her strength was almost at an end, Kennedy drew on every bit of fury and anger she had within her to raise the cylinder again. "This is for my husband and baby, you son of a bitch."

She slammed the extinguisher into his face. Blood spurted, splattering against the walls and all over her. His eyes rolled back in his head, and Adam fell hard, onto his back.

Breathless but triumphant, she stood over the man, who, without any conscience or remorse, had taken everything from her. His eyes were half open, his mouth and nose a bloody mess. He looked weak, pitiful—not a man but a willing pawn for his even more evil father. She searched for compassion, forgiveness. Found none.

"And this one's for me." Even though her strength was almost gone, she found enough to lift the extinguisher once more and slam the base into Adam's groin. His squeal of agony bounced against the walls, echoing skyward in the empty staircase.

"Kennedy!"

Her breath coming in fits and spurts, she looked down to see Nick racing up the stairs, fire blazing in his eyes.

Giddy with triumph and blood loss, she grinned. "We did it," and pitched forward, unconscious, into his arms.

CHAPTER FORTY-SIX

Sunshine brightened the interior of the oversized hospital room. Brilliant bouquets of flowers covered every flat surface. The outpouring of good wishes from friends, old and new, along with people they didn't even know, was overwhelming and surprising. Who knew so many people would be happy to see Adam Slater go down?

Nick sat in a chair beside Kennedy, who was lying on the hospital bed. Other than the times she was attended to by nurses or doctors, he hadn't released hold of her. Didn't plan to ever again.

The nightmare of her covered in blood, collapsing in his arms, wasn't something he'd get over this century or the next. Most of that blood had come from Adam, who had been in the stairwell above them, where Kennedy had left him bloodied and rolling around on the floor, crying for his daddy.

Thankfully her arm injury was just a flesh wound, but she'd lost a fair amount of blood. The bruise on her cheek was minor, too, and for that alone Nick wished he'd had the chance to spend a few minutes of quality time with Adam Slater. Kennedy had made that unnecessary as she'd definitely taught the man a lesson he was never likely to forget.

The gunshot wound, along with the trauma she'd endured, prompted the doctors to insist she stay a couple of days in the hospital. Being able to hide here was a blessing since news reporters were clamoring to talk to the woman who had uncovered a mountain of Slater corruption.

The explosion of events over the last twelve hours had left all of them reeling. Mathias was dead, Adam had been arrested, and Jonah Slater was alive. The entire Slater empire had been turned upside down, and much of it was due to the delicate and lovely woman beside him.

"Do you think I should call Julie?"

Out of all the things that had happened, seeing Julie again was the one thing Kennedy seemed the most focused on.

"When you're feeling better, we'll go see her."

"I feel so badly for treating her that way, but I had no choice."

"And I'm sure she'll understand that."

"What in the world was she doing here in Dallas anyway?"

Since he didn't want to spoil a surprise that he hoped would be happening soon, he shrugged and said vaguely, "Must've been the fundraiser. Remember I told you she had been elected to some charity boards?"

Kennedy nodded. "I guess so. I just hate that I was so rude to her. I just didn't know what else to do."

About to reassure her again, he stopped abruptly when the television attached to the wall across from them showed the face of Mathias Slater. Nick grabbed the remote and turned up the volume.

"The state…the entire country is mourning the loss of multibillionaire Mathias Slater, who was found murdered in his home last night with a gunshot wound to his chest. No suspects have been arrested, but there is strong speculation that a longtime employee, Cyrus Denton, was responsible for his death.

"In an apparently unrelated event, Denton was reportedly shot to death in an attempt to kill Nick Gallagher, a former Houston homicide detective, who was working undercover. There are unconfirmed reports that Gallagher was on special assignment with the Dallas Police Department.

"Additionally, Adam Slater, son of Mathias, has been arrested on drug-trafficking charges. As our viewers may remember, three years ago Jonah Slater, Adam Slater's youngest brother, was tried and convicted of smuggling drugs into the United States from El Salvador and was sentenced to twenty years in prison. A source close to the investigation has revealed that evidence was found in Adam Slater's office showing that he framed his brother for the crime and was the actual perpetrator.

"Jonah Slater was believed to have been murdered in prison only a few weeks ago, but in a stunning development, it has been revealed that his death was faked. Though Slater was rearrested, he is out on bond and is reportedly at an undisclosed location with the rest of his family.

"Adam Slater has also been charged with conspiracy to commit murder of Houston Police Detective Thomas O'Connell, who was killed two years ago in what was thought to be an armed robbery attempt. Additional charges linking Slater to the murder of three young men of the Delano gang in Houston are pending. We will continue to keep you updated as more developments are uncovered.

"Now, for a look at today's weather, let's go to…"

Nick clicked mute on the remote and glanced over at Kennedy. She was still too damn pale for his liking, but her bright smile reassured him.

"I still can't believe Jonah is alive. Did you know about it?"

Nick shook his head. "Had no idea. I talked to Justice last night. He got the information a week or so ago and shared it with Eli. They wanted to keep it to themselves until we could get what we needed on Adam."

"Where on earth did the police get all that evidence on Adam? We searched every place we knew to look."

"That's a question even Adam is asking," a male voice said.

Their eyes turned to the door, where Grey Justice stood, holding a large fruit basket. He squeezed his gift between a potted plant and a bouquet of daisies, then turned to Kennedy. "How are you feeling?"

"A little sore but incredibly, astoundingly, fabulously wonderful, too."

"You did an outstanding job." He shot Nick a glance. "You both did."

"How's Adam?" Kennedy asked.

"Broken nose, three chipped teeth, busted mouth, cracked ribs, along with an agonizing groin injury he's going to feel for weeks. He's on the second floor, handcuffed to his hospital bed and crying for his daddy."

Nick had no sympathy for the bastard. If it had been his choice, Adam would have been rotting in hell with Mathias.

"So, where did the evidence on Adam come from?"

"No one seems to know. My sources tell me files detailing numerous illegal activities were in plain sight at all three of his offices, including the secret one he thought no one could find."

"You have some theories?" Nick asked.

"Yes. Both Eli and I think that Mathias had the evidence planted. Adam had earned his father's displeasure by losing over two million dollars. Mathias was nothing if not creative in the punishment of his sons who displeased him."

"So he was going to frame Adam?" Kennedy said.

"Looks like it. Since Jonah was dead, Mathias probably got a kick from the ironic twist. He could use the same crime and frame his other son, too."

Kennedy nodded. "And he could also get all sorts of sympathy for having a son who had been convicted of a crime he didn't commit and then murdered. That's the kind of publicity he would have eaten up."

"Exactly," Justice said.

"That was one sick bastard," Nick said.

"Yes, but no longer physically sick. Apparently, the real reason he went out of the country last month was for an experimental treatment. It worked."

"Meaning he felt free to punish his son since he was going to live," Nick said.

"That's the theory. Hard to know for sure what was going on in his devious mind."

"So why did Cyrus Denton kill Mathias? Does anyone know?" Kennedy asked.

"The dead tell no tales," Justice said. "Evidence suggests they had a falling out, and Denton shot Mathias in the chest. There were no witnesses."

His cop's instinct kicked hard. "What evidence?" Nick said.

Justice looked him straight in the eyes. "Several of the servants said they heard the two shouting, then a gunshot. Mathias was found dead on the floor, and Denton was nowhere in sight."

As a homicide detective, Nick had investigated too many murders to accept such threadbare details. Justice was a damn good poker player but was hiding something. Who was he protecting? Had Jonah killed his father in retribution for Teri Burke's death?

"I'm sure Eleanor and DeAnne Slater are in shock," Kennedy said. "How are they holding up?"

"About as well as you could imagine under the circumstances. Even though Mathias was responsible for so much death and destruction, bringing all of that out in the open would serve no purpose. Eleanor has suffered enough already. What's done is done. Mathias is in hell where he belongs."

"So what happens, now? Will Jonah be completely exonerated?"

"Not yet, but he will be soon. With the evidence Mathias so kindly provided for us, Adam will be charged with those crimes, along with being responsible for your husband's murder. The recording you made of his confession sealed his fate on that."

"What about those three gang members the news reporter mentioned?" Kennedy asked. "Why were they killed?"

"That was my last case before I was shot," Nick said. "I suspected it wasn't just a gang shooting but could never uncover what happened. One of the men—Frankie Chavez—was a friend of Jonah's, wasn't he, Justice?"

"No. He was a low-life snitch for Cyrus Denton, but when Adam didn't get everyone out of the way as quickly as his father thought he should have, Mathias ordered the kid killed, along with two of his friends."

"So, basically, Mathias cleaned up his son's mess and cleaned house," Nick said.

"So it seems."

Though it galled that Mathias Slater would never pay publicly for his crimes, Nick had never been happier over someone's death. The bastard's evil reign was finally over.

Justice glanced at his watch. "I've got an appointment across town, so I'll leave you two alone. When things settle down and you're feeling better, Kennedy, I'd like to discuss some employment opportunities. If you're interested."

She glanced over at Nick and smiled. "Thank you, but I think my undercover days are over."

"There are lots of other opportunities that don't involve undercover work. Specialty jobs I think you would enjoy."

"Then, yes, I'd definitely like to talk with you."

"Excellent." He put his hand on the door and then glanced back over his shoulder. "By the way, there's a young woman outside who seems rather anxious to see you."

"Irelyn?"

A bleak look appeared in the man's eyes for barely a second. "No. It's someone you didn't get to speak with last night."

Nick released a relieved breath and smiled his appreciation. He'd made the call early this morning but wasn't sure it would work out. Justice had used his contacts to uncover the hotel where the one person he knew Kennedy was dying to see was staying.

The instant the door opened, a frazzled-looking, sobbing Julie rushed into the room. Her arms open wide, she squealed, "Kennedy…I knew it was you!"

Feeling like a brand new person, Kennedy parked in her driveway and allowed herself a moment to savor the sensation. A day at the spa doing nothing other than "spa" things had done wonders. Two nights at the hospital plus an emotional reunion with Julie, followed by several exhaustive days of police and news reporter interviews had taken their toll. Last night, when Nick had presented her with a complimentary spa day, she'd practically screamed with gratitude.

The massage, facial, mani-pedi, mud bath, and herbal skin treatment had left her skin glowing, her muscles relaxed and her energy renewed, but it was the hair treatment that she was the most excited about. What would Nick think?

The instant the door opened, she knew something had changed. What, she didn't yet know, but there was a different atmosphere. She took three steps into her foyer and skidded to a stop. Nick stood at the entrance to her living room. She'd never seen that look on his face before—a mixture of uncertainty, nerves, and love.

"Did you enjoy your day?"

She beamed at him. "It was wonderful. Thank you."

"Your hair. You changed it back."

Self-conscious, she touched her newly darkened tresses. Though still short, she loved returning to her natural color. "Do you like it? Or do you prefer a blonde?"

"I prefer you any way I can get you. But I'm glad to see your natural color."

"It feels good to be getting back to normal." She frowned and looked around. Everything seemed the same but not. "What's going on?"

"I did something today. If you don't like it, we can change it back."

"You do know there's nothing you could do that would make me love you less. Right?"

His cocky grin returned. "Good to know."

Backing away from her, he said, "Come on in."

More curious than ever, she went toward him and then stopped at the entrance to her living room. Where before it had been sparsely furnished and decorated, the room was now full. But not just full…it was full of her home from Houston. The things she'd had to leave behind when she'd left. The grandfather clock that had hung in the entry way was now over her mantel, the large screen television and DVD player from her living room now sat in the corner. Three boxes of books had been placed in front of the bookshelves, just waiting to be categorized and shelved.

Her throat threatening to close with emotion, she said huskily, "You've been busy."

"We never talked about it, but I figured you had your stuff put in storage." He shrugged. "I wanted to give you back as much as I could. Most of the stuff I had moved to a storage facility about five miles from here, but I had a few things delivered I thought you might like."

"How did you know where to look?"

"Not too many people in Houston have the name Casper Scooby."

Casper the Friendly Ghost and *Scooby-Doo* had been her favorite cartoons when she was a child, before she'd lost her parents. When she had arranged for her house to be emptied and her things stored, she had used those two names as much for comfort as anything else.

"There's so much you know about me. Things I barely remember myself."

"There's a whole lot more I want to know…if you'll let me."

"And there's tons more I want to know about you."

Wickedness in his eyes, he held open his arms. "I'm an open book. Come read me."

She flew toward him, and he caught her close, capturing her mouth with his. How she loved this man who had loved her for so long, searched for her, and helped her find justice for Thomas.

His lips, tender and passionate, stayed on hers as he swept her up and carried her into the bedroom. Laying her on the bed, he settled beside her and propped himself on one elbow. His eyes roamed over her, loving, adoring, the need in them sending a flood of heat through her bloodstream.

Surprising her again, he said, "I also picked up some law school brochures. I know it's two years later than what you had planned, but I thought you might want to go back."

Oddly, that wasn't something she had even considered. Two years ago, going to law school had been a dream come true. Now, her priorities had changed…her entire life was different.

Before she could thank him and explain that she had different goals now, he went on, "And I know we haven't talked a lot about our future together…I understand if you need time, but—"

"No." She pushed hard at his shoulders so he would move back. When he did, she switched their positions so that he was lying down and she was over him. Nick needed to hear these words from her as much as she needed to say them. He was looking up at her curiously, maybe a little confused. And it hit her hard—he really had no concept of how wonderful he was or how deeply she loved him.

"I don't need time, Nick. I don't need things…all I need is you."

"You lost so much. I just want to give you back as much as I can."

She shook her head, unsure if she could ever express adequately how she felt about him. "I love you, Nick Gallagher. More than I ever thought possible. You've given me so much already. Friendship, a shoulder to cry on, passion, laughter, peace, security. Without your love and support…" Her heart so full she could barely speak, she continued thickly, "You gave me my life back."

"How so?"

"I was in a vacuum, just existing. My life was empty. Then you showed up, all grumpy, grouchy, grim."

"Hey!" he protested.

"Incredible, wonderful, considerate, gorgeous, and deliciously, fantastically sexy."

"Oh yeah?"

"Yeah."

She slowly unbuttoned his shirt, spread her hands on his warm, hard chest and closed her eyes at how exquisite he felt beneath her fingers. She wanted to explore every inch of his amazing body, give him everything he needed, wanted. All of herself—body, heart, devotion, love, tenderness, loyalty—everything she had now belonged to Nick. She was totally and completely his.

With delicate precision, she licked the raven tattoo on his chest, tracing the edges with her tongue. A shudder went through him, and she smiled her delight. The times they had made love before had been all about her pleasure or satisfying a hunger. Nick had always been the giver…she had been the taker. Today, she wanted him to understand she loved and desired him…the man. Not just for what he had done for her, but because he was an amazing, wonderful, complex and utterly beautiful man. Perfect for her in every way.

His voice grumbled beneath her mouth. "Like the tat, huh?"

"Like the tat, love what's beneath it."

"Oh, you mean my manly chest?"

She smiled against his skin. "Oh yes…definitely your manly chest. But more than that, I love your beautiful heart."

He pushed her away slightly to look up at her, clearly surprised. "No one's ever told me that before…that I have a beautiful heart."

"Good. I like being the first."

His eyes darkened with emotion. "You were my first for a lot of things."

Unable to stop herself from kissing that beautiful, unsmiling mouth, Kennedy pressed her lips to his. With a groan of approval, he pulled her close and opened his mouth, allowing her inside. In seconds, clothes disappeared and sighs, soft demands for more, sobbing gasps of pleasure, whispers of fulfillment that only lovers can hear and understand, filled the room.

Wrapped in Nick's arms, secure and content, tears flooded Kennedy's eyes. How blessed was she to have had the love of two phenomenal men? Thomas had been her first love, and she would treasure her memories of him for a lifetime.

Nick would be her last love. Husband, lover, partner, friend, and father of her children. Her future, her life. Forever, for always.

Thank you for reading *Nothing To Lose, A Grey Justice Novel*. I hope you enjoyed it. If you did, please help other readers find this book:

1. This book is lendable. Share it with a friend who would enjoy a dark and steamy romantic suspense.
2. Help other people find this book by writing a review.
3. Sign up for my newsletter at *http://christyreece.com* to learn about upcoming books.
4. Come like my Facebook page at *https://www.facebook.com/AuthorChistyReece*

Other Books by Christy Reece

Rescue Me, A Last Chance Rescue Novel

Return To Me, A Last Chance Rescue Novel

Run To Me, A Last Chance Rescue Novel

No Chance, A Last Chance Rescue Novel

Second Chance, A Last Chance Rescue Novel

Last Chance, A Last Chance Rescue Novel

Sweet Justice, A Last Chance Rescue Novel

Sweet Revenge, A Last Chance Rescue Novel

Sweet Reward, A Last Chance Rescue Novel

Chances Are, A Last Chance Rescue Novel

Writing as Ella Grace

Midnight Secrets, A Wildfire Novel

Midnight Lies, A Wildfire Novel

Acknowledgements

Special thanks to the following people for helping make this book possible:

My husband for his loving support, gifts of chocolate, and numerous moments of comic relief.

My mom who housed me during the hair-pulling parts of writing this story. And to Billie and Marlin for opening their home on the river for me to finish the book.

Joyce Lamb for her copyediting, great advice and input.

Marie Force's eBook Formatting Fairies, who answered my endless questions with endless patience.

Tricia Schmitt (Pickyme) for her beautiful cover art.

My first readers, Anne, Crystal, Jackie, Kara, Hope, Kris, and Alison, for their insight and wisdom. And one more extra special thank you to Anne for going above and beyond!

And, as always, thank you to my readers. Without you, this book and all the others, past and future, would not be possible. You make my dreams come true!

ABOUT THE AUTHOR

Christy Reece is the award winning and New York Times Bestselling author of dark and sexy romantic suspense. She lives in Alabama with her husband, four precocious canines, an incredibly curious cat, a very shy turtle, and a super cute flying squirrel named Elliott.

Christy also writes steamy, southern suspense under the pen name Ella Grace.

You can contact her at *Christy@christyreece.com*

Praise for Christy Reece novels:

"The type of book you will pick up and NEVER want to put down again." *Coffee Time Romance and More*

"Romantic suspense has a major new star!" *Romantic Times Magazine*

"Sizzling romance and fraught suspense fill the pages as the novel races toward its intensely riveting conclusion." *Publishers Weekly, Starred Review*

"Flat-out scary, and I loved every minute of it!" *The Romance Reader's Connection*

"A brilliantly plotted book. Her main characters are vulnerable yet strong, and even the villains are written with skillful and delicate brush strokes haunting your mind long after the book is done." *Fresh Fiction*

"A passionate and vivacious thrill-ride! ... I feel like I've been on an epic journey after finishing it.... Exquisite." *Joyfully Reviewed*